CARUTHERS

WITHDRAWN

K546ti
Kienzle, William X.
Till death /

WORN, SOILED, OBSOLETE   2000

D1014960

Presented
to

FRESNO
The County Free Library

by

Ray & Joy Bircher

TILL
DEATH

Also by William X. Kienzle

The Rosary Murders
Death Wears a Red Hat
Mind Over Murder
Assault with Intent
Shadow of Death
Kill and Tell
Sudden Death
Deadline for a Critic
Deathbed
Marked for Murder
Eminence
Masquerade
Chameleon
Body Count
Dead Wrong
Bishop as Pawn
Call No Man Father
Requiem for Moses
The Man Who Loved God
The Greatest Evil
No Greater Love

TILL
DEATH

William X. Kienzle

**Andrews McMeel
Publishing**

Kansas City

Till Death copyright © 2000 by Gopits, Inc. All rights reserved. Printed in the United States of America. No part of this book may be used or reproduced in any manner whatsoever without written permission except in the case of reprints in the context of reviews. For information, write Andrews McMeel Publishing, an Andrews McMeel Universal company, 4520 Main Street, Kansas City, Missouri 64111.

ISBN 0-7407-0489-3

Design/composition: Kelly & Company, Lee's Summit, Missouri

For Javan,
my wife and collaborator

Acknowledgments

Gratitude for technical advice to:

Colleen Baird, B.S.N., C.C.R.N., Michigan Heart and Vascular Institute, Ann Arbor, Michigan

James Bannon, Deputy Chief, Detroit Police Department (retired), Detroit, Michigan

Sister Bernadelle Grimm, R.S.M., Pastoral Care Department (retired), Mercy Hospital, Detroit, Michigan

Jerry Hodak, Chief Meteorologist, WXYZ-TV, Detroit, Michigan

Patricia Kamego, R.N.

The Reverend Bill King, Lansing Diocese, Lansing, Michigan

The Reverend Anthony Kosnik, S.T.D., J.C.B., Professor of Ethics, Marygrove College, Detroit, Michigan

Mickey LeCronier, Senior Writer, Organic, Inc.

Charles Lucas, M.D., Professor of Surgery, Wayne State University, Detroit, Michigan

Irma Macy, Religious Education Coordinator, Prince of Peace Parish, West Bloomfield, Michigan

Sergeant Mary Marcantonio, Detroit Police Department (retired), Detroit, Michigan

Grey Papke, Student Meteorologist, St. John Lutheran School, Rochester, Michigan

Werner U. Spitz, M.D., Professor of Forensic Pathology, Wayne State University, Detroit, Michigan

Any technical error is the author's.

With special thanks to Jordan Pizzuro, whose timely assistance helped Father Koesler immensely.

In memory of Father Michael O'Hara.

Prologue

LATE AUTUMN. In Michigan, nature had staged its annual show of shows. No artist living or dead could have matched God's broad strokes of color in stands of trees.

Now it was gone. Brilliant leaves had faded in turn to dull and fallen to earth.

There are those for whom spring signifies birth; summer, life; autumn, death; winter, burial. Followed by nothing. For others, the very perpetuity of the seasonal cycle attests to summer as life; autumn, death; winter, burial; and spring, rebirth into eternal life.

Father Robert Koesler belonged to the latter school.

And those were the thoughts he mused on as he stood very much alone in the Holy Sepulchre Cemetery.

He shuffled his right foot, allowing the chilly breeze to waft some leaves, uncovering a grave marker set flush with the ground. The chiseled inscription provided minimal information, a name and two dates, the earlier commemorating birth; the latter, departure from this life.

In the span between these two dates was a life that changed many others.

Actually, this story began some forty years earlier.

Father Koesler, then a young priest, was appointed the unlikely editor of the *Detroit Catholic,* the archdiocesan newspaper. The *Detroit Free Press,* reporting the appointment, termed the paper "influential" and was patently surprised that this inexperienced inner-city priest had been given the job.

Concurrent with the appointment, Koesler was directed to live at the rectory of St. Ursula. St. Ursula's could have been designated an ethnic parish, having been erected in a neighborhood almost entirely

Italian. By the time Koesler moved in, it was almost equally Italian and Polish, with a mix of African-American.

The most distinctive feature of St. Ursula's was its pastor, Father Angelico, who succeeded the affable Father Pompilio.

In the early sixties, the Second Vatican Council was about to break forth upon the world. Few could have guessed the changes it would bring.

At this time, the clergy were split not along conservative and liberal lines; rather, the line was drawn between pastors and their assistant priests.

Father Angelico was the one of a trio of east side pastors recognized as notorious tyrants. He virtually imprisoned the two priests assigned to him as assistants, and dictated their daily schedule down to the very minute. In this he was not blocked by current Church law.

With rare exception, each priest who served under Father Angelico emerged from his five-year stint with a severe case of shellshock or battle fatigue. Whatever one cared to term their condition, they were rubbed raw.

The one who uniquely escaped Angelico's tender mercies was Father Koesler. Angelico had no pigeonhole for him. Koesler was not a defenseless assistant. He was "in residence." Whatever the hell that meant, Angelico had no idea what to do with him, nor what his role might be in the pastor's fiefdom. For all Angelico knew, Koesler might be a chancery spy.

So, Bob Koesler ended by, in effect, writing his own ticket. He offered daily Mass and assisted on weekends.

Father Koesler could not help but be acutely aware of the shameful treatment accorded Angelico's assistants. Had he been more experienced he would have intervened—although what he might have accomplished was questionable. The chancery, with ultimate clout, though aware of the situation, did nothing.

Once Koesler left St. Ursula's, he tried to bind up the wounds of shredded dignity inflicted by its despotic pastor. As part of this effort, he established an informal group dedicated to supporting those who had served under Angelico or were presently imprisoned there.

The nuns who staffed St. Ursula's school were in worse condition than the parish's assistant priests. Not only were they browbeaten and cowed by Angelico's pervasive presence, they were also dominated by their rigorous religious order. Not until nuns began leaving religious life in large numbers in the wake of the Council were these women free to join the recovering Ursuline group.

In the beginning, the organization was more or less ad hoc—called upon as needed. Gradually, as a result of the growing priest shortage, fewer and fewer priests were assigned to St. Ursula's. Then Father Angelico died. The group's raison d'être began to wane. Eventually, the group—or what was left of it—met only once a year, on the first Wednesday of June.

Now, in the year 2000, fewer than ten of the Ursuline club remained. And a peculiar chemistry marked their relationship.

At this point, Koesler was able to do little more than observe their interaction—an interaction that tore asunder committed pairings and forged others. An interaction that led to death for one of the members and possible complicity for others.

He felt sorrow for the one at whose grave he now stood and prayed.

He felt sorrow for just about everyone involved on that fateful day: the first Wednesday in June.

One

Never get sick on a Wednesday.

Why not?

Because the doctors and priests will be on the golf course.

Lil smiled at the memory of the old wheeze as she peeled strips of bacon from the package and slid them into the frying pan.

It was very much an "in" joke for Catholics of long standing who could count themselves well within the loop. Once upon a time, when Catholics fell ill a priest might be summoned as routinely as a doctor. While the doctor scribbled a prescription, the priest would confer the appropriate sacrament, and assure the family of his prayers as well as those of the other parishioners.

Nowadays, doctors don't make house calls, and priests, an ever more endangered species, are buffered from callers by answering services. Nonetheless, Wednesday is still a popular day off for those able to arrange it.

Lil wore only the top half of a man's pajamas. The man, still snoozing, wore the bottoms.

The sun was creeping into the basement studio apartment. The tiny dwelling comprised a kitchenette wall, one bath, and an all-purpose space that was foyer, living room, dining room, and bedroom.

This Wednesday in June promised to be a pleasant day, the type that invited one to get out and enjoy the weather. Many of those left behind at this suburban apartment complex after the majority went off to work—mostly mothers and young children—would gather poolside.

Not this couple.

Lil and Rick had to be extremely careful.

This caution did not concern Rick nearly as much as it did Lil.

He was by nature carefree, spontaneous, and relatively fearless. She envied him these traits. Still she feared they'd be found out. Her fear was more for him than it was for her. But she too had high stakes in their relationship.

After all, Lillian Niedermier was principal of St. Enda's elementary school. She wondered how long she would hold that position if it leaked out that she had for the past ten years been half of a significant-other relationship.

The marital status of parochial teachers and principals had been taken for granted in the era when Catholic schools were staffed almost totally by nuns. Religious brothers served a few schools; priests—Jesuits, Basilians and the like—taught at some other schools as well as at seminaries.

That considerable dedication—for that was what it was—solved any number of problems.

There were no unions in Catholic schools. There was nothing to be negotiated. There were no interviews of prospective teachers to sap the pastor's time. If St. Paraphanucious school was slated to have twenty-four Dominican nuns, there they were: twenty-four dedicated women all in black-and-white habit.

None of the twenty-four had volunteered for a specific parish. The pastor did not select any of the nuns. They were sent.

Like so many other changes in the Catholic Church since 1965, when the Second Vatican Council concluded, things were radically different in today's parochial schools.

Formerly there was no challenge in finding *the* layperson on the Catholic school faculty. She was the only one wearing ordinary clothing.

Now there was plenty of challenge. The nun—if there was even one on the faculty—probably couldn't find a religious habit to save her soul—literally.

So, layperson Lillian Niedermier found herself principal of a parochial school in a northwest suburb of Detroit.

She could have made lots more money teaching in the public school system. Her choice to go parochial was partly because her schooling had been Catholic and also because here she could achieve the rank of principal. A position for which she would have had to wait many more years had she been in the public system.

But what would the parishioners of St. Enda's—let alone Father

O'Leary, the pastor—think if they were to discover that she had a live-in boyfriend? Marriage and its rules and regulations had for centuries been, and continued to be, an obsession with the Catholic Church. It would not take a canonical major to conclude that Lillian was "living in sin." St. Enda's students were not the only ones likely to earn an A.

Lil began cracking eggs into a bowl. She dropped four slices of bread into the toaster. The essentials were ready to go. All that was missing was a hungry man. Her man would have to wake up to feel hunger.

As if on schedule, stirrings and grunts emanated from the bed. "Do those sounds," Lil called over, "mean that you are about to favor me with your presence?"

There was a pause while he rolled over onto his back and rubbed his eyes. "If you play your cards right . . . maybe."

She turned up the heat under the frying pan. After some moments the distinctive aroma of sizzling bacon permeated the room.

"Sweetie," he said, "you just dealt a royal flush!"

She smiled as she flipped and flopped the strips in the pan. He liked his bacon uniformly well done.

Her back was toward him and she swayed slowly as she busied herself at the stove. He studied her appreciatively.

Her straight dark hair, parted in the middle, fell to the base of her neck. Her shoulders and upper torso were, he thought, incredibly narrow. Yet she was surprisingly strong. On those occasions when a heavy object was too hefty or bulky for him to lift alone, Lil bore the load every bit as equally as he.

His pajama top was many times too large for her slender figure. The garment hung to approximately mid-thigh. It reminded him of a mini skirt. Below her wasplike waist, the pajama top clung to her hips and suggested the rounded firmness beneath.

No doubt about it, she was one beautiful woman. And he was one lucky guy.

Breakfast would be prepared without his participation. Not that he couldn't prepare food; actually he did that with some regularity. And when he himself was chief cook and bottle-washer, he welcomed the involvement of others.

Not so with Lil. When she was in charge she firmly warned all others to steer clear of "my" kitchen.

He'd learned his lesson. He would not approach the kitchen area until everything was on the table. Meanwhile, he would feast his eyes on her generous beauty. He'd never met a curve in her body that he didn't treasure.

His thoughts flowing in free association, he contrasted her youth and perfect form with what he brought to this relationship. His gift, he thought, was not all that much.

In his prime—Lil's age and younger—he had been a trim athlete. If it bounced he'd played it: baseball, football, basketball, hockey, tennis, racquetball. Come to think of it, even if it didn't bounce, as long as it was a game, he'd played it.

Now his exercise was limited to bowling, golf—when the season and weather allowed—and sporadic visits to a fitness gym.

His upper body testified to his youthful athleticism. A thick neck and strong, sloping shoulder and chest muscles suggested strength and sinewy toughness. But that was the end of that. Over the years, he had developed a paunch that now threatened to sag over his belt.

Well, he said to himself, what could you expect at age sixty? Gravity, as well as other forces such as inertia, tended to remind one of the passage of time. Belying a drooping middle was his rigidly square face displaying the storied map of Ireland, accentuated by brilliant blue eyes and a full head of still-red hair.

All in all not too disgraceful for a man of sixty years.

Sixty years! When he was on the way up at thirty, forty, or fifty—even fifty-nine—sixty had seemed ancient. Well, what was sixty supposed to feel like? It all depended on health. He had known men who were old in their thirties and forties. While others—yes, some even in their sixties—were still young.

However, further complicating things was Lil, twenty-five years his junior.

Sixty years against thirty-five. Some might say it was the embodiment of a May-December relationship, that he was robbing the cradle. From time to time, he himself wondered.

On such occasions, Lil would attempt to kiss away his troubled thoughts. And each time she would succeed. But he proved unable to return the favor.

Lil worried. He was reminded of it more often than not. She worried not about the difference in their ages, not a bit about their love for one another. Lil worried because she was principal of a Catholic school. And because he was a priest.

Father Richard Casserly, Roman Catholic priest of the Archdiocese of Detroit. Pastor of St. William of Thierry parish in the city of Detroit. Vicar of the East Side Vicariate. A substantial representative of the archdiocese.

If Lil had her way, no one on earth would have any idea that Father Casserly and Ms. Niedermier were an item. As it was, and due largely to her precautions, precious few suspected and actually only one other person knew for certain.

The situation demanded constant vigilance. The effort primarily was Lil's. In her mind, the alternative was disaster. If their secret were to be known by her pastor, or by the archbishop, undoubtedly she would be fired. And Rick? That was pretty much up in the air.

At very least he would suffer some sort of ecclesial punishment. Suspension, perhaps, which would demand that he not exercise any priestly function for some specified period—a month, a year, whatever the archbishop, Cardinal Mark Boyle, imposed.

Compared with what other bishops in other dioceses would do in this situation, temporary suspension was pretty mild. That was because Boyle was not confrontational. He would level such a penalty only if backed into a canonical corner with the media's glare turned on.

All of this, she thought, Rick could take.

But there was more.

The authorities would insist that their relationship be terminated. And that, Lil was convinced, Rick would refuse out of hand. In that sort of confrontation, Rick didn't have a ghost of a chance. Whatever form of penalty would follow—suspension, excommunication, laicization—he would face the loss of his priesthood, undoubtedly permanently.

The priesthood or Lil. It would be a gut-wrenching decision for Rick.

Frequently both would reminisce about how this had begun. The thread that bound them had originated at St. Ursula's, Rick's first assignment after his ordination in 1965. Rick became a popular priest in the inner-city parish that had for some time been held captive by a despotic pastor.

Against the pastor's wishes—he could not make them orders since his policies were even more harsh than restrictive Church law—the attractive, young Father Casserly had instituted an athletic program in the parish high school, regularly visited the grade school, preached well, and was as open and as healing as possible.

So popular was he that years after his hitch at St. Ursula's he was still called back to witness weddings and perform funerals for the friends he had made there.

It was impossible for the pastor to overlook Rick's profound popularity. And so he was welcomed back only reluctantly for such parish events as confirmation, Forty Hours, and the parish festival.

On many such occasions Father Casserly would meet and greet both the old and new parochial employees. One of these was Lillian Niedermier, who taught in the parish school from 1984 to 1987.

It wasn't love at first sight. It was respect, interest, and appreciation. The relationship deepened slowly. At the time she was nearly twenty, he in his mid-forties. He tended to treat her as a daughter, a chronological possibility.

Metaphorical incest never crossed her mind. He had an aura of wit, good humor, and intelligence, as well as physical attractiveness and an Irish gift of gab that charmed her completely if gradually.

For him, being a priest in the eighties was vastly different from being a priest in the fifties; for her, being a parochial teacher in the eighties contrasted greatly with being a Catholic schoolgirl in the seventies.

In the sixties, both priests and nuns were slowly emerging from their cocoon of clerical clothing. The Catholic Church, as well as the country, was in turmoil. But tradition, along with a residual discipline, held most of the Catholic clergy in place.

However, by the time Lil was in high school, the priest drain was in full force.

Still, even in the eighties, when Lil began teaching, Rick was very much a priest and Lillian was in awe of his priesthood.

So they began by being peripherally aware of each other and conscious of the comfortable feeling they had with each other. On rare occasions they might take in a movie or a concert. They took pains not to appear to be together, often even sitting apart in the theater.

The more they knew of and about each other, the more their initially platonic attraction grew and evolved.

By 1990, their love had become physical and total. Three years later, he moved some of his effects into her small apartment, while maintaining his residence in the rectory.

They were together almost every moment they were not on duty: evenings when he had no meetings or sacramental responsibilities; Saturday mornings and early afternoons; Sundays after morning Masses; Tuesday nights and—his regular day off—Wednesdays all day.

Nothing in Lil's schedule conflicted with his availability except Wednesday, when, of course, St. Enda's school was open for business as usual. She was able to clear her Wednesdays only because she was principal and had complete confidence in her assistant principal.

Indeed, the two educators were so close Lil almost shared her deepest secret. But in the end she could not break the *omerta* even with her best friend. That was the gigantic fly in her ointment. She could share her secret, her happiness, with no one—not her family, not her friends, not even her closest confidante.

She was beginning to feel sorry for herself. That would never do. It was a fine day; the forecast was sunny skies with a high in the mid- to upper seventies. She didn't have to go to work. Neither did her sweetheart. But even with a beautiful outdoors beckoning, they probably would spend the day in the apartment. That was their usual M.O. It was easier than being tensely on guard.

As long as they were together. She had her man.

She heard the bathroom door quietly close.

She removed the bacon from the pan, replacing it with the eggs.

Scrambled eggs were her forte. Her recipe called for a humongous amount of milk to be added to the eggs and the whole scrambled vigorously until the mixture became fluffily firm.

She didn't hear him approaching. So she was startled when she felt his lips on her neck—startled and pleased. She turned to him and they embraced. She leaned away from him. "Good morning. I love you."

"Good morning. I love you," he replied.

They grinned and kissed.

This morning ritual they had borrowed from one of their favorite movies, *Tarzan and His Mate*. The first time Rick and Lil saw that film together, they adopted Tarzan and Jane's morning greeting for themselves. As it happened, Wednesdays were the only mornings they awoke to each other, apart from vacations and unforeseen good luck.

It had been Johnny Weissmuller's second crack at playing the Ape Man. As far as Rick and Lil were concerned, the only authentic Tarzan was Weissmuller. Above and beyond his spine-tingling jungle call—later imitated repeatedly by Carol Burnett—Rick considered, "Me Tarzan. You Jane." the two most perfect declarative sentences in the English language.

Rick seated himself as Lil served breakfast. Over his pajama bottoms he wore a robe. It was one of his many thoughtfulnesses that she prized. She would not have appreciated nor found appetizing a broad, hairy chest opposite her during meals. They had never discussed it, although coming from an all-macho environment, he might be expected to be oblivious of her sensibilities. But he was not like that. And she was grateful.

"These eggs are terrific," he said. "I don't know how you do it."

"It's the milk. Why won't you believe me?"

"I know. I know. But when I see all that white milk in the pan barely diluted with a touch of egg yellow . . . I just can't believe it."

"Oh, ye of little faith."

She finished eating well before Rick did. That was due to a combination of factors. Twelve years of his young life he had spent in a seminary where food was carefully measured out—never quite enough to satisfy hungry, growing boys. He often claimed that if it had not been for peanut butter, he might well have starved. When he was ordained, he was a reed-thin young man.

As a priest, he was served just about anything he wanted. Witness the stomach folds he now wore.

Lil, on the other hand, was never hungry; she ate only sparingly. Thus, she was likely to retain her perfect body indefinitely.

There were two elongated half windows in the apartment's easterly exposure. The windows were half the normal height because that was all the space there was between the ground outside and the ceiling inside.

The casual passerby might have been able to peer in. But he would see nothing because Lil had had one-way glass installed. It gave them an extra measure of the privacy they desired.

Rick finished the toast. It was the last morsel on his plate. "Well, honey, what would you like to do?"

Lil yawned. "Oh, I don't know. Hang around here. I've got some teacher evaluations to go over." She lowered her eyes seductively. "We could squeeze in a little lovemaking, couldn't we, Ollie?" She mimicked a character from Erich Segal's *Love Story*.

"How pressing are the evaluations?"

"Not urgent." Her brow knitted slightly. "You want to spend the entire, blessed day in bed?" She hesitated. "I mean it's certainly all right with me . . ." Her voice faded.

"Looks like a super day." He gazed at the filtered sunshine peeking through the wide, stunted windows.

She sighed. It *was* a super day. Her thoughts turned to the pool that had been open for a couple of weeks now. She used the facility only when he was not there. They tried—successfully, they believed—to avoid giving the impression that they lived together.

Rick had been a priest, functioning publicly, for thirty-five years. It was easily possible that someone who knew him as a priest might be living in this apartment complex. That he was residing both here and at the rectory was nothing to wonder at; lots of priests had abandoned rectory life in favor of a house, a condo, or an apartment. The practice left many rectories—and convents, for that matter—vacant.

So, if someone—a former parishioner for instance—were to meet and recognize Rick . . . well, it was not all that out of the ordinary—as long as he was by himself, or at least not with Lil. This huge complex did not invite much neighborly fraternizing. However, poolside togetherness might prove a giveaway.

"It *is* a super day," she replied. "But we can't risk the pool."

"I wasn't thinking of the pool. I had something bigger in mind . . ." He halted, waiting to see if she would guess correctly.

For a few seconds she gazed at him, expecting to be told his plans. As she waited, she pondered. Then her eyes widened. "The boat!"

He nodded. *"Das Boot."* He used the German title of the popular movie.

"Will Tom let us use it? You asked him! Why didn't you tell me? We could have packed our stuff and been out of here long ago!" Unbridled enthusiasm from Lil.

"Take it easy, sweetie. Tom's having some work done on it this morning. We can pick it up and take it out this afternoon. We've got plenty of time."

Tom Becker, owner of the power boat in question, had been Casserly's seminary classmate through high school and college. He had dropped out after his first year in the major seminary.

Indeed, that was the primary function of seminaries: to, on the one hand, enable students to choose whether to make a commitment to the priesthood and, on the other, enable the faculty to accept or reject the candidate for ordination.

After nine years, Tom Becker, following much prayer and soul-searching, decided the priestly life was not for him. Exceptionally talented as a carpenter and builder, he went on to study architecture at the Lawrence Technological University in Southfield, Michigan.

Dedicated to the poor, after graduation he began a career in housing restoration. He was a one-man army, going through run-down neighborhoods rehabilitating once-proud houses, making them sound and attractive again. Then, after selling them for a pittance to poor families, he taught the new owners the finer points of maintenance and repair.

In this he was years ahead of Jimmy Carter's popularizing Habitat for Humanity.

His income came almost completely from various governmental grants and private foundations. This definitely did not make him a wealthy man. When he married and began a family, it was time to earn some real money.

He joined an architectural firm and quickly climbed the executive ladder. In less than fifteen years he founded his own company. He was, of course, president and CEO. He built an impeccable reputation and made millions. Along the way he offered employment to some men leaving the priesthood.

He retired astonishingly early, and almost immediately, to combat boredom, he planted roses and started a tree nursery, which he eventually expanded into a highly succcessful landscape business.

Through it all, Tom Becker and Rick Casserly remained close friends. Becker was the only person Casserly trusted enough to confide in. He proved a source of dependable support. As far as he was concerned, his friend was at most a bit premature. After all, married Episcopal priests as well as other married ministers were, *mutatis mutandis*, allowed to function as Catholic priests. Soon—and inevitably—in order to supply much-needed priests, the Church would be forced to offer ordination to married Catholic men.

Becker's only regret was the pressure Rick and Lil were under to keep secret their . . . what? . . . common law marriage.

"We can have the boat all to ourselves this afternoon?" Lil's eyes danced.

"It's ours. The boat is booked for tonight; otherwise we could have had it all the way through this evening."

"Honey, no," Lil cautioned.

"No? No what? No boat? No afternoon? No evening?"

"We've got an engagement this evening. Don't you remember?"

Rick's brow furrowed. "Oh yeah: the St. Ursula party. That's tonight?"

"The first Wednesday in June. That's today. The annual bash is tonight."

"Well," Rick reflected, "you could hardly call it a bash."

"True. It's more like the remnant returning . . . like the Jews coming out of the Babylonian Captivity."

"Time takes its toll," Rick said. "The number of guys and gals who served their term under dear old Father Angelico has dwindled. So many have moved away. Some died. Some just lost interest over the years."

"Refresh me: How long has this commemoration been going on?"

"Oh, wow! Let's see: I think it was Bob Koesler who started the thing. Must be almost forty years now. And he was just in residence there while he was editor of the *Detroit Catholic*. He didn't have to take all that crap from Angelico. Observing it was medicine enough for him."

"Forty years! I had no idea it's been around that long."

"It was a cathexis. You needed at least a once-a-year day to blow off steam. Even after the assignment board moved you the hell out of there, it still helped. Sort of like getting together to nurse old wounds.

"Over time it got to be a kind of convivial gathering—especially once the old tyrant died. It's been thirteen years now. He died after you got a new job at another parish." He grinned. "Somehow, you must've killed him."

Lil smiled. How easy it was to call to mind her years with the second-graders at St. Ursula's. How impressionable were their innocent minds! And how legalistic and dour were the regular visits to her class by the pastor, Father Angelico. It seemed his aim was to block every direction set by the Council.

Typical was the battle over the order of confession and Communion. In pre-Vatican II times, Catholic children were introduced first to confession—then known more properly as the Sacrament of Penance, now called the Sacrament of Reconciliation—closely followed by Communion—then, as now, more properly termed Holy Eucharist.

However, after the Council and before a Vatican ruling, most parishes reversed the order.

In the prior practice, a mistaken connection was drawn between confession and Communion. Catholic children, most of them second-graders, were prepared for these two sacraments almost simultaneously.

So, most Catholic adults carried over what they'd learned as children. Many felt unworthy to receive Communion without first going to confession.

It led to confusion on a massive scale.

Children, whose peccadilloes could not rank with the transgressions of the occasional serious sinner, were making up sins for the confessional because—well, because they had to say *something* to prompt the priest to give them absolution.

Adults grew up with this routine of going to confession on a Saturday and Communion the next day. This was followed by three communionless Sundays until time for the monthly confession.

After the Council, parishes regularly prepared children to receive Communion. Then, after a period of a year or more, the youngsters were taught to appreciate the Sacrament of Reconciliation. Some of the fire and brimstone doctrine disappeared, to be missed only by a very vocal traditionalist minority.

Short of some interferences from the Vatican, children were welcomed to Communion at every Mass in which they participated. To attend Mass without receiving Communion was compared to going to a banquet and not eating. Confession was another matter entirely.

But not at St. Ursula's. Not under the regime of Father Angelico. This, as well as so many other anchors driven into the past, was brought home to the fledgling teacher Lillian Neidermier once she learned that she was expected to teach from the Baltimore Catechism, a book of religious questions and answers. The questions were fundamental. So were the answers.

"Who made you?"

"God made me."

Everybody studied and learned from the Baltimore Catechism. Among other frightening bits of doctrine was the view of God that held our Creator as a harsh judge ready and able to snatch our lives an instant after the commitment of a mortal sin (a pork chop on Friday), and consign us to eternal damnation.

It was unfortunate that Lil left St. Ursula's before Father Angelico died. Otherwise she might have come to understand that religion could be a loving experience.

Eventually, of course, her knowledge of God as Love did come about. But how neat it would have been to experience this in a St. Ursula's newly bereft of Father Angelico.

"It wasn't a case of my killing Father Angelico . . ." Lil laughed lightly. "I always thought if we both stayed in the same parish long enough, he would kill *me*. That look! When the skin stretched across his bony face, I could never guess whether he was smiling or furious. I learned in the school of hard knocks that most of the time he was barely containing rage."

Rick's brow was knit as if he were thinking through a complex problem. "To understand Father Angelico properly you should remember that if you were convicted of heresy, Father Angelico would have accompanied you to the pyre. He would have prayed with you, and then he would have lit the fire."

She laughed heartily. But, as her chuckles subsided, her face grew thoughtful. "By the way, honey, you do want to go to the party tonight, don't you?"

"Oh, sure. I just forgot."

"We each got an invitation—sent to our separate residences naturally."

"What can I say after I say I'm sorry? I forgot. I barely remember getting the invite. Where's it supposed to be?"

"Old St. Joe's downtown."

"Hmm. I wonder why."

"Well, for one thing St. Ursula's is no more. We couldn't have it there."

"Did you ever think"—Rick stretched elaborately—"when you worked there that the day would come when the old place would be closed?"

"Mmm"—she pondered—"I guess I wondered why they bothered building it." She smiled. "But not why they would bury it."

"But the memory lingers on. Thus, tonight's party." He rose from the table and slipped out of his robe. "We've got plenty of time before we can get the boat. What do you want to do?"

"I haven't the slightest idea," she replied impishly. "But I'm sure we'll think of something."

Two

"WHAT DAY OF THE WEEK is this?" Jerry Anderson asked loudly.

"Wednesday," Dora Riccardo answered just as forcefully.

"Then don't get sick."

"Because all the doctors and priests will be out golfing?"

"You got it!"

In her office at the far end of the editorial room, Patricia Lennon looked up, startled. Then she smiled. She hadn't heard that old bromide since her days at Marygrove, then a Catholic college for young women. Now it was coed but still very much alive deep into Detroit's northwest side.

Pat Lennon was continuing her long and distinguished journalism career in Detroit. She'd been at it approximately thirty-five years.

In her time she had worked at both Detroit daily newspapers, establishing a reputation of excellence. In a profession where bylines on news stories were routinely overlooked, her authorship was consistently recognized.

But when she reached age fifty and looked back at thirty years of pressure, deadlines, and the gradual demise of professionalism among many of the younger crop of journalists, she decided to pack it in. With very few regrets, she gladly accepted the golden parachute and was off on a leisurely, extended vacation.

No sooner did she return to her high-rise apartment in downtown Detroit than she was contacted by a man she knew all too well.

Chris Reynolds was considered by many as Michigan's Donald Trump. Responsible for the proliferation of strip malls throughout the state, he also owned chains of movie houses and many varied publications.

Whenever possible he was a hands-on manager. But the sheer number of his enterprises made it impossible for him to attend to everything personally.

At the time Pat Lennon called it a day in newspaper journalism,

Reynolds was on the brink of closing his *Oakland Monthly*. The magazine primarily served Oakland County, the third wealthiest county in the United States. Oakland County provided a substantial answer to, Where do all those fabulously rich auto giants, high-priced lawyers, inheritance-heavy people live? Some of the old money dug in at one or another of the Grosse Pointes. Much of the fast-lane wealthy staked out Oakland County.

So, Reynolds asked himself, why should a magazine featuring this toddlin' county fare so poorly in circulation and advertising revenue? No one seemed to have the answer. But Chris Reynolds was determined to solve the puzzle before or instead of shelving the magazine.

One of his many vice presidents informed him that Pat Lennon was voluntarily unemployed.

Reynolds was familiar with Lennon's high standards and professionalism. He discovered that she had next to no managerial experience. Reynolds had no problem with that; lots of managers he knew could not manage.

After considerable thought, he decided that for weal or woe Lennon would be the ultimate answer to the survival of *Oakland Monthly*. So he put on the full-court press.

A personally conducted tour of the wonderful world of Reynolds' kingdom; done lunches; invitations to wheeler-and-dealer parties; a most generous salary offer with incentives, and, finally, a free hand in editorial decisions.

Pat smiled her way through it all. Never before had she been the target of such a cunningly contrived campaign.

In the end, she was won over mainly by the opportunity to run this organization—especially with no one peering over her shoulder.

She made certain she would not be second-guessed by Reynolds or any of his lackeys. She had established some ground rules in their relationship several years before when she'd done a feature on him for the paper.

The feature had run as a series. So she'd had to spend a generous amount of time with him. That time, for her, was strictly business. But Reynolds had had something more in mind.

It happened toward the end of their time together. He invited her to his headquarters. She intended to track statistically his far-flung empire. He intended to give her a scenic tour of a lavishly elaborate office that, with the push of several buttons, transformed into a seductive bedroom.

This was by no means the first pass she had fielded cleanly. Afterward she had to admit that he *could* take no for an answer.

So their negotiations were all business—if friendly business—and she accepted the role of editor-in-chief and associate publisher of *Oakland Monthly* magazine.

It was now five years into her contract. Reynolds had been true to his word; he had been an absentee owner. One of his lieutenants had stopped by early on to check on progress or lack of such. But a word to the boss from Pat had put an end to that.

Besides, she *had* turned the business around. *Oakland Monthly* was operating in the black.

Having been distracted by the interplay of Jerry and Dora, Pat gazed out of her glassed-in office. Things in editorial were bustling. Everyone seemed busy. Just as it should be.

In the beginning, Pat had cleaned house and hired her own people. She particularly had confidence in the woman she had brought on board as advertising manager. Her confidence was not misplaced; ad sales had soared.

Pat allowed herself a few moments to reminisce.

Early on she had been aware that she was strikingly beautiful, first as a child, then as a teenager, then as a mature woman. All along, she had remained determined that her good looks would not undermine her intelligence nor her abilities.

She married early and, as it happened, not wisely. One tragic mistake was quite enough. In her dealings with men, she was never casually romantic. There were several liaisons, none of them close to one-nighters—more like significant commitments.

A talented colleague, Joe Cox, had come closest to becoming a spouse. His immaturity eventually was his Achilles' heel. Currently he was seeded highly as a reporter for the *Los Angeles Times*.

Out of sight, out of mind; they no longer even exchanged Christmas cards.

As good a journalist and writer as Joe Cox was, his personality type was what Pat most wanted to avoid in her search for new talent.

The magazine's previous administration had been in the habit of hiring, mostly as freelancers, everything from college students to fledgling writers with no training and/or experience. Too often most of the freelancers turned in generally unacceptable work. But they did come cheap. The unused money in the editorial budget found its way into administrative staff pockets.

No wonder the publication had been on its final glide path.

Early on, Pat had hired first Dora Riccardo, then Jerry Anderson. These two and those who followed them into *Oakland Monthly* fit Lennon's standard, to wit: A professional in journalism—or any like field—having accepted an assignment, turns it in (a) on time and (b) in acceptable condition.

The freelancers who had been used before Lennon's arrival—and only briefly after she took charge—were the antithesis of this. They needed to be cajoled, coaxed, wheedled, humored, threatened, warned, intimidated, scared, bullied, yelled at—in short treated like any badly behaved two-year-old.

Pat Lennon had no children and she was not about to take any on now.

However, Jerry Anderson and Dora Riccardo were just the type Lennon wanted. While neither had an extensive background in journalism, both were strong academically in English, and Anderson had experience in creative writing, and in directing small publications.

Perhaps . . . just maybe . . . it didn't hurt that he had been a priest and she had been a nun. Lennon chuckled when she thought of her employees' background: Who would have thunk it?

What were the odds when she was a student at Marygrove, breaking every rule on that Catholic college's books, as well as some laws that had not yet even been invented, that she one day would be boss of a priest and a nun?

Five years ago when he was hired at the magazine, Jerry Anderson was fresh from a Detroit inner-city parish. He had been a priest fifteen years.

In a way it helped that Lennon was cleaning house at that time. Positions were open across the board. And most of the hirees had not known each other. Anderson did not have to work around longtime friendships and cliques. He, as well as the others, could start on a level playing field. He needed this as a buffer to his previous calling.

He referred jokingly to this postclerical position as his "first honest job." Not that he hadn't worked as a priest. But now he was entering the mainstream of American life.

Pat Lennon, of course, knew of his background. It was all over his résumé. He and she decided it was better that his former occupation not be concealed. For one thing, many of his coworkers were investigative reporters; they undoubtedly would have sniffed it out early on. Better to be open about it.

Dora Riccardo, on the other hand, had left the convent in 1990, about five years before the sweep at *Oakland Monthly.* For her first five years after leaving the religious life, she had been a Kelly Girl. So she was pretty much at home in this mainstream.

The reaction of the duo's coworkers was merely a passing interest, and some amusement: Not one of them had ever dreamed that one day he or she would be working shoulder to shoulder on even ground with a priest or a nun.

From time to time, while brown-bagging lunch or on a coffee break, the subject of religious life would come up. Of the two former religious, Anderson was far more open about his previous lifestyle.

Three

JEROME ANDERSON was born in 1955, about a decade before the Second Vatican Council began. He entered St. Joseph Minor Seminary, a high school and college whose only purpose was the training of young men for the priesthood. He was ordained in 1980 to serve wherever sent in the six-county Archdiocese of Detroit. His first priestly assignment was to St. Ursula's parish. He considered this appointment a challenge. The pastor, Father Angelico, was notorious; so his disposition came as no surprise to anyone condemned to work with him.

Anderson was not eager to accept the unhappy challenge. In this he was far from unique. No one in the diocese would be masochistic enough to find pleasure in being sent on such a mission.

His sentence ran from 1980 to 1985. Father Rick Casserly had been rescued a full ten years before Anderson's arrival, having served from 1965 to 1970. St. Ursula's was the maiden voyage for each of these two priests; interestingly—amazingly—neither had been embittered by the experience.

When Anderson appeared on the scene, even though Casserly had been out of the picture for a decade, his reputation still flourished. Casserly was known by many parishioners as "the priest who smiled"— an allusive commentary on the atmosphere that prevailed in the face of Father Angelico's irascible despotism.

Anderson turned to Casserly for direction and support. Both were professionally offered.

Privately, Anderson considered this assignment punishment for his sins. If fracturing seminary rules and regulations had been sinful, he might have had grounds for this conclusion. However, by the time he went through the seminary, discipline was on the wane. As the years of his training passed, fewer and fewer rules remained.

Nonetheless, he'd never encountered a regulation that he hadn't flouted or tried to violate.

Ostensibly, seminary rules had weakened and grown fewer in number mostly because the student population also was decreasing. The seminary administration decided that possibly it was the rules and regulations that made it a challenge to recruit and/or retain students. Eventually the thinking was that if there were no rules whatsoever, many more young men would be attracted. The faculty actually reached that point and found that it didn't work.

Jerry Anderson's personality was such that, metaphorically, he needed to kick against the fence of rules and regulations. When the rules disappeared so did his fence. But the testing, challenging spirit lingered on.

In moments of serious reflection, he wondered why they'd ever accepted him into the seminary. A far deeper puzzle was why, even after all that mutual exposure, the seminary faculty had recommended him for ordination.

His academic grades were merely adequate. His attitude toward rules was confrontational. His classroom demeanor, while attentive, bordered on disdain or downright hostility. Particularly when hard moral questions were raised he was wont to argue against the institutional Church—especially against the presumptions of Church law that almost always favored the institution, hardly ever the individual.

On the positive side, he was a compelling speaker. Highly motivational, he related exceptionally well to youth. He had a good sense of humor, a quality not easily glossed over.

He claimed to be six feet tall. Close; actually he was more like five foot ten. He loved sports and participated at every opportunity. It was no surprise his body was firm and well muscled. His blond hair was full, though almost brush-cut short. His originally prominent nose had been broken twice, once playing football, the other time on the basketball court. His style of play raised basketball from a noncontact game to a collision sport.

In any case, after the second fracture, a plastic surgeon gave him a new and more classically perfect profile. Fortunately his nose had not been broken since.

All of this, together with a ton of naiveté, Anderson had brought with him to his first assignment at St. Ursula's parish.

For a while, Father Angelico had Jerry Anderson cowed, though Anderson was not easily intimidated. That it took some time for him to flex his own personality spoke volumes for the depth of the pastor's meanness. But by three years into his five-year tour of duty, Jerry Anderson had gotten his feet solidly beneath him.

It was at this time that, in one of their routine changes of personnel, the teaching order of Theresians brought in a new face to teach a freshman high school class. Her formal name was Sister Mary Perpetua, Religious Sisters of St. Theresa (RSST).

It could not exactly be called love at first sight. Because all Father Anderson could see was a face—pinched by an unforgiving wimple that made it look as if Sister had just been sucking a lemon—and hands.

Sister Perpetua belonged to a very strict religious order. Relatively recently almost all religious orders had been given the option of wearing either the habit (traditional or modified) or lay clothing. It had been a decade since the conclusion of Vatican II and things were moving, seemingly, for just about everyone but the Theresians: They had stuck with the past.

Along with the traditional habit, the Theresians appeared to have taken some sort of vow to stamp out good cheer, which was why Sister Perpetua, together with Fathers Casserly and Anderson, stood out amid the crowd: She smiled.

There was absolutely no way of discerning what Sister Perpetua really looked like under those yards and yards of dark brown cloth; even her face was distorted by the tight wimple. The founders of the older religious orders intended to make chastity easier to observe by making their followers pretty much asexual. In the unlikely event of an assignation, the players would be pretty much spent by the time Sister had been helped to disrobe.

One thing was incontrovertible: Perpetua was tall. She stood five foot eight. Whatever other proportions she possessed were hers alone to know; everyone else had to guess.

Sister Perpetua and Father Anderson got along well—better as time passed. They smiled at each other. Even when there wasn't much about which to be happy.

The smiles were noted by the other Theresians as well as by Father Angelico. Perpetua paid for her indiscretion by having menial jobs heaped upon her until her back was almost literally broken.

Anderson would have suffered a similar punishment except that he was now in the process of self-emancipation. No longer would he be indentured to Angelico. Not since the stewardship of Father Casserly had the pastor had this much trouble controlling an assistant.

Not only was Anderson casting off the yoke of servitude the pastor forced on those associated with him, Jerry was also becoming choosy about which Church laws to impose on the laity. He was particularly incensed by the Church's marriage laws. His distress grew in the ten years he continued in the active ministry after moving on from St. Ursula's. It would be the proximate reason he would leave the priesthood.

That and his imagination as to what Sister Perpetua looked like under that enshrouding habit.

As was the case with many priests who left, Anderson was offered a job with Tom Becker. Jerry had expected as much since he and Rick Casserly were both members of Father Koesler's St. Ursula's alumni group. Casserly made certain that Tom, his former classmate, would at least offer a position.

Anderson was grateful. As he put it, quoting more than one ex-priest who had joined the mainstream, "Life gets pretty tough when Mother Church removes her nipple from one's mouth." He gave serious and grateful consideration to Becker's offer.

Then, suddenly, in a manner of speaking, all his ducks, like a syzygy, were lined up in a row.

Jerry Anderson had had some success editing and writing a series of parish bulletins. He'd had letters published periodically, a couple of them in the *New York Times*. Chris Reynolds was trying to save his magazine. And Pat Lennon, with the approval of the boss, was cleaning the slate.

Several of Jerry's former parishioners, aware of his interest in writing, urged him to apply for a job in that field. And then came lunch with Sister Perpetua—now having reclaimed her pre-Theresian name of Dora Riccardo. She arranged for his interview with Pat Lennon at *Oakland Monthly.*

He landed the job—the only one of those he'd applied for that he really wanted.

And, as frosting on the cake, Dora Riccardo worked in the same office.

God was good.

Four

THE YEAR WAS 1960. It was the beginning of a decade of awakening, revolt, mistrust, divisiveness, assassinations, and Vietnam, among many other interesting and provocative events.

It was the year Dora Riccardo was born in Hamtramck. Her father was Italian, her mother Polish.

Hamtramck is a largely Polish enclave completely surrounded by the city of Detroit. Catholicism might just as well have been the state religion. The family belonged to Our Lady Queen of Apostles, known colloquially as Q of A, largely to distinguish it from the many other parishes dedicated to "Our Lady."

Dora's environment ensured that she thought of herself as Polish, that she dismissed her paternal Mediterranean ancestry, and that she was much closer to her mother than to her father. The father tried to close this gap by lavishing presents on her. It worked to a degree; he ingratiated himself with both wife and daughter. As Dora passed from childhood to pubescence, she grew increasingly convinced that she could get anything she wished if she just played her cards winningly.

It might have been different had her parents achieved what they desired. When they had married, the priest asked them ritually if they would accept all the children God would send them. Enthusiastically they consented. But despite every effort and the assistance of the medical technology of their time, Dora proved to be their only child.

She did well in Q of A's parish school, particularly in religion courses. The nuns—Theresians—who taught her decided that they detected a religious vocation in little Dora. Tacitly, Dora agreed. In fact, at that time, Dora wanted nothing but to become a nun. The thought of being a priest never occurred to her because—well, because she was a female. She knew of few girls who wanted the priesthood. As far as Dora and the Theresians were concerned, such girls did not know their place.

At her earliest opportunity she was off to the convent. The vocation drain was just beginning, although the Theresians, unrelenting in their inflexibility, were affected to a much lesser degree than most other orders. However, since warm bodies were needed to replenish the thinning teaching ranks, training was telescoped. Instead of academic degrees, Dora was equipped with little more than the glorious package of poverty, chastity, and obedience—vows she had taken in order to enter the Community of Theresians.

Having made her profession, Dora, at the tender age of eighteen, was shipped off to teach at St. Ursula's school.

Somehow the Theresians had managed to keep a full complement of nuns in this school. St. Ursula's was among the very few parochial schools at that time still completely staffed by nuns. Even so, at one time the assistant priest—with no training or certification—was sent to teach religion in the high school.

Father Casserly's contribution to this program—emphasizing love, forgiveness, and joy in religion—nearly undermined the party line that was expected to be taught at St. Ursula's.

Later, Father Anderson took up where Father Casserly had left off. The upshot was that toward the end of Anderson's tenure his instruction of religion was discontinued. The assistant priest's contribution to the education of the children of St. Ursula's was supplanted by that of the pastor, the fearsome Father Angelico.

That's what Sister Perpetua walked into. And that's when the trouble began.

Many teaching orders of nuns routinely inserted their new members into classrooms as quickly as possible, leaving it up to many years of summer school to gain graduate degrees. Sister Perpetua was not alone in being turned loose to teach with very little training.

It was hectic trying to stay ahead of the textbooks and at the same time enforce necessary discipline on the kids. It was demanding. But when the occasional undemanding moment occurred, Sister Perpetua was conscious that something was wrong.

She was lonely. She hadn't expected that. After all, she was living with eleven other women. How could anyone be lonely in such a sizable group?

She hadn't counted on being in a semicontemplative order. As a pupil, she had been accustomed to the Theresians talking in the classroom. Sometimes they had even shouted.

But since she hadn't asked any questions, she'd never realized that Theresians had permission only rarely to speak when in the convent. Aside from a half-hour recreation period after supper and on Sunday afternoons, the Sisters needed permission from Mother Superior to speak to anyone, even each other.

So there she was, still a young girl actually, in an alien situation. She felt so all alone, with no one to talk it over with but Mother Superior, who didn't wish to be bothered.

Sister Perpetua wanted to run. Just get up of a morning and, instead of going to chapel for meditation and morning prayers, somehow get a car and drive away. Anywhere, as long as it was away from this dead-silent convent with its elderly, silent nuns.

But she couldn't do that. At least she didn't think she could.

One early morning she felt she had no alternative; the choice was escape or suicide. She went to meditation and morning prayer with the intention of splitting immediately afterward. On the way to chapel, she pocketed the key to the nuns' only car.

But the theme of this morning's meditation was from Luke's gospel. Mother Superior read the text: "Yet another said to him, 'I will be your follower, Lord, but first let me take leave of my people at home.' Jesus answered him, 'Whoever puts his hand to the plow but keeps looking back is unfit for the reign of God.'"

This text struck Sister Perpetua as if it were a personal revelation.

She had put her hand to the plow when she entered the convent. To look back to her life as it had been, to take the plow in hand and then leave it—for whatever reason—was to make oneself unfit for the reign of God.

Stealthily, after morning prayer, she returned the car key to its hook. She then followed the other nuns in the short walk to St. Ursula's church for Mass.

There was only one other reason that argued against her leaving the religious life: Such a departure would, especially in her family's neighborhood, be a disgrace. She and her mother would be the target of gossip and shame. Her father, inasmuch as he was able, had opposed her entering the convent. If she were to return home now, he would not badger her. But his silent "I told you so" would be manifest and unequivocal.

Even so, she could have pulled it off if it had not been for what she considered to be the will of God. The will of God through Sacred Scripture in the place of prayer.

All of that could not have been a mere coincidence.

So she continued to go forward, one foot ahead of the other, finding some form of fulfillment in the children she taught.

Then she began to take notice of the young assistant, Father Anderson. He was in his fourth year at St. Ursula's. The rest of this year plus all of the next and he would have served his hitch.

At a time when there was considerable experimentation in Liturgy elsewhere, Mass was strictly kosher at St. Ursula's. It wouldn't be otherwise given its pastor. Nonetheless Father Anderson made his performance come alive. He had good presence. And his sermons were captivating, relevant, and sprinkled with humor. After a few of these— just to make sure it wasn't a fluke and that his homilies were always good—Sister Perpetua began to smile.

It did not take the other nuns long to notice. If Sister Perpetua had thought life was closing in on her before, she could have had no concept as to what would happen when her Sisters began to ratchet up their contempt for her frivolous behavior.

She simply stiffened her resolution. She would not disgrace her mother. She would not allow her father to win. Mainly, she would not take her hand from the plow. But she had to turn to someone. Otherwise she would implode from all the external pressure.

Who else but Father Anderson?

The revised Code of Canon Law had been published a year ago. But even in the old 1918 Code, with its call for "regular confessors" for nuns (regular in the sense of an assigned priest to hear nuns' confessions every week), even then nuns could select any priest they wished as their confessor. And no one could say them nay.

So Sister Perpetua began going to confession to Father Anderson.

Of course St. Ursula's confessionals were yesterday's model with three compartments: the center cubicle for the priest and one on either side for penitents. Even when the sliding panel was opened, a grating and a curtain still separated confessor and penitent.

There'd be no fooling around with a confessional room and communication face-to-face. Not while Father Angelico was at the helm. If the guarantee of anonymity was good enough for the past few centuries, it would survive the next millennium.

Even with the barrier of door, grate, and cloth, it was sometimes impossible for the priest to recognize the identity of the penitent. If not by name at least from the routine sameness of the style of speech. There was the woman, for instance, who always added the phrase "more or less," as in "I ate meat on Friday four times, more or less." And, yes, the inevitable would happen from time to time—as in, "I missed Mass once, more or less."

It did not take Father Anderson long to recognize that one of his penitents was a nun—and, in short order after that, that the nun was Sister Perpetua.

What gave her away initially was what Anderson liked to call the "eau de nun." It made sense, since every nun wore the same sort of clothing (differing only in size), that the same detergent be used for all laundering. So every nun, at least in this school, smelled exactly like every other nun.

But there was more.

Twined about her cincture was the rosary. Not the beads of the five-decade rosary many Catholics carried and some actually used. The nuns wore the full fifteen-decade variety with large beads. If not for the beads, nuns would have been completely noiseless when they walked. However, with the beads hanging loosely from the cincture, nuns clicked when they walked. They also clicked in the confessional when they fidgeted about trying to find a comfortable spot on which to kneel.

There was still more.

Nuns confessed things practically no one else ever mentioned. As when one would confess anger with her children. Just out of curiosity the priest might ask how many children she had. And she would answer, "Sixty." It may be possible that only a nun ever confessed failing in "promptitude"—meaning she had been late for one or another ritual function.

Put these all together in the dark recesses of the confessional and you have a nun-penitent.

One further deduction on the part of Father Anderson—that no other nun assigned to St. Ursula's would think of using Father Anderson—led to the conclusion that this had to be Sister Perpetua.

At first her confessions were run-of-the-mill: impatience with the children; resentment toward some other nun—or all of them; inattentiveness during prayer; and, of course, the ever-popular failure in promptitude.

Gradually, her reserve broke down. She announced that she wanted him as her spiritual director. He consented. This created an entirely different plateau in their relationship. She was no longer confessing sins—or rather, peccadilloes. Now she was consulting him on the level of her spirituality. He should be steering her on a path that would mark progress in her spiritual life. She should confide in him with deepening trust.

This new plateau further dampened what had been no more than a unilateral platonic affair, alive only in his fantasy life.

To date, her only contribution to their relationship had been a smile. Not much to fuel a genuine love affair. Her participation in this relationship might or might not be active. He had no way of knowing.

His fantasies were extremely entertaining. But now they had to be put on a back burner.

As for her spiritual life, after some initial progress, things had bogged down. The crucial question became whether or not to remain in her present position.

They talked about it regularly—interminably.

It was her life, the only mortal life she would have. Was she throwing it away on mindless rules and regulations? She was still a young woman. She could have children of her own. But if she stayed put, years would pile up to the point that she would have dried up and her children would not be.

The argument for leaving was compelling.

And Father Anderson was growing more convinced from each session with her that she should, indeed, put an end to this struggle and go. He was not of a mind to vacillate with no hope of a resolution. A favorite incident he'd witnessed involved a gentleman, one Ferris Fain by name, who had played first base for the Detroit Tigers. An opposition batter bunted. The second baseman ran to cover first, resulting in a collision. The two players shouted at each other, argued with each other and cursed each other—until Fearless Ferris Fain hauled off and decked the runner. Fain had become weary of "all the jawin'" and determined to end it. And so he did.

Fain was one of Anderson's heroes; he and the first baseman were both men of action.

Perhaps it was because Perpetua was playing devil's advocate. The harder Anderson pressed his argument for leaving, the more she dug in her heels. Inevitably their sessions took on a sameness.

There was no question that their get-togethers had to be beyond suspicion. In the confessional, out walking openly, rarely in the convent's parlor, it really didn't much matter: The mere fact that each was young, of the opposite sex, and evidently interested in the other was enough to fuel evening and Sunday afternoon gab sessions.

Then something happened that redirected the attention of the faculty. The pastor and Mother Superior decided that the school needed a kindergarten and therefore an additional teacher. The ongoing census indicated a bumper crop of preschoolers coming of age. Their parents pressed for adding a kindergarten to serve them.

Compared with other teaching orders, the Theresians were fairly well stocked with nuns; nevertheless, the supply was not inexhaustible. Even Father Angelico had to pull in his horns every now and again when confronted with a strong and determined Mother General.

The request for an additional nun was denied. *Soror locuta est.* Sister has spoken. Case closed.

As a result—and much to the interest of the faculty—instructors qualified to teach primary grades were now being interviewed. That took a lot of heat off Sister Perpetua and Father Anderson. She was obsessed with the question of whether to stay in or bug out of religious life. He was busy trying to counsel her while wrapping up the loose ends of his stay at St. Ursula's. Though only his first assignment, this surely had been an education.

Eventually—with indifference on the part of Perpetua and Anderson and great curiosity on the part of the rest of the faculty—a young woman named Lillian Niedermier was hired to teach the second grade.

Finally, it was time for Father Anderson to leave St. Ursula's.

It was the custom in almost every parish to host a send-off for the departing clergyman. The purpose of such an event was to elicit donations that would speed the recipient on his way and soften the blow of moving. In some parishes this collection was called a purse.

Associated with this procedure was the following probably apocryphal story.

It involved a pastor and his assistant who got along with each other much as did Angelico and Anderson. Actually, the two were at the point where if one more straw were to fall the relationship would self-destruct.

The sanctuary of this particular church was the traditional type with the high altar near the rear wall. The tabernacle held the consecrated wafers for Communion, as well as the single large wafer used for the Benediction service. This tabernacle could be opened from the front or the rear. The rear opening afforded access when there was an emergency sick call while services were being conducted—thus obviating the disturbance or interruption of the service.

One Sunday evening the pastor was concluding Benediction service. At the end, in dramatic fashion, all the church lights, except the spotlight on the tabernacle, were dimmed. The congregation was singing, "Good Night, Sweet Jesus" as the pastor opened the tabernacle to repose the Blessed Sacrament. At this very moment, the assistant was at the rear door preparing for a sick call.

So there they were: the congregation singing, "Good Night, Sweet Jesus," the pastor and his assistant looking at each other through the open tabernacle.

The assistant said, "Good night, Joe."

Shortly thereafter, the assistant was assigned to another parish. As he left the rectory, carrying his few earthly possessions, he said to his now former pastor, "So long, Joe. And, Joe: No purse."

Father Anderson did not get a similar bum's rush. His time had been paid in full. The only striking similarity was in the farewell collection: There was none.

In baseball, the on-deck batter swings either several bats or a special weighted bat. The extra load makes the single bat to be used at the plate seem light as a feather by comparison. In parochial assignments, serving under a Father Angelico made almost any subsequent parish seem like a little bit of heaven.

So it was with Father Anderson. His next parish after St. Ursula's was Nativity. In location and congregation it was not unlike St. Ursula's. The difference was in the pastor. Though of the same vintage as Angelico, he did not look over his assistant's shoulder. Anderson was given certain responsibilities and was left to his own devices as to how to respond to them.

Anderson appreciated being treated as an adult. However, this new-found freedom would grow into what some might describe as a mixed blessing at best.

Back at St. Ursula's, Father Angelico expectantly awaited his next assistant. His patience was not at all resilient. In less than a month he began contacting the chancery about a replacement for Anderson. He drew a grimly bleak if realistic picture of a large parish being served by a single priest.

As it turned out, Angelico simply lived in an unfortunate time frame.

When he had served his apprenticeship as an assistant there were many priests to staff many parishes. A change in assignment required nothing more than a letter beginning with the words: "Dear Father So-and-So: For the care of souls I have it in mind to send you to . . ." And there followed the name of one's next assignment where one would work for no more than the next five years.

Times had changed drastically. In a word, there just simply were not enough priests to go around. And assignments were no longer made by letter; now the transferee had an active voice in the circumstances of his own future. In this seller's market, the first to be shunned were despots like Father Angelico. The irascible tyrant importuned the chancery people via mail and phone, until, worn down by the onslaught, they had to respond.

The task of informing the irate pastor on the present way of life fell to a young priest—low man on the hierarchical totem pole.

After stating the simple truth that St. Ursula's was not going to get a replacement for Father Anderson, the young cleric responded to Father Angelico's, "Why not!?"

"Because," the fledgling priest replied, "no one will serve with you."

Angelico seethed, fussed, and fumed. It didn't matter whether a priest wanted to come live with this pastor: Send him!

In fending off all these objections, the chancery official held the trump card: the factual truth—no one would serve with the cantankerous old pastor.

Five

MEANWHILE, a vacuum had been created in the spiritual life of Sister Perpetua.

Her spiritual director was gone. Not irretrievably—she and he still shared the same city. Yet, to try to maintain their relationship would complicate things. The city's bus service left much to be desired. Twelve nuns shared the one car allotted to St. Ursula's convent. Jerry Anderson had a car, of course. But it was unrealistic to expect him to visit her. He had more than enough to do acquainting himself with his new parish.

It was June. The traditional time for graduation celebrations and, of course, June brides. Both sorts of events saw the return of Father Rick Casserly. Even after all these years, he was still called upon occasionally to witness a marriage at his former parish. He also agreed to attend St. Ursula's high school graduation.

Feeling the loss of Father Anderson, Sister Perpetua's attention turned to Father Casserly. Given a choice between Casserly and Anderson—all other things being equal—Perpetua would have chosen Father Rick for her director.

In the cold light of reality, Anderson had been no more than a convenience: He had been handy when she felt the need of spiritual direction. Now that Anderson had departed he was no more handy than Casserly—who would have been her first choice had that been convenient.

She phoned Father Casserly and explained the situation. The main problem, if he accepted her plea, would be transportation. But before any concern about how to get from here to there, Casserly would have to agree to become her director.

He was well aware that his primary responsibility was to his present parishioners. Of course one neither could nor should cull nonparishioners out of the confessional line nor screen phone calls. But taking on an individual for a relationship as sensitive as personal spiritual direction could develop into a time-consuming task.

Casserly had lived through a similar misery during his days at St. Ursula's. Perhaps, on second thought, not so similar; there he'd had to deal merely with the pastor. Perpetua answered not only to the pastor but much more nitpickingly to the Mother Superior, plus ten other equally dissatisfied nuns.

He reached for the phone just before it rang. It was Sister Perpetua.

"I was just about to call you." His assured tone was that of a self-confident priest. "I've given your request a lot of thought. And prayer," he added, although not at all sure that his considerations had actually included prayer. "I'd be glad to help you. And I think I may have a solution to the transportation problem."

"But—"

"I have quite a few friends at Ursula's," he continued over her interruption. "I'm sure I can get one of the women to drive you back and forth. I haven't actually contacted anyone yet. I wanted to find out first what you think about it. Frankly, it's about the only way this can work."

"There's more . . ." She sounded bewildered. "There's another problem."

"Oh?"

"It happened just today. Mother Superior called me in this afternoon—just a few minutes ago."

"What is it?"

"I'm being transferred."

He was about to ask if she had been consulted about the move when he remembered the Theresians operated in the old, strict fashion: One was told nothing more than where one was going and when one was expected to arrive. "To another school?" The Theresians staffed a few hospitals. It was easily possible that a nun such as Perpetua with several years of teaching under her belt could be sent to a hospital to start from scratch.

"I think the parish has a school. Mother didn't say—and I was too shocked to ask."

"Has it got a name?" Perpetua's information so far had not been very helpful.

"St. Adalbert's."

There followed a long silence. "Adalbert?"

"Yes."

Another long silence. Then: "Do you know anything about St. Adalbert's?"

Perpetua was not one given to asking questions. "I never heard of it before."

Again, silence.

"Adalbert's," he said finally, "is kind of famous—or rather, infamous."

"Not another Ursula's! I don't think I could take that."

How to soften the news? Casserly thought it wise not to dump too much reality on Perpetua all at once. St. Adalbert's convent had been a Waterloo for many an undecided, confused Theresian nun. Deep within him, Casserly held a secret hope that Perpetua could weather this and endure. But the matter of this assignment had to be handled delicately.

"It's not another Ursula's." He didn't sound as self-assured as he had in the beginning of this conversation. "It's along similar lines. But not the same. Listen: You've got your walking papers. I know from my exposure to this group that there's no reason to expect a review or an appeal. You have to go where you've been sent—or start a procedure to leave religious life."

"*Leave? Take my hand from the plow? Look back?* I can't do that! I've got to hang on!"

Similar thoughts had occurred to Casserly. He did not want her to give up. Especially without giving this assignment her best shot. "Look," he said, "when are you scheduled to go to Adalbert's?"

"Mother Superior didn't say. She didn't give a specific day. She just said to be ready . . . that somebody from the mother house would come by and take me there."

"Anything else?"

"Uh . . . like what?"

"Did she say anything else about where you're going?"

"No. Now that you mention it, there was a long period when she didn't say anything. Like she was waiting for me to say something. But I couldn't think of anything to say. It came as such a shock. I was just trying to absorb the thing. I don't think I grasp the whole situation even now. I called you . . . sort of instinctively. You're the first one I've told . . . not even my folks."

"Okay. Get your things packed."

"That won't be hard."

Ah yes, he thought, the vow of poverty. Women religious generally seemed to take it much more seriously than male religious. Casserly was a diocesan priest. So he had taken no vows. Even so, he had few possessions.

"I think it's going to be imperative that you come to me on a regular basis. You have every right to choose me as your director. Put your foot down. Something you're going to have to do much more often now. They'll have to provide you with transportation. If they out and out refuse, get in touch with me. We're playing hardball now."

She hesitated. "What am I getting into? You're scaring me . . ."

"Don't worry. We're going to see this thing through together."

The last statement quieted her fears. Until this suggestion that he intended to support her in this new and frightening venture, she had felt desperately alone. "Okay. I'll do everything you say. But after I settle in, what happens next? Do I contact you?"

He considered the question briefly. "Better you leave the first move to me. I've got a lot more clout than you have. Not that my influence could move a mountain or anything. But I'm completely out of their jurisdiction. And as far as guiding you, I've got Church law in my pocket."

She sighed audibly. "Thanks. I really mean it. Before I talked to you I didn't know which end was up. Now I feel lots more confident. I'll go to Adalbert's and wait for your call. Thanks and thanks again."

He signed off, then leaned back in his chair. His mind was cluttered by the turn of events. Before this phone call, he had foreseen no problems in granting Perpetua's request.

Casserly knew firsthand the difficulties of staffing St. Ursula's parish and/or school. But it was not impossible. Perpetua herself was a walking example of that. Her current assignment had been not only Perpetua's first teaching position but also she had embarked upon it fresh from the novitiate—a brand, spanking-new Sister turned loose on nun-baiting school kids.

Yet Perpetua had carried it off. In the face of these challenges, she'd stuck it out for seven years.

But now she was about to face the greatest crisis the Theresians could mount. Its name was Adalbert, and its purpose was geared to be a launching pad—sending Perpetua out into the lay world.

St. Adalbert had begun as a legitimate parish in Detroit's far west side, actually straddling the border between Detroit and Dearborn. Neither Detroit nor Dearborn was willing to out and out claim the territory. Its atmosphere comprised the cinder belched from the gigantic Ford Rouge Plant that turned out cars and soot. It had not taken long for the St. Adalbert's plant—church, rectory, school, and convent, all very small—to become encrusted with the automotive giant's spewing waste.

In short, the neighborhood grew to be an undesirable place to live and to support a Catholic parish. The parish plant did one favor for the diocese: Instead of become an imposing white elephant it remained tiny.

As for clergy staffing the parish, even in the Church's heyday in the 1960s—when priests were abundant—St. Adalbert's never had more than the one lonely pastor.

As for the convent, gradually, the Theresians managed to post there the order's most cantankerous, irascible, obnoxious, peevish, bad-tempered, disagreeable Sisters—with a mean age in the mid-to-high seventies. Thus did the Sisters of St. Adalbert's form a chute to the outside world.

Young women, such as Sister Perpetua, would from time to time mistakenly enlist in the Theresians. Usually, any Theresian convent to which such hopefuls were missioned quickly and easily—one might even say, with relish—made them see the error of their ways. And the once idealistic candidate would leave the order.

The Sisters of St. Ursula's had done their darnedest to ease Perpetua out of their company. They undoubtedly would have succeeded had it not been for her little miracle in the form of a relevant Gospel text for meditation. Armed with that revelation, and supported by the counseling of her director, Father Anderson, Perpetua had kept her feet on the path despite the undertow created by the Sisters.

Thus the religious powers that be decided that Perpetua needed the St. Adalbert's convent to catapult her out into the mainstream of American life.

Within the week Perpetua met her van—it wasn't a large van—but then she scarcely needed much space.

Notified that Perpetua was now ensconced at St. Adalbert's, Casserly made his phone call to Mother Superior. He came on strong. He wasn't asking for any favor. Sister Perpetua had voluntarily and spontaneously requested that he be her spiritual director and he intended to do just that. He had even taken the trouble to check with the chancery; it was fine with the boys downtown. And so Mother Superior, as head of this convent, had better make transportation available.

At the first words of Mother Superior's response, Casserly was willing to confess to overkill.

She couldn't have been more agreeable. Of course she would take care of the necessary details. All she needed was to know when such transportation was desired.

Casserly was almost speechless. He didn't know what to make of this spirit of cooperation.

For her part, Mother Superior was simply confident that the spirit of the St. Adalbert's nuns would win the day. To date, it had never failed.

Dumbfounded, Sister Perpetua learned no one was putting any barrier between her and her spiritual director. Could Father Casserly have been misinformed? He had come on so strongly about the pitfalls that awaited her at St. Adalbert's.

Casserly shared her wonderment.

Mother Superior couldn't have been more cooperative. Initially, Casserly and Perpetua met once a month. The convent's Damoclean sword seemed to call for nothing oftener.

Like the storied Chinese water torture, the campaign at the convent started slowly. These Sisters, like all Theresians, were semicontemplative. But during the prescribed periods when speaking was permitted, no one spoke to Perpetua.

At first she didn't tumble to what was going on. Of an evening or a Sunday afternoon she would sit in the convent's common room, keeping busy with knitting. Everyone seemed to be working on something. But no one spoke to her. No one even acknowledged her presence. If Perpetua asked a question, no one replied. If she commented on something another Sister said, it was as if she hadn't spoken.

At first she was willing to tolerate any number of eccentricities. After all, these were very elderly women. Some gave evidence of Alzheimer's disease. She rationalized, coming up with excuse after excuse.

She mentioned this phenomenon to Casserly in their monthly meeting only because he probed for problems. He could not believe the convent's reputation was ill-founded; there had to be some basis for all the rumors.

He hit pay dirt when he asked about socialization, camaraderie. There wasn't any—at least not for Perpetua.

She assured him that she could take it. Encouraged, he urged her to continue her counteroffensive. Keep talking. Keep asking. Keep being pleasant. He was certain of her eventual victory, the triumph of goodness over rank pettiness.

Heartened and reassured, Perpetua clung patiently to her Scripture motto: Whoever puts his hand to the plow but keeps looking back is unfit for the reign of God. She would not turn away. She would not turn back. She wanted to endure. Her spiritual director wanted her to endure.

But it was far easier to say than to do.

She wondered what her Sisters had in mind. What were they doing to her. Ostracizing? Shunning? It was as if she were a ghost. She was there in the convent, but no one seemed to notice. As far as the other nuns were concerned, she simply didn't exist. It was nerve-racking.

But in time she began to adjust. If she could endure, maybe they would let up. Maybe it was just a test. They would accept her in time. If only she could wait them out.

The parish school was a token effort. The first through the sixth grades were functioning. These six grades contained only a few children. Of all the nuns at St. Adalbert's, Perpetua was, by far, best able to handle a full class burden. But she was the only one not participating in the school in any way.

Bored nearly out of her mind, Perpetua sought to get involved. Perhaps she could visit the sick, care for them at home. Perhaps she might tutor slow students.

Each and every one of her overtures was rejected by Mother Superior, who reminded her that she had already been given permission to leave the convent for spiritual direction. That, on a continuing basis, was much more latitude than any of the other Sisters were granted. Or had even requested for that matter.

But she desired more responsibilities? Watch the bulletin board, Mother told her.

Perpetua did just that. Her name began appearing on the duty roster. She was given care of floors, toilets, and of some of the more dependent Sisters—who actually required more nursing care than "assisted care."

At least, she hoped, these nuns for whom she cared would spare her a word or two.

That was not to be.

The little miracle began to fade. It was all good and well to remain faithful to one's commitment to God and not turn back. But she could not envisage what she was enduring here as any sort of Godly commitment. She was being horridly treated by a group of women who called themselves religious.

She was beginning to enter onto the path that had been her destiny from the beginning. Subconsciously, then consciously, she was preparing to leave the convent and religious life.

The only mind that had not been changed was that of her spiritual director. There was never any major change in the direction he set for her.

Everything appeared to have deserted her. Her desire not to embarrass her parents by quitting had perished in the face of the grungy toilet bowls she continued to keep immaculate. Her special Scripture lesson probably would make sense in some setting other than the Theresians.

That left standing only Father Casserly.

Six

Over the months of counseling, the relationship between Sister Perpetua and Father Casserly evolved. It had to. She was revealing her inmost soul.

Gradually she began seeing him in a different aspect. She had never been this candid with anyone—parents, girlfriends, even Father Anderson. When she'd been under his direction, she had not been undergoing the enormous stress that the Adalbert group was now inflicting.

Looking back on their work together, she would have to guess that, for whatever reason, Father Anderson had been more interested in her than she was in him. Perpetua and Anderson had operated on the surface. When he was sent to another parish and she was exiled to Adalbert's, there had been no emotional tugs—certainly none on her part.

Not so her dependence on and feeling for Rick Casserly. For both obvious and subtle reasons she felt more emotionally involved with him.

And so she stayed and suffered and soldiered on, almost entirely for Casserly's sake. He was determined that she would, with his faithful help, make it. They would conquer.

Slowly, quietly, steadily, her feelings for Casserly deepened. She had given him her soul with all its hidden places, strengths, and weaknesses. She didn't say it—she didn't dare think it—but she was about to give him her body. It was all there was left.

But how?

It couldn't be as simple as removing clothing and hopping into bed. Not for people like Rick and her.

What if she had badly misread Rick's feelings for her? What if she were to offer herself to him and he rejected her? She couldn't imagine him doing anything like that. But what if . . .?

She had to fantasize a plan—if she were indeed mistaken, that would give her a face-saving way out.

Good Lord, she had never even read a romance novel. Never mind. She had an active imagination.

For the first time, Sister Perpetua was grateful for the isolation imposed by the other nuns at St. Adalbert's. Instead of suffering cabin fever, she was planning an assignation. She was aware that customarily the male was the instigator in a tryst. But, hell, it was the 1980s—a time for women to take charge. Or so she'd read.

The simple act of planning this very special get-together provided stimulation. She'd never done anything like this before. She found she had some latent talent for plotting.

In the end, this is how it should play out:

She would ask for the keys to the car. She was going to consult with her spiritual director. (That much was at least partially true.)

Although as a member of the Theresians she had never had occasion to wear one, she did possess a swimsuit—modest and functional, rather than openly seductive. She would put it on, then stand under the shower. After she drip-dried she would don her full outer habit and drive to Father Casserly's rectory.

It would be a Saturday afternoon, so he should be there making last-minute preparations for the evening Mass.

He would answer her ring. "Sister," he would exclaim, "what are you doing here? I mean, did you make an appointment? Did I forget something?"

"Noooo . . ." She would be smiling broadly. "It's like they say, I was in the neighborhood and I thought I would just drop in for a while."

"Well, I don't quite understand. But . . . come on in." He would lead her into the living room.

The rectory was a two-story building with full basement. Originally it had been built to house at least five priests. Four suites had once been occupied by four priests. There was an extra suite for the housekeeper that could have been converted to rooms for a priest, if they'd ever gotten the desired assistant. They never had.

Father Casserly now lived on the main floor, using the deserted housekeeper's quarters for himself.

"Well," he would say as they settled themselves in chairs they always used for the counseling sessions, "we didn't have an appointment. How did you get out?"

"I just had to. I couldn't bear to be locked up there another day."

"You are going back. I mean later today . . . aren't you?"

"Yes. Yes. I just had to tell a few lies to get out."

"Harmless lies, it sounds like to me. White lies? Something we can deal with in your regular session next week?"

"Oh yes, they can wait."

"Can I get you something? Iced tea? A cookie?"

"No, nothing."

"Well, then, what have you been doing on your marvelous day off?"

"I went swimming." He would buy the swimming excuse only because he had no idea how terrified she was of the water.

"Swimming!"

"Yes. Just the thing to do on a hot summer's day."

"Granted. But how did you pull it off?"

"Pull it off?"

"Yes . . ." He would gesture toward the habit. "You're not exactly dressed for the sport."

"It really isn't that difficult. The idea is to put your swimsuit on under the habit. Then all you have to do is find a little spot for privacy and slip the habit off. With all the practice I've had, that can be done in the twinkling of an eye."

He would blush slightly. "You mean after you got done swimming, you put the habit back on over the swimsuit?"

"Uh-huh."

"It must be terribly uncomfortable. I mean your suit must still be wet. Isn't it?"

"Well, yes. I didn't count on the discomfort."

"This is going to get dicey, I think, isn't it? By the time you get back to the convent you are going to be dry-cleaned. You will be wearing practically a sauna."

She would smile nervously. "I guess I didn't plan this very well."

"Well . . ." He would hesitate for several moments. "Why don't you get straightened around before you leave? You can use my shower. Get rid of the swimsuit. Then when you're dry you can put the habit on and it'll be lots more comfortable by the time you get back."

"Well, if it's not too much trouble . . ."

"No trouble at all. You've never been in the back of the rectory. I'll show you around."

They would go into his bedroom. "Excuse the messy bed. I wasn't expecting guests."

"Without a woman's touch, things tend to get this way."

By this time, his face would be almost the color of his hair. What had begun as an innocent offer of aid would be developing into the threat of serious sin. "Here's a fresh towel and there's the bathroom and shower. Take your time. I'll be in the living room."

He would go back to the living room and pace nervously, hoping that this would not explode.

But explode it would.

That would happen when she walked in wearing only the towel.

Her hair would be wet because she had taken a shower. Her smile would be forced and plastic. Two people would be standing in the living room, both deeply embarrassed. The silence would last a few moments. Then she would say, "I hope you don't mind. I wanted to give the habit a chance to dry."

From that point on, the scenario could go in any number of directions.

She would wait for him to make a move. But not too long. If he approached her, she would throw herself into his arms. From that point they could allow passion to carry them through to that rumpled bed.

If he did not make the first move, she would drop the towel. Just observing him over the years had left her with no doubt whatsoever of his masculinity, his ample testosterone level. If she stood before him naked, he would never be able to resist her.

If he were willing, he could mend her life, which had become so fragmented. What would happen after their first sexual adventure only time would reveal. As far as she was concerned, they could simply exchange the counseling sessions for romantic interludes. Fortified with tangible, expressed love, she would be strong enough to field whatever cruelties the nuns would invent for her.

And Father Casserly? He would achieve his goal of helping her to stay the course in the face of the Theresian plan. Included in this package was a missing fulfillment for him.

It certainly seemed a satisfactory solution for everyone. The nuns could lay on the punishment as thick as they wished. That should make a group of sadists happy. She would draw strength from Rick and their lovemaking. And she would make sure he was a happy camper.

She just needed a little time to get used to her plan. As far as she was concerned, this was a drastic step; she was not prepared to put it into action immediately.

So she stayed with the status quo. She was obedient to every crazy and monstrous command and demand made by the Sisters. Her delight in what was to be sufficed. She was at peace in the anticipation of Rick's love.

In her counseling sessions her mind would wander in fantasies that would one day become realities. She would undress him with her eyes—an action once the province of the male. Yes, there was something to this new feminism.

In due time she was ready. She waited for the next sunny, warm Saturday—one that would make credible an outdoor swim. Such an opportunity arose ten days later.

Since it was Saturday, the convent's one and only old car would be used for shopping. But Saturday afternoons were virtually the only times that one could be quite sure Father Casserly would be at home and unencumbered by appointments. Knowing Mother Superior might forbid the car's use even for spiritual direction, Perpetua decided to ask for it anyway. After all, this could be God's will. She had to give it a chance.

The frown could have meant that Mother was displeased at the request. Or it might have been her standard expression.

In any case, permission was granted with a curfew no later than four in the afternoon.

Perpetua paid no mind to the curfew. If her plan did not develop the way she had expected, she would be back in plenty of time. If, on the other hand, it worked substantially if not perfectly, nothing Mother Superior could do to her would matter.

For her part, Mother could afford to be patient and confident. It was always possible the young nun would break and conform to the demanding obedience that characterized the Theresians. Occasionally a rebellious Sister would change her life and stay with the Theresians. Something like a wild horse being broken to human use. But wild horses learned to conform much more reliably than young women.

Perpetua could escape the convent to visit her director. It made little difference to Mother. The impetuous young lady would return and the persecution would proceed to break her—or send her packing.

After receiving permission and the car keys, Perpetua dug out her bathing suit and slipped it on. It fit loosely. She had lost significant weight in these almost two years at St. Adalbert's. It didn't matter. According to her plan, Rick would not see her in the suit. Either she would be wearing the habit or nothing.

She showered with the suit on, then patted herself down. Her extremities were dry but the suit was sopping.

She parked in her familiar spot in the church lot. She remained in the car, waiting for her breathing to return to normal. Once that was accomplished, she went to the rectory door and rang the bell.

It was like living a dream.

He was dressed in black slacks, shoes, and a white T-shirt. He was surprised to see her. He supposed this was his fault—that she had made the appointment but he had failed to recall it.

She disabused him. She told him of going swimming and getting the keys. She did not mention the curfew; it just wasn't relevant.

She was sure he would have some reaction to the genuine fact that beneath her habit she was wearing a wet bathing suit. It was also a fact that she was chafed and miserable.

Just here, according to her scenario, he was supposed to offer his shower and an opportunity to lose the wet swimsuit. Her heart raced in anticipation.

"Well . . ." he said, and hesitated, as she'd planned. But instead of showing her to the bathroom and offering her a fresh towel, he began talking to her about the convent.

It was only a matter of time, he predicted, before the Theresians would have to catch up with the post-Vatican Church. She herself was contributing to this progress by her very presence in the convent. And when, inevitably, the change came about, Perpetua would be there to celebrate the victory. All she had to do was persevere. He urged her to remember that divine lesson that she had learned at prayer: Stay the course. Don't turn back.

All the while he was talking, he seemed insensible of her uncomfortable condition.

She felt like a balloon whose air was slowly escaping. It hadn't worked. He had not caught her signal. It had gone well over his head.

She was lost. All this time Rick Casserly had been her preserver. The only strength she had left was in his arms. Love seemed banned in her convent. She was starving from denial of compassion.

Rick continued to extol the virtue of patience. But his words fell on a distracted mind. With great difficulty, she held back heated tears. She blinked some of them away, brushing the escaping ones aside with furtive gestures.

Rick concluded his monologue by noting that he had to be getting over to church to prepare for Mass. As he let her out, he added one more pitch for restraint and prayer for her religious life. He assured her he would join her in that prayer.

He shut the door and retreated to the back of the rectory. Thus he did not see the forlorn figure walking dejectedly to her car. He did not see her sitting in the car, shoulders shaking from gut-wrenching sobs.

Now she was completely alone. Her final hope of finding a compassionate ear and a loving body had just been dashed. She was despondent and terribly, terribly depressed. The battle was over. Rules without humane mercy had won.

She was in no condition to drive. Nevertheless, she turned the ignition and put the car in gear. She hoped she would not harm anyone as she drove. Other than that, she didn't care.

Seven

Rɪᴄᴋ ᴄᴀssᴇʀʟʏ automatically prepared the church for the first of the weekend Masses.

Light the candles. Don't forget the Paschal candle. Turn the lights on—though on this bright, sunny day they were hardly needed. Check the microphones to make sure all are working.

While he followed the familiar routine, his thoughts returned to his unexpected visitor.

He was puzzled. It just didn't make sense.

Why would she lie about having an appointment with him? Just to go swimming? The two of them had talked of many things in the counseling sessions. Lots of extraneous subjects were discussed. Never once was there a mention of water sports.

He had no notion how many layers of cloth went into a full religious habit. But he was pretty sure that there was room enough, if one were familiar with the garb, to wriggle out of a bathing suit without having to remove the habit.

If that were true, why would she say she was wearing a wet bathing suit? Anyone wearing a wet suit under the bulk of that habit would have to be extremely uncomfortable. He'd thought it strange the moment she'd mentioned her discomfort.

At the time, he almost suggested she use his shower. Once she was dry and the suit was removed, all would be well. He didn't act on that thought because he instantly realized that course was fraught with danger.

There was no doubt about it: The two of them by themselves in a rambling rectory could spell trouble. Of course that was always a possibility when Perpetua came for spiritual direction. However, the setting for those meetings had been structured to ensure decorum.

But if they were alone and she was naked, look out!

The thought took only a moment to materialize. By the time the

54

thought became a temptation, he knew better than to start the ball rolling. That path led to disaster.

For one thing, he was her spiritual guide. As part of that designation, he heard her confession during each visit. If they had sex—even once—it would destroy that relationship. Not only that: If they were to sin together and he absolved her, he would be automatically excommunicated—a sin reserved to the Pope for absolution. Which meant, among other things, that he would confess to a priest who would have to notify the Holy See of the sin—all the while preserving Rick's anonymity. Absolution would be granted by a Vatican office acting in the name of the Pope. The penance demanded by Rome had been known to go as high as, "Father will cease acting as a priest and disappear."

All of that had flashed through Rick's mind in the few seconds it took him to reject the very strong temptation to offer Perpetua his shower and a towel.

As he went in a different direction, trying to convince her to keep a stiff upper lip and hang in there, he could see the tears welling in her eyes. He wasn't reaching her despair and he knew it. He had the strongest urge to take her on his lap and just hold her. Let her cry it out.

But that, he feared, would only return them to the shower and the towel.

So, in effect, he did nothing. This day she had brought him a tortured soul. She took away with her a troubled mind, to go with the tortured soul.

It had been no picnic for him either.

He knew Perpetua as well as or better than anyone else. He liked her. He liked her a lot. It would not have taken much to move from platonic friendship to a romantic relationship.

There had been sexual dalliances in his past. Nothing terribly serious. Inquisitive minds and responsive bodies; growing up experimenting with the opposite number.

In the twenty-five or so years he'd been a priest he had never violated the chastity required of him. But it was getting harder rather than easier as the years passed. Deeper than the drive for sexual fulfillment was the need for companionship. He was lonely.

Neither condition would have to last much longer if one could believe what was being written and bandied about. Almost anytime anyone mentioned the Catholic priesthood it was in reference to the priest shortage and the possibility of an optionally celibate clergy. That possibility seemed just around the corner. Eastern Uniate churches never had ruled against a married clergy. Most of their clergy were married. And their churches were in complete union with Rome.

Then there was the latter-day phenomenon with some of the Protestant clergy, notably those of the Episcopal and Lutheran faiths. Some of their priests and ministers were requesting inclusion in the Catholic priesthood. And some were welcomed—along with their families. Someplace along the line it must occur to the Catholic Church at large that if some men from other sects are welcomed to function as priests along with their wives and children, the option should be open to everyone.

Meanwhile men like Rick Casserly kept denying themselves the pleasure, comfort, and responsibility of married life.

He did not think of this often. But an occasion like this, when a woman every bit as lonely as he came to him, drove the lesson home: He did not dare even hold her hand.

The church was filling. Mass was scheduled to begin in just a few minutes.

Soon he would have to focus on the church service. Especially his homily. He'd been at this a quarter of a century now—a long, long time. His sermon preparation was not as it once had been; he had so much experience that his sermons no longer needed the research and preparation that he'd given them in his early years.

However, his recent conversation with Sister Perpetua had disquieted him. She had taken him unprepared and—he hated to admit it—he was confused. Had he handled her visit correctly? Both he and the nun admittedly were lonely people. He was supposed to guide her. The blind leading the blind.

He was limping psychologically. He understood loneliness but lacked the integrity to lead someone out of that dark night. Just as he limped when counseling in marital situations. He had never lived in the demanding closeness of marriage.

He felt he might correct this weakness by the simple process of getting married.

But that was not to happen anytime soon. As much sense as a married clergy made, there was no indication that the present Pope was paying attention to the plea that sprang from clergy and laity combined. On the contrary, His Holiness was building walls around celibacy and the question of female clergy by trying to preclude even a discussion about these solutions.

Father Casserly began to vest for Mass.

One final distraction: Suppose he were free to marry, who would have him at his age? And, if he had a choice, whom might he select?

These were such ridiculous questions that he could not help but chuckle.

He was surprised by the name that came to his mind.

He'd met her five or six years ago. And he'd encountered her occasionally since. They had talked and seemed to enjoy their conversations. Really there was not much of anything beyond an innocent friendship. But she did seem to like him. And he certainly liked her.

But the age difference was so great and their relationship had been so casual, that it seemed absurd even to think of such a thing.

Nonetheless, Lillian Niedermier, second-grade teacher at St. Ursula's school, was easy on his mind.

Wouldn't it be wonderful if something were to grow from this rudimentary relationship?

It might solve some of his problems. On the other hand, it might create some for her. What were the odds?

Astronomical.

Sister Perpetua parked in the port reserved for the nuns' car. She had no recollection of how she had gotten from Father Casserly's rectory to what passed for home. But here she was and there had been no accidents. For this she was grateful.

At least she was aware of one thing: The battle was over. Her days and nights with the Sisters of St. Adalbert's were finished. She might just as well put her vocation out of its misery. She just wasn't sure exactly how to do that. But it needed to be done, so, as she turned in the keys, she asked Mother Superior for a meeting.

Instead of addressing the request, Mother said, "You were unusually long with your director. Never mind, we've still got time for the shopping."

She seemed to be dismissing Perpetua. But the nun didn't budge.

"I need to talk," Perpetua said in a no-nonsense tone. "I need to talk to you now!"

Mother removed her glasses and slid them into their case. "Very well, Perpetua. What is it?"

Perpetua had not been invited to be seated. And in the Theresian order, one needed such an invitation. Otherwise one stood. She took the straight wooden chair opposite Mother.

A thin smile passed quickly across Mother's lips. Perpetua missed it entirely. From the tone of Perpetua's voice and her presumption of sitting without permission to do so, Mother guessed that this was the end. Perpetua would not be broken to the Theresian mold. So it would be farewell, Perpetua. Either conclusion would have been acceptable; it did not much matter to Mother.

"Mother," Perpetua began, perfectly calmly, "I feel that I have given the religious life a full effort on my part. It's not working. It will never work. Of that I'm now certain."

"You speak of the religious life not working. Did you think our life was somehow going to give you something? You were expected to serve this community, this way of life."

Perpetua was not going to cry. That had taken place in the car. She felt nothing but numbness. This meeting with Mother Superior was like purgatory. It was meant to be painful, but eventually it would be over.

"You are as a child," Mother continued, "compared with the other Sisters in this parish. Did you ever consider the years they have given to our order? They did not demand that the Theresians give them something. They have given their all to the order. They have held nothing back. What have you brought to us? What have you given?"

Perpetua considered these questions rhetorical; she did not bother to respond. She just wished it would be over.

"You refuse to answer!" Mother threw restraint to the winds. "Because you have no answer. You have agitated not one but two Theresian houses. I wish it were in my power to dismiss you as we did in the golden years before that wretched Council."

"How was that?" Just as a matter of curiosity, Perpetua raised her head and looked directly into Mother's eyes.

"We would have treated you as dead. You would be asked to leave sometime in the early morning hours, so the Sisters would not be aware of your departure. They would have retired with your presence in their home and awakened to find you gone as if you had been buried. We would have put a patch of cloth over your picture in the Mother House. Your name would never again be mentioned by the Sisters. If we cannot treat you thusly now, I assure you we will not think of you once you've left us."

"Just how do I do that, Mother?" Perpetua reached back to her initial reason for asking for this audience. There had to be a drill. Surely she was not the first to leave the Theresians. She knew for a fact that there was not a year when at least one hadn't left the order. Additionally, she now understood the role St. Adalbert's had played in this dance of religious death. All she wanted was to leave as soon as she could while following the proper procedure. She didn't want any trace left of her experiment in the religious life.

Mother retrieved her glasses, put them on, searched for and found a sheaf of papers. She slid the papers across the desk to Perpetua.

"This," Mother said, "is your first step."

Perpetua studied the pile. "What am I supposed to do with these?"

"There are forms to fill out and there is the petitioning document. You must fill them all out."

"How long after that will it take?"

"Nothing can be done until you complete the forms. Particularly, you must give good reasons why you are seeking this dispensation."

"Are there any so-called reasons cited in here? I don't want this held up because I didn't have the proper reasons."

"There should be no problem on that score. Put down your reasons to be dispensed from your sacred vows of poverty, chastity, and obedience as well as from your obligations to the order."

"That's all I need to do?"

"Yes. Fill out all the forms. Follow the instructions included."

"After I do this, then what?"

"I will send your petition to Mother General. She will send it, along with her recommendation, to Rome. There it will go to our Cardinal Protector at the Vatican. Finally, the Holy Father will grant the dispensation through the proper channel."

"There's no chance, someplace along that line, that the petition will be denied?"

Mother slowly shook her head. "Rome used to be more strict in matters like this. Not now. Particularly since both I and Mother General will add very strong recommendations that the petition be granted."

"You will?"

"We want you out. You are the round peg in the square hole."

"What shall I do while I wait out this process?"

"Nothing."

"Not even the janitorial work I've been doing?"

"Nothing. You may attend prayers if you wish. It will no longer be required. You will eat with the Sisters. But you must remain in your room during every talking session. The other Sisters would find it awkward to have you in their company during recreation."

"I guess they've found me awkward from the beginning. They've never talked to me."

"That should have given you a clue. You either had to conform to the Theresians or leave. You could have made your choice long ago. Now that you have, you will be in a sort of limbo. We will have no advance information as to when your dispensation will come. Be ready. For the moment it comes, you must go. Is this all clear?"

"Yes, Mother."

"Then you have my permission to leave. And may God have mercy on your soul."

Puzzled, Perpetua left the office. What sort of dismissal was that?

From the movies and TV shows she'd seen in the past, these were the types of words used when a judge passed the sentence of death on a convicted person.

Did Mother actually suppose that leaving this convent was like death? It was more evident that life was just outside these walls.

She entered her room—the nuns called them cells, which was more appropriate—and leaned back against the door. This had been quite a day. Quite a day. She took off her habit as well as the swimsuit, which by now was dry, as was the habit.

While she was nude she took stock of herself. Not bad. Not bad at all. She would have preferred a bit more meat on her bones. The result of a stress-filled time in the wrong place, living with the wrong people.

She would take care of that, perhaps even before she left this place. The food was not all that bad for institutional fare. Now that she knew her "Sisters" would be advised not to speak to her, much of the tension should be eased.

She put on a robe and spread the documents out on the desk. Truly there were a lot of forms to complete. She would stay up all night if necessary. She desperately wanted this over as soon as possible.

As she worked at the petition, she reflected, as she had many times, how accidental it was that she had found herself a member of the Theresian order.

She had attended a parochial school staffed by Theresians. She had wanted to serve God in a special way. Devout Catholics looked upon women who became nuns as "brides of Christ." Dora had found the concept fascinating and extremely attractive. The Theresians were, naturally, the religious order with which she was most familiar.

Thus, with this compelling urge to enter religious life, the only natural outlet was the one she knew best. It was not until she had been accepted and had begun living the Theresian rule that she realized that she had embarked on the completely wrong path.

Had she applied to almost any other religious order, she would most certainly have avoided this entire mess. Any other order and she would have had a satisfying and rewarding life.

She had only one more request of her religious superior. She wanted to consult with her spiritual director one more time.

Mother thought the request odd. When last she and Perpetua had met, the young nun definitely had made up her mind to leave. And this was only minutes after she had seen the director. Why, Mother wondered, would she not have told him of her decision then?

No matter. It was only a brief time before the troublesome one would be no more. Permission granted.

Rick Casserly was saddened and disappointed. He'd thought they were making steady if halting progress. He'd tried his best to convince her to hang in there. Evidently, his best was insufficient.

He had to admit, the game was over. No use trying to make this horse run. It was dead standing up.

So he tried to be upbeat.

He told her all about the Ursula club. Having served time in that parish and school, and now out of the parish and the convent as well, she was eligible to join.

There was a bit of gender inequity here but it was virtually unavoidable. Priests who had served at St. Ursula's could join the club, founded many years ago by Father Bob Koesler, either while they were there or after they had served their time.

Nuns stationed there could not join any club. The Theresian rule would not permit such a thing. Only someone like Perpetua, who left the order, could belong to the club. And there weren't many such cases.

They were about to part when he said, "I suppose this will be our final meeting."

"I think so. They are just tolerating my presence at St. Adalbert's. I think Mother—and maybe the rest of the Sisters—would rather not see me if they can help it. So I'd better not press my luck in asking to see you again."

"I don't think that's fair. But it may be wise."

"One more thing," Perpetua said. "After this is over, can I still come and see you . . . maybe regularly?"

He hesitated. Her previous visit had been fraught with possible problems. But, hey, those problems were covered by Perpetua's being in, for her, a bad habit. That shouldn't be a problem anymore. "Sure," he said with conviction. "Why not?"

In time, both might live to regret this continuance.

She returned to the convent to bide her time until Rome would set her free.

Since childhood, Dora had believed she could get anything she wanted if only she played her cards right. Now she wasn't so sure.

Eight

WHEN FATHER ANDERSON left St. Ursula's parish, he had traveled light.

In the five years since he'd been ordained, he had accumulated few possessions. And, as mentioned previously, there were no farewell gifts. The parishioners gave what they could to the parish. There was nothing in their budget for presents for priests who moved in and out of their lives like ships in the night.

That was all right with Jerry Anderson. Escaping intact from Father Angelico was gift enough.

Nativity parish, his second assignment, was, as one priest noted, a plum. A little wrinkled but a plum. That it was wrinkled was a comment on its age and obvious need of upkeep. The fruity metaphor was a tribute to its pastor of that time. Not that the pastor was especially holy, a good administrator, or a dynamic leader. It was just that he knew that the assistant pastor supply was running dry. Father Anderson could very well be the final extra priest for this parish and the pastor wanted to keep him for as long as possible.

So Anderson had pretty much carte blanche as to what he wanted to do.

A priority, since Jerry had been a stellar athlete himself, was to revive the parish athletic program.

In time, that program grew so substantially it overshadowed the parish that was the mother of it all. Before Jerry Anderson had arrived hardly anyone outside the parish had been acquainted with Nativity of Our Lord. Now, due almost entirely to its basketball program, almost everyone who at least read the sports pages or did not switch channels when the sports segment of the TV newscast came on was familiar with "Nativityville" and its director, Father Jerry Anderson.

Amateur basketball teams were formed all over Detroit, especially on the city's east side. Such teams quickly joined Nativityville's league.

X numbers of kids were practicing and playing basketball instead of looting or mugging. The city officials, particularly the police, loved the effort and gave it preferential support.

Frequently seen in the gym were scouts of every stripe: collegiate and professional. The import of this was not missed by kids who were well aware of the skyrocketing salaries in the pro leagues.

The parish's pastor operated in obscurity. This pleased him greatly as he was only a few years from retirement. He wanted to live to see that day. Nativityville was granting him immunity from any attention that might affect him adversely.

Oddly, a sports program such as this should have been the product of a powerful and popular parish. As it happened, the basketball league made the parish known and solvent—the tail wagging the dog.

As time passed, the sports program was able to function without Father Anderson's constant attention and presence. A manager was found and hired. The league continued to flourish. Jerry Anderson spent more time doing that for which he had signed up: being a priest seeing to the care of souls.

He revived the parish's St. Vincent de Paul Society. It became effective in finding shelter, food, employment for those in need, and, in general, putting skin and bones on works of mercy and Christian love.

What troubled him most in the day-to-day operation of the parish were the people with marriage problems. They came in three sizes: Those who were living together but growing apart. Those who were divorced and contemplating another marriage. And those divorced who already had attempted another marriage. Those in the latter category were referred to as "living in sin."

Jerry Anderson grew more and more estranged from the Tribunal—the archdiocesan department that processes marriage cases to determine whether a petitioner should be granted or refused a declaration of nullity.

The Tribunal, over very recent years, had become more user-friendly. So much so, in fact, that Rome grew irritated with the Church of the United States over the great number of annulments being granted.

For Anderson, the increasing annulments constituted a small step in the right direction. But it was a long way from the ultimate solution, which, in his mind, was abolishment of the entire process. He believed that anyone who had endured a failing marriage and been bloodied by a divorce should be welcomed openly by the Church as the People of God.

Instead, anyone applying for an annulment faced being bloodied again, this time with more embarrassing detail, more delving into the private and personal aspects of his or her relationship, more expenditure of time, more embroilment of friends, relatives, and acquaintances.

In his seminarian days, this ecclesial approach to marriage had seemed unnecessarily complicated. Never once had he doubted the permanence of marriage. But he did have to wonder about exactly what constituted marriage.

Church law dealt almost exclusively in positives. Were both parties free to marry? There was no previous marriage for either bride or groom? Neither was crippled psychologically? Neither brought any other impediment to the covenant? Both freely exchanged consent? The marriage was consummated?

Instinctively, young Anderson believed there must be more than this.

Where was love? Growth? The sense that, in the face of worse, poorer, and sickness, the union was working? There had to be more to matrimony than what the Church explicitly expected.

Then conscience stepped in.

A union might fragment. In which case Church law demanded: Prove it was that way from the very beginning.

But the conscience . . . the conscience knew. The inner voice told whether or not the marriage was true.

When, after careful, after agonizing prayer, the conscience concluded "nice try" but it just isn't working, then what to do?

Take the case to the Tribunal, Anderson presumed.

Or, if the person's conscience was strong enough to rely on, follow the dictates of the inaudible voice.

Just as one cannot be a little pregnant, so, one cannot be a little married. Either a couple is married or not. Anderson's conclusion was that conscience knew better and more accurately than the Tribunal.

His advice to couples who were blocked by Church law from marrying, as well as those already living in a canonically invalid marriage, was to follow their conscience. And if these consciences ruled that all was well with the marriage, then follow that dictate.

What if they were kidding themselves? Could they fool the priest? Most certainly; it was not that difficult to pull the wool over priestly eyes. However, God would not be deceived. Following one's conscience in opposition to law is tricky business. Pretending to follow conscience when one knows it is lying is fatal.

Father Anderson would lead troubled souls through this maze and, after their successful completion of this spiritual journey, he would advise them to recognize their extra-ecclesial wedding and continue to receive the sacraments. They must remember: Conscience has spoken, they are not a little married, they are a lot married.

All of this was accomplished in what is called the "internal forum."

The internal forum was located in the confessional, the rectory office, places where confidences are confided and secrets kept.

There was no church building, no altar, no side altar, no aisle to walk, no music, no flowers, no ceremony, no pomp, no circumstance.

It was a silent decision made by a man and a woman, ratified by a priest.

To move out of that internal forum into an external forum easily could become canonical suicide. After all, the woman, the man, and the priest are, in the eyes of some, operating against the law or, in the eyes of others, outside the law.

Yet it was Anderson's experience that although some couples could reach the conclusion that they were free to marry even though church law held they were not, still they needed a ceremony. And that ceremony they needed moved the matter into the external forum. At which point those involved—especially the priest—became open targets.

Anderson was well aware that as long as things remained in the internal forum, he was safe from recrimination or censure; the matter was more protected even than a lawyer-client or doctor-patient relationship.

Nevertheless, when couples needed a ceremony of some kind to dot the i's and cross the t's of conscience, Anderson would comply.

Going for him in this dangerous move was the obscure status of his parishioners. The people he served in Nativity parish were not tycoons. They watched and read the news; they did not make the news.

So, chances were no one was going to make a public display of the occasional simple ceremonies Anderson provided to make everyone comfortable. No doubt, even in these circumstances, conducting any of this business in the external forum was risky. But Anderson's own conscience would allow him to do no less.

It was his impression that the internal forum solution was used often in the Detroit archdiocese. It was known popularly as the Pastoral Solution.

Very, very few dared offer a public ceremony.

Doubts lingered as to what would happen if he were to be publicly exposed as having challenged Church law. Doubts due only to the forbearance of the local archbishop, Cardinal Mark Boyle. Lowering the boom abruptly was not Boyle's style. Backed into a corner, he could punish as firmly or as severely as any bishop. He tried to steer clear of that corner.

By his fifth year at Nativity, Anderson had transformed the creaking parish into a mecca of year-round basketball called Nativityville. He also had soothed uncounted troubled consciences.

As succeeding years rolled by, Father Anderson had become a parish institution. And then one day what he feared might happen did happen. He had almost convinced himself that it was so improbable it was impossible.

It started with the telephone. The pastor was out making hospital calls. Anderson picked up the ringing phone. "Nativity," he identified.

"This Father Anderson?" The voice was familiar. It had a manly, professional tone.

"Yes. And you are . . ."

"Dea. That's spelled D-E-A. Pronounced DAY."

Anderson put it together. "Dana Dea. The TV guy?"

"The same. I wonder if I could have a little of your time?"

Anderson hesitated. The call caught him by surprise. "Can you tell me what it's about?"

"Better face-to-face, Father. Got some time?"

Anderson consulted his calendar. "How about late tomorrow afternoon? Say, five?"

"Not so good. How about after dinner today. Say, eight?"

"Uh . . . okay."

"See you then." Dea hung up.

Anderson wanted more information. The connection had been broken too abruptly. He tried to guess at the reason for the call. The only thing Nativity had that could be construed as newsy was the basketball program. Although nothing out of the ordinary was going on in the program currently, it was the only newsmaker he could think of. It must be sports.

Promptly at eight the doorbell rang. In cassock and clerical collar, Anderson answered the door. Unlike many of his colleagues, he routinely wore the uniform. He needed it to work his little miracles such as witnessing weddings without benefit of Tribunal.

Dea in the flesh was more impressive than he was on TV—though he was handsome enough in the medium. At a little over six feet, he was several inches taller than the priest. Thinning hair had given him a widow's peak. His teeth caught the light and reflected it tenfold.

He extended his hand. "Dana Dea," he identified himself once more. "And this," he indicated his companion, "is Trish Murrow."

As tall as Anderson, she was strikingly beautiful. Her thick black hair fell in waves to her shoulders. Her skin was not merely black, but deep ebony—almost purple. He guessed she was a model.

Dea completed the introduction. "Trish is my fiancée."

Uh-oh. Anderson's inner antennae went on alert. This, he thought, could be the start of something dangerous.

Anderson led the couple into his office. After everyone was seated around Anderson's desk, he looked at them, waiting.

"I introduced Trish as my fiancée, Father, because we want to get married."

"I could have guessed."

Dea's smile sparkled. "It's that transparent, eh, Father?"

Anderson nodded. "Would it be safe to guess that Dana Dea is not your real name? It sounds so perfect for TV."

The smile never quit. "It is now. Had it changed legally when I started making it big in television. You need my real name?"

"For the moment, Dana Dea is fine. You want to get married. I guess the appropriate question is, Why are you here? We get a pretty good crowd for the weekend Masses. But you two are outstanding. I can't believe you've been attending our Masses and I never noticed you."

"Right! We're from Grosse Pointe Farms."

The Farms sounded like the proper place for this couple. The clothes these two were wearing would cost probably a whole month's salary for a Nativity parishioner.

"When last I looked," Anderson said, "there were four parishes in the Pointes. So, once again, why here?"

"We live in St. Andrew's parish." Dea said. "We talked it over with the pastor. He didn't hold out much hope."

"There's a problem?" Anderson could have predicted some sort of problem the moment he'd met them at the door.

"We didn't think there was a problem. It came as a complete surprise."

Anderson was aware that Trish had not said word one. "Cutting through to the heart of this, what was the problem the priest at St. Andrew's found?"

"I was married before," Dea stated.

"Oh."

"But it didn't count. I was sure it didn't count. But that other priest said it counted."

"Odds are it did count. Gimme a rundown on it."

"I got married about five years ago. I got divorced four years ago. That should count for something . . . I mean, the marriage only lasted a year."

"Maybe," Anderson said cautiously. "Tell me some more."

"Well, not only did we stick it out for just a year, but I'm not a Catholic."

"Was your first wife a Catholic?"

"No. Methodist."

"And you?"

"Episcopalian. Neither of us practiced any religion."

"You were married by . . . ?"

"A judge. You see what I mean, Father?" Dea spread his hands in an explanatory gesture. "There wasn't anything religious about it. The Catholic Church had nothing to do with it. Now we want to be married in the Catholic Church."

"Why?"

"Trish here—he nodded in her direction—is Catholic."

"You are a baptized Catholic, Trish?" Anderson swiveled toward her.

"Yes, as a baby, Father." Her clipped accent was as attractive as she was.

"You've never been married?"

"No, Father."

"See," Dea cut in, "she was born and raised in Haiti. She emigrated to America when that priest was elected president."

"Father Aristide," she supplied.

"Yeah. It didn't take her long to sign up with an agency as a model. You can see she really looks the part."

"Yes, indeedy." Anderson rubbed his eyes. He had had a busy and demanding day. Very much like any other ordinary day. "Well, let's do the drill."

"What?" Dea didn't understand.

"I'll just ask you some questions. From that we ought to know how your case would stand up at the Tribunal."

Anderson's questions were right out of Church law. They were comprehensive and covered every possible impediment that would have rendered Dea's first marriage invalid. Nothing emerged that would provide grounds for an annulment.

At the end of the interrogation, Anderson shook his head. "I'm sorry, Dana. I wish I could tell you you could build a case to challenge your marriage. But there's nothing there."

Dea inched forward in his chair. "These questions were just about the same as the other Father asked. I can't swear that they were exactly the same. But you both were in the same ballpark."

"Dana, did you think we made these things up? When it comes to Church law, we've all got the same books on our shelves."

"Okay, I thought maybe there'd be a difference. You know, like going to a doctor and then going to another one . . . to get a second opinion."

"Sorry."

"But you can do more."

Just as Dea had inched nearer to Anderson, the priest now retreated by pushing his own chair back a few inches. Anderson suspected what Dea had in mind. The Pastoral Solution.

Ordinarily, at this point, when he was dealing with any of his parishioners, it was he himself who brought up the noncanonical solution.

But this one was different.

Actually, he was not fully aware of what was different. But it had something to do with the status of this couple. They were not the obscure blue-collar people with whom he was used to dealing. These two belonged with the movers and shakers of local society. These were celebrities.

The Pastoral Solution was a subject for the internal forum. This couple probably wouldn't recognize something of any importance in secrecy if they found themselves immersed in it.

On the other hand, what could be the consequences if either or both went public? They were free to do so. It was their secret as much as his. No matter what they did, he was in a position neither to affirm or deny it.

It wasn't as "safe" as if he refused to help them. That way there could be no negative outside reaction. But if he did help them, and if for whatever reason it reached the external forum, and he refused to comment, he was convinced, still there would be no repercussion. He would leave Cardinal Boyle an escape hatch. The Cardinal would not push the incident. If Father Anderson decided not to comment on the matter, then neither would his archbishop. Boyle would respect the inviolability of the secrecy just as he would were the matter protected by the seal of confession.

All this inner argumentation took only a few moments. At this point

Anderson had not even ascertained that Dea was proposing the Pastoral Solution. "What do you mean, I could do more?"

Dea hesitated. "To be completely aboveboard, I don't really know. The word I got was that you could fix things up."

"Where, may I ask, did you hear that?"

"I don't remember the name. Maybe I didn't even get the name. It was about a year ago, a little less, maybe. I do remember it was raining like hell—uh, excuse my French, Father."

Funny, Anderson thought, if this guy were talking to anybody else, he wouldn't have apologized. A clerical collar wasn't everywhere. But God was. "You were saying . . ."

"It was raining. I was doing a standup on one of the overpasses on I-75. I had trouble keeping the umbrella steady and holding on to the mike at the same time. The story was that some guy had killed his wife—threw her out of his car on the freeway. All because she refused to lie so he could get a Church annulment. There was a guy who was just standing there taking it all in. Before I went on, he said something like, 'Is that all the jerk needed? He could've got that from that maverick priest at Nativity.' I thought it was an interesting comment. I tried to get him to stay and be on camera. But he slipped off in the crowd.

"I didn't think, at the time, I would have use for that scrap of information. But here I am." Dea was grinning. "So, Father, you *can* do more. I just don't know how much more."

Anderson sighed deeply. Push had come to shove. "Okay, there is another step possible. It's called a Pastoral Solution."

He felt comfortable in having thought the problem through in this situation. Still their celebrity status made him uneasy.

So, he explained that it was not precisely against the law; it was merely a simple admission that there were certain marriage cases which Church law did not address. He led them, step by step, through the entire process.

"You mean," Dea stated, "that all we have to do is get married by a judge, a J.P., or a minister and we can count ourselves really married.

73

And Trish—she's the one we're most concerned about—she can still be a Catholic and can practice her faith?"

"That's about it. I'd like to go through that explanation with you one more time so you're really clear on it. It's kind of hard to grasp what we're doing. I want to make sure you understand everything."

"Sounds good to me," Dea said. "Real good."

Anderson could tell by the expression on her face that something was disturbing Trish. "What is it, Trish?" he asked.

"You mean," she said, "that getting married by a judge is as good as getting married by a priest?"

"In this instance, yes."

"How can that be?"

"Think in terms that you're on an island with Dana. There isn't anybody else on the island. You want to get married. What would you do about getting married?"

She hesitated. "I guess we would just say the words to each other. You know: I take you as my husband for better or worse, for richer or poorer, in sickness and health, until death do us part."

"That's exactly right. And then you would be not . . ." He paused.

". . . a little bit married, but a lot married."

He smiled. "So, in those circumstances, having no priest around to witness your words would be as good as having one."

Trish shook her head. "On the island there isn't anyone else. But we're not on an island. We're here in Detroit. There are lots of priests around." Tears welled in her eyes. "What am I supposed to do when I come to confession? What am I supposed to say? That I got married by a judge but that it's okay?"

"Why would you bring it up at all?" Anderson said. "In the confessional, we deal only in sin. Your conscience—yours and Dana's—tells you that you are free to marry. No matrimonial Tribunal can crawl inside your conscience. Your conscience tells you one thing. The Tribunal would tell you quite the opposite. As long as your conscience is sincere, you follow it and you don't sin. So, you don't have to mention in the confessional how you were married. You will be really married. Just as you would be really married if a priest had witnessed it.

74

You wouldn't confess the way you were married if a priest had performed the ceremony, would you? Because it's a real marriage. Well, it's a real marriage, in your case, either way—priest or judge."

She said nothing. She searched in her purse, found a handkerchief, and wiped her eyes. "I understand, Father," she said. "And I agree with everything you said. But there's something . . ."

"What is it, Trish?"

"My upbringing, I guess, Father. Marriage, a priest, and a church all go together—if you know what I mean."

"I know what you mean. It's the way I was raised too." Anderson turned to Dea. "What do you think of all this?"

Dea shrugged. "None of this matters much, as far as I'm concerned. I never even think of my first wedding as a marriage. It collapsed. You could hardly even say it was a good try. We had a good . . . physical relationship. I think we thought it would get better if we got married. It got worse." He grimaced. "I don't want to go into all the lurid details. It just didn't work. We were driving each other nuts.

"So, it was a . . . it was a surprise to me when the priest said I'd have to prove that wreck was a wreck. And he, just like you, went through all the possible reasons why the Church might agree it was a wreck. Neither of you found anything that would make the Church agree that the marriage was a farce.

"On top of that, if we did get this cripple up and off the ground, we'd have to get testimony from a whole bunch of relatives and friends and especially from my ex.

"My conscience was clear going into this that I am free to marry. I must admit I am surprised that we found you and that you agree with us.

"I'm clear on this deal. And I'm grateful. But, then, there's Trish. She grew up Catholic—I guess you'd say traditional Catholic. She's used to having a priest around for the big events of her life. Marriage certainly would qualify as a major event." He looked at Trish, then turned back to the priest. "Maybe I can get her to change her mind. But I doubt it. You gave it a pretty good shot."

All three were silent for several moments.

Anderson knew what step had to follow. He could understand Trish's reaction to attempting marriage without benefit of a priest.

Some Catholics who seldom if ever attend Mass—which is the core of the faith—wanted—demanded—a priest to baptize their children, to give them absolution, to anoint them when they were sick or dying—and to witness their marriage.

Trish gave evidence of being a far more faithful Catholic than that. She desperately wanted a priest to witness her marriage.

But Anderson was loath to get more deeply involved than he already was.

Again, the problem was their celebrity. They were not ordinary people. They were, at least on the local scene, Very Important People.

Indeed, he had performed marriage services for people who were canonically barred from a Church wedding. However, no way would those weddings have attracted any public attention.

But Anderson had to be open and honest with this couple. That's the way he was.

"There . . ." He paused. "There is another way. If I am going to be forthright with you and apply the same standard to myself as I have to you, I must admit that my conscience speaks to me too. From your attitude and all you've told me, I must confess I believe you. Specifically, I believe that you can be married validly. No more validly, mark you, than if the ceremony were to be witnessed by a judge. That last statement is true only because Church law doesn't recognize your freedom to marry. That circumstantial technicality allows you to marry validly even if your marriage is performed by a judge. Naturally you would be validly married also if a priest performed it. Except that Church law not only prevents you from having such a marriage, it also specifically forbids a priest from witnessing it." He paused to let this be assimilated. To this couple, what he had just explained must seem like tortuous Byzantine complexities.

Dea broke the silence. "Have you ever done it? Performed a ceremony like this?"

Anderson nodded slowly. "I have. Not often. Usually people are content with the internal forum solution. And I include myself among the people who are happy when that does the trick."

"Well," Dea said, "let me ask you this. I don't want to insult you, but are you reluctant to perform the ceremony because deep down you really don't believe in this conscience thing we've been talking about? You don't want to get involved . . . you want the couple to be totally responsible?"

"No, Dana." There was a touch of impatience in Anderson's voice. "I don't want to actively participate in the wedding because I want to cover my ass. Pardon my French!" Turnabout not only was fair play, it brought a sense of satisfaction.

It was clear that Dana and Trish were momentarily shocked.

"The people," Anderson continued, "who are members of this parish, who live in these neighborhoods, don't travel in the fast lane. They live quiet lives far from a spotlight. It's less than likely that a wedding in this parish would attract any publicity. But there's always a chance. That's why I'm reluctant to take an active role in one of these noncanonical weddings."

"What would they do to you?" Trish seemed genuinely concerned.

"I'm not sure. It would depend on the circumstances. From what I know of Cardinal Boyle, he wouldn't want to have to do anything, like leveling some kind of penalty. He might even be sympathetic—although that I'm not at all sure of. But none of that matters. He is a loyal Churchman; if he had to act, he would—and he has done so in the past."

"What do you think would make him act?" Trish asked.

"If knowledge of the situation became public. I don't anticipate this—but it's always possible. As I said, it's happened in the past." Anderson shook his head as he recalled a couple of cases that had resulted in Boyle's suspending a priest who had performed "scandalous" marriages.

"Publicity about your wedding would not only be possible . . . it would be probable. And that is exactly what I want to avoid."

"I understand." Trish appeared resigned.

"Does this mean," Anderson asked, "that you agree to no Catholic wedding but, following your conscience, you will continue with your faith?"

Trish hesitated. "No. I don't think I can do that. I'll have to think this through. Either we will be married in the Church or we won't be married at all. I can't think of marrying anyone without a priest performing the ceremony."

Anderson cringed inwardly.

"Look"—Dea was trying to control his temper—"to me this is a tempest in a teapot. I want to marry this woman. I *really* want to marry her. I couldn't care less how we get married. "But you've seen how much she needs to have her priest there. Look, Father, it's not our fault we're well known. Isn't this a classic case of reverse discrimination? Okay, you're reluctant to do this for your parishioners. But you *will* do it if your people want you there. If they *really* want you. If they want you as much as Trish wants you. But lots of people have seen her in ads. Lots of people see my mug on the local news. Is it fair that you would grant a couple's request because they're not celebrities and refuse us because we're well known? Is that fair?"

Anderson did not reply. But he thought hard.

"Dana," Trish said softly, "it's the man's career at stake."

Anderson sat silent.

"Come on, Trish . . ." Dea started to rise from his chair.

"Wait," Anderson said. "Wait a minute. Can you guarantee there'll be no publicity?"

Trish brightened.

"The word I'm uncomfortable with is 'guarantee,'" Dea said. "There's a limited number of things I can cast-iron guarantee."

"I'm not talking about guaranteeing the sun will rise tomorrow. You know what I'm asking."

Trish spoke with feeling. "I can't guarantee that no one will know any details about this internal/external business. But I can promise we will do everything we can to help you 'cover your ass.'" She smiled—a model's disarmingly jaunty smile.

Anderson tapped his pen against the desk thoughtfully. He would have laughed at Trish's usage of his colloquialism, but this decision was too important. The consequences could run from zero to God knew what.

This was dangerous territory. But he was moved by Dana Dea's argument. There definitely was something to be said as far as reverse discrimination was concerned. No, withholding his presence at their wedding would be cowardly.

He dropped the pen on his desk and looked at them. Both wore expressions of hopeful anticipation.

"Okay," Anderson said. "Let's do it. Your place or mine?"

Nine

Quite naturally, they first considered Nativity church for the wedding. But true to their promise to maintain a low profile, they decided to invite a minimum number of relatives and friends. Such a small group would rattle around in the mammoth edifice. So the wedding would take place in a friend's suburban apartment. It was spacious and could easily accommodate the small group.

At two in the afternoon of an overcast Sunday, everyone had assembled.

As one of the talented guests played the "Wedding March" on the grand piano, the assemblage fell silent. Father Anderson stood before a window wall that displayed a typical suburban panorama of trees interrupted by strip malls and parking lots.

He was thinking of how egregiously illegal this entire procedure was. At the root of its illegality was Dana's first marriage—nonannulled. Following that, Anderson had not requested delegation from the priest at St. Michael's parish within whose boundaries this ceremony was taking place. Plus by Church law the engaged couple were supposed to live apart for nine months before a marriage. Anderson had not explored their living arrangements. Obviously they had been cohabiting for some time.

Father Anderson was not overly concerned about such details. He was not about to tell the happy newlyweds that for two out of three reasons this ceremony was invalid; the unannulled marriage was enough to eclipse the other technicalities.

Dana wore a dinner jacket, as did the majority of the male guests. Trish eschewed a traditional wedding gown in favor of a simple white, calf-length sheath.

Accompanied by the pianist, a woman whom Frank Sinatra would have labeled a saloon singer rendered several appropriate popular songs. Between musical numbers, the priest offered pertinent Scripture texts.

The couple exchanged their consent in self-composed form.

The assembly applauded the newly joined couple, and the good times began to roll.

Anderson was unnerved when he caught sight of one of the guests recording the ceremony with a TV camera. His concern was further intensified when several other guests took photographs. But Dea reassured him that the pictures were for private use only. Shortly thereafter, the priest took his departure.

Even for someone who was used to flying in the face of Church laws that he regarded as antithetic to Christ's command of love, this wedding was upsetting. Clearly, what tipped the scale was the celebrity status not only of the participants but also of many of the guests.

To ease his anxiety and help clear his mind, he joined a couple of priest friends for dinner at a Southfield restaurant. Never once during the meal did he mention this afternoon's canonical crime.

The conversation bounced about, touching on such clerical topics as:

- Who is next in line to become bishop? In 1978, there were 3,714 bishops worldwide. Soon there would be more than 4,000. The ratio between priest and bishop is narrowing to such a degree that it might call for giving more than one of the auxiliary bishops his own diocese before Detroit ended up having more bishops than priests.
- If Detroit comes up with one more fund-raising project, we will find faithful Catholics in the poorhouse.
- Clustering parishes is the latest reaction to the priest shortage. Already there's about one-quarter of a priest per parish.

And last but not least:

- What are we going to do about women?

The priests were gracious enough to leave the waitress a generous tip. She deserved it if only for all the trips she took to refill coffee cups.

Father Anderson arrived back at his rectory a little before 11 P.M. Just time to settle in for the late news, and then to sleep. He prepared a nightcap, fell exhaustedly into his recliner, and punched the remote switch. Two innocuous faces beamed at him from the small screen. Both newscasters, male and female, had lots of hair, prominent teeth, and seemingly sunny dispositions.

They grew quickly serious as they dug into the seamy side of the news. There had been a shooting—what else was new? There was a recapture of a fugitive who two days ago had conned his way out of the custody of the Detroit police.

There were commercials. Anderson yawned elaborately.

There was a weather forecast. Some areas would have precipitation. Others would be dry. It didn't take a genius.

More commercials.

There was sports. Some teams won. Others lost.

The news had been read. The banter had been exchanged. There was time only for one last, light touch.

The male newscaster, smiling even more broadly than usual, began, "I'm sure all you fans of Dana Dea are wondering what happened to him. Ordinarily he would have occupied this chair for the weekend wrap-up. Well, Dana took a big step today—right into matrimony."

There appeared on the screen Dana, Trish, a panorama of their guests, and, as one born out of due time, Father Jerry Anderson. The voice-over glided on as the camera continued to record the event. It was a short, good-night piece of fluff. Still, they managed to name the officiating priest.

In an instant, Anderson knew he would not sleep tonight. He got up and began to pace. The phone rang. Unusual for this late hour. He pressed the receiver to his ear. "Nativity."

"Is this Father Anderson?"

"Yes. And you?"

"My name is Mike Geller. I'm director of the eleven o'clock news at Channel 5."

The voice gave little provocation. Yet Anderson was seething. "Is Dea there? I want to talk to him!"

"He's not here, Father. He and Trish are off on their honeymoon. He tried to reach you earlier but you weren't in."

"Go on."

"He told me about the need to keep the wedding details secret. And we had it worked out to do just that. Then the station manager got wind of it. He found out we had pictures.

"Dana had just about convinced us not to run it at all. And believe me, he really tried. Then the station manager entered the scene. When he gets a fix on something he's like a bulldog with a bone. He won't let it go.

"Anyway, Father, that's what happened. Honest, Dana did everything he could. But the game was up just as soon as the manager made up his mind. Dana and Trish felt awful about it. They wanted you to at least know what happened."

"Okay," Anderson growled; it was clear that Geller had spoken his piece. "Thanks for the call."

He had to assess the damages.

The phone rang again. He knew the pastor wouldn't pick up and he himself sure didn't need the distraction. He activated the answering service. He was sure they would log some calls. Undoubtedly a few of his priest buddies wanting to rib him for his quick entry into the wonderful world of TV celebritydom.

Still, with a little bit of luck . . . with a little bit of luck . . .

Nothing in the TV presentation had even hinted at Dea's previous and unannulled marriage. Absent that detail, there was no reason for anyone to question the kosher quality of the wedding.

Maybe, just maybe, he could squeeze out of this pickle. Maybe he would get some sleep this night after all.

He did. But not much.

He was up early to check the local TV and radio stations to see if there was any further mention of The Wedding. He thought of this ceremony as unique and thus worthy of upper case.

He listened a bit absently while preparing a breakfast of cereal with bananas. As was his habit, he scanned the morning paper per page— spending only a short couple of minutes—reading not much more than the headlines on most pages.

Until page A5. The three-column picture showed the handsome couple, Mr. and Mrs. Dana Dea. And there was he himself blessing the rings.

The story said it all. The ceremony had taken place in a Southfield apartment. Damn! The pastor of St. Michael's in Southfield would know that no delegation had been requested. Anderson was certain that even at that very moment that pastor was phoning the chancery to wash his hands of any responsibility for all this—and to question why Father Anderson had not requested the necessary delegation.

The story revealed the most damning aspect of the event: that Dea had been previously married. Double damn! Now the pastor of St. Andrew's would be phoning the chancery, charging Father Anderson with improperly and invalidly marrying a couple who were unmarriageable as far as the Church was concerned.

Anderson was just getting over this shock when the news came on Channel 5. It was the final nail in the coffin. How could this have happened? How had they been able to capture the central truth of this story? And so fast?

He placed a call to Nelson Kane, a friend who was managing editor of the morning paper, and an occasional member of Father Anderson's congregation. "How did this happen, Nellie? I mean I talked to a guy named Geller at Channel 5 last night. Know him?"

"Yeah."

"He explained how the story got on their eleven o'clock news. But he didn't have the whole thing. You have the whole thing. Did you get it from Geller?"

"No, we got it on a silver platter. One of your guys called after the TV news broadcast and in time for our late edition. I'm sorry, Jerry. Really. We had no choice. He had chapter and verse. If we hadn't run it, the other guys would have."

"Wait a minute. You said one of our guys gave you the whole story. What do you mean 'our guys'?"

"Name is Foley." There was a pause while Kane riffled through a deskload of notes and wire service copy. "Name is Monsignor Dennis Foley, pastor of St. Andrew's in Grosse Pointe. That's all I know just now. But while I've got you on the line . . ."

Anderson hung up firmly.

No sooner had the receiver hit the cradle than the phone rang. "Yes!"

It was probably another media person. Anderson was furious with the lot of them.

"Father Anderson?" a familiar female voice asked.

"Yes."

"Hold everything for Bishop Donovan."

The next and no-nonsense voice belonged to the bishop. "Jerry, you busy this morning?"

"Well, yes I am, Bishop. I—"

"Well, cancel your appointments. I want to see you right away downtown."

"Okay. Right away." Anderson, even if he'd had hours to decide how to respond to the bishop's demand for his presence, could only have replied affirmatively.

Before leaving for the chancery, he stopped by the dining room where his pastor was assembling breakfast. "I'm on my way down to the chancery. I have no idea when I'll be back. I just wanted you to know."

"Wait! What's this all—" Before the pastor could finish his question, Anderson was out of the rectory.

There was no waiting. Anderson was ushered immediately into Bishop Donovan's office.

"Sit," Donovan invited. "Nasty bit of news this morning."

"I couldn't argue that, Bishop."

"Is it true? The paper's account?"

"Not to the last dotted i. But essentially, yes."

"This is something the boss would ordinarily handle. But, as you know, he's in Rome."

Actually, Anderson had forgotten. Cardinal Boyle had gone to Rome together with a select group of United States bishops for a meeting.

Since there was no response, Donovan continued. "That wasn't a smart move, Jerry. Just in case you are wondering, we are aware downtown that you don't give the Tribunal much business."

"According to the scuttlebutt I get, Bishop, I'm not the only local priest who takes pity on the Tribunal."

Donovan nodded. "A few. Not as many as you think."

Anderson shrugged. It didn't matter, nor was it germane how many priests did or didn't make use of the Tribunal to process marriage cases.

"As far as we know, none of the men let this stuff get into the external forum. We can't do anything about that." Donovan made no secret about his fidelity to the Vatican position on just about anything. He, like Father Angelico, was another who, if someone were convicted of heresy, would walk with the condemned to the stake. But, unlike Angelico, he wouldn't bother praying with the doomed soul; he would proceed to light the fire.

"Sometimes, Bishop, the internal forum just doesn't do the trick."

"For a loyal priest, it never does the trick." Donovan took a deep breath and exhaled slowly. "Well, I got in touch with the boss just a short while ago. We talked it over. We agreed that something had to be done. He accepted my opinion. So, Father, you will be suspended for a period of two months. During this time you will not confect any of the sacraments—well, you know the details: Short of ministering to someone in danger of death, you will not act as a priest. You can just forget you are a priest for the next two months, beginning now!"

"I don't know . . ."

Donovan cut him off. "Later this morning, I will conduct a briefing for the media and announce your penalty. You will have no comment. If you wish, I can get you into a monastery for an elongated retreat. That's optional. The essence is that you will not function as a priest for two months. What else you do during this time is up to you. Personally, I don't care."

Anderson fixed his gaze on Donovan's well-shined shoes. He made no move to leave or even speak.

"I think this matter is concluded." Donovan said.

"Not quite." Anderson looked into Donovan's eyes and held the gaze. "Suspension is a punishment for sin. I believe I have not sinned in witnessing the wedding of that couple."

"That's not even debatable."

"Even then, I don't think Cardinal Boyle would punish me publicly."

"To be honest with you, he didn't want to at the outset. But when I told him how publicly you flaunted it, he had to agree to the public sanction."

"Publicly? Flaunting?" Anderson almost leaped out of his chair. "I wasn't responsible for all that publicity. Your man did that!"

For the first time in this meeting, Donovan seemed flustered. "Our man? What are you talking about?"

"Dennis Foley! He was the one who alerted the media. He was solely responsible for that article in the paper."

"Are you sure?"

Anderson nodded once decisively. "He provided them with every detail in that story."

"How did he know all this?"

"He was the son of the bitch who refused to witness their wedding in the first place."

"As well he should," Donovan stated. But inwardly, for the first time, he had some doubts. "How can you be certain this leak came from Monsignor Foley?"

"Nelson Kane. I called him. He told me." Anderson did not need to further identify the source. Kane was the tough-talking equivalent of Mother Teresa for Detroit journalists. "Call and ask him yourself."

"I will." But even as he spoke, Donovan had no doubt Anderson was being accurate. This information cast a new light on the matter. Donovan would prefer keeping Foley's role a secret. He was certain Cardinal Boyle would be far more angry at Foley for forcing this issue than at Anderson for violating the law.

But the bishop quickly decided this sort of secret did not easily lend itself to being kept. Much better for everyone—except, of course, Anderson—that the Cardinal be advised of this added complication. "In good time," Donovan continued, "the boss will be briefed on how this happened. The media has got hold of the story and they're not going to let it go until some action is taken. Your suspension stands.

"You may, naturally, appeal this decision in the diocesan court; the Tribunal would handle the appeal." Donovan barely suppressed a smile thinking about what the Tribunal would do to this clerical loose cannon if it got the chance. "I don't really think you want to pursue this." The bishop paused a moment. "Does that pretty well finish this matter?"

Anderson's shoulders slumped. "I guess so." He rose and took a step or two toward the door, then stopped as another thought came to mind.

The matter was not finished by any means. He thought of all the people he had conducted on a tour of the internal and external forums. He had helped many of them in good faith form their consciences. They—many of them—had been convinced on his word alone. What would they think when they learned that he was being punished for what he had told them and what he had done for them? Would those tender consciences be troubled again?

Anderson returned to the chair and sat down.

Donovan was startled. They had covered all the necessary ground. He would have treated Anderson gruffly. But the poor bastard was on the ropes. While toying with his episcopal ring, the bishop leaned forward.

"I'm not going to accept the penalty. It was meant to punish sin. And, as I've said, I don't consider what I did sinful. Rather than accept, I will resign my priesthood."

Donovan was completely taken aback. "You'd do that!"

"Yes."

Donovan studied the desktop. He did not want to go to the mat on this one. The conclusion had been clear at the outset: The Church would slap Anderson's wrist. He would accept the verdict and go into temporary exile. Later he would come back chastened, a little bit older and a lot wiser.

Anderson would be made to know that he couldn't get away with this sort of aberrant conduct.

All would be well.

But the whippersnapper was upsetting the applecart. What's more, there was very little time left before the scheduled news conference.

What to do?

It was too late to contact the Cardinal. The bishop would have to improvise.

"This is not going the way I want it to go," Donovan said.

"Sorry. But I'm not going to give in on that punishment."

Donovan thought again. Maybe it didn't have to be a flat-out sanction. Maybe there was a way of getting the message across without the penalty.

The bishop folded his hands on the desk. "How about this? I state that Church law was violated. And that you have requested and received permission to take a leave of absence. You will use up to a couple of months to rethink your position. You are still a priest in good standing but you will take a spiritual retreat before returning to the archdiocese."

Anderson considered that. He had taught his people that they were indeed violating Church law. But only because said law could not address their situation. So, he could accept the statement containing language that a law had been broken. It was a little iffy. But after all the time he had patiently worked with these troubled people, they ought to be able to take this language and run with it.

But there was something more to be considered: his mother's tender conscience and her pride in him as a priest.

It was not uncommon for Catholic parents to feel fulfilled in a very special way when a son became a priest. Generally this feeling was more intense for the mother than the father. So it was in Anderson's family. His father definitely was pleased. His satisfaction had grown over the years of Jerry's priesthood. But his mother was ecstatic. She remained so to this day.

It was also not uncommon for a Catholic young man to remain in a seminary or the priesthood solely out of respect for his parents, who would be terribly hurt if he were to quit.

The sentiment is similar to that of a married couple who remain together only for the sake of their children.

In either case, the end result of this charade frequently was disaster.

Anderson's father had died five years ago. Jerry, assisted by many of his priest classmates and friends, had offered the Resurrection Mass. His mother's loss was buffered by all the priests, especially Jerry, who stood by her and at the altar.

To this date, Anderson had been a priest over fifteen years. His mother would be shocked that her son would violate a Church law. Both she and he could survive that. And there was no threat connected with his being granted a sabbatical leave of absence. But this would not be the end of the matter.

The handwriting was clear on the wall. The next time he would be dragged into the public arena for a similar sidestepping of Church law, the boom would be lowered. The next time he would, in all probability, be facing anything from suspension to being returned to the lay state. The latter punishment was more popularly known as defrocking.

In all of this, Anderson's sole certainty was that there would be a next time. Whether it would be a troubled couple of parishioners, or the son or daughter of one of his many friends, someone would bring him a situation that was beyond the scope of Church law. There was no possibility he could turn such people away.

He was on a collision course with Canon Law and the Institution held all the cards. Futility held no attraction for him at all. The deal was done. He needed no more time for consideration. He had to leave the priesthood he so loved.

The question was how. Of the possible courses of action there had to be one that would best tie up all the loose ends.

He thought he had it. "Bishop, suppose you say in your press conference that I am taking a leave of absence in order to contemplate the place of Church law in my ministry. Perhaps you can say it's open-ended."

Donovan considered the proposal. "I think we could live with that."

"All right. Then what I want to do is start immediately a petition to be granted laicization."

Again Donovan was surprised. As far as he was concerned, this would be the preferred conclusion. Even with the scarcity of priests, the Church didn't need the Andersons to challenge authority at every turn.

Donovan had neither suggested nor demanded that Anderson be returned to the lay state. The bishop was fairly certain that neither the Cardinal nor the priest would have gone for that. But now that Anderson himself had requested it . . . fine. "If that is your wish"—Donovan shrugged—"you won't find any opposition here. In fact, you picked a good time. Rome is in the mood to grant laicizations pretty freely now. And I have some connections at the Vatican."

"What do I have to do?"

"See Father Arsenault. He'll take you through the paperwork . . ." He halted and looked at Anderson searchingly. "Are you sure you want to do this?"

Anderson nodded. "It seems to fit the bill. There'll be no mention of a censure. During the leave, I will presumably reflect on my attitude toward Church law. That I don't return after my leave will not be surprising. Scores of priests have taken a temporary leave that became permanent."

"I agree. But my question is: Why the laicization?"

"Because if I were to return, the watchdogs of the diocese would have me under virtual surveillance. It *would* happen again. And, to paraphrase the Bible, my last state would be worse than my first. Does that answer your question?"

"Partially. What I'm really puzzled by is why you are voluntarily going through due process. It no longer is any secret that you have no regard for Church law. Why go through a procedure that is governed by a law that you definitely don't believe in? Why not just leave the priesthood? Just walk away—with no paperwork at all. Scores of priests have done that too."

Anderson stood, but did not turn to leave. "My mother is going to be hurt terribly—at best. I'm trying to soften the blow as much as I can. She would have been wounded by the talk of a Church sanction. That's smoothed over by calling my disappearance a leave of absence. She's going to be devastated when I do, in fact, leave. The only thing I can think of to help her over that is to go by the book. So I can be a Catholic in good standing. It's the only thing I can think of to help. It may not work, but it's my best shot.

"And now, Excellency, all I can think to say is good-bye."

Anderson turned and left the room. The bishop did not return the soon-to-be former Father's farewell.

Bishop Donovan sat motionless behind his desk. A smile began to spread. How things could change!

When Anderson had arrived at the chancery this morning, as far as Donovan was concerned everything had been cut and dried. The priest had violated a serious Church law. He would be punished by being suspended for two months. This had not been Donovan's best scenario, but it was the most severe sentence he had been able to squeeze from Cardinal Boyle.

But then Donovan long had thought Boyle was too soft a touch. The Cardinal would not have agreed to any penalty at all had the case not drawn all this publicity—publicity that Foley would pay for once Boyle got back in town.

Now, instead of the foreordained conclusion that Donovan and Boyle had agreed upon, Anderson himself had orchestrated an ending that Donovan had preferred all along. How the Cardinal might feel about it was something else. But it had been Anderson's choice, so . . .

The bottom line now was the resignation of Father Anderson. And since he was applying for laicization—and Donovan would make certain he got it—Anderson would never again function as a priest.

A canonical situation like this was rare but not unique. Donovan knew that few priests would dare go beyond the Pastoral Solution. But some would try to witness a clandestine, invalid marriage. Most would fail. The bishop reckoned that as long as there were laws and mavericks there would be trouble.

The bishop shook his head. He didn't understand what made a man like Anderson tick. But Donovan would see to it that *Mr.* Anderson would never run again.

Ten

SOME STORIES HAVE LEGS. They run longer in the media. All stories run down eventually.

Reporters tried to milk the Anderson/Dea/Murrow story. But with just about no cooperation from anyone, it died after a couple of days.

The relatives and friends of the newlyweds were happy and satisfied. Even though Mr. and Mrs. Dana Dea were not responsible for the notoriety, they didn't mind it. Their business, after all, was to be in the limelight. And so they were. The underlying philosophy was: Feel free to use my name; just spell it correctly.

The friends, relatives, and supporters of Father Jerry Anderson were much more somber and concerned.

Jerry's first task was to make peace with his mother. It took a while but eventually he accomplished it. It was difficult for her to understand how her son, the priest, could break a Church law. She worried, too, about how her fellow parishioners and daily Mass attendees would react to this scandal. In the end, either she finally understood—or pretended she did for his sake. Anderson was not sure which was really the case.

The other shoe that remained to drop in Mrs. Anderson's life was her son's laicization. Outside of someone's being in danger of imminent death—or an extremely improbable change in the Vatican mind-set—Jerry would never function as a priest again. That would be a tough pill to swallow for Mrs. Anderson. Jerry was counting on the effect of laicization that would at least allow him to be a layperson in pretty good standing with the Church.

Meanwhile, he had to find a job. Others might think that a "leave of absence" was temporary. That's what the dictionary implied: permission to be absent from duty or employment. Initially, these people would expect him to return. In time they might forget he was gone.

As far as Anderson was concerned, he had two months of, in effect, paid vacation in which to find employment, not to mention a continuation of health care insurance.

He was not surprised that there was little interest in a theology major on the part of business or industry. Nor was he unduly concerned when no one broke down his door to offer a job.

One offer did come forward, prodded by Father Rick Casserly. Tom Becker, friend and former classmate of Casserly, mildly recruited Anderson. Becker didn't need any more employees at that time. In fact he was being forced to lay off workers. Additionally, Anderson had neither experience nor particular interest in flowers or trees.

However, it was a bona fide offer. If all else failed, he could learn the business. He felt he could become scab labor rather than starve. He put Becker's offer on the back burner with gratitude to both Becker and Casserly.

Over the years, Anderson had lost touch completely with his former penitent, Sister Perpetua. He had not seen her since their ways parted from St. Ursula's. Out of curiosity, he learned that she had chosen Casserly to succeed him as her spiritual director. With all Anderson had to do at Nativity, culminating with his citywide basketball program, he was happy to know she had found a skilled and reliable director.

He did not know that Sister Perpetua had returned to being Dora Riccardo.

But she had not forgotten him. He was no stranger to the local sports scene. She read about his program in the papers and caught the occasional interview on radio or TV.

Finally, she read about the celebrity wedding he'd almost gotten away with. She understood what his ceremonial leave of absence really meant.

Dora had just managed a switch from Kelly Services to *Oakland Monthly* magazine. She had applied for a secretarial position with the publication, but had done so well in technical skills that she was hired as a copy editor.

She was familiar with Anderson's experience with writing, limited though it might be. Among his duties at St. Ursula's, he had been editor of the parish bulletin. To his credit, he had turned that house organ

throwaway into a genuine means of communication within the parish—
and an interestingly written paper to boot. He'd had letters published
in prestigious newspapers and magazines. Through the programs he
created and continued to monitor, he had name recognition, something that would get him through doors if he were researching or
developing a story. Mostly, Dora knew that Anderson would be every
inch a professional along the lines that Pat Lennon was recruiting.

She debated with herself. Which would be the better way to inter-
cede for him? Go directly to Pat Lennon? Or, sound him out to see if
he did indeed want a job on the magazine?

Dora decided to begin at the top. She made a strong case for Anderson's dependability and thorough professionalism—after Pat's interpre-
tation of that quality. Though Lennon had grave misgivings regarding
Jerry's experience—or lack thereof—she agreed to interview him.

That left Anderson's interest in this job yet to be discovered.

Dora called the Anderson home. She figured correctly that Jerry
would be financially strapped and unable to afford an apartment.

His mother, who answered the phone, was very guarded when it
came to answering questions about her son. And she was very inquisitive about "this woman" who was interested in her son—still and
always her son the priest. Finally, Mrs. Anderson consented to give
Jerry the message to return the call.

Which he did that evening. He was surprised and delighted even to
think about Sister Perpetua—Dora Riccardo—once again. Both were
open for lunch the next day. In fact, though he didn't mention it, he
was wide open all day for any sort of meeting. They agreed on Pea-
body's on Woodward south of Maple in downtown Birmingham in the
heart of Oakland County. Dora thought the location particularly
appropriate since they would be talking about a possible position at
Oakland Monthly.

They were to meet in the lobby about 11:30 A.M.—"to beat the
crowd." They never would have made contact had it not been that
Anderson had not changed all that much. A bit of gray in the side-
burns, hair receding ever so slightly. Still an athletic physique. An
attractive gentleman all in all. Of course he was wearing civvies, but

that was not much of a disguise; he was still recognizable. Had she not approached him, he never would have recognized her. His entire experience had been with a creature consisting of face and hands, and all else sealed in wool.

She was everything he had fantasized. Her face was every bit, if not more, open, friendly, and beautiful. Her hair was tossed and curly. This was the first time he'd seen her crowning beauty, now unboxed by religious headgear.

After they were seated, Dora told the waitress it would be a while before they ordered. She cheerfully brought coffee and promised them all the time they needed.

Anderson was smiling like a kid who had hit his first Little League home run. "I can't get over it. After all these years . . . I almost called you Sister."

"That's okay. I'll probably slip and call you Father before lunch is over."

He broke a breadstick. "We both left Ursula's about the same time. Where did they send you?"

"To hell!"

"That bad!"

"You ever hear of St. Adalbert's?"

He thought briefly. "I think so. Tucked in the west side of Detroit?"

"More like Dante's second circle."

"Wow! That must have been some assignment!"

"Oh, it was. Nothing that anyone could do to me for the rest of my life could equal that."

"That's a shame. But you . . . what? . . . resigned?"

"What was left of me after the Theresians picked the bones clean."

"Seems to me I spent most of our time together urging you to quit."

Dora nodded. "I was too pigheaded to seriously consider following your advice."

"You wanted to stick it out because of your parents. And . . . something else . . . that I can't recall right now. Some kind of mystical experience, wasn't it?"

Dora blushed lightly. "A Scripture text that said, in effect, once you're on the road to following Jesus, you shouldn't turn back or you are unworthy of the kingdom of God. I happened to be exposed to that text at a time when I was about to call it quits—to turn away from Jesus."

"That sort of thing can be a powerful motive to stay or go or do or don't do just about anything." He was beginning to feel self-conscious.

The waitress returned to see if they were ready to order. It reminded him that Dora was on her lunch hour, whereas he might as well be on an infinite coffee break.

Both ordered Caesar salad. It seemed the simplest. They were there to talk more than to eat.

She buttered a roll. "Our first item of business revolves around your leave of absence."

He winced.

"Are you really going back?"

"No."

"Absolutely?"

"No chance."

"That firm!" she exclaimed. "I kind of thought so."

"Yes. You were right."

"I don't mean to pry, but are you getting married?"

He smiled. If only she knew. He probably would marry some day. It was a real long shot but if it was at all possible his bride would be Dora Riccardo. "No plans right now."

"Then, why?" she wondered. "Is it all about that wedding you witnessed?"

"The private little ceremony that the couple assured me would be kept quiet to the point of being clandestine. Yes, that's why—at least partly."

"You'd rather not talk about it?"

"No, it's okay. I saw it coming when we were in the seminary. But I refused to look at it. I just wasn't going to enforce Church law. Especially regarding marriage. I should have quit right then. Here I was advising you to get out and there I was hanging in."

The waitress brought the salads and refilled their coffee cups.

"What if you change your mind?" she asked. "It's possible. One of the things I've learned is never to say never."

"I agree with you . . ." He nodded as he chewed absently. "But sometimes circumstances tend to reinforce one's resolutions."

"Hmm?"

"I'm laicized—or, I will be in another week or two."

Her eyes opened wide. "So soon? I thought it took a long time. Months. Years! Maybe never."

He smiled ruefully. "Seems I applied for just what the bishop thought I should have. On top of that, he has friends in high Vatican places. All in all, my laicization may set all-time speed records."

She shook her head in disbelief. "Cardinal Boyle did that to you? It doesn't sound like him."

"It wasn't he."

"But you said, the bishop—"

"Bishop Donovan. The Cardinal was in Rome when that wedding hit the fan. Before I got to Donovan's office, he had talked to the Cardinal. I was supposed to be suspended—put on the shelf, so to speak. And that because of all the publicity. To cut this short, I wasn't going to accept the penalty. So I brought up the subject of quitting.

"The Cardinal might have spoken a few kind words. Maybe asked me to reconsider. But the Cardinal wasn't there. I handed Donovan my head on a silver platter. Bishop Donovan couldn't have been happier if he had danced for the trophy.

"On top of that, Donovan doesn't have to worry that he did not adhere to the procedure that Boyle had cleared—that I would be suspended. I asked for it!"

For several moments they ate in silence.

"Getting back to my original question," Dora said, "what does laicization have to do with your never going back to the priesthood no matter what happens? You know: Never say never?"

He put his fork down and gave her his undivided attention. "There's a clause in the contract you're supposed to sign. In effect it says this is for keeps. Once you have been reduced to the lay state, you can never go back. As far as the Church is concerned, you remain a priest, but you never again can function as one. Unless, that is, somebody gets very, very ill.

"This—putting your priesthood in permanent mothballs—is the price you pay for Rome's dispensing you from the celibacy demanded by the Latin rite."

"And," she said, "if you didn't get laicized, what about marriage? What about your status in the Church?"

He began eating again. "Well, then, that's a whole other kettle of fish. Without the laicization document, I'd really be on a leave of absence. Unless I got married—or, as the Church prefers, attempted to get married—I would be on an extended leave.

"Attempted marriage would excommunicate me. And I wouldn't be much of a candidate to be welcomed back to the active ministry."

"Let's see if I've got this straight. If . . . well, when . . . you get this document, technically you'll be as much a priest as ever. But you can't use your priest powers. But you can get married . . . in the Church . . . validly?"

"If I want to. Yes."

"And if you hadn't applied . . . ?"

"I would be in a sort of limbo. I'd need to be called back. Then I could function as before."

"If you weren't laicized and you got married?"

"The Church wouldn't recognize the wedding and I would be excommunicated. And I would be dead in the water."

"Right now, you're not considering marriage?"

"Right now? No. But I haven't asked: You married?"

"No."

"Close?"

"No."

God was good, he thought.

"Now"—she sat back as the attentive waitress cleared away her plate and replenished her coffee—"about work—a job."

"I told you last night on the phone about Mr. Becker's offer."

"And you said it was on your back burner. I think that's wise. We who have been employed, sort of, by the Church, have to keep our options open."

He was only a bite or two from finishing. The waitress was hovering vulture-like. "It's a different world. There isn't anybody saying, 'I'll get that for you.' Or, 'Let me take over for you, Father.' I suppose you've had the same sort of experience."

"Well, not really. Nobody does anything for the Theresians. Now that I think of it, everybody was dumping on me."

"But you're doing all right now."

"It worked out. The Kelly Services program was okay. But I couldn't see my doing that kind of work the rest of my life. I was lucky I found *Oakland Monthly.*"

As he placed his fork in the now otherwise empty plate the waitress swooped to scoop up both dish and silverware.

"Last night," she continued, "I didn't have time to tell you much about the magazine."

"Only enough to make me wonder why your editor/publisher would consider me. My experience shouldn't attract her interest."

"Maybe you're selling yourself short."

"The old *Nemo judex est in sua causa,* eh?"

"Don't press me on the Latin. We didn't have enough of it."

"Sorry. 'No one is a good judge in his own case.'"

"Exactly." She removed a credit card from her purse.

"No, no," he protested. "I'll get the check."

She covered the check with her card. "I'm the one who has a job. I'll pick up the tab . . . *this time,*" she insisted, laughing. "Pretty soon you'll have a job and the check will be all yours."

He thought of that time in a very vague future. Oh yes, he'd like to treat her. He'd like to date her. He'd like to marry her. Easily the most attractive aspect of a job at the magazine would be working with her. Leaning over her desk. Smelling her perfume.

"All of this is very kind," he said. "To think of me at all. To consider me for a job. To clear the way for an interview with your boss. To think that I could qualify for the magazine. But—and I don't think I'm selling myself short—I have no experience in the real world of journalism."

The waitress needed her signature on the credit card receipt. Dora added the tip and signed. Jerry was going to say something more but she held up a hand.

"I've been studying Pat Lennon's hiring practice. I applied for the job at the secretarial level. She saw I could do much more. She hired me as a copy editor. It's worked out well for the magazine and for me. And that makes it work well for Pat Lennon."

"But—"

Dora glanced at her watch and interrupted him. "What I'm getting at, Father—oops, there I go. What I'm getting at, Jerry, is that Lennon is building her own team. She wants quality workers as a first priority. With that and their decent background in writing, she thinks she can build an efficient and quality staff."

They were silent a moment.

"I would like that job," he said. "I can't deny it." He paused again. "Okay," he said, enthusiastically. "I'll call this afternoon to set up an interview. I guess I've got nothing to lose."

"Good. I've got to get back now." She slid to the edge of the booth. "Jerry, I wish I could actually get you the job. The best I could do was get you an interview. I just have this strong hunch you're going to do very well."

She reached across the table, took his hand, and squeezed it. It was a small gesture. But it marked the first time there had ever been any physical contact between them. He felt a rush of blood to his head.

"You really helped me when we were at Ursula's. I was never able to thank you for everything you did for me. I must have been a pill, bothering you so frequently. I don't mean that going to bat for you evens the score—nothing like that. I'm just happy I might be a help to you for a change."

The flush receded quickly. The last thing he wanted between them was a counting of favors they did for each other. That was not the path that led to affection, togetherness, and love.

They left the booth and walked toward the exit. He held the door, but didn't leave with her.

"I've got a hat to retrieve," he said. "I'll keep in touch . . . let you know how the interview goes."

1037669114

"Thanks. I want to know." Dora turned and began walking down the path leading to the parking lot and her car.

As she walked, she felt someone's gaze. It was as clear an impression as if she were looking at the person face-to-face. It was Jerry Anderson, her intuition was certain.

She turned her head sideways, as if she were looking at the busy Woodward traffic. Actually, in the periphery of her vision, she caught sight of Jerry still standing in the doorway, allowing the door to close slowly. She could feel the layers of her clothing peeling off under his scrutiny.

Well, why not? She hadn't applied all that makeup, worn a form-fitting suit, and added a touch of delicate perfume just to be ignored.

Was she fooling herself? she wondered. In anticipation of this luncheon, she had taken more care with her appearance than usual. Even to the point of wearing black lingerie. Not that anyone would see it. But it did make her feel sexier.

Seducing Jerry Anderson was not foremost in her mind. She liked him. She'd liked him from the moment they'd first met at St. Ursula's. She had been and remained grateful to him for all the help and direction he'd tried to give her.

And he had been correct: Being in the Theresians put her in the wrong place, no matter what. She should have taken his advice, left life in the nunnery, and forgotten the Theresians.

But that was as far as it went.

A physical relationship with Jerry Anderson? Did he expect it?

When she took his hand only moments ago, she could sense that he was moved. Moved far more than one might think appropriate. Far more than she had intended.

And now, as they parted, what had alerted her that surreptitiously he was giving her a lusty look? Intuition. And she had learned to rely on that intuition.

A physical relationship with Jerry Anderson?

Possible. Definitely possible. He was a very attractive individual. In their spiritual relationship at St. Ursula's, he had proved to be gentle, caring, giving—and demanding nothing in return. Not bad traits in a friend. And, yes, in a lover, in a husband.

Possible but not probable.

Years ago she had given herself, body and soul, to Rick Casserly. He didn't even know it.

After she left the convent, she had continued consulting Father Casserly for spiritual direction. She didn't know whether he found that arrangement cluttered. She most definitely had. There was something about being alone with him—even in a confessional setting—that complicated everything. In all likelihood he was in cool possession of himself. He could be objective in their relationship. She could not.

She told him that they had gone about as far as they could in her spiritual life. She had to be on her own for a while. He understood entirely and, indeed, agreed with her analysis and conclusion. They parted amicably.

So amicably that she had volunteered to work with him in his parish's catechism program. That way she could see him at least once every week, as well as during quarterly meetings, and periodically during the summer months.

The one mistake she dreaded was any possibility of repeating the wet bathing suit incident that had been a near disaster.

To this day, Rick still was the only person for whom she might take off her clothes.

But she couldn't rush or force that gift. This she had discovered that afternoon when she had orchestrated a seduction that mercifully was aborted. She blushed. As she always did whenever that memory surfaced. It was rewarding reliving that incident if only to ensure it wouldn't happen again.

Since she'd left religious life these five-plus years ago, she'd had her share of dates. Frequently the guy would simply assume that the evening would end with both occupying the same bed. After all, the argument went, this was the millennium. Gone was the innocent kiss, the awkward touching. All-the-way scarcely described what was expected from today's woman.

Sometimes, though rarely, she found it very tempting. But she was a one-man woman. And that man was Rick Casserly.

She was a virgin and she had every reason to believe Rick was also. Of course she was hardly with him all the time, or even most of the time. But she had that gift of inspired intuition. She could, and did, rely on it.

It would all work out. All she had to do was play her cards right.

Jerry let the door close in front of him. The meeting just concluded was supposed to be a business luncheon. For him it had been pure pleasure.

This was the first time he and Sister Per—uh, Dora—had been together as laypersons, civilians. They didn't have to be cautious, conscious of a religious habit, clerical clothing. It was great.

He was grateful that she had gone to bat for him. He could use all the help he could get.

Was he reading too much into this? Maybe. Maybe not: After all, she wasn't trying to find him employment just anywhere. If this deal came together, they would be working side by side. Did she want it that way?

As he watched Dora move toward the parking lot, he marveled at her perfection. There was sex in the way she walked. The way her head bobbed. The way her arms swung. The way her hips undulated. How much of this was objective he was in no position to judge. As far as he was concerned she left nothing to be desired.

She turned the corner and disappeared into the parking lot. He stood at the door several more moments, memorizing every detail about Dora. Then he turned, retrieved his hat, and left. He didn't see her in the lot; she must have already pulled out.

Adding to his belief that Dora might intentionally want to work with him—or at least work in the same office with him—was the fact that his experience in journalism was slim to nonexistent. There had to be some basis in fact that the Lennon woman wanted to build her own team. Otherwise there would be no reason why she would consent to interview him.

Dora was, he thought, pushing things a bit. But there was no way to tell without a meeting.

He would call Pat Lennon this afternoon. He wanted this job. The desire was growing. If Lennon wanted someone who was dependable, reliable, and thoroughly professional, he would be the perfect candidate. Journalism? He was willing to learn.

He wanted to be close to Dora. Without a doubt that was the principal attraction.

Short of a job offer at *Oakland Monthly*, he wanted some means of employment. He had to get out of his parental home. The atmosphere there put him directly back to childhood. His mother, God love her, was doing as well as could be expected with her son's midlife career change. She understood little of what was going on. Laicization threw her. But if Jerry said all was right between him and the Church, she believed him.

However, she was screening his phone calls. It was a stroke of luck that Dora's call had reached him. Life would be taxing enough as it was without having to relive his adolescence with Ma.

He needed to be free to have guests over. Specifically, he needed to invite Dora to visit. He could just imagine entertaining Dora—any girl—with Mother hovering about. Not a very encouraging picture.

So, priority one: Get a job, preferably with the magazine. Priority two: Move out. Priority three: Establish rapport with Dora Riccardo.

But, please, God, don't make a move toward Dora until the right moment.

At lunch he had touched the subject very lightly, he thought. She wasn't serious about anyone. He couldn't have asked for a better break than that.

He was a virgin. He hoped Dora was. But that really didn't matter; after all, she had been out of the convent these five years. And this was a new era: A girl was expected to put out. The concern with virginity was a thing of the past. All that was necessary as far as he was concerned was that she love him, or grow to love him.

It was no accident that so many former priests and nuns became attracted to each other and married. They were not merely Catholics;

they were dedicated, consecrated to a life of service to others. And they were not merely consecrated Catholics, they had risen beyond that commitment. Each had his or her reason for entering the seminary or convent. And each had his or her reason for leaving that life and re-entering "the world."

Anderson was in a special position to understand Dora's religious history. She'd fallen in love with a myth. There were those women who taught her. They exuded discipline. They themselves lived disciplined lives and they demanded discipline from their students.

They were revered by just about everyone, Catholic or otherwise. They wore a dress called a habit. The habit set them apart from what might be called a normal life. From men, from other women, from courtship, from marriage, from having children.

They were truly set apart.

Dora had been so very young. All she knew was that her nuns had a firm grasp on things heavenly if not on things mundane. She didn't know that the Theresians, the only religious order with which she was familiar, were semicontemplative. She wouldn't even have known what semicontemplative involved.

Dora wasn't alone. Many children fall in love with a uniform, the idea of a life of luxury and wealth, a life of selfless service, a life of material success, a life of spiritual success. When Dora had made her choice she was too young, too uninformed. And she had chosen the Theresians, an order so mired in the Middle Ages that it was moribund.

She left the order simply because the members who surrounded her made it impossible to stay.

Jerry Anderson had entered the seminary for many of the same reasons that had attracted Dora to the convent.

Unlike Dora, Jerry had years of study and testing facing him. Like a car racing a train to a crossing, Jerry ignored the red light signal that was Church law. He ran the signal and paid the price many years later as witness to a well-publicized clandestine wedding.

Nuns and priests prayed alike, were trained to serve others, lived dedicated lives, wore distinctive uniforms, were generally respected—very much alike. Many contemporary nuns and priests worked together in close collaboration, at an intimate level they had in the past been taught to avoid. Many of them fell in love and left their religious vocations to marry.

Others—Jerry and Dora among them—left for other reasons. For them, just as for ordinary laypeople, falling in love, getting married, and having a family was the natural progression of life.

Whatever reason priests and nuns had for leaving their vocations, once having left it was only normal for them to marry. Just as marriage was a normal step in adult life, so it was for former priests and nuns now that they had returned to the lay state.

Jerry Anderson had been squeezed out of his priestly life. That was behind him. It was gone. No longer was there any reason for him to live as a single man for the rest of his life. In the normal progression that he picked up now, he would find a woman, they would fall in love, they would be married. They might or might not begin a family. At their age, having children could be a dicey decision.

But putting one foot in front of the other, Jerry had found his woman. She would no longer be a part of his fantasy life. She was real. And her reality excited him.

He would have to force himself to go slowly. The wrong word, the wrong move could prove disastrous.

One thing was certain: He knew what he wanted. He would do anything to make it happen.

Eleven

"WE SEEM TO BE DOING the right thing," said Father Robert Koesler. "It's Wednesday, we're priests, and we're playing golf."

Father Zachary Tully looked about him. "Kind of crowded," he observed, "but I'll bet you there aren't any other priests here. And certainly no doctors."

"That, my dear friend," Koesler said, "is a tribute to the caliber of our golf game. They wouldn't let us loose on a good course."

They were a twosome playing on a Detroit municipal course notorious for its topography. It was as flat as a poorly chosen parish choir. Each fairway was set off from another by a row of widely separated trees. Occasionally a groundskeeper would water the greens. God took care of the rest of the course. And, sometimes, even He didn't care.

It was known to be a shooting gallery, in that it was advisable to hit your ball and duck; someone on an adjacent fairway was likely to hook or slice and take your head off. In short, it was not a championship course. The players were not scratch golfers. They were hackers before the term described computer interlopers.

The greens fees, though modest, for all that were still exorbitant.

Father Koesler, having reached the age of seventy a couple of years before, was now retired from priestly service in the Archdiocese of Detroit. Or, to use the official term, he had achieved the status of a Senior Priest.

Perhaps the approved description was closer to the truth. Retirement connoted inactivity. As in: What are you going to do in your retirement years? Nothing. Whereas the average senior citizen, having reached a certain age, would avail himself or herself of some cut-rate benefits and continue on with an active life.

Koesler mused that he might have shrunk an inch or so. Just a few weeks ago he'd met a young man whom Koesler judged to be one inch or so taller than he. He liked guessing the height of others, particularly if the person was taller. "Six foot four or five?" the priest had asked.

"No," the young man had said, "Six three."

"Impossible," Koesler had gasped. "*I'm* six three. I have been since high school."

"No," the man had insisted, "six three."

Koesler was so sure of himself that this caused doubt to creep into his mind. He'd heard of shrinkage in older years. Could it be happening to him? He would wait till his next visit to the doctor and get weighed and measured on accurate instruments.

Whatever, he was tall enough to see the foursome ahead was walking off the green. On this par three hole, golf etiquette allowed teeing off when the green was clear or if the preceding foursome was in trouble and waved the following group on. "You're away," he told Father Tully, who had won the previous hole and had honors.

Neither Tully nor Koesler had ever had a golf lesson. If there were any doubt, all one needed was to watch them play.

For example, Tully used a driver for his tee shot on a par three hole. A bit too much club, but Father Zachary needed all the help he could get. Instead of soaring high in the air, Tully's shot skipped merrily down the baked fairway. Despite his overclubbing, the ball stopped well short of the green.

Koesler had never grasped the fundamental difference between golf and baseball. In both games one used a ball and a club. Actually golf appeared less demanding than baseball. After all, no one was throwing the ball toward you. It just sat there on the ground waiting to be hit.

Although Koesler aimed his tee shot well to the left of the fairway, it sliced onto the fairway to the right.

They parted to address their respective balls. They would meet again, inevitably, on the green. Needless to say, neither would come close to par on this or any other hole, except by accident.

They played the ninth, a par four hole, in remarkably the same manner as they had the eighth—well over par for both holes.

Nine holes constituted the beginning of a golfing day for genuine players. For these two hackers, nine constituted all the exercise they needed.

They repaired to a nearby restaurant for a well-deserved lunch. Each ordered a tuna sandwich and a Miller Lite. Both were saving themselves for tonight's dinner party.

Father Tully had been ordained a priest in the Josephite religious order, a group whose mission was to the poor, especially to poor African-Americans. He was unique in being the only Josephite ever to transfer to the Archdiocese of Detroit.

His father had been African-American, his mother, white. His father died soon after the boy's birth. So, Zachary grew up knowing next to nothing about his father's background. Since his mother's family were fervent Catholics, the boy was raised Catholic.

He'd been working a parish in Dallas when he was sent on a business trip to Detroit. Then it was that he had learned from an aunt that his father had had a previous family in Detroit. The only member of that family still living in Detroit was Zachary's half-brother, Alonzo Tully, a police lieutenant in Detroit's busy Homicide Department.

Zoo, the lieutenant's nickname, shared Zachary's father but not his mother. Zoo was dark-skinned. Zachary, a mulatto, while sharing many characteristics of his brother's physiognomy, could easily pass for white.

As luck would have it, Zoo, a backsliding Baptist, had married a committed Catholic. This was Zoo's second marriage. He had five children from his first marriage, all of whom lived with their mother, outside Michigan. He had no children with Anne Marie, his present wife.

Both Alonzo and Zachary had been amazed to meet each other for the first time so far along in life. But in no time they were getting along famously—each meddling in the other's territory whenever it was appropriate.

By a geographical chance, and to be close to his newfound brother, Father Zachary on his initial stay in Detroit had billeted in Father Koesler's rectory.

Then, after sending Koesler on a well-deserved vacation, Zachary had baby-sat the parish. By a strong turn of fate, during Koesler's absence, Zachary became involved in a murder investigation his brother was handling—and eventually helped solve the case.

Koesler himself was no slouch when it came to amateur detection. More or less annually, beginning in 1979, he either blundered into or was invited into a homicide investigation.

Not that either Tully or Koesler were in the same league with professional police officers. It was just that periodically there seemed to occur a murder with a decidedly "Catholic" cast to it.

As yet the police had not developed their own expert on religion in general or Catholicism in particular. So they had come to respect and utilize the expertise of, first, Father Koesler, and now Father Tully as well.

Each Detroit priest, at the age of seventy, was offered the status of Senior Priest. By mutual consent of the Archbishop and the said priest, he could, in effect, retire. Or he could continue in full service. Some priests could scarcely wait for the opportunity to retire. Others simply plowed on, treating their seventieth as no different from their sixty-ninth—or their fiftieth, for that matter.

Father Koesler had chosen to accept retirement, while continuing to work pretty much full-time. Now, he was able to pick and choose where he felt called to be.

Both priests had been sipping at their beer and exchanging small talk when the sandwiches were served. Koesler studied the plate. "Potato chips," he said. "I hadn't counted on that."

"What's wrong?"

"Salt."

"Salt?"

"Yes," Koesler said. "I try to stay away from salt. They put so much of it in food, it's almost impossible. Add the salt to the greasy chips and I can almost watch my arteries shut down."

"Does that mean you're not going to eat them?"

Koesler looked at the other priest and smiled. He pushed his plate toward Tully. "Enjoy."

Smiling in return, Tully scooped up the rejected chips and added them to his own pile. "You make this seem sinful," he complained in jest.

"Not at all, Zack. Eat up. But I'm afraid I can't say: Eat them in good health."

They finished lunch in leisurely fashion. Wednesdays were Tully's day off. Koesler no longer restricted himself to a specific day off. Still he managed to keep busy nearly all the time.

This afternoon a meeting at Blessed Sacrament Cathedral was Tully's sole appointment.

Koesler was aware of the meeting. But since he wasn't required to attend, he wasn't going to. Not attending meetings—diocesan, vicariate, parochial, or what-have-you—was the prime luxury of his retirement. Instead, he had a list of former parishioners and friends who were either hospitalized or were infirm at home. These he would visit. As time passed, more and more of his friends and acquaintances were finding that old age was not for sissies.

For now, the two priests had time to relax and enjoy each other's company.

"It was very kind of you," Koesler said, "to host our Ursula party tonight."

"Not at all," Tully said. "There's just no end to what I have to learn about this archdiocese. I didn't know there was a St. Ursula's parish." He paused to chew deliberately. "As a matter of fact, I don't even know much about Ursula. She was a martyr, I presume."

Koesler chuckled. "Nobody knows exactly who this Ursula was. Most books on the saints list her as having lived in the fourth century. And that's followed by a question mark. The way the story goes, she was the daughter of a Christian British king. She was going to be given in marriage to a pagan prince. But she was allowed a three-year postponement because she really wanted to remain a virgin."

Tully covered his mouth as he began to laugh. "What would a measly three-year delay do for her if she wanted to remain a virgin?"

"I don't know," Koesler confessed. "But that's the way the story goes. Anyway, she spent the three-year period sailing around—mostly the Mediterranean. Then she and her companions ended up somehow in Cologne, where they were martyred by the Huns for their Christianity."

"How did the Huns get in the story? And what happened to the pagan prince?"

"No one seems at all sure. Ursula appears to have bought the farm because she refused to marry the chief of the Huns."

"I guess there is a moral to that story"—Tully continued to enjoy the tale—"virgins should be more flexible. That's one. And Ursula must have been quite a looker if princes and chiefs wanted to jump her bones."

"She always reminded me," Koesler said, "of a story in a lovely little book called *St. Fidgeta and Other Parodies*. The story was about an apocryphal saint called Pudibunda. If I remember the story correctly, it went this way: 'St. Pudibunda on her wedding night decided that God had called her to a life of spotless virginity. The causes of her death that very night are not known. But the pious may guess at them.'

"And the moral of all this," Koesler continued, "is that it's certainly not your fault that you were unfamiliar with this obscure saint. It's not even your fault that you are unfamiliar with the Detroit parish of the same name. Both the doubtful saint and the obscure parish were tucked away in a corner of oblivion."

Tully squeezed a handful of potato chip morsels into his mouth, where he chewed them into a gummy blob. When he had swallowed that, he said, "Okay. Now I know what little is known of the saint, and just a little bit more than that about the parish named for her. But what of the club? What was so special about the saint or the parish to have this club named after she . . . it . . . them?"

"The club," Koesler explained, "was in memory of neither the saint nor the parish. Rather, the club was dedicated to the parish's erstwhile pastor, Father Antonio Angelico. And thereby hangs the story."

Tully was ingesting the crumbs—all that was left of two heaps of potato chips—much more delicately. "I think we've got time for a short story, at least, about St. Ursula's parish. The management of this place doesn't seem to be in any hurry for us to clear out. And my meeting's not till mid-afternoon."

"Actually"—Koesler had finished his lunch some minutes ago—

"you'll probably get a pretty good notion at tonight's party of how things were. But maybe I can give you some background."

"It'd help."

"Okay. Well, I have no idea exactly when St. Ursula's was established as a parish. The way the Detroit diocese functioned back then was to anticipate the development of new neighborhoods, buy property in those areas, then wait for the people to build their homes, move in, and start producing families."

"Excuse me," Tully interrupted, "but how did the local Catholic administration know where Catholics were going to migrate? What if the diocese made a mistake? What if the property just stood barren?"

Koesler nodded. "A good point. It all worked out rather well for a number of reasons. The priests who were given responsibility for these developments were assisted by Catholic laymen who were experts in demographics. That's one. And two, they could hardly miss: One community grew almost on top of the other.

"St. Ursula's, or the property purchased for some sort of new neighborhood, happened to be in a mostly Italian cultural area. As you can imagine with a predominantly Italian section of the city, there were loads of Catholics there. So, they sort of grew up together—the neighborhood and the parish.

"Father Angelico was the second pastor. By the time he got there, things had shifted around. The parish still comprised a majority of Italians. But Polish families had moved in until they had become a solid minority. And before Father Angelico died, the parish went from almost exclusively Italian to about forty percent Italian, forty percent Polish and ten percent black. By the time Father Angelico was no longer, African-Americans made up almost the total population.

"Back when Angelico was thriving, the relationship between pastor and assistants differed from parish to parish. All Church law had to say about it was that the assistant was 'below'—*subest*—the pastor. And some pastors took flagrant advantage of that positioning.

"Some pastors were very good shepherds—good to their parishioners, good to their employees, good to their assistants. Some of them were very poor managers. Of course they weren't supposed to be managers; they were supposed to be 'other Christs'—*alter Christus*. But a few of these guys were small-time tyrants. They were notorious. And among them was Angelico."

Father Tully sipped his beer. The bottle had a long way to go before it would be a dead soldier. "I've heard that from time to time. But it's always in the context of history—like this type of pastor went out with the Ice Age."

Koesler eyed several small potato chip crumbs that Tully apparently had missed. Tempting but not compelling. "Funny," he mused, "I'm just running the presbyterate—as we are called from time to time— through my mind. It used to be that I could freeze-frame on certain pastors as fitting the infamous mold. That doesn't happen any longer.

"Not that I think that human nature has changed that much. It's more that there are fewer rear ends to kick."

"You mean," Tully said, "that the object of their sadism—the vanishing assistant—is not around to be brutalized?"

"Something like that. But in the days of yore, pastors—at least a handful of them—could be a menace."

"Didn't they ever pick on anyone but assistants?"

"Of course. I can think of one—now in that great offertory in the sky—who had the ushers puncture the tires of every car parked on or over the yellow line in the parking lot."

"Outrageous! The following Sunday there were no improperly parked cars because no one went to Mass there?"

"You'd think that." Koesler nibbled on one small potato chip crumb and was disgusted with himself. "But those were the days when territorial boundaries were vital. Most parishioners, even the ones with punctured tires, would attend *their* parish no matter how tyrannical the pastor might be. And, if it came to the point where they really had had it, they would still need a letter from the pastor to 'switch parishes.'"

"What if the guy hopscotched over his pastor and didn't bring a letter from Daddy? If he just went to another parish to sign up there?"

"Then the priest of that parish was not supposed to permit him to join."

"Seems preposterous!"

"By today's lights, definitely. That was a different time."

"I'll say. Personally, I'm happy all my folks—that used to be your folks—show up of a Sunday. It's nice if they register. But that's entirely up to them."

"Yep," Koesler agreed. "That's the open-ended approach I favored. But getting back to the original thought, hardly anyone today would consider causing needless insult to the faithful. The same pastor, the one who had tires punctured, was refinishing the interior of his church. Turns out he received only a partial delivery of the new pews he had ordered. So he put all the spanking new ones in the church's main section, and left the old, shabby pews in an old side section, and had parents with small children occupy that space."

Tully was shaking his head. "What a winner! He could solve the priest shortage by cutting back on the number of Catholics belonging to parishes—thus reducing the proportion of the faithful compared with the number of priests left to go around. Didn't these guys ever take on someone their own size?"

"You mean pastor to pastor?"

"Uh-huh."

"Rarely. But when it did happen it was like a couple of bulls, a couple of lions having at it. No, the butt of choice were the assistants. They were a well-defined target."

"And you?" Tully beckoned the waitress to bring the bill. Waving aside Koesler's attempt to pay, he studied the bottom line briefly then slipped some money on the table. "Keep the change," he said. It would be a generous tip. The waitress could never again bad-mouth stingy clergymen.

"And you, Bob? Did you ever serve with any of these guys?"

"Well, of course, there was Angelico."

"I mean beside him."

"No, thank God. I don't even have to knock on wood. I'm well beyond the stage of having anything even remotely resembling that happen to me."

"How was it with you and Angelico?"

"Different than anyone he had living with him before or after."

Tully was smiling. "Because?"

"Because I was the first—and the last, as it turned out—who wasn't an assistant. I was 'in residence.' I was the newly appointed editor of the diocesan paper. He didn't really know what that entailed, how much clout I had with the administration. It was all lost in the mist of 'downtown.'

"I think the poor man may have suspected that I was sent to spy on him. It was unlikely he could be charged with anything that resembled misfeasance of any kind. He didn't steal any of the parish's money. If anything, he squirreled it away against a rainy day.

"He had no problem avoiding sexual misconduct. He distrusted, even disliked women and boys and girls"—he chuckled—"just about everyone, for that matter, except the men he drafted into the ushers' guild. Them he handpicked.

"He took no chances with the weekly collection. None but the consecrated hands of a priest could touch the Sunday collection. So, with three priests counting—the pastor, his two assistants, but not me—the money would be banked sometime Monday afternoon.

"Outside of sheer general crankiness, his principal vice was the demeaning abuse he inflicted on his assistants. He never gave any indication that he considered anyone sent to work with him as fully human, let alone fellow priests."

"They weren't allowed to exercise their ministry?" Tully wondered.

"They were commanded to exercise *his* ministry. Or, at least, what he considered his ministry.

"Take this for example. The two assistants were not supposed to leave their one-room chambers—at all!—except to say Mass, to take devotions like Perpetual Help, to answer emergency sick calls, to bring Communion to shut-ins, to give instructions to converts . . . you get the picture."

"Wow! They might as well have been prisoners."

"Exactly. I was many times his junior. I didn't feel it was my function to get in the middle of this mess. Over the years, I have come to have second thoughts: I should have intervened. Of course, the chancery downtown knew what was going on. They should have corrected him—no matter the cost. But, for whatever reason, I should have gotten involved. It was a major failing on my part. The best I could do, I thought, was to form the Ursula club. It may not have been the best idea I ever had. But I think it did some good.

"Originally it was intended as a haven for priests and nuns who had spent any time at all under Father Angelico's thumb. We had no dues, no rules or regulations, not even a clubhouse. Just a get-together to lick wounds, let off steam, find comfort from shared misery.

"Many years ago most of the membership consisted solely of those priests who were actively assigned to the parish. After a guy had moved on, he tried to forget, and once he'd been reassigned, he rarely needed a group to get over the experience.

"Nor did any nuns belong to the club. First off, they would never have had a chance to escape the convent to gather with the rest of us. Secondly, most of the nuns of that order probably thought that Angelico was a saint.

"But as is usually true, time heals all wounds. And Father Angelico has, for lo these many years, passed on to his eternal reward—or whatever. Now, only a few who were contemporaries attend. It's more a social event dedicated to keeping tabs on each other and, inevitably, recalling the stories of the way it used to be. Only in retrospect were the good old days actually good."

Tully checked his watch. The afternoon's clergy meeting loomed. "By the way," he said, "thanks for inviting my brother and sister-in-law. They're looking forward to it." He stopped and smiled. "At least Anne Marie is."

Koesler smiled. "I know you want to include them in everything you do . . . as much as possible."

Oddly, Koesler had known Zack Tully's brother and sister-in-law longer than Zack had. Father Koesler and Zoo Tully had collaborated in solving several murder investigations and had become friends. Through Zoo, Koesler had come to know and appreciate Anne Marie for the treasure she was.

In subtle ways, Koesler, Zack, and Anne Marie were trying to interest the detective, a Baptist backslider, in things Catholic. They were careful not to push too hard. For none of the three conspirators was it essential that Zoo convert. If it happened, it would be a tasty frosting on the cake.

"I just hope," Tully said, "that they won't feel like fifth wheels. After all, they'll be the only ones there who won't be alumni—or alumnae—of the parish."

"Well, not really," Koesler responded. "Just so they won't feel like outsiders, I invited another couple who were never affiliated with the parish or with Father Angelico."

"Oh? Who?"

"Tom and Peggy Becker. They're friends of Rick Casserly. Matter of fact, Tom and Rick were seminary classmates. Tom left the seminary something like three years before ordination."

"They the ones with the landscape business?"

"You know them?"

"I've read about Tom Becker. But I've never met him or his wife."

"I think you'll like Tom. He started out practically giving away housing to the homeless. Then he married and started a family. At which point he got serious about money—and from then on he had the Midas touch."

"That part I'm familiar with. How about the wife?"

"Peggy? She's a good wife and mother for all I can tell. But I think she let the winds and sands of time pass her by."

"How's that?"

"She's on the other side of changes in the Church."

"Impervious to Vatican II?"

"Exactly. Tom moved with the changes. Peggy did not. Either they have established a delicate balance or all is not perfect in paradise. I don't think they have much in common anymore—at least not as far as the Church is concerned."

"Okay." Tully looked quickly at the waitress. She seemed in no hurry. Nor were there many customers in the restaurant. He felt there was no pressing need to clear out. "Everyone else at the party will know each other. Right?"

Koesler nodded.

"Then, how about I introduce my brother and sister-in-law to everyone and you do the same for the Beckers wherever they need an introduction."

"Fine with me."

"You can start right now," Tully said, "in giving me a quick rundown on the rest of our guests for tonight."

"Sure." Koesler glanced at his watch. Something he had always done with great regularity throughout his adult life. "I know you've got a meeting to attend. And I should get in a few hospital visits before evening. So, it'll just be thumbnail sketches.

"There's Rick Casserly. I think you know him."

"God's gift to vocation recruiters? I should say so. Seems like all the little boys who know him want to grow up to be Father Casserly. I don't think our archdiocese knows what a gem they have in this guy. If they did, they'd center most of their recruitment efforts around him."

Koesler chuckled. "I guess you do know Rick! And you've identified him perfectly. He's the next best thing to Bing Crosby, Father O'Malley in *Going My Way*. He's big and brash and handsome and Irish. He makes friends with everyone. He's reverent with the sacraments, especially Mass. He's established a reputation as an effective spiritual director. In short, if Hollywood wanted a perfect priest, central casting would send for Rick Casserly."

"And," Tully added, "he could do it without makeup."

"Right. And, let's see, the others. There's Dora Riccardo—formerly, Sister Perpetua of the dreaded Theresians. She joined us almost immediately after the order helped her make up her mind whether to leave or stick it out.

"I must confess, she surprised me with how quickly she came to us. Almost as if she left the order *just* to join the club. That couldn't be . . . but I still wonder about the speed of it.

"Well . . .

"Then there's Lillian Niedermier. She has the distinction of being the only nonreligious ever to join the club. She taught at the school for three years."

"Enough time to experience the wounds and develop the scars of

Angelico, I'd say . . . sort of a kissing cousin of the stigmata," Tully said. "Where is she now?"

"Principal at St. Enda's. And doing very well from all I've heard. If the Church will let her climb an ecclesiastical ladder, she ought to have a bright future."

Tully shook his head sadly. "Yes, I'm afraid the Church has got as impenetrable a glass ceiling as any nonepiscopal organization. Good luck to Lillian."

"Lil, she prefers."

"Lil it is. Any more?"

"Our newest member," Koesler replied, "Jerry Anderson. You'd have to be living in a cave not to know who he is."

"True. But I didn't know he had been with Father Angelico."

"A few years ago. And that explains his eligibility to join us. Once upon a time he served under Angelico. That entitles him to become a member of the club. But it doesn't account for his joining us just now. I mean, he could have joined while he was with Angelico—and believe me, he had good reason to do so. The pastor was as rough or rougher on Jerry as on any other assistant. But Jerry didn't get in touch with us then, even after he left the priesthood."

"He left the priesthood?" Tully was surprised. "I thought he took a leave of absence."

Koesler shook his head. "In this archdiocese, ninety-nine percent of the time, when a priest takes a leave he's not coming back. The phrase is nothing but a euphemism for quitting. In all the time this term has been in use, I think only two or possibly three priests actually returned from a leave."

"Why not just say he resigned?"

"It looks better. It softens the blow. People read that this or that priest is on leave of absence. They don't reflect that never—or almost never—is there a notice that the priest has returned."

"So," Tully asked, "nobody knows why, after that huge time gap, Anderson is joining this club now?"

"Not really . . . not that I know of. But," Koesler toyed with his napkin, "I think it has something to do with Dora Riccardo."

"The former Sister Perpetua?"

"The very one."

"What's the connection?"

"I must have too much time on my hands," Koesler confessed. "Or maybe it's just fun searching for anwers to puzzles. And all I have is circumstantial evidence; there's no smoking gun . . ." He hesitated. "My Lord, would you listen to me? I must be watching too many reruns of *Law and Order.*"

"You've certainly got my attention. Proceed, counselor."

"Okay." A small smile played at the corners of Koesler's lips. "Dora . . . Perpetua . . . served time with both the Theresians and Father Angelico while Jerry . . . Father Anderson . . . was assigned to St. Ursula's. He was her spiritual director. I know that because when they left for new assignments, he passed her on to Rick Casserly. In one of our gatherings around the hot stove, he happened to mention that.

"Now," Koesler warmed to his story line, "by the time Anderson picked up all that publicity and left the active ministry, Dora was working for that *Oakland* magazine. She gave him an entreé to the magazine. And he applied and got the job. He followed her into the lay life. And now . . ." He paused.

"He's following her into this little club. You think this could become a relationship made in heaven?"

"Kind of strikes me that way. He certainly doesn't need this club. He had plenty of time to join us during or immediately after his stint with Angelico. One would have to think that he did just fine with his own rehabilitation. Those wounds were healed. But there was something the magazine and the club have in common . . ."

"Dora Riccardo."

"Uh-huh."

"Sort of paints the picture of basketball's full-court press."

"I think so. It shows every promise of ending in marriage."

"But," Tully objected, "he's still a priest. I mean canonically. He's still bound to celibacy. If that isn't enough to deter him, how about her? Maybe Dora isn't quite ready to be excommunicated . . ."

"At this stage in their lives it may not make a lot of difference. Besides, it's always possible that Jerry has applied for laicization. Most of the guys who do just don't talk about it."

Tully thought about that for a moment. "Generally, there's no other reason for going for laicization than getting married. There's no ecclesiastical penalty, as such, for leaving the priesthood; just for getting married."

"So," Koesler continued the thought, "if the rumor is true, then Jerry probably does plan marriage. And, again, probably, the bride will be Dora Riccardo."

"My . . ." Tully spoke with mock wonder. "There are circles inside circles in this club."

"Puzzles and mysteries add spice to life."

Tully leaned forward. "Let's see, we're expecting Tom and Peggy Becker; my brother and Anne Marie; Rick Casserly; Jerry Anderson; Lil Niedermier; Dora Riccardo—and the two of us, right?"

"Well, the caterers are preparing for a generous serving for ten, yes. The 'generous' label should take care of any last-minute guests. I know it was an RSVP invitation, but I can think of one or two more who might just wander in without reservation." Koesler checked his memory. "Matter of fact, I can think of one who has attended these meetings religiously. So I kind of expect him."

"Who is that?"

"Father Harry Morgan."

It was Tully's turn to check his memory. "Can't say I've ever heard of him."

"I'm not surprised. Harry Morgan is my classmate."

Tully was startled.

"Yes"—Koesler grinned—"that old!"

"I didn't mean . . ." Tully fumbled.

Koesler laughed. "It's okay. Just remember: As we are, so you one day will be."

"It's not that," Tully insisted. "It's just that I've tried to familiarize myself, particularly with the guys who are my senior. I really should have recognized Morgan. Even if I didn't know much about him, I should have recalled the name."

"Don't feel bad. Harry has given new meaning to the phrase 'keeping a low profile.'"

"He's retired?"

"No. He's administrator of a tiny mission called the Pietà."

"Doesn't sound like much of a job. He's not a pastor. And the mission isn't a parish."

"All true. But Harry is dedicated to a quest . . ."

Tully smiled, "Like Don Quixote de la Mancha."

"Something like that. Except that Quixote found the gold in dross. He found Dulcinea in Aldonza. Harry more likely would see Aldonza in Dulcinea."

"He sounds interesting."

"He's fascinating in many ways. I had—gratefully—moved out of Ursula's several years before Harry was sent there as an assistant. Of all the priests who served under Angelico, Harry was the only one who clearly enjoyed it."

"Enjoyed?"

"Hard to imagine after all you've heard about the place, isn't it?"

"I should say."

"Lots of priests tried to prepare Harry for what he was about to suffer there. Really, in all Christian charity, they tried to soften the experience. Even I briefed him and, in fact, urged him to confront the pastor early on. And he seemed affected by all this concern.

"Then he moved in and got acquainted for himself. In a couple of words, he loved it."

"No!"

"Uh-huh. It was as if somebody had cloned Angelico and got Harry Morgan. In fact, he outdid Angelico; he was more stern and strict than the pastor ever dreamed of being. In time, Angelico built up enough confidence in Harry that he was allowed to roam free. On his own initiative, Harry took the damned census for several hours every day.

"Voluntarily he quarantined himself in his upstairs room. They say that Angelico actually invited Harry to use the sacred living room as often as he wished. And, why not: For Angelico, having Harry around was like looking into a flattering mirror."

"That's almost spooky."

"Really! It was weird. Harry still looked like Harry Morgan. But there were expressions—facial expressions—that were uncannily reminiscent of Angelico. For instance, it was hard to tell when Harry was smiling—which was not often—and when he was furious. His lips were always drawn tightly across his teeth—something altogether new for Harry.

"And it changed his life. We thought that maybe when Harry left Ursula's, he would return to his own personality. Give him a few months, a year at best, and he would be the Harry Morgan we'd known for all those years in the seminary.

"But it was not to be. Angelico had, in a sense, taken possession of him. Harry was never the same again."

"Incredible," Tully exclaimed. "What's happened to him?"

"I think it would be fair to call his ministry undistinguished. He was an assistant in several parishes. He was pastor of a couple of parishes in the boondocks. Actually, he was one of the last—as a matter of fact, the very last—in our class to get his own parish. In fact, if the priest supply had held up and there hadn't been a priest shortage, he might never have become a pastor."

"You make it sound as if he should never have been ordained."

Koesler pulled his jacket tightly around his neck. There was no need for the restaurant's air conditioning to be turned on, but it had been. With the noon crowd having thinned out, he was beginning to feel the chill. "In 1954 when we were ordained, to go by the book was to steer a safe course. And a safe course was to take no risks. When we delivered practice sermons, a critique of being 'bookish' was the equivalent of a passing grade. So, being strict and stern and rigid and 'bookish' by no means disqualified a seminarian from ordination.

"Besides, most of the narrow-minded among us mellowed in time. Who knows; Harry might have turned out entirely different if it hadn't been for Angelico.

"But Harry did become a new edition of the old man. Much to the detriment, I think, of souls. He might have become more forgiving; instead he gained a reputation as a harsh confessor who confused mercy with vengeance. And if you were in the pew, and he was hearing confessions, you might hear Harry shout, 'You did *what?!*'"

They both laughed even though they knew the reality of that example was anything but funny.

"I'd say," Tully observed, "that we have quite a cast of characters for this evening. Before we had this talk, I must admit I didn't anticipate much interest in the party. But now . . ."

"But now, " Koesler supplied, "you can see that there may be an interesting interplay among the guests—if not fireworks."

"And I'm dying to meet the clone of Father Angelico."

Twelve

THEY STOPPED at a Holiday Inn for lunch.

Pressed as to why he had chosen this motel for a meal, he would have confessed it was their slogan, "No Surprises."

Indeed, Tom Becker did not enjoy surprises. His life was ruled by set goals, not happenstance.

He had entered the seminary with the goal of discovering whether or not he had a vocation to the priesthood. His goal was not to become a priest but to learn what God had in store for him.

It took almost ten years, but he achieved his goal. When he finally made up his mind to leave, there wasn't a single doubt in his decision. Both the seminary faculty and student body had plenty of doubts concerning that choice. The consensus was that he would have made an excellent priest. Still he himself had no doubt whatever. One morning he was there for meditation; the next morning he was gone.

Some who left the seminary before ordination made a production of their decision. Days if not weeks were used to tell as many as possible that this young man was departing. Sometimes there was a not too subtle message in this dramatic leave-taking. That occasional message was, "Here I am, a decent enough man. I'm leaving because I don't consider myself worthy of this calling. And what makes you think you're better than I. Why don't you do the honorable thing and quit?"

The majority who left did so as Tom Becker had: silently slipping away.

It didn't seem to matter what course a departing student took. Most seminarians were convinced that, on the one hand, the vocation to which they aspired was sublime, and, on the other hand, that they were not perfect enough to dare attempting it.

Through years of prayer, study, thought, and direction, Becker became convinced he was not suited for the priestly life. He would not

127

become a priest. But he had achieved his personal goal: He was convinced his resignation was God's will.

His next logical step was to inform his parents, the rector, and his spiritual director of his decision to leave.

The general feeling of everyone who was affected was that an excellent candidate had resigned spontaneously. A lot of consciences were searched. A lot of agonizing was sustained. In the end, and after a suitable time for mourning, Tom Becker was forgotten throughout the hallowed halls. And life went on.

For Tom, after that most important of all goals was reached, the rest was easy. The ensuing objectives were: to rehabilitate homes for the poor; marry; gain academic degrees; succeed as an architect; retire; own and operate a landscape business. The goals followed like dominoes.

For all of this he was grateful. And, unlike some, his gratitude expressed itself in generosity. He responded to many of the seemingly infinite requests. Come Christmas, he hunkered at his desk writing checks for those charities nearest and dearest his heart.

In the early years of their marriage, Peggy Becker routinely would respond to the question, "Do you work?" with, "No. I'm a housewife." It did not take much thought—but it did take a lot of time—for that brief response to change to, "I'm a homemaker." Most recently, lots of women had acknowledged that being a mother, a cook, a wife, a psychologist, an accountant, a disciplinarian, a peacemaker, and more was, indeed, work. But now, women joined the workforce just like men. But for less pay and with a ceiling on their promotions.

In the face of all this, Peggy remained a housewife. And did so with pride.

Those who knew the Beckers, even intimately, considered their marriage near perfect. They were close physically. They were comfortable financially. Rarely was heard a discouraging word. Both were very spiritual. They were committed Catholics. Their children were exemplary. Everyone knew nothing could be this perfect. But if there was anything wrong, it was buried and hidden.

So, everyone would be surprised that at this moment Tom and Peggy were suffering through one of their rare arguments. It concerned tonight's party with the Ursula crowd. They were studying their menus in sullen silence.

"Look, dear," Tom motioned, "they've got your favorite, Caesar salad." This time around it was his turn to try being the peacemaker.

She scanned the menu until she found the listing. She considered it. "It's more than I want now. Maybe the chef's salad." She could not be angry with him. At most she was impatient.

The waitress came. Tom ordered the chef's salad for his wife and soup and a sandwich for himself. The waitress asked if he wanted a beverage. He felt like having a glass of wine. But . . . he knew water would be fine.

They didn't speak for a few moments. Even after all these years, the protocol was not clear as to which one should take the initiative.

"You know you didn't have to come this evening," Tom opened. "We're not too far from home to turn back. You can have some time to yourself while I run off to this dinner meeting."

"I thought of that." She delicately broke off the end of a breadstick and nibbled. "But you'd probably try to return late tonight."

"Either with or without you, I might try."

"Exactly! I don't want you driving alone that late. If you insist on coming straight back. I can be with you and be company for you."

"Okay. Come along. I'd like your company."

"Even if I'm grouchy? She met his eyes with a mixture of love and snappishness.

"I understand. It's just that I can live with tonight's cast of characters and you've got a p oblem with some of them."

"'Some of them,'" she repeated. "That's entirely true. But you know a couple of rotten apples can be contagious."

"Maybe part of my problem," Tom said, "is that I'm not completely clear which of tonight's guests is on your list. I seriously doubt that either of our hosts causes you a problem. Father Koesler? Father Tully?"

"No, of course not. Father Tully is a dear. And Father Koesler has a long track record. He is everything a priest should be."

"The policeman and his wife?"

"Oh, come on. We've never even met them."

"You don't mind meeting them for the first time in this setting?"

She thought a moment. "I don't think so. Time will tell. But I'm not anticipating any problem there."

"How about the young woman, the principal?"

"Ms."—she emphasized the modern pronunciation of the identification—"Niedermier? You are going at this process in concentric circles, aren't you?" She smiled. "You do intend to get down to the problem area eventually, don't you?"

He returned her smile. "Can't take anything for granted. Let's take them one at a time. Ms." he mimicked his wife, "Neidermier?"

"No. If anything, I feel sorry for her. She certainly is eligible, isn't she? Such a pretty girl. I wonder why no one has scooped her up."

The waitress brought their orders, asked if anything was wanting, then left to service her other tables.

"I couldn't agree with you more," he said. "Lillian is a very attractive woman. But we don't know how many proposals she may have had. In any event, you have no problem with Lil?"

"None."

"That brings us to Father Casserly."

She shook her head and sighed. "You're really leaving the problem area till last, aren't you?"

He smiled broadly. "Got to touch all the bases."

"How could anyone not like Father Casserly? Superpriest. Athletic, handsome, marvelous sermons, deep thinker, renowned counselor."

"You sound as if you could be his agent."

She laid down her fork and gazed out the large window at the dark green grass of a fairway. "Lots of women would consider his celibacy as a waste."

"Do I have to worry about you?"

She laughed. "'Lots of women' does not include me."

"You think they still would find him attractive?"

"Certainly."

"He's my age. Sixty. That's a little long in the tooth, don't you think?"

"So what? Women find you attractive too."

He laughed. "You're too kind. But I love it."

"It's true. It's also not fair. When women age and their skin is not tight, they become ancient, no longer sexually appealing. Men don't age or grow old; they *mature*. All I'm saying is that Father Casserly has matured and continues to mature wonderfully."

"I'll have to tell him. It may boost his morale."

"Don't you dare!"

Strange, Tom thought. Things seemed to be changing, but there was a lot of truth in what Peggy said. Women tend to try to mask the signs of age. Some wear clothing tight enough to threaten asphyxiation. They apply makeup to hide the wrinkles. They've forgotten the original color of their hair. It's not so much that they try to appear young. It is much more that they feel they must remain young.

Men can go to pot, literally, and still feel no need to go to women's extremes. If thinning hair is a concern, there's always a rug, or combing over the thin spots. Or, much more simply, just be like Sean Connery— or go totally bald and join forces with Yul Brynner, Telly Savalas, and Patrick Stewart.

Youth seems to be a priority with television newscasters—national, network, cable, or local. People who travel around the country can turn on the local TV news at six and see seemingly the same list of characters from city to city. Males may be young or maturing, but the females must exude youth. Water Cronkite could have anchored CBS News to the absolute end of "That's the way it was." His maturation signified reliability, wisdom, and experience. But Lesley Stahl had better be smooth-skinned, slim if not taut, one of the shades of blonde, and have teeth sufficiently sparkling to cause eye damage.

Tom Becker wondered if he would live long enough to witness the inevitable triumph of gender equality.

In the Catholic Church that would mean that for the Third Vatican Council, bishops would bring their wives. And for the Fourth, bishops would bring their husbands.

Tom Becker also wondered whether he had been correct when he had decided not to tell Peggy about the unorthodox living situation of Rick and Lil.

How would Peggy react if she knew? It was anyone's guess. Tom understood his wife far better than did her closest friends and relatives. His estimate was Peggy would drop the priest like a hot pizza. A beautiful friendship would be destroyed—needlessly, as far as Tom was concerned.

All the attractive attributes would melt away. In Peggy's eyes, Rick would no longer be a superpriest. He would not be even superman. Just another guy—and one who didn't even have the courage to stand up publicly for his lifestyle at that. Tom was certain this was the way things would play out.

His decision to keep Peggy in the dark had its repercussions in their own relationship as well.

Long ago, before they were married, Tom and Peggy had agreed that there would be no secrets between them. Tom was sure of two things: One: Peggy had not broken that trust. Two: He had.

He shuddered to think of the meltdown in their ability to share. Life with Peggy without trust would be no life at all. At this stage of the game there was no compromising. Tom had to make sure Peggy never learned about Rick and Lil. And, by extension, of Tom's breach of trust.

They finished their lunch expeditiously and in silence. By now the ice had been broken and it was a friendly silence.

He always drove unless they had attended some event or program that exhausted him. That was not the case now. Tom slid behind the wheel.

He had been deferring any mention of her attitude toward Jerry Anderson and/or Dora Riccardo. He hoped something unforeseen might happen and the conversation would veer away from the final couple. That hadn't happened. So clearing this final problem was an event that was going to happen.

They drove in silence for several miles. He swung onto southbound I-75, the freeway that would lead them into downtown Detroit, then slipped into cruise control and aimed the car at the Motor City. He broke the silence. "I'm waiting for the other shoe to drop."

"Other shoe?"

"Jerry Anderson and Dora Riccardo."

Peggy didn't reply.

"They're the ones you're having a problem with?"

After a lengthy pause she said, "Yes . . . you could say so."

"But you don't even know them."

"You do?"

"I know Dora. Well, maybe a little bit."

"Oh?"

"Sometimes when I've visited Rick Casserly in his rectory, Dora has been there. She helps with the catechetical program. She's quite good at that. She was a nun, you know."

"I'm painfully aware of that."

"What's that supposed to mean?"

"It means . . ." Peggy turned toward Tom. She knew that unless she chose her words carefully, there'd be another breakdown in communication between them. "It means," she repeated, "that once upon a time she made vows to God. They were for life, if not eternity."

"I suppose you have the same problem with Jerry Anderson."

"I don't know why you are calling what these two have done *my* problem. If anything, it's *their* problem."

"Come on, Peg. *Their* problem? There are circumstances."

"Maybe we'd better not talk about this."

"Maybe. But I don't think so. As long as we're going to dine with them this evening in an atmosphere of enjoying a party, we'd better air out our feelings. After all, our hosts are two priests you like very much. We don't want to embarrass them. And that's not to mention Rick and Lil and the Tullys."

"Don't fret. I'll be on my best behavior."

"I'm not worried about that, dear. I don't for a moment think that you would intentionally wreck the party. And I'm told the small talk at these affairs is about the old days and the atrocities under Father Angelico. So there's not much chance that we'll get into a serious conversation on controversial subjects. But it's always possible. And if that happens you may be tested beyond your patience. So why not try to reach some sort of agreement, at least between us, on what Dora and Jerry did?"

Peg looked out her side window and absently regarded endless fields just beginning to produce new crops. "What they did seems to me so transparent," Peggy said finally. "It's like explaining an axiom . . . I mean, you don't have to be Sherlock Holmes to draw a logical inference from their affair."

"You make it sound so tawdry."

"Isn't it?"

"Peg, they followed—or, in Jerry's case, are following—the rules and regulations set up by the Church."

"To clean up a mess. Not to be righteous."

Tom sighed deeply. "They just happened to be placed in the same parish at roughly the same time. For both of them that was their first parochial assignment. Dora was in much deeper trouble than Jerry, so he tried to help her."

"He helped her right out of the convent!"

"Peg, she didn't leave religious life until years after they had gone their separate ways."

"The seeds were planted well."

"You make it sound like a time bomb."

Peggy fidgeted. She searched for a more comfortable position. It was not just a physical need. She was uneasy traveling over familiar religious ground that led—she knew from experience—into a dead end.

"A time bomb," she acknowledged, "is not a bad analogy. She left the convent in plenty of time to find a job where, soon enough, she could prepare a job for him at the same place. I guess the time factor is a pretty good simile."

"There's nothing wrong, no impropriety in what you've described. They worked in the same parish. But not together. She left religious life. There is no way we can know why—or what influenced her decision. He left years later. And anyone who follows the local news knows why he left when he did. She smoothed the way for him to get a job. What's wrong with any of the above?"

"What's wrong, my dear, is that she took vows. He took vows—all right, all right, he made promises." She corrected herself before Tom could. "They leave a trail of broken vows and promises. That's what's wrong."

Tom shook his head. Peg didn't see the motion—both were looking ahead at the roadway.

"Peg, we can't be more Catholic than the Church."

It was at this point that their argument always bogged down.

She labeled his approach to moral judgment "situation ethics." He countered that she refused to consider circumstances that could alter the morality of an action.

He was a student of both Fathers Casserly and Koesler. In their school of thought there was nothing that was intrinsically evil. Every action had to allow circumstantial forces.

For Peg many actions were indeed evil through and through and could not be mitigated by any other consideration. In this she was in agreement with the official position of the Church. For the life of her, Peg could not understand why, since it was the official Church teaching, Tom, the two priests—plus anyone else in agreement with them—could question her conclusion.

Tom had all but given up citing the case of Galileo Galilei, who had in effect been forced to deny the truth that his own eyes had seen. Peg's response was that whether the sun circled the earth or vice versa was not a matter of faith or morals; the decision had to do with astronomy. Tom insisted that the path of sun and earth had been an "official" teaching of the Church because the Church made it so. And unless Galileo recanted his insistence on heliocentricity he would be punished as a heretic.

Both Tom and Peg sensed that it would be futile to continue their difference of opinion. However, experience had taught that it was good for them to vent their feelings. "So what about tonight, Peggy? There's no absolute reason we have to attend this party. If you feel the least bit uncomfortable, we'll just skip it."

She weighed the offer for a few moments. She strongly leaned toward skipping the party. Despite all the excuses one could marshal to justify that couple's decisions, she could not buy into any of them.

Ever since Vatican II, there had been a flood of women religious either radically changing their original commitment or leaving religious life entirely. Teaching nuns, once the mainstay if not the driving force of the parochial school system, had all but disappeared. Many of them had switched careers while remaining nuns, branching into fields such as social work and parish administration. The majority, however, had simply left religious life and returned to lay life. In time the process of moving from one vocation to the other grew easier. There was a serious threat that women religious would become extinct.

Peggy Becker could understand none of it. For almost all her formative years, she had been taught by nuns. Only with resolute purposeful concentration was she able to address her former nuns by their given and maiden names. She found it difficult to consider the possibility that these women who almost constituted a third sex would be no more.

She would have a hard time this evening relating to Dora Riccardo without prejudice. Peggy would call the woman Dora but she would be thinking Perpetua.

It would be even more difficult accepting Father Anderson as Jerry. He had broken just about every one of the conceivable rules and regulations binding Catholics who were getting married.

The clerical gossip line, into which Tom was plugged, had it that Anderson could have dodged the bullet if he had accepted an ecclesial punishment that would have been no more than a slap on the wrist.

He could have remained an active priest so simply. Peggy definitely held it against him that he hadn't. Anderson made it sound so brave and principled. For a stand about which he would not compromise, he would surrender the life he had chosen.

Peggy didn't buy it. Her version had it that Anderson had not only fully approved the bogus wedding but that he had encouraged all that publicity. It was something like the phenomenon of "death by cop." People determined to self-destruct, but lacking the will to pull the trigger on themselves, confronted the police and made it necessary for an officer to do the deed.

In this case—according to Peggy's scenario—Anderson wanted to leave the priesthood, but lacked the courage to quit. So, through his actions, he would, first, compel the Church to level a punishment against him. Then, when he refused to accept the penalty, the Church would have to laicize him.

As she considered Father Anderson's ploy—a ploy she had concocted for him out of her own ideation—words sprang to mind: hypocritical, deceitful, hollow, dishonest, crooked, tricky, deceptive, treacherous, and traitorous.

"Okay," she responded to Tom's open-ended invitation to attend or not to attend this evening's dinner. "Let's go to the party." But, she thought, Jerry Anderson had better be a long way from gloating. Or the party just might explode in everyone's face.

Thirteen

THE MISSION OF THE PIETÀ was figuratively buried on Detroit's southwest side.

The building itself was small and primitive, with room for possibly 250 worshipers. To clean it after all these years of neglect would require more elbow grease than any of its members could muster. The wooden floor squeaked with any movement, whether one was kneeling, walking, or even merely shuffling. If anyone shifted his or her weight while standing, the floor groaned.

Minimum requirements for a music director were that the person could at least play a piano legato as well as have the stamina to pump air into the ancient pump organ.

The smooth asphalt surface of the parking lot bespoke, not caring maintenance, but rather a barely minimal use. Between the entrance and exit drives of the parking lot stood a poor likeness of Michelangelo's famous sculpture of Mary cradling the dead body of her son, Jesus. The original, known as the *Pietà,* was on display in St. Peter's Basilica in Rome. Since the time the original was attacked by a madman with a hammer, it had been protected by a heavy transparent shield.

No such precautions were needed at the Mission of the Pietà. The only threat posed to the parochial status was from one or another of the youth gangs that populated the area. And they seemed spooked when it came to the unguarded religious icon. The word was that anyone who fooled with that sacred hunk of cement would be cursed with big trouble—akin to breaking one's mother's back by stepping on a crack. As it turned out, Mary and Jesus were the safest personages in the area.

The parking lot separated the church from the rectory, which had been built at the same time as the church, in the late eighteenth century. The rectory creaked in harmony with the church.

Almost everything in the house was an antique of greater or lesser value. No one cared to evaluate the furniture, paintings, statues, silverware, utensils, bric-a-brac. Time enough for that when, inevitably, the Mission would be closed.

All that was keeping the Mission open now was the presence of a priest, Father Harry Morgan.

The arrangement made some sort of sense. Father Morgan was of an age to achieve Senior Priest status, as it was termed. At this point he could put himself on the shelf or remain selectively active; it was entirely up to him. He chose to man the Mission. He informed the chancery that he would work the place until he dropped. It was consoling that Father Morgan would never die alone; the Mission of the Pietà would go with him.

Both served a hodgepodge of clients or parishioners, whatever one cared to call them. First and foremost were the poor and/or the elderly.

Extremely fortunate, the Mission boasted an active and effective St. Vincent de Paul chapter. Most members of the S.V. de P. were themselves elderly former parishioners. They responded to every plea, discerning between the genuine needy and the frauds.

Most who still attended the Mission as their parish had long since moved out of the area. The resultant vacuum invited teen gangs and drug houses. No one, not even those who clung to the Mission, would have been shocked or disillusioned had Father Morgan abandoned ship.

The thought scarcely ever crossed his mind. Not only was he not tempted to leave, thereby dooming the Mission; he hardly ever even left the rectory. No vacations, no cruises, no picnics, at most an occasional "G"-rated movie. Not even—ever—a day off.

The constant procession of the elderly was relieved only occasionally by one or two young persons wandering in. Usually they were trying to escape the demands of their families; sometimes they wanted a sacrament, usually matrimony, beyond their parents' knowledge.

It was nine o'clock, just one hour before his bedtime. The doorbell rang. Most unusual. Visitors were rare at any time. But after about five in the evening it was as if the drawbridge were raised and the moat flooded.

Almost anyone else in his position would have ascertained the identity of the caller before opening the door. But Harry Morgan felt no danger. He was doing God's work. God would protect him.

Whether or not God was actively involved, the couple at the door appeared innocuous. He was Xavier (pronounced Ha-vee-aír)—"call me Havie"—Martines. She was Maria Sanchez. They wanted—what else?—to get married. Though English was their second language, they spoke it well enough. Father Morgan invited them into his office.

The priest's mouth was shut, his jaw clenched. Xavier was concerned. This priest might be suffering a stroke. Or, it might be his way of smiling. It was a toss-up. If it proved to be a heart attack, or anything similarly crucial, he and Maria would be out of there. Xavier didn't like the odds of a Mexican couple on the scene with a dead priest when the cops came.

But the priest clutched nothing and appeared not to be in discomfort. He was wearing a long black cassock, black cummerbund, and spotless white Roman collar. That was nice. Xavier liked it when people who should be in uniform were.

The jaw unclenched. "What brings you to the Mission of the Pietà?"

"We want to get married, Father," Maria said proudly.

"Yeah, Father," Xavier seconded.

The chair squeaked painfully as Morgan leaned back. "So, you want to get married."

Both nodded vigorously.

"I repeat," Morgan repeated, "why come to the Mission?"

The couple looked at each other. Neither was sure how to answer the question. At length, Xavier said, "We wanna get married in the Church?"

Morgan rocked in the chair, which squealed madly. If he had made this racket on a putting surface, he would have destroyed his opponent's concentration. But, of course, he scarcely ever played golf. After several moments of silence, the priest spoke. "You know, not many people come to the Mission for Mass. I'm sure I would remember a handsome couple like you. But I don't. Never at daily Mass, of course. Never at Sunday Mass. Not even Christmas or Easter. Have I overlooked you on any of these occasions?"

Xavier lit up like a neon sign. "No, no, Father. You got twenty/ twenty." He shot a glance at Maria. "We did talk about going for Christmas. But . . ." His explanation trailed off. He could not think of an excuse for not coming to honor the baby Jesus.

"Maybe," Morgan probed further, "you go to another Catholic church in the neighborhood?"

"Oh no, Father," Maria said. "We live only a few blocks away."

"Then"—the priest focused on Xavier—"Havier . . ."

"Call me, Havie, Father. Everybody does," Xavier said brightly.

"Noooo." Morgan drew the word out. "You bear the name of a great saint. A credit to Catholicism and to your country. I shall call you Havier."

"No sweat, Padre."

"Then," Morgan returned to his previous thought, "then it would be safe to say that you don't go to church at all."

"Yeah, that's about it, Padre," Xavier said.

Maria was growing edgy. She was beginning to anticipate where Father Morgan was going with his little quiz. She was correct. Morgan was playing a game of cat and mouse. Xavier and Maria were the doomed rodents.

"Well, then," Morgan said as he took from a desk drawer a pad of paper, "first things first. You'll want to register."

Xavier's eyes shifted nervously. "What is it, this register?"

"Become parishioners of the Mission."

"Join? The parish?"

"How else can we begin talk of a wedding?" From the same drawer, he extracted a box of collection envelopes.

That rang a bell. Long, long ago Xavier had seen a similar box gathering cobwebs in his parents' closet. One day he asked about it. His father explained that those small envelopes were the ticket that had gotten Xavier baptized.

His parents had been no more faithful to their parish than was he. But when he was born, they'd wanted him christened. Why? As far back as anyone could remember, all babies were baptized. No one was very clear why this custom continued. It had something to do with the baby's ticket to heaven. Without baptism, if the baby died, it would go to a place called limbo where it would be "naturally" happy forever. While limbo didn't sound at all bad, people were assured heaven was better because that was the only way one got to see God.

While the argument didn't sound too compelling, most parents bought it. In that era, being a Latino was almost synonymous with being Catholic.

As Morgan slid the envelopes across the desk, Xavier did some rapid reasoning. Holy blackmail! he thought in remembrance of Batman and Robin. He made no move to touch the box of envelopes. In fact, he recoiled from it. As if it were some sort of bomb that would explode and hurt him if his fingers met it.

The collection envelopes were self-explanatory: One put money in them and then placed them in the collection basket the usher shook insistently in front of one's face.

There was a problem here. Neither Xavier or Maria had any spare money. Maria's income came from baby-sitting. Which, in that part of town, would not contribute to a lavish pension. Xavier did menial tasks in a small neighborhood market.

He could have accepted the envelopes and let them gather dust in some remote closet, as had his father. But Xavier was not the type to dissemble. Slowly, and as respectfully as he could, he slid the box back to Morgan.

"Father, I know you gotta eat, and all that. But we ain't got no money. We both got jobs. But they don't pay nothin'. If we pay for any kind of wedding, we're gonna be in hock for a long time. And I want Maria to look good as a bride. She's gonna wear her mother's wedding dress. But it needs work. And then, there's the ring . . ." He was lost in thought as he contemplated the financial quicksand that could undermine their lifestyle into the foreseeable future. The reception. The hall. The food.

"Havie's right, Father." Maria's brow wrinkled with furrows of concern. "We don't have no extra money at all. Maybe we could owe you and pay you a little bit at a time."

Morgan looked intently into Xavier's eyes with such solemnity that the young man was forced to look away. "I think," Morgan said, "we have come down to, as they call it now, the bottom line. We can waive the expense of the marriage liturgy."

"But . . ." Xavier tried to interrupt.

"No, no," Morgan continued, "hear me out. We can waive the wedding expenses. As it happens, you can be a parishioner here without its costing you anything. And being a parishioner means you would be entitled to be married and buried in a Catholic ceremony. And your children could be baptized and confirmed and go to confession and receive Holy Communion." Morgan paused. "You do intend to have children." It was more a statement than a question.

"Yes, Father," Xavier quickly responded. "But not now. Later when we get more money."

Morgan shook his head sadly. "Well, we will talk more about that later." He extended his hand to the collection envelopes and gave the box its third trip across the desk.

Xavier was perplexed. "Father," he said, "we got no money. I just told you. We got no money."

Once again, was Morgan smiling or grimacing? Xavier couldn't tell.

"These envelopes," the priest explained, "are good for more than one use. Those who can contribute should use them for a donation. We must remember that God has been good to us. We must be generous with God. But, realistically, not everybody can give anything. I am willing to take your word that you are indigent."

"Father?"

"Poor."

"Oh." Xavier did not argue the point. Nor was he embarrassed. He was poor. There was no argument there.

"But," Morgan continued, "these envelopes serve more than one purpose."

"Oh?"

"Yes. They tell us about your attendance."

"Attendance?"

"Yes. We check not only how much a parishioner contributes, but the fact that the parishioner was there. If an envelope contains money, we record that. If the envelope is empty, we record that. If the envelope is not there, we conclude that the parishioner was not there either. So, take the box. When you can contribute, fine. At least we can record you are here."

In his mind, Xavier saw that box of envelopes in his father's closet. Xavier imagined the prototype of this present meeting. If his father had not accepted those envelopes, Xavier might never have been baptized. Further, his dad might also have been told to record his presence in church by at least turning it in empty.

Probably his father had promised everything, anything—without the slightest intention of following through. Suddenly Xavier thought much less of his dad. It wasn't right. Lying wasn't right. His father—but mostly his mother—had taught him that. "Father," Xavier said, "I don't wanna bull—I don't wanna tell you any lies. We don't plan on all of a sudden changing the way we live. We ain't gonna be going to church. Maybe later. Maybe when we have kids. But even that is maybe."

"Havie," Maria said, "maybe I will go to church. Maybe that will be enough."

Xavier shrugged. "Come on, Maria, you know how it's always been with us. Remember Christmas Eve? We were all set to go to church. Then we both fell asleep watching TV.

"Father"—Xavier turned toward Morgan—"we work hard. We don't get paid much. But we work hard. When we get the chance, we sleep instead of goin' to Mass. What happens, Father—what happens if we don't take them envelopes?"

Morgan did not respond for a few long moments. Then, "Why do you really want a Catholic ceremony? You are not serious about the Church. You don't even put the Mass ahead of some shut-eye. You seem an honest young man, Havier. So, why?"

It was Xavier's turn to hesitate before answering. "It would make our parents very happy. All our relatives, on both sides—at least almost all our relatives—got married in church. It would really piss off everybody if we didn't get married in church."

Morgan pushed himself away from the desk. "I thought as much. Well, listen, my young people. The holy, Catholic Church was established by Jesus Christ, Our Lord. He did not die on the cross so that you could avoid 'pissing off' your relatives.

"Get married as best you can. A minister. A judge. You can even shop around for another parish where some misguided Catholic priest will witness your marriage. But it's not going to happen here. You are not my parishioners. You never have been. You're not now. And, from all you've said, you never will be.

"You spoke the truth, I'll give you that, Xavier. Maybe—just maybe—you might consider going to church regularly. Maybe later, when you deign to come for the sake of the children.

"And what about those children? What would you say when, in the Catholic marriage ritual, the priest asks if you will accept the children God entrusts to you? Then, will you tell God, 'maybe'? Or when you get better jobs? Where is your faith, Xavier . . . Maria? Where in God's great heaven is your faith?" Father Morgan uttered a sound that was halfway between a growl and a sigh. "I'm afraid this matter is concluded. You may leave. And don't ever return unless your 'maybe' is 'now.'"

Wordlessly, the young couple left the rectory. Maria was in tears. Xavier was angry. The old priest could have let them down more gently given he was not going to marry them after all that.

All Xavier had to do was take the damn envelopes. They could have gotten married at the Mission. Everybody would have been festive. Then he could have put the box of envelopes in an unlooked-at hidey-hole and let them molder.

Well, the hell with this priest and the hell with his Church. He and Maria would make it on their own.

That was last night. Father Harry Morgan still felt he had done the right thing. He seldom, if ever, second-guessed himself.

Over the years he had set two standards for himself. One of those had been the example of Father Angelico of happy memory. The other, the method of operation of his classmate Father Robert Koesler.

Morgan had never cared for Koesler.

They were among the charter members of the class of '42, high school freshman. The vast majority of that class would leave before ordination in 1954. Others, particularly discharged World War II veterans, would replace those who left. But even they would suffer a drastic dropout rate.

Bob Koesler and Harry Morgan got to know each other very well in the twelve years they shared in the seminary.

They had little in common. Koesler was a jock, Morgan was not. Morgan was a serious scholar. Koesler was not—not until the final four years of theology.

Not that there was any enmity between them. But they traveled in different circles. Aside from the burning desire to be a priest, they had no other common interests. Yet that goal of ordination was so strong that they got along fairly well.

In addition, the seminary of that day mirrored the Church of that day. The seminary and the Church of that day were not kind to inquisitive minds. One did not question theology; one learned it.

So, there was no disagreement between Bob and Harry concerning the "official" teachings which they were to use in instructing the faithful. There was no difference in substance. There was, however, a wide expanse—miles—of disparity between their method of dispensing these teachings.

The pivotal blow to their relationship was struck when Koesler was awakened by the Vatican Council while Morgan was cloned by Father Angelico.

Once their separate courses were set, Koesler became a very approachable, popular symbol of a happy, fulfilled priest. And Morgan withdrew inside himself, content to be there, yet bitter that so few consulted him. Koesler became a leader. Morgan was not.

Morgan had just finished the noon Mass. He settled in for a little brunch before his only appointment this afternoon. No one had a problem with the scheduling of Masses at the Mission of the Pietà; Mass was at noon every day, weekdays and weekends.

In this age, when popular belief held that hellfire was *not* the lot of the Catholics who skipped Sunday Mass, it didn't help to needlessly confuse the faithful. No one who belonged to the Mission could claim that he or she forgot what time Mass was. Noon. Every day. Every season. Every year. Except, of course, for Good Friday.

Mass was offered in Latin. Not the Tridentine form that had been proscribed by Pope Paul VI. The form that had replaced the ancient Tridentine was first experienced in Latin, then translated into the various vernaculars.

Elsewhere throughout the Detroit archdiocese, Mass was offered in the new English form. Morgan offered it in Latin. A better case might have been made for using Spanish, the vernacular of most of the Mission's neighborhood.

Father Morgan placed the plate containing his carefully prepared toasted cheese sandwich on the kitchen table. This was another of his invariables. Normally a few vegetables accompanied the sandwich. Today, he cut back, mindful of the party tonight. On an occasion such as that, he was wont to eat more than he was accustomed to.

He was trim, to the point of being too thin. It was another lesson he had gratefully learned from Father Angelico. *Mens sana in corpore sano,* as the Latin had it, a healthy mind in a healthy body.

The thought of cutting back at lunch reminded him again of tonight's party. He never looked forward to the periodic Ursula get-together with any sort of joy.

He certainly qualified for membership. He had served his time under the watchful eye of the pastor. Yet he was unique in having enjoyed it. It had been the signature event of his life.

He attended the get-togethers mainly to defend Father Angelico's reputation and methods. With this in mind, such occasions kept him busy. At times, it was as if his entire body were riddled with buckshot. He would spend the evening figuratively pulling out pieces of the charges against the ancient pastor.

But it had been eleven years now since the priest had passed on. Time, as it often does, had bestowed a healing process. In recent years, parochial problems and the taking of sides in theological debate had gradually replaced Father Angelico and his barbaric behavior as topics.

Morgan felt that the Ursula crew was on its last legs. Not only had

Father Angelico been dead these many years but the crowd was thinning out. Morgan had given consideration to not attending this year. It would be his first absence. There was less and less reason for him to be there.

If Bob Koesler had not volunteered once more to be the host, Morgan probably would have called it quits. But Morgan enjoyed baiting his classmate. This year, the subject of his taunting would be the retirement issue. Of course, other considerations might arise as the evening progressed. But retirement would do for openers.

Koesler had retired and was beginning his second year as a "Senior" Priest. Morgan had not retired. And there was the rub.

Morgan could cite their own generation. Priests, before The Changes, did not retire. Either they died in harness or they had been put on the shelf. Priests had a corner on the market of wearing out rather than rusting out.

So Koesler had put himself on the shelf while Morgan remained— on the job. He would have the upper hand. If truth be known, he needed the upper hand. Koesler was blithely unaware of it, but Morgan felt compelled to measure himself against his classmate in a most peculiar way.

Last evening, for example, Morgan had refused a sacrament to a couple who had every legal right to it. The decision was his and he'd made it. Then, as if he needed justification, he wondered what Koesler would have done under the same circumstances.

Koesler had a reputation of being free and easy with rules and regulations. Not when it came to himself, but as applied to others. At first guess, the presumption was that Koesler would have performed the wedding. Had Morgan gone that route, then, by some weird inverted logic, Morgan would have felt he himself had made the wrong decision—because Koesler's decision would, of course, have been wrong.

But last night's case was a close call. It could have gone either way. He could imagine even Bob Koesler refusing a couple who were only misusing, manipulating the Church. He would have told them to "make a statement"—tell the precious relatives that this is the way it's going to be. Don't expect us to live as practicing Catholics; we don't believe in it, and we're not going to be hypocritical about it.

Undoubtedly Koesler would have let them down more compassionately than Morgan had. But the bottom line might well have been the same. And that's what troubled Father Morgan.

Maybe tonight at the party the subject of marrying the unchurched would come up. If he saw the opportunity, he certainly would introduce it. Then he could find out what Koesler would do in a situation like that. If, by chance, Koesler would have performed the ceremony, Morgan's decision not to marry them would be justified.

The doorbell rang. It would have to be the expected appointment. For a change, this meeting had been requested by parishioners, the Oliverios.

Dressed clerically in his cassock, he greeted three members of the Oliverio family: Federico, the father; Louisa, the mother—both in their mid-sixties—and Carmen, the daughter, in her mid-thirties and unmarried.

He greeted them in his best friendly mood reserved for faithful parishioners. In her phone call, Louisa had stated that they wanted to arrange for a funeral. She would not go into any detail. She wanted to discuss the arrangements in a face-to-face meeting.

Morgan got his visitors settled in the dining room. Neither of the two offices was large enough to accommodate a foursome. He then waited expectantly.

"Father," Louisa began, "my dear brother passed away day before yesterday."

"Sorry." He uttered it with the same sincerity as the automated, Have a nice day.

Louisa nodded. "We want to arrange for the funeral, Father."

"There are a few questions before we get to that." Morgan shifted in his chair. After a great many years of doing this, boredom had to be suppressed. "The deceased . . . his name?"

Louisa took a frilly handkerchief from her purse and dabbed at her eyes.

Carmen, the daughter, spoke. "My mama is under a lot of strain. She and my uncle were real close. My uncle's name was Alfredo Salvia." Clearly, Carmen was going to do the talking. Federico, the father, gave every evidence that this was torture he was being forced to undergo. And Louisa was emotionally overcome.

Morgan turned toward the daughter. "Where did your uncle live?"

"With us." "Of course" was left unsaid.

"I was just wondering," Morgan pursued. "I am familiar with you and your mother. But it's always just the two of you. I see your father, but it's only Christmas and Easter. I don't believe I've ever seen your uncle."

"Uncle 'Fredo didn't go to church much. Maybe never."

Morgan was sizing up Carmen. She should get married, have an army of kids, and rule the roost. She was a natural for the part of matriarch. "Well, if your uncle never went to church, why should we take him there now?"

Carmen shrugged. "Because it would break Mama's heart if he didn't have a church funeral."

Fortunately, Morgan knew exactly how to deal with these people. He had been carefully taught by the master himself, Father Angelico.

Angelico was Italian, of course. He knew their ultimate fear was being denied a church funeral. Morgan literally had heard Angelico's threat: "And when you die, you will be buried like a dog!" Morgan had seen the "conversions" after that.

"Sometimes," Morgan said, "hearts have to be broken before worse things happen. Like hellfire!"

Louisa burst into deep sobs. The sound would have melted a flinty heart. But not Morgan's. Better some pain now than later. "We will not force Alfredo into a place he would not visit if he were alive. As he lived, so shall he die."

Louisa was near collapse. Carmen had her hands full supporting her mother, assisting the older woman to rise as she herself shouted curses in Italian. Federico was stumbling about. He had knocked over a chair trying to rise and escape this damned place.

"And you!" Morgan extended an arm and pointed like the avenging angel at Federico. "You had better change your life and come to the church as you should. Or you too will be buried like a dog!"

As Carmen, the last of the threesome out the door, turned back to face Morgan, she exclaimed, "You have seen the last of us. You pig-headed jackass!"

Morgan closed the door behind them.

He had done the right thing. Shock them into the faith now rather than watch them sink into hell.

He had done as Father Angelico would have. And he was confident that Koesler would have done just the opposite.

Koesler buries everybody.

Fourteen

THE BOAT WAS IMPRESSIVE. It was a Regal Commodore 322. Length 32 feet, dry weight 11,800 pounds, and fuel capacity 172 gallons. Tom Becker insisted that the tank be refilled after each use.

There were three keys. Tom had one. His wife had none. One of the maintenance men had one. Tom had given the third to Rick Casserly.

It was one indication of the trust and friendship Tom had for Rick. The craft cost in excess of one hundred thousand dollars. Although it was fully insured, one did not give carte blanche access to one's dream boat—literally—unless the trust was complete.

Throughout the morning of this first Wednesday in June, the maintenance man and his crew had given the boat a thorough checkup. They didn't leave until all was well. But they left in plenty of time for Rick Casserly and Lil Niedermier to board for a leisurely afternoon cruising the Detroit River and Lake St. Clair.

Rick was at the helm, letting the craft virtually idle. He was content just to know the cruiser was capable of better than 50 mph.

Lil was in the galley whipping up a snack that would serve as lunch and hold them over until dinner. She shook her head when she recalled that the word "galley" was often associated with the word "slave." She certainly didn't consider herself a galley slave. How could you when culinary facilities on board this boat were better than what she had in her own kitchen?

She looked about her as the hot dogs sizzled in the microwave. Stainless sink, two-burner electric stove, coffeemaker, concealed refrigerator, and Corian countertop set off the open salon. In all, not an inch of space was wasted. It was a happy blend of luxury, utility, and efficiency.

Lil brought the hot dogs on deck. Two for Rick, one for herself. "There's more," she announced.

"Lemme get these down and we'll see."

The river was so calm and the boat was moving so slowly that Lil climbed upon the forward deck and sat at the tip of the prow like the figurehead on a sailing ship of yore. Or the heroine of the movie *Titanic*.

She was directly in front of Rick, who sat at the helm and steered with one finger. She did not block his view. On the contrary, he loved to look at her. Now in her mid-thirties, she probably would always look young.

She finished her hot dog and crumpled the paper napkin in her fist. She did not toss it into the water. The river appeared too pristine to defile.

Why was she depressed?

The weather was picture-perfect. For this afternoon at least she could pretend they were wealthy enough to actually afford a cabin cruiser this grand. She and Rick had their health, and each other. She was more or less looking forward to this evening's party. She wasn't overjoyed with the entire cast of characters. But it was a singular occasion when she and Rick could be together with others legitimately. Both of them qualified as members of that exclusive club—people who had served time at St. Ursula's under Father Angelico. In only a few more days her school would close for the summer. God was in Her heaven, all was right with the world.

So, why was she depressed?

Could it be because her life seemed to be drifting toward a dead end?

She should be married. She should be a mother several times over. Well, at least once. She should be living in a neighborhood. Not an apartment complex where people shuffled off to work only to drag themselves home each day. She should be free to walk openly with her husband arm in arm. They ought to be able to attend concerts, movies, exhibitions, parties together. They shouldn't have to be vigilant all the time, worried sick that someone might recognize and report them.

Complicating everything was the outlook that their situation was more like hell than purgatory; these conditions would endure for the length of their lives, not just for a few years. Experts conceded that under the present Pope the Church laws regarding a celibate clergy—with exceptions that would not include Rick—would not be changed.

But none of these considerations ever seemed to bother Rick.

Of course, he had just entered his sixties. She had no idea what that might be like. But from her vantage point sixty seemed almost ancient. In that age bracket one ought to be approaching life's end.

Maybe, she thought, that's why none of these depressing considerations seemed to bother him: From this point on, he did not have as long to live as she.

Why was she depressed? It was the whole damn thing!

This is the sort of day to drift down the Detroit River and come back again upstream into Lake St. Clair. This is the day the Lord has made. Let us rejoice and be glad in it.

What could be nicer? Absorbing the sun's warm rays. Not a care in the world. Some satisfying disputation and debates with the gang this evening. Watching, with controlled amusement, Harry Morgan take on the whole, changing world.

Everything going well in his parish, everything under control. The gym and auditorium, contained in one building, had been completed just before Rick's predecessor had retired, leaving Rick with the bill for construction. But he'd paid it off.

In short, he felt good—maybe even great.

He was just entering his sixties. He remembered how foolishly concerned he'd been when he had hit various milestones. Thirty, the credibility gap. Thirty-three, the biblical number of years, reputed to be the age at which Jesus had finished his salvific work on earth. Forty, when certain aches and pains became noticeable. Fifty—half a century.

Now, sixty. It hadn't laid a glove on him. If anything, he had a better appreciation for things than ever before. Chief among those things was that glorious creature just now rising from where she'd been sitting on the boat's prow. His life had been sweetened immeasurably by her presence.

She was wearing brief white shorts, calling attention to her shapely long legs. A pity to have one's attention arrested by just one aspect of her body. Everything was worthy of appreciation. However, he was well aware that Lil definitely was not all body and no brains. On the contrary, he valued their serious conversations, her insights, even her intuition.

If only he could convince her to relax more. These past few years, they might just as well have been married. All they lacked was some paperwork, a priest, and a very different Pope. The facts were that with the present Pope chugging along, no priest would dare try witnessing their marriage and there wasn't enough paper in the world to fix things up and clear the way.

But, all in all, this was such a beautiful day and he was feeling so good that Rick believed he might prefer their present "third way" to a canonically approved marriage.

Lil climbed down from the prow and sat next to Rick. She further crushed the paper napkin in both hands and vehemently flung the wad into the cockpit. Clearly, she was not happy.

Sometimes when she was like this, Rick would suppress any comment that came to mind and wait for her to clear the air, get it off her chest. This was not such a time. Later he would wish he had followed his first instinct and waited her out.

"Something the matter?"

She didn't respond.

He didn't push. "A beautiful day."

"Uh-huh."

"It doesn't do anything for you?"

"I'm feeling down."

"A beautiful day gets you down?"

"I just decided . . . it's the whole damn thing."

"That's funny. I just decided I was happy due to the whole damn thing."

Silence. The boat's engine purred.

"Honey . . ." Lil turned to him. "How many years do you figure I've got?"

"For what?"

"To live." She was feeling some anger toward him. He was playing dumb. He knew damn well to what she was referring.

"What do you mean? How would anyone know?"

Silence. Eventually Rick felt he should say something. "Who knows? Forty years? Maybe more." Pause. Then he said, "What's bugging you, honey?"

A longer pause. Then she said, "I got my period yesterday."

For the life of him, Rick could think of nothing to say. Except, So what? But that would not speak to the emphasis Lil was placing on *this* period. "Is there something special about this particular period?"

"I was thinking . . . Ever since I was twelve I've been having periods. Regular as rain. You could set your watch by them."

Rick almost laughed out loud. Her metaphor was funny. But her tone and demeanor made it quite clear that she was not in the mood to be humorous. He remained silent.

"In ten or so years, I'll go through menopause."

"That's a long way off. Are you scared? No need to be. I guess it affects different women differently. No way of knowing how it'll be for you. It's just too early to give much thought to it."

"That's not the point!" Lil said peevishly. *Men! Why do they have so much trouble understanding women?*

Women! Rick thought. *Why is a simple conversation such a guessing contest with them?*

"You've heard of the 'biological clock'?" She looked at him almost challengingly.

Aha! He thought he understood. "Of course I have. After menopause there's no fertility."

"Exactly!"

"Honey, we've talked about this before. You want to go through it all again?"

"That's just it: We talked about it a long, long time ago. I was lots younger and the reality of being childless didn't hit me then. In just a few more years I'll have sealed whatever chance I ever had to be a mother."

Rick nodded. "That's the conclusion we've reached whenever we discussed this."

"Things change." She turned away from him but spoke loudly enough to be heard. "Take your experience, for example."

Briefly he wondered what in his experience had anything in common with menopause.

"When you were ordained, there was no doubt your life would be monastic as far as sex and women were concerned. And so it was until the Council happened and you no longer saw any value for you to live a celibate life.

"Just about then I came along. We fell in love and would have married but for Church law. You didn't want to leave the priesthood and I didn't want you to leave. So we got as married as we could get. And here we are."

Pause.

"So?" Rick considered Lil's little speech an accurate historical narrative. He just didn't know where she was going with it.

"So," she said, "you saw things one way when you were very young. But with age, more experience, and that redoubtable Council, you've changed your mind. And now, darling, I'm telling you that I've changed *my* mind. Or that I *am* changing it."

"You mean . . ."

"I mean I'm sick of having these tiresome if predictable periods. I want a child. I want *your* child."

Rick couldn't stop the boat dead in the water. But that, figuratively, was the state of his mind—frozen and immobile. Her statement was completely unexpected. "How about another hot dog?" he said.

"What!"

"You said there were more."

"I am proposing having a child and all you say is 'another hot dog'?"

"It'll give me a chance to think."

Lil shrugged and stepped into the galley. She emerged with the dog on a bun slathered with mustard—the way he liked it.

Rick held it in a paper napkin. It was too hot to chew. He let it cool in the brisk breeze.

"Well?"

Lil waited for a response to her demand.

"We've been over this. Lots of times."

"I know. The question is still the same. But I've changed."

"To me, it's moot."

"What?"

"Whether you've really, radically changed. Or whether your 'female problem' is depressing you."

"You're referring to my 'curse'?" she responded sarcastically.

"Just that your reawakened concern may be a passing thing."

Lil attempted to comment but Rick held up his hand. He wished to retain the floor. "Granted," he said, "I am not now nor have I ever been a woman. So all I know about your 'biological clock' is secondhand at best. Nor have I experienced any of what goes on during menstruation. So, I guess I can just sympathize from a distance—"

"I'm well aware you're not a woman. Matter of fact, I'm grateful you're all man. But I assure you, the plain and simple truth is I want a child. My present period is just a nagging reminder of the fact that I am barren—childless. And I don't want to be that way."

Rick bit into the hot dog. It was tasty and just the right temperature. But his mind was too occupied to appreciate the savor.

They had, indeed, been over this question many times. He did not wish to flog a dead horse. But Lil gave every indication that she would be satisfied with nothing less than a definitive conclusion. Even if it was the same conclusion they had reached at the end of all previous similar disputes.

"First off," he began, "we don't know we're both fertile. We know I'm potent; we know we're both orgasmic—plenty orgasmic. But neither of us has ever proven fertility—"

"So, we go to our doctors and take simple tests."

"Fine for you. As far as your doctor is concerned, you need to find out because you're planning a child and you want to know what your chances are.

"But me? I go to a doctor to discover whether I'm fertile. Or exactly how fertile I am. And just why does a priest need to know this?"

"You've got this backward," Lil protested. "We—you and I—don't go running to our respective doctors. It's far more simple than that. I merely go off the Pill. We don't even have to change our relationship. We make love when we want to. Maybe a little more often when I ovulate. We don't visit a doctor, unless, after a few months of trying to conceive, nothing happens. With any luck there won't be any visit to any doctor. We'll be an ordinary couple. We'll be parents."

Rick finished the hot dog. He wadded the paper napkin and pitched it into the river. As the paper left his fingers he remembered that Lil had much stronger feelings than he about littering. For once, she didn't call him on what he'd done. She was too involved in their conversation.

Despite the cooling breeze from the river, Rick was perspiring freely. Sure, that's all they'd have to do: She could cease taking the birth control pill and they could take their chances. Both of them were healthy adults. Of course he was in his sixties. But that didn't make much difference—or so he'd read. Men, unlike women, could become parents at almost any age.

For the first time in their relationship he felt pressured.

He had enough trust in Lil that if he were to veto her proposal, he was confident that she would not deceive him. She would stay on the Pill. Plus, they would continue to be cautious during her fertile period.

Maybe he could yet convince her that parenthood probably would prove to be a disaster for them. "Suppose—and this is purely hypothetical—that you found yourself pregnant. Then what?"

"Then what what?"

"We won't be able to get married. You don't, all of a sudden, want me to leave the priesthood, do you?"

"Heavens, no!"

"Then, again: What? You become a single parent? What about your job at St. Enda's? Do you suppose Father O'Leary is going to tolerate an unmarried mother being principal of his parochial school?"

Lil shook her head decisively. "I would resign."

"Nice! And live on what?"

"I'd line up a job in a public school. With my résumé and experience that shouldn't be so tough."

"And the baby? You gonna take him to school with you?"

"Nursery school, day care, Montessori. There's lots of places—good places—for a child while the parent or parents work. I'd have him with me in the evenings and early mornings. You'd be with us at least as often as you're with me now."

The invisible noose was tightening.

"And when the baby is old enough to know, with all the implications, that its father is a 'Father'?"

"By then, who knows? It might not be all that uncommon for priests to have families. We'll just be a bit ahead of the game. And, if not? He, or she"—for the first time she introduced the possibility that their baby might be a girl—"whichever—in any case, we will have been good enough parents that our child will be able to deal with this lifestyle."

She paused. Then: "What happens to children whose parents are ex-priests and ex-nuns? What happens to the Episcopalian priests who convert to Catholicism and bring their wives and children with them?"

He continued to sweat profusely. This was not off the top of Lil's head; this was something she had long thought about and planned.

"Lil, honey, this is a momentous decision. If we were to go ahead with your idea, our lives would change completely . . . radically. This isn't the kind of thing you bring up during a pleasant ride on the river."

Neither spoke for several moments.

Then Rick said, "Look, why don't we think about it? Talk about it some more? Later?"

"When?"

"I don't know. Give me a chance to consider the possibilities. We don't need a timetable or a scheduled meeting or anything. Just let it rest for a while."

"Is this your way of putting this on an eternal back burner?"

"Of course not. It's just not something to rush into. There are lots of things to think about, to talk about. There's . . . there's . . . uh . . . adoption. We haven't ever discussed that."

"You mean you'd be willing to adopt?"

"I didn't say that!" he responded hurriedly. "It's just another facet of what might be open to us." He was taken off guard by her seeming acceptance of the notion of adoption.

"Be up-front honest with me, Rick: If I agree to put this matter on hold, will we ever seriously consider it again?"

"Of course . . ."

"Rick, love, up-front honest!"

His brow was creased in painful thought. "Probably . . . not," he admitted.

"It doesn't matter how important this is to me?"

"I'm banking that in a little while you're going to look at this in an altogether different light."

Lil smiled with absolutely no humor. "I see. It's like if a Catholic doesn't agree with the Pope: He's advised to go pray until he sees the light."

She'd struck a nerve. It was this sort of slavish, forced agreement with the teaching office of the Pope that Rick abhorred. "No, of course, that's not what I meant. And it's unfair of you to accuse me of trying that on you."

Their tempers were drawing short. They were on the verge of heated disagreement, something they seldom experienced with each other.

"I would not do anything underhanded to you," she protested. "You know that without your consent I wouldn't take any chances—like fooling around with the Pill."

"Does the lady protest too much?" The line was delivered reeking with sarcasm. She was offended, but he didn't care.

She studied the river until its rapid current became a sort of mantra. He saw no reason to continue this conversation. Not in the direction it was going. So they sat in silence. There was no sound but the lapping waves, the cries of the seagulls and the soft purr of the motor.

Without looking at him, Lil said, "Do you ever confess us?"

He figured her period was giving her more than the usual inconvenience. "Do you mean," he restated, "do I go to confession to a priest and confess our relationship?"

"Uh-huh."

"That's the first time you've ever asked me anything like that. You're treading on pretty private territory."

"There were supposed to be no secrets between us."

"With an exception every now and again."

Again time passed in silence.

The boat was nearing other water craft. Rick steered away from them. The maneuver once more reminded them of their state of virtual solitary confinement. A wave of pity passed over him. Their companionship was much more trying for Lil than for him. She was still young. Yet she was deprived of a normal existence.

It was only natural for her to think of having a baby. But Rick was confident that this craving for a child, this too would pass. The trick was to maintain their union during this crisis. Maybe a little sharing of himself with her would help. "The question, darling," he began, "is not do I confess you—us. The question is: Do I confess? And the answer is that I haven't. Not for a long time."

She surely had not expected that. Truth to tell, her status vis-à-vis the sacrament of penance was about the same as his. Even so, she was surprised that he was not confessing regularly.

Rick had grown up as a Catholic about a generation before Lil. He was a practicing Catholic and more. He had been a seminarian on the way to becoming a priest. Normalcy for him called for confession every week. More casual Catholics confessed every month. In that era, Catholics who confessed only once or twice a year were marginal by anyone's measuring.

"You haven't been to confession in a long time?" she said with wonder. "How long?"

"You're not my confessor, nor my spiritual director."

They were quiet for another while.

"I have nothing against confession," he said finally. "It's just that I came to the conclusion that the sacrament is put to much better use if it occurs when events call for a radical change in one's habits or behavior."

"Like me entering your life?"

"No, actually not. If the Church would wake up and face reality, you long ago would have been Mrs. Rick Casserly. I don't see any reason why I need to turn away from you, to exclude you from my life. It's not a sin. Just because we have been denied a priest to witness our marriage doesn't mean we're not married. We are—certainly in the eyes of God if not the Church." His expression evinced a mixture of entreaty and irritation. "We've been through this many times, Lil. Will you ever be at rest in this matter?"

"If you," she said firmly, "are so certain sure that we are man and wife before God—if we are Mr. and Mrs. Rick Casserly—then why can't we have a family—one child—to seal our relationship?"

Only with difficulty did Rick control his anger. He had bared his soul to her and she had taken advantage of his openness. "Honey," he said with finality, "we are not ever going to have a child. Not ever. So just get that out of your mind. Now and forever!"

"Fine!" she responded in the same tone. "Then you can take me in to shore."

"Now, Lil, there's no reason—"

"I said take me in! Now!"

Wordlessly, he veered sharply toward shore.

She disappeared into the forward berth. She packed her things, leaving his gear and the supplies they had brought aboard.

As he eased the boat into its slip she stood on the foredeck. The instant it touched, she was off the ship and on the dock, striding away from the boat and Rick.

Angrily he reversed and pulled back into the river's flow. This time he opened the throttle to peak speed. He wished for the rushing wind to blow away his frustration. Where had this day gone? It had started so beautifully. Until she brought up the idea of a kid, things were moving along in routine fashion. This whole mess was due to that damned period! She looked at it with the fear that life was passing them by. That damned biological clock! If he'd had any thought relating to her period, it was that each one was another step toward menopause. Once they achieved that, there would be no more talk or even thought of having babies.

This was by no means the first argument they'd had. But it certainly ranked among the most heated.

She'd get over it. He'd get over it. But it would take time.

Meanwhile there was that crazy reunion of the Father Angelico club. He wondered whether Lil would attend after their tiff. Maybe seeing what was left of the old bunch would get him into a brighter mood.

Time would tell. He glanced at his watch. Just a little more time.

Fifteen

FATHER KOESLER AND TULLY were alone in the basement of St. Joseph's rectory, a structure that had witnessed many significant events over the past several years.

Tonight, in Koesler's opinion, would be the final meeting of the St. Ursula club. It wasn't just the dwindling membership; by this time the get-together of the informal group had pretty well served its purpose. Persevering with the organization was akin to endlessly pumping embalming fluid into a well-aged corpse.

Feeling that he would have little to add to whatever would be said this evening, Father Koesler resolved to be the thoughtful observer. With a few exceptions, tonight's guests should prove to be quite articulate and thus in no need of Koesler's help. Besides, he had long since learned that it was more blessed to listen than to speak.

Father Tully glanced at his watch, an act more characteristic of Koesler. "It's time," Tully announced. "Nobody's here." He sounded as if all was lost: Not only was no one here, no one was coming.

Koesler smiled. "The only one I'm not totally certain of is Harry Morgan. The rest will show up, I'm sure."

As if in response to his declaration of faith, the doorbell rang. The priests could hear the scurrying of feet against the ancient floors of this old house. That sound was followed by the banter of mixed voices. One of the caterers evidently had admitted some of the guests.

By the time Alonzo and Anne Marie Tully and Tom and Peggy Becker reached the basement, the couples had introduced themselves. Everyone in the foursome already knew the two priests. Alonzo and Zachary Tully were brothers.

After greetings were exchanged, the group split into threesomes: Zoo with Zack and Tom Becker, Koesler with Anne Marie and Peggy.

Zoo was the glue that held his group together. Becker was fascinated by Zoo's police work. And Zack, as usual, could not get enough of his brother. Becker's questions grew longer as Zoo's answers become more concise. The officer was a man of few words.

Koesler, despite his resolution to remain in the background, found himself chattering to fill in awkward silences of two women who had little in common. Peggy was a homemaker, while Anne Marie was an employed and very active teacher.

The remaining guests soon straggled in. Koesler noted the arrival of Father Morgan—the fly in the ointment. However, once the crowd gathered, Koesler was able to retreat to his observation perch.

Predictably, Harry Morgan was the sole guest who was doing his best to be unconvivial.

Everyone was invited to concoct his or her own preprandial drink. These ranged from tonic water for Peggy Becker to a double Scotch for Father Casserly.

Koesler took note of the potency of Rick's drink. It seemed awfully strong for this early in the evening, especially on an empty stomach.

Also, Casserly was rather sunburned, even for a red-haired Irishman. The only other guest nearly that red-skinned was Lillian Niedermier. That condition seemed a bit premature for early June. Odd perhaps that Lil and Rick were the only ones who'd had too much sun. Coincidence undoubtedly.

Little by little, small groups emerged from the conglomerate mass. Koesler, Niedermier, Casserly, Riccardo, Anderson, and Morgan were the core of the participants. They were those who at one time or another had been stationed at St. Ursula's. They were those for whom these annual get-togethers were held. With rare exception they came together at least once a year—the first Wednesday of June.

There were others—many others—who qualified for membership. Some had never responded to the invitation. Others had attended for a while, only to tire, lose interest, or for any number of reasons simply let the occasion fade and die.

A caterer passed among the group, offering hors d'oeuvres.

Koesler alone wandered uncommitted. On his way, he picked up snatches of conversation.

Someone mentioned the concept of *ne potus noceat*. Koesler, of course, was asked to explain, since not everyone was conversant with Latin. The literal meaning was "lest the drink harm" and was an ancient fast day excuse for eating some solid food when drinking alcohol, rather than imbibing on an empty stomach.

Not a bad idea. Particularly at a party such as this with an open bar and various liquors and liqueurs available on an easily accessible shelf.

The caterer seemed similarly concerned as she moved swiftly among the group pushing trays of cheeses and crackers, followed by a tray of small shrimp and dip. What with one thing and another, all seemed to be holding themselves in check as far as sobriety was concerned.

In a group of six, Rick Casserly was reminiscing about the status of the census during his stay in the parish. "It was a joke to the priests. Word got around that St. Ursula's parishioners were better counted and identified than the Jews under Caesar Augustus. But in reality, it wasn't close to being complete, let alone perfect."

Before Casserly could continue his attack against the storied lists, Father Morgan jumped in to defend Father Angelico. "Maybe it wasn't completely perfect, but that wasn't Father Angelico's fault. It was the fault of the assistants. They failed to go house to house as they were instructed. The plan was for the assistant priests to take turns handling the census and, after the whole parish was canvassed, we were to start over."

"We know what the plan was." Casserly focused complete attention on Morgan. "You forget, Harry, that we were there. We weren't getting this secondhand. We were told by the old man to hit the bricks. Otherwise we were supposed to confine ourselves to our rooms until needed."

"But you didn't do as you were told!" Morgan insisted. "I did. I obeyed my pastor, just as it says in Canon Law. If everybody had obeyed Father Angelico, the census would have been perfect!"

Casserly drained his glass. All that remained of the double Scotch were a few impregnated ice cubes. His cheeks were slightly flushed. "Harry, Harry, the damn thing wouldn't work because people moved in and out of that neighborhood faster than we could keep up with them.

"For the working-class family that moved into that neighborhood, it was a stepping-stone to better things. Most of the Italian and Polish parishioners were on their way up Gratiot from Ursula's to upper-middle-class homes in parishes like Assumption Grotto. As soon as they could afford to, they got out of the *Caca Lupo* area."

"*Caca Lupo*?" Peggy Becker asked. "What is that? I don't think I ever heard of that."

Her husband attempted to head off her question, but it was voiced quickly.

"*Caca Lupo*?" Casserly grinned. "It's a pun in Italian. Either it refers to the corner where the streetcars used to turn around. Or, it can mean wolf shit."

It was a mildly offensive word, one that Casserly ordinarily would have avoided in mixed company. Koesler wondered whether the liquor was reaching his younger friend. Fortunately the caterer was in the vicinity and Casserly accepted a couple of finger sandwiches.

Koesler, relieved that Casserly was taking food, immediately grew concerned when Casserly, having downed the canapés in just a couple of bites, moved to the liquor shelf and refilled his glass.

Fortunately at this point, Father Tully announced that dinner was ready. It was a buffet and well served. There were no place cards, so the guests seated themselves at either of two round tables in the haphazard order in which they filled their plates.

At the first table, in clockwise fashion sat: Tom Becker, Father Koesler, Peggy Becker, Father Tully, and Lillian Niedermier.

At the second table, again in clockwise order, were: Zoo Tully, Father Casserly, Dora Riccardo, Jerry Anderson, Anne Marie Tully, and Father Morgan.

Lieutenant Tully was about to dig in when he noticed that everyone else seemed to be hesitating. He aborted his movement and waited.

There was an awkward moment when no one did anything.

Father Morgan made as if to speak but was cut off at the pass by Father Koesler, who feared there might be a misunderstanding regarding who would offer the before-meal prayer.

"We have with us this evening," Koesler said, "three active pastors,

Father Casserly, Father Tully, and Father Morgan. How about we ask the resident pastor to say grace?"

Zack Tully caught the urgency of the moment and immediately offered the traditional prayer: "Bless us, O Lord, and these Thy gifts which we are about to receive from Thy bounty, through Christ Our Lord."

"Amen," all affirmed. Plates filled and no dishes to pass, everyone dug in. Koesler was glad to see the food being eaten. He resolved to talk to Father Tully about the questionable wisdom of an open bar.

Father Tully opened the conversation. "I know I'm the resident pastor. But if this dinner were being held back in the early sixties, I'm afraid I would be an assistant rather than a pastor."

Koesler, having tucked away his first mouthful, smiled. "You're right there, Zack. Back in the sixties even I would have been an assistant—if I hadn't been assigned to the *Detroit Catholic.*"

"The sixties," Tom Becker said in an almost reverential tone. "That was an exciting time. And you did a great job with the paper."

Koesler waved off the compliment with an empty fork. "I had very little to do with it. I just happened to be there during the Council and all that civil unrest . . . Vietnam, the assassinations, the campus protests—all that and more. In a job like mine, all you really had to do was get out of the way and let the breaking news come in."

"Don't sell yourself short," Becker insisted. "There were lots of Catholic papers that looked the other way when the Council was on."

"Well . . ." Koesler intended the interjection to close the topic of his direction of the newspaper. "In any case—to get back to the original subject—that was the beginning of the end of the vocation glut."

"Bob took me on a walking tour of the Detroit seminary." Father Tully was referring to Koesler. "He darn near had me on the ropes, the place was so huge. But what really impressed me was not so much the old buildings—though they are spectacular. What I've never forgotten was the new building, the Cardinal Mooney Latin School. It was erected for the overflow of high school seminarians in 1962. The old buildings couldn't hold the crowd anymore. And it boggled my mind that they were thinking of putting up a second gymnasium."

"Yes," Koesler said, "and in the next decade the seminary population began to drop. So there wasn't any need for a new gym. Come to think of it, no need for the new high school building either. The boys just stopped coming."

So far, this, the principal conversation, emanated from table one. Lesser conversations involving chitchat went on among the others, in groups of twos and threes. But at this point, Father Morgan spoke up, forcefully challenging Koesler's statement and, in so doing, uniting, for the moment, the two tables.

"It's not so much that the young men stopped coming as it was that there were priests who backed away from their commitments and left the active ministry." Morgan, eyes narrowed, looked directly at Jerry Anderson.

Of the multitude who had left the priesthood, Anderson was the only one in this room. He rose to the bait. "Oh, come on, Father. Even with all of us leaving the active ministry, it wasn't the priest drain that caused the vocation crisis. It was all those empty places in the seminary. I don't know that anyone has fingered the reason recruitment fell off. But the kids stopped coming."

"I'm not so sure it was all that cut and dried," Casserly said. It crossed his mind—which was a little clouded by Scotch—that he was agreeing with Harry Morgan. That was something he could not have anticipated.

"You take the sixties and seventies," Casserly continued. "It seemed like every week, maybe every month, more and more priests were leaving. And their departure was euphemistically described as 'taking a leave of absence.' Call it what you will, it was a phenomenon that was well recognized by the people in the pews."

"So," Anderson defended his position, "what's that got to do with the kids who were not showing up in the seminary?"

"Just this," Casserly responded. "Who wants to book passage on the *Titanic*?"

"What?"

"Certainly. When we were growing up—and I'm sure Bob will corroborate this—when we were growing up, we saw priests confident and sure of themselves. They were satisfied and self-assured. That's the image that the entertainment industry projected. You think Bing Crosby or Barry Fitzgerald had the slightest doubt about their vocation?

"Now, it's just the opposite. For, I guess, a whole bunch of reasons, there's no longer that permanence. I mean, the Church is still demanding a lifelong commitment, but that's not the image that's being projected by the guys who quit."

"I think I have to agree with Rick," Father Tully said from the other table. "Take for example law schools. They're overflowing, just as seminaries used to be. Why do so many people want to become lawyers? Partly to serve the cause of justice. And partly to make a lot of money. The first part of that reason seems to be breaking down. Mind you, once either of those motivations begins to fragment, the law schools will be darn near as empty as the seminaries are now."

All eyes turned to Jerry Anderson. He alone in this room was on "leave of absence" from the diocese. Everyone here was aware that his "leave" was permanent.

Father Koesler attempted to steer the conversation away from Anderson. "What would Father Angelico think?"

"If the dear Father were here and were still an active pastor," Dora Riccardo said, "he probably would be wondering why he was working his parish alone and why the chancery couldn't just send someone."

"Sounds good," Koesler said.

"By the way, Father Morgan," Dora continued, "I suppose I and my inactive Sisters are responsible for the near death of religious life?"

"Out of your own mouth you have said it!" Morgan replied.

"Maybe . . ." Tom Becker's tone was hesitant, as if he wasn't sure he should be speaking now. ". . . maybe this is the beginning of something new. Maybe the era of the laity. Oh, I don't mean that the laity will, or should, take over priestly tasks. But there are lots of administrative jobs that priests find themselves doing now that could be done better by the laity than by the ordained. Now maybe that's not a permanent solution. But it could be something to tide us over until, in God's good time, the situation corrects itself."

"I'm not sure I have this all straight," Peggy Becker said, "but isn't that something that's going on now? I don't mean getting the laity more involved. Personally, I have lost enough of my husband to the Church. I do not intend to lose him completely."

Unsure how irritated she was about her husband's generous contribution in time and money, most of the guests chuckled politely.

"What I'm getting at," Peggy continued, "is supplying instant priests."

"Instant priests!" Tom exclaimed.

"Those Anglican or Episcopalian priests who are entering the Catholic Church. Aren't many of them becoming Catholic priests?" Peggy said.

"The Anglican converts." In Father Tully's tone there was no question. "There aren't that many of them. It's sort of like applying a Band-Aid to a ruptured elephant."

That got a laugh.

"Besides," Tully said, "most of them feel more at home in the Catholic Church that doesn't allow women priests."

Casserly, about to add a word, noticed that Harry Morgan was almost salivating in his eagerness to lead a charge. Rick was interested in the direction Morgan's conservatism would take. He knew that, on the one hand, conservative if not traditional Catholics looked on the Protestant Churches in general and the Episcopalians in particular as heretical and separated from the Pope and thus from the "One, True, Catholic and Apostolic" Church. (He chuckled to himself, recalling that some wags always added to the four marks of the One True Church, another mark, making it "One, True, Catholic, Apostolic, and Bingo.")

On the other hand, Rick knew also that such Protestant crossovers have, by their lights, one of the best reasons for leaving their sect and becoming Catholic. Such action was ipso facto a strong protest against a female clergy of any sort, whether deaconesses, priests, or, saints preserve us, bishops. The Anglicans, the Presbyterians have all of these. Meanwhile the Pope stands firm: Only those who resemble Jesus Christ can be His priests. Besides, Jesus chose twelve *men* to be his Apostles.

This could have posed a dilemma for Morgan.

If Casserly had to bet on the outcome, Morgan would side with those who opposed women clergypersons. And he would, if he had to, tolerate the Episcopalian clergy's bringing with them their families.

Morgan wagged a finger at Father Tully. "That, young man, is perhaps the most forceful argument against a female clergy. Our sympathy with these men leads us to accept them and even their wives and children rather than see them forced to share their priesthood with a bunch of women. Imagine having to concelebrate the Eucharist with women priests!" Morgan fairly spat out the last two words.

Anne Marie Tully caught her husband's eye and lifted her empty wineglass. He nodded and went to the shelf where the booze still rested.

Outside of a few initial pleasantries, Zoo and Anne Marie had not contributed to the principal conversation, even though most of the heated verbal exchange sprang from around their table. The couple's dearth of contribution was due partly to the fact that neither could get a word in edgewise and partly because both were out of their league when it came to the inner workings of the Catholic faith.

As if reminded that there was more liquor available, Rick Casserly followed Zoo to the wet bar. A journey noted by Father Koesler; he watched as Rick eschewed ice, let alone water, and poured himself a Scotch, neat.

En route back to his seat, Casserly stumbled. No damage done; he didn't even spill his drink. But Koesler resolved to get between Rick and the alcohol supply. If he drained his present glass he would likely be a candidate for a volunteer chauffeur.

"It would be a sad, sad mistake," Morgan persisted, "to think that the few Episcopal converts could possibly fill the ranks that have been left vacant by our turncoats who have abandoned their posts." As he finished he was staring directly at Anderson. Who, in turn, gazed back unflinchingly.

"Turncoats!" Peggy exclaimed. "Isn't that a rather strong term for those who leave the active ministry?" Not to embarrass her husband, she determined to moderate her comments concerning Jerry Anderson.

"Ask one!" Morgan's glare had not swerved from Anderson.

"What?"

"He means me," Anderson said.

"I don't understand," Peggy looked around the room, seeking clarification from her fellow guests. "He can't be referring to you, Father. Oh, excuse me, I guess I can't stop using your title. But, still, it's not you. We read about you in the *Detroit Catholic*. You asked for a leave of absence!"

"It's a euphemism, dear," Tom Becker said. "Most of the time it means that the priest won't return." He felt like patting his wife's hand, but he was one person—Father Koesler—removed from her at the table.

"True," Casserly said. "Nine times out of ten it's the same as a resignation. But I'm with Peggy: There's no call to use a pejorative term like 'turncoat.'"

"I agree," Koesler said. "Jerry took one step beyond counseling a pastoral solution. He took a chance and got shot down. It was a bold possibility . . . but it hardly deserves such a harsh label."

"Did you apply for laicization, Jerry?" Casserly asked.

"Did I apply for it?" Anderson's tone was sardonic. "I got it!"

"What!" Casserly exclaimed. "My information is that the Vatican is routinely denying all requests. And you've been gone—what?—something like five years!"

"The die was cast the minute I refused to accept suspension. The bishop practically handed it to me over the table." Anderson paused. "I'm exaggerating. But not much; it was a matter of weeks."

"That's incredible!" Koesler said. "Even in the days—long ago—when Rome was of a mind to grant the request, I never heard of anyone cutting through the red tape as quickly as you did."

"I got a boost from the bishop," Anderson said. "He said he had friends in high places—and he evidently does."

"The floodgates are open, do you think?" Father Tully asked.

"I don't know," Anderson replied. "You mean the gateway to getting laicization?"

"Uh-huh."

"Again, I don't know. Mine may be a special case. But our Church is strong on the setting of precedent. I think somebody who wanted laicization—if he was in our diocese—might well cite, and argue from, what happened to me."

"How is anyone going to know what happened to you?" Father Tully said. "*We* wouldn't have known if you hadn't just told us."

"Good question," Anderson said. "And I don't know that answer either. It's way too esoteric for the secular media to be interested in it. And the chancery would prefer that it be hush-hush. I guess the only way it'll be spread is by word of mouth."

No one spoke for several moments. Father Morgan seemed to have curled up in a metaphorical corner to nurse his wounds. Since no one in the group agreed with or even took seriously his condemnation of Jerry Anderson, Harry Morgan beat a strategic retreat.

"I hope this isn't too personal," Father Tully said finally, "but whatever made you go for laicization? Did the bishop bring it up? Did he force you into it?"

Anderson smiled. "None of the above. It was my idea. He was willing to live with whatever I did, as long as I left the priesthood. He seemed to relish the fact that I was not going to accept a Church penalty. That meant that my 'leave of absence' would be permanent. Once that fact was established, it was I who requested the process. He merely expedited it."

"But," Tully persisted, "why *you*? You couldn't have had any love for the rules and regulations of Canon Law—not and witness that wedding. I mean, why would you bother with laicization? You felt you needed it? I just don't understand."

Anderson stared at his fingers splayed on the tabletop before him. "Mother. She was so proud of her son the priest. Well, so was I—proud, I mean. But that's neither here nor there. It's just that she wasn't going to understand why I would leave what she sincerely believed was the greatest calling heaven had to offer.

"I stood a better chance of calming her down if I was okay with the Church. I dotted all the *i*'s and crossed all the *t*'s in the petition. And I got the document which says that while I am 'reduced to the lay state' I am still in the good graces of Mother Church. With all that, I can tell Ma that I'm square with the Pope." His lopsided smile was an ironic one. "Don't get me wrong. Mother is pretty torn up by everything that's happened: the wedding, all the publicity, and all the trouble with the chancery and even Rome. But I gave her the document to read. It sort of mollified her. Fortunately it was in English so I didn't have to translate from the Latin. I was talking to one of the brethren who left a long time ago. He said the document he got was in Latin." This time his outright laugh was between a snort and a chuckle. "They stopped doing that 'cause some of the guys didn't know Latin well enough to completely understand what they were signing."

"Getting laicized," Casserly said, "may prove to be the smartest thing you could do. And not just for your mother's sake."

"How's that?" Anderson asked.

"I think you'll find, Jerry," Casserly replied, "that, for one thing, you'll be playing on a level field. People may applaud or deplore your leaving—but you will have kept the rules. They have to give you that. Whatever else you might be, you are a 'Catholic in good standing.' So no one has any right to call you a renegade or"—Casserly shifted his gaze to Morgan—"a turncoat. Harry!"

Father Morgan growled softly. He never should have used that sobriquet. Not that he did not believe that Anderson deserved it and more. Going through the proper channels gave Anderson the appearance of having voluntarily done the proper thing. But inwardly he knew it was all a sham. Oh yes, Jerry Anderson richly deserved to be called turncoat, renegade, hypocrite, and more. But not in this largely sympathetic group. Not at this time.

One thing about Harry Morgan: He knew on whose side God was, by damn!

The caterers had long since cleared the last of the dishes, packed up the remnants of the dinner, and gone on their way. They had left bowls and plates of finger food. Koesler noted that Rick Casserly had been snacking on nuts and cheese and crackers. This would not help his weight but it might buffer the booze somewhat.

"Maybe"—Peggy Becker seemed determined to put a happy face on this evening's affair—"one day you'll be able to come back. I know lots of people will miss you. You were—uh . . . *are* a good priest. You never know what the future might hold."

All of the priests present, except Harry Morgan, gave a collective sigh.

"True," Anderson said, "there's no telling what may happen. But it is highly unlikely that I'll be invited back."

"How can you be so sure?" Peggy pressed.

"Because," Anderson replied, "it's part of the deal. See, a priest applies for laicization. If the Church grants it, then it's their deal. And they name the game. There is a list of things you *can't* do. You can't teach religious subjects. You can't do this and this and this. But most of all you can't come back. Rome shuts the door. Outside of being able to give the sacrament of the sick 'in case of emergency,' you can never again function as an active priest."

Peg Becker, Zoo, and Anne Marie hadn't known of this restriction; the others had.

When no further clarification seemed forthcoming, Lieutenant Tully spoke for the first time in this latest interchange. "Excuse me. If you were talking police procedures, I would be in my element. Now, I'm willing to admit that I'm in strange waters with all the Church rules and regulations. But one thing I can dig: Jerry Anderson seems to say that he won't or can't enforce some of these rules. So he's leaving his position in the Church. That makes sense. If you're not going to be a cop, don't wear the uniform. Lots of these things I've heard my brother comment on. But there is one thing that really has me puzzled."

"What's that?" his brother asked.

"You've got a priest . . . no . . . make that *two* priests. Both of them decide to quit. One of them goes through all the red tape that the Church seems to require. The Church is satisfied that priest A did it by the book and grants priest A his request.

"Now you got priest B. He just packs up and leaves. He doesn't touch the red tape. He's not playing by the rules.

"One difference between these two priests is that the one who went though every step the Church wanted can never come back and be a priest again. But the one who just walked away without paying any mind to the drill of leaving, he can somehow, someday, be a priest again."

"Maybe," Father Tully said.

"Maybe?" his brother repeated. "How would that ever work out in real life?"

"Supposing," Zack said, "your priest B who just walked away didn't actually do anything that would alienate him from the Church. Like he didn't join some other religion. Or commit some felonious crime. Or, mostly, he didn't get married. Now, after whatever time . . . months, years . . . he wants to come back. He's never been 'reduced to the lay state.' But mostly, he didn't get married. That's the biggie. The only thing he's done wrong is walk away without the Church's by your leave.

"In this case, and since there is this God-awful priest shortage, he probably will find some bishop who'll take him back.

"Whereas, your priest A has gone through a special process. By solemn decree, he can no longer function as a priest. That's something that didn't happen to priest B.

"So it doesn't really matter whether the priest who's been laicized gets married or not. The Church has decreed that, for all practical purposes, he is no longer a practicing priest no matter what happens."

Silence.

The lieutenant began to regret having tried to clearly comprehend the practical consequences of an arcane discipline. "So," he said, "the guy who does what the Church wants him to do ends up a nonperson. While the guy who thumbs his nose at the rules can be accepted back—full honors."

"Yep."

Zoo looked around the room. He was aware, as he had been many times during this evening, that he was the only non-Catholic in the bunch. "Don't you people have a constitution? A bill of rights?"

The Catholics looked at one another.

"We have," Casserly said finally, "laws. We have a body of principles, rules, standards, norms—canons—laws. The Code of Canon Law. At the beginning of the last century we had 2,414 laws. By the end of the last century those had been revised down to 1,752 laws. That's all we have—laws."

"That's all we need," muttered Father Morgan.

"If," Father Tully said, "we were to have a constitution from which we drew our laws—like the United States has—the next question would be: Who would write the constitution? The way things are now, the same men who wrote the canons would end up writing the constitution. I doubt that the outcome would be very different."

The scraping sound came from Tom Becker's chair as he pushed it from the table. "It's been a long evening and a long day. We've got a long way to go home."

Tom proved himself a leader. Everyone began preparations for leaving. There was a lot of handshaking—even on Father Morgan's part—and promises—mostly empty—to get together again soon.

Fathers Tully and Koesler led the way up the stairs and to the kitchen door, which opened to the lighted parking lot. When the last of the departing guests had gotten into their cars, Koesler noted they were two shy. "Did you notice," he said to Father Tully, "that only seven people have left?"

"Who's missing?"

Koesler needed only a moment. "Rick Casserly and Dora Riccardo."

"I wonder what's keeping them?"

"Let's see."

In no particular haste, the two priests ambled back to the basement. There they found Rick and Dora still seated where they had been throughout the dinner. To Koesler's shock, Casserly was sipping from a freshly filled glass. But it wasn't Scotch, his booze du soir. Wrong color; this was darker. "Watcha got there, Rick?"

Koesler affected joviality in order to disarm Casserly.

"Johnnie Walker Black." Casserly raised his glass aloft as if making a toast.

"What happened to the Scotch?" Koesler moved in slowly. He picked up the bottle of whiskey and placed it far back on the shelf.

"You ran out of Scotch," Casserly explained. "Not exactly the wise thing to do—especially when you invite priests to a party. Fortunately, there was this full bottle of Walker. Fortunately, because if you had run out completely"—he wagged his finger at Koesler—"word would have gotten out!"

"Well, we've learned one thing, anyway," Tully said.

"What's that?" Koesler was moving cautiously toward Casserly's glass.

"When Rick gets loaded," Tully said, "he is a happy drunk."

"Hey!" Casserly looked in astonishment at his empty hand.

"You've had more than enough, my friend," Koesler said.

"I hope you don't think I had anything to do with this." Dora spoke for the first time.

"Of course not." Tully was reassuring. "Things just got out of control for Rick."

"If it just hadn't been for that damn boat!" Rick said, slightly slurring the words. He shook his head and lost a few of the cobwebs.

"Boat? What boat?"

"Keep it going," Koesler stage-whispered. "While you keep him occupied, I'll get these bottles put away."

"The boat, the boat, the boat!" He had made an original ditty to go with his original lyric. Neither was very good.

"Were you on a boat, Rick?" Dora prodded. "Is that where you got that sunburn?"

"I should have stayed home. Then none of this would have happened." He was growing maudlin.

"Let's get him home now," Tully said.

"No need for you to get involved in that," Koesler said. "You're home now. All you've got to do is go to bed. No sense in your driving way out to the far east side and back."

"For all practical purposes, you're home too, Bob," Tully said. "This is your home away from home. You've got some of your stuff upstairs. You can stay here tonight."

"Why can't everybody go away and leave us alone?" Casserly was trying to hold on to some measure of sobriety.

Dora's eyes darted from Koesler to Tully and back again. "Why don't I take him home? Neither of you needs to go anywhere. I live out in his direction. I can drive him home. He can figure out how to get his car from your parking lot in the morning."

"Well," Tully said slowly, "this is an awful imposition on you."

"Are you sure you can do it?" Koesler asked.

"Of course. Nothing to it. I'm going in that direction anyway."

"You can get him into the rectory?"

"I don't think there'll be any trouble. I'll leave the car windows open on the way. The fresh air will help."

"Well," Tully hesitated, "if you're sure . . ."

"I say," Koesler said, "thanks a heap, and safe home. Come on, Zack. let's load our friend in Dora's car."

They did not have to carry Casserly. But they did support him from either side. Meanwhile, Dora opened her car's four windows and helped settle the priest in the passenger seat.

Like an odd couple, the two priests stood in the parking lot, waving good-bye until the car turned the corner.

Tired and somewhat exhausted, Tully and Koesler bade each other good night and retired to their rooms on the rectory's second floor.

Once upon a time, this rectory and this parish had been Koesler's responsibility. For years he had slowly but surely increased the parishioners until what had been a virtual relic had become a thriving parish—at least by inner-city standards.

A couple of years ago he had reached the magic age of seventy and had retired. But, as was his intention, he stayed active in the diocese. There was a crying need for priests, and he could at least answer a whimper. He even managed to help the police with their investigations into "Catholic homicides" when possible.

Father Koesler was remembering all of this as he climbed the creaking stairs to what, when he was pastor, had been the guest room. At Father Tully's gracious invitation, Koesler kept some clothing, pajamas, and toiletries here.

Now, he seated himself in the room's one and only upholstered chair and mentally ran over the evening's proceedings. He had, he thought, been accurate in predicting that this would be the final meeting of the St. Ursula survivors. There weren't that many participants left. And tonight's near fiasco could quite logically be the capper.

The conversation regarding memories of Ursula and Father Angelico had faded quickly and descended into the never-ending controversy over the Second Vatican Council. It had even led to name-calling. Though Father Harry Morgan had attended all the previous meetings, he had never been so belligerent. Much of this, Koesler thought, was triggered by the presence of a freshly unfrocked priest.

Koesler was in no way surprised that almost all the conversation involved the clergy present. That's the way it invariably developed when priests were the principal guests.

Topics tended toward religion and the back-room machinations of the clergy and—especially juicy—the hierarchy. Add to the priests—Koesler, Tully, Casserly, Anderson, and Morgan—Tom and Peggy Becker, who were most at ease in this sort of setting, and you had practically all of tonight's conversationalists.

He hadn't expected a lot of participation from Zoo and Anne Marie Tully. But the virtual silence of Lil and Dora had not been expected. Each of the two women had seemed to be in her own, separate world this evening.

Dora had listened to all that transpired—how would one describe it?—aggressively. She hung on every word. Her eyes darted from side to side. She contributed only sparingly during the early light conversation. But once the heavy artillery began, she had reacted like an eager student hungering for everything that each speaker revealed about himself or, in the case of Peggy Becker, herself.

Lil, on the other hand, seemed to be pouting. She gave every indication that she would rather be almost anywhere else in the world but here.

This struck Father Koesler as odd. At previous gatherings when Lil was present, she had always emerged as the life of the party.

Some sort of chemistry was going on in that basement room tonight. Something he felt sure was in the developmental stage. This chemistry would need a catalyst. It would be Dora or Lil or both. This situation needed watching.

But not tonight. He was tired. He hadn't done all that much today. But he'd been a priest for almost fifty years; the old energy just wasn't there. His get up and go had just about got up and went.

He turned out the light and safely found the welcome bed by the light of the street lamp.

His last conscious thoughts concerned Dora and Rick. He hoped and prayed she would have no trouble getting him home.

Sixteen

THE FRESH, LATE SPRING BREEZE did not seem to be doing much for Father Casserly. His head lolled against his chest. Every so often he would awaken, look out the open car window, mumble something, and drop off to sleep again.

Dora Riccardo drove up well-traveled Gratiot Avenue only hazily aware of the passing scene.

Gratiot was a mockery of its former self. Dora wondered at the percentage of closed businesses and boarded-up shops. The present mayor of Detroit was doing yeoman's work in waking up the city. But he had a long way to go.

She glanced at her sleeping passenger. Ordinarily, in a situation like tonight's, she would have had eyes for no one but Rick Casserly. But the items being debated this evening she had found arresting. So, until nearly the end of the conversation, she was unaware that Rick had been drinking so much. By the time she did notice it was too late for her to do anything about it—if indeed, she had been able to alter the course of tonight's events.

At the close of the evening when the hosts and their guests were filing out of the basement, she noticed that Rick seemed determined to stay right where he was.

She watched as he refilled his glass, chugalugging the booze until the glass was only half full—to the eyes of an optimist. At that point, she guided Rick to his seat and managed to distract him from downing the rest.

Then, mercifully, Tully and Koesler returned and at least put an end to any further alcoholic damage self-inflicted by Rick.

After that Dora determined to play whatever cards were dealt her. This device—opening oneself to chance or divine providence, depending on one's faith—was something she practiced often. So it was that her heart skipped a beat or so as both sober priests excused each other from any obligation to leave the rectory confines to drive Rick home.

Even their disclaimers were amusing. They wanted to be sure that if there was any problem with her being chauffeur, it would be her responsibility, not theirs. Only when their hands were squeaky-clean would they load Rick into her car. As she drove Rick home, she made it perfectly clear to God that this was His scenario. She would just follow in any divinely sponsored direction.

As she swung her car onto Outer Drive she marveled again at the size of the church, let alone the rectory. One priest rattling around in that huge home seemed completely out of proportion.

She parked next to the garage. She could not enter and park in there. The door was automatic and she had forgotten to take the remote control from his car. That would be okay as long as Rick could at least try to help himself from the car to the rectory. She no longer had a man assisting on either side of him. She would miss Tully and Koesler. They would be self-tucked-in for the night. Nothing was too good for Father.

She took the keys from Rick's pocket and opened the rectory's front door. So much for the remote preparation. Now to accomplish the deed. "Come on, Rick . . ." She eased him out of the car. She draped his right arm over her shoulders and wrapped her left arm around his waist. It was dark. No nearby lights, not even any moonlight. It was possible that some neighbor might see them. But that chance was remote.

She progressed well enough, despite all the while swaying from one side of the walkway to the other.

They entered the rectory as one. They did it relatively smoothly. On the second floor were five bedrooms, each with a sitting room and bath. Once they had all been occupied. Now they spoke of a day gone by and likely never to come again.

They reached the first-floor master suite. The bed had not been made up. Clothes were draped on chairs rather than hung in closets. Dora could not know that Rick seldom slept here. For her, this was a typical bachelor's apartment. She didn't know for sure, but she figured there were far more Oscars than Felixes in the world.

Now what, God? Better undress him. If he becomes sick during the night, at least he won't soil his clothes.

She sat him down on the bed. He promptly collapsed supinely on it. This would not be as easy as it first seemed. Maybe it would be better to try to bring him to. He could contribute something to the process if he were even just a little more conscious.

Maybe talking would help. Just a few minutes ago she had successfully talked him out of the car and into the house. Talking couldn't hurt. "Come on, Rick, you've got to help me a little if you're going to hit the hay. And, God knows, you've made yourself quite a bundle of hay."

He stood up. A little wobbly, but he was standing. She began to unbutton, unzip, and discard.

He was struggling for consciousness. "That's it, Rick," she encouraged, "try and help me."

"You got a problem?"

She giggled. She couldn't help it. She wondered if he was remembering a time when he had been her spiritual director. Little had she known that one day she would be disrobing him and tucking him into bed.

"No," she said. "For a change, I haven't got the problem. You do."

"What? What's my problem?"

"You've had a little too much to drink. Well, actually, you've had way too much to drink."

"That's okay. The potatoes will sop up the booze."

My God, she thought, he doesn't know the drinking and eating are in the past. "The party's over, Rick. There's nothing more to eat or drink."

"Sad. Now that's sad."

He reached for her and fumbled with the buttons of her blouse.

She was startled. She pushed his hands away.

Smiling crookedly, he persisted.

Memory clicked in. She recalled when she had come to him clad in the outer garments of her religious habit, and beneath that only a bathing suit. What was happening now had been one of her fantasies then.

A romantic interlude was not God's will then. But it appeared to be His will now.

She stopped pushing his hands away. She removed the last of his clothing. Encouraged, he now worked feverishly to disrobe her. It wasn't a smooth operation for him. He was still fighting the insensibility of drunkenness.

Together they tumbled onto the bed. His hands were all over her. He concluded through a drunken haze that women built larger than Lil could also be more curvaceous.

Their frantic foreplay gave new meaning to the phrase, a roll in the hay.

In moments it was over.

He lay on his back, snoring softly.

She was no longer a virgin.

She threw a sheet over him. She pulled the coverlet up about his shoulders. It was a fairly cool night.

She dressed and left the rectory, making sure the front door was locked.

She would not sleep tonight. Not a wink. She felt cheap, used. And yet, she wondered, was this God's will? Could it possibly be God's will?

At one point she felt that she had been manipulating him, at another that he had been using her.

Certainly lovemaking was not all that she had expected. In most of the romance novels she'd read, there was passion, deliberateness, tender, loving concern for one another. The lovemaking she'd seen on the screen—movies or TV—frequently was explicit. But unless it was a rape, filled with violence, it usually contained at least some of the romance qualities.

She couldn't stop thinking of the song: Is that all there is?

Well, clearly, tonight's adventure was not typical of what the experience could be were both parties sober.

She began to think that this really had not been the will of God. Maybe she had manipulated God. She had wanted Rick Casserly so much and for so long a time that her desire had muddled her normally dependable reasoning.

On the other hand, who was she to, in effect, second-guess God?

What this could develop into over time no one could know. She recalled the aphorism, If you want to make God laugh, tell Him your plans.

Still, a long time ago she had decided that Rick Casserly was the only man for whom she would undress. And so it had been. If only he had been abstemious early in the evening.

On the other hand, if he hadn't been drunk it was safe to assume nothing between them would have happened.

So, the ice had been broken. It only remained to be seen who would fall in.

He woke with a start. Where moments before he had been deep in a dreamless sleep, now he was instantly wide awake.

He looked at the clock on his nightstand. Eleven o'clock. A.M. or P.M.? The sun was shining brightly—A.M. How could he have slept so long? The last time he had slept to midday was . . . last summer's vacation.

He hated this feeling. He was completely vulnerable. He didn't know what had happened. He didn't know how he had gotten into his bed. He threw back the covers and tried to stand. He staggered backward onto the bed. His head throbbed. He wouldn't try that again right away.

He lay back on the bed slowly and carefully. Gently he lowered his head to the pillow. Gradually, the events of last evening came into focus.

The St. Ursula gathering. The food was good. The alcohol better. Argumentation and debate. The clash of Morgan and Anderson.

Becker broke up the party by announcing that he and Peg had a long trip ahead of them.

That was it. He remembered watching everyone leave. And then things got fuzzy.

Was it possible he had actually driven himself home? In such a condition? If he really had done it, it had to be a major miracle or the prayers of his dear late and sainted mother, Bridget Casserly.

Cautiously, he raised himself again. Last night's clothing was flung carelessly on top of previously worn clothing. He might have been able to do that. If he were lucky enough to have driven himself home, disrobing would have been child's play.

He looked down and studied himself. Dried, caked semen. What could have caused that? He hadn't had a wet dream for ages.

Had someone driven him home? Probably. Was someone responsible for all the rest of this? Probably. But who? Who would know?

He dialed Father Koesler. Good old dependable Father Koesler.

"Bob," Casserly began, "you're going to find this hard to believe, but I just woke up."

"I believe that to the same extent that I believe Zack Tully is going to have to replenish his liquor supply. You drank almost all of it."

Casserly groaned. "What happened after everyone else left?"

"You were pretty well out of it by then." Koesler went on to explain the discussion between himself and Father Tully concerning how to dispose of the body—Casserly's. He concluded by citing Dora's offer to take the body home. "So that," Koesler said, "is how you got from here to there. Don't you remember any of it?"

"Pieces. And that not very clearly." Casserly had no intention whatsoever of mentioning that he was naked, nor the bit about the semen. "Look, Bob, I'm sorry. I'm really sorry about messing up the party."

"Actually, you didn't. You contributed rather nicely from time to time. It was as if you timed it carefully. You were holding your own—albeit a bit marginally. The ultimate damage was done as the guests were leaving. You were left alone in the basement with Dora. You filled a glass with whiskey and downed half of it before anyone could stop you. Zack and I arrived too late to call a total halt."

"Half a glass of booze!" Casserly said it with almost a sense of awe.

"Take it easy today, Rick. Time is about all that will help."

"I don't think I'm capable of anything more. Oh, by the way: My car?"

"In Zack's parking lot next to the church."

"Thanks. All I can say is you *can* teach this old dog new tricks. I'll never let this happen again."

They signed off.

Things were getting a bit clearer. Not anywhere close to normalcy. But improving.

Dora! Dora, Dora, Dora! So she brought me home, he thought. Armed with this essential information he tried once again to put the pieces together. For quite a long time, though in the end fruitlessly, he tried to recall the drive home. Nothing. He must have been completely unconscious.

Okay. She got him home, somehow. He remembered how difficult it had been for him to walk to the rectory and up those stairs—even with help. That must have been Dora.

After climbing the stairs there was another blackout.

He remembered feeling cranky initially when someone made him stand while peeling off his clothing. That very definitely was Dora. At the time he remembered wanting to participate and he had focused all the concentration available to do just that. Now, hours later, he had to concentrate again to recall what had happened.

But now he cut through to it. He remembered reciprocating.

She had looked terrific. With the possible exception of Lil, Dora was the most breathtaking sight he'd ever seen. She had made herself a gift to him. He had been in no condition to resist it. One glimpse of the essential Dora and his resistance was gone.

He remembered the frenzy in bed . . . then the lights went out again. Everything after an ungainly intercourse was blacked out. Everything until he'd awakened with a start minutes ago.

Feelings of embarrassment assaulted him from every angle.

He was embarrassed that he had so badly lost control of himself and drunk so irresponsibly. It was likely that only Zack, Bob, and Dora knew how very bad the situation was. Casserly was certain that the two priests would keep the incident to themselves. Undoubtedly they had helped a drunk more than once. Possibly even a drunken priest. Besides, they were men used to keeping secrets and confidences.

Dora, the central character in last night's fiasco, was an X factor.

Good Lord, he thought, if his alcohol-saturated memory could be trusted, he'd had intercourse with her! There was no way that animal response could be called lovemaking.

He knew, principally from counseling and listening to confessions, as well as from books and movies and TV, that what had happened between them last night would have a far more potent effect on Dora than on him.

He could feel bad that it had happened. He also could put it out of his mind fairly soon and more or less completely. It could become no more than a lascivious memory—something developed into a fantasy.

He couldn't totally understand all that this sexual activity could mean for Dora. He would have to be a woman to comprehend that. All he knew—and of this he was certain—was that it had meant, would mean, more, much more, to her than to him.

He considered the event no more than a drunken mistake. She probably would view it as at least the beginning of a commitment.

And that led to the source of his third embarrassment: Lil.

She must have left with the others. So she couldn't have known how falling-down drunk he'd been. Above all, she wouldn't know about Dora.

He had reassured Lil time and again that they were married in every sense except for some official paperwork. Either he had been kidding himself and her, or he was serious.

And if he was serious, he had just committed adultery.

Lots of times he had counseled married people who had strayed and were repentant, truly sorry for it. And always he had counseled them not to confess to the spouse. Telling what happened would more than likely open a can of worms that might better be buried.

Now, for the first time, he was challenged by the same choice.

To top it off, he had the mother of all headaches.

There was no alternative than to tough out this indisposition and face the music.

The last time he'd been with Lil, she had been mad as hell at him. She didn't know it, but she had an even better reason for anger now. She probably figured that his absence from their apartment was merely a continuation of their quarrel. Fine. Let her continue thinking this. They would be getting together eventually.

Better to have her on the back burner and try to get a handle on how Dora was going to react to last night.

Seventeen

As it turned out, Thursday, mercifully, was a nothing day. Casserly spent the hours nursing this gigantic hangover and fearing that anyone—especially Lil or Dora—might call.

The telephone didn't ring all day. A small miracle for which he was duly grateful.

Friday was something else again. At any rate, it was something that made him grateful for Thursday.

Friday opened the gates to the little rabbit punches of life.

The janitor reported on the church roofing. It was deteriorating with great dispatch. Casserly assured him that help was on the way. Even as they spoke, the geniuses downtown were debating funding.

He didn't tell the janitor that Tom Becker had volunteered to finance the fix-up. Casserly had dissuaded his friend from doing so. Were Becker to underwrite the project he would be dragged inexorably into endless repairs and rebuilding.

Far more important to Rick now was this evening's meeting of the Catechetical Committee. Dora Riccardo, always faithful to these meetings, would surely be present. This would be their first face-to-face since Wednesday night's debacle. He was not looking forward to the encounter.

While trying to think of how he might relate to Dora after what had happened, the phone rang. He was about to let the answering service pick up, then had second thoughts. He recognized the voice immediately. It was Lil. And she knew it was he.

He lit a cigarette, then coughed. After a hiatus of some twenty-five years, he was smoking again! He promised himself that the recidivism would be temporary—just till he was able to work through this crisis.

Lil identified the sound of his inhaling. It caused her mixed emotions. She was angry that he had returned to the habit that could shorten his life. And she felt guilty that she might have caused this backsliding.

"Lil," he said with warmth and genuine relief, "it's good to hear your voice." They had been apart only a day but, considering how they had parted in rancor, it was a long time.

"I was beginning," she said, "to think you were going to be stubborn and not call. So I decided to break the ice." After a short pause, she continued. "Right off the start, I want to apologize for what I said. You don't need that kind of pressure. Wanna make up?"

He smiled. "Making up is fun."

"Tonight?"

"I've got that Catechetical meeting tonight, honey. After that I'll be where I want to be—with you."

"The world seems better now, doesn't it? We . . . I have to focus on how lucky we are having each other. No more negatives. Okay?"

"Definitely okay."

They hung up.

He blew smoke rings. It's like riding a bike, he thought; the ability comes right back to you. He would smoke this cigarette down to its bitter end—literally—for the sole reason that cigs cost so very much more than they did when last he'd had the habit.

He knew that Lil could tell he'd taken it up again. She'd said nothing. Which probably meant that she had unilaterally declared a cease-fire.

He cautioned himself not to become too addicted to the weed. He did intend to quit again as soon as this mess got straightened around.

And when would that be? As soon as he possibly could arrange it. And that would depend on what needed to be done about Dora. He had neither seen nor talked to her since . . . well since, through a foggy memory, he saw her naked.

Maybe he could smooth the waters and settle the matter tonight. For that he hoped. And for that he prayed.

It was a party more than a meeting. The catechism program was over for the summer. The catechists were celebrating a successful year. A few routine business matters were brought to meaningless votes.

Chicken salad and coffee were served. Conversation was light. The teachers exchanged anecdotes about some of the funnier doings and sayings of the students.

As often as Father Casserly glanced at Dora Riccardo, she was beaming at him with the adoration of Nancy Reagan. That would have to stop. Anyone who cared to could surmise something was going on, at least from Dora to Rick.

The gathering broke up early. People began leaving about eight-thirty. Casserly did not encourage dawdling. By nine o'clock everyone had left but Dora and Rick.

Neither said anything. There was an awkward pause. "About the other night . . ." Rick began but did not finish. He hoped to throw the verbal ball into her court.

She said nothing.

So he continued. "I want to apologize. I'm ashamed of my behavior. I ask your forgiveness."

Dora said nothing. But her eyes narrowed and seemed to cloud over.

"Look, Dora, I was totally irresponsible. I got drunk. You helped me. I am grateful. It got out of hand. For that, I'm sorry."

"You took advantage of me!"

"I was drunk."

"You can't tell me those moves you made toward me were not your complete responsibility."

"What can I say? I was drunk!"

"You were like a combination of a raging bull and a drowning man. You wanted me! You wanted me desperately! You can't deny that."

"It's not a matter of denial or affirmation. You were undressing me. I was aroused. What I did an animal would do. I wasn't acting rationally. I wasn't even acting humanly. I admit all this freely. And I want to apologize and get on with life." He lit a cigarette. This was becoming his worst-case scenario. He had to get things down to a more basic level. "Dora, you are a beautiful person."

"Nobody should know that better than you."

He almost laughed. It was a funny line. But not in this context. "Dora, I've known you very well for a very long time. I know you are a

193

beautiful person, inside and out. Don't you think it's time for you to get a life?"

She glowered at him.

"There's nothing for us in this. I am a priest. I intend to be a priest till the end of my days. We can't get married. You know that."

"Who said anything about marriage?"

That set him back on his heels. Two women. Neither knowing about his relationship with the other. It was the stuff from which French bedroom farce was made. He inhaled deeply. In a few moments smoke came cascading from his nostrils. "I was hoping . . . friends," he murmured.

"Friends!" she snorted. "Is this the way you treat your friends? Strip them and screw them?"

His hands were trembling slightly. He hoped she hadn't noticed. "Maybe . . ." he offered tentatively, ". . . maybe we are just too close to this thing. It was just the other night. Maybe we have to give this incident time."

She cocked her head to one side. "How much time?"

He sensed a tone of conciliation in her voice. He clung to it like a life preserver. "I don't know, Dora. Just give it a period to breathe. Maybe if we think and pray over it, a solution will occur."

Her expression was noncommittal. "Can you deny you found me attractive?"

He shook his head slowly, sincerely. "No, Dora. You are most attractive. That's why I suggested you select someone more eligible than me—"

Anger flashed. "It sounds like your mind is made up way before we try your suggestion to keep an open mind!"

"Sorry . . . sorry. You're right. We go slowly. Okay?"

She stood. From the look on her face it did not appear that she was about to consider life without Rick. She moved toward him as if for a kiss good-bye. Then, having thought again, she turned on her heel and walked away.

As she did so he could not help but notice how her hips undulated. Then he forcefully looked away. In the situation he was in, admiring her physical beauty was not moving in the right direction.

Outside the rectory, Dora sat in her car. She had not started the motor. She just sat and thought.

She hadn't planned it this way. When she arrived for the meeting some hours ago, she had half anticipated something romantic might develop for Rick and her. So, instead of parking in the church lot, she'd pulled into an empty space on the street. She didn't want to chance having her car be the only one left in the lot for . . . what? The night?

By happenstance she had parked equidistant from two streetlights. The light from neither reached her vehicle. Thus, in the dark she was practically invisible.

Just two nights ago the incident she would never forget had occurred. She could see the garage. She had parked at the entrance of one of the doors. She had helped him into the house and up the stairs.

Was it God's will? Of course. She'd had no plans. Certainly no plans for what had happened. She was only trying to help someone in need. That someone happened to be the man she had long loved.

It probably was not his fault either. Admittedly he had been seriously drunk. Just as he claimed.

It was God's will.

But how would she be able to demonstrate this to Rick's satisfaction?

She placed the key in the ignition. She was about to start the car when she hesitated.

The garage door opened, turning on the inside light.

Rick, in civvies, got into his car. He backed out, the light disappearing, as the garage door slowly came down behind the car.

She made an instantaneous decision. As he drove down Outer Drive toward Gratiot, she followed at a discreet distance.

She'd seen this done countless times in the movies. The object was to stay in the traffic's flow but not so closely as to arouse suspicion. She was amazed at how easy it was. The fact there was not much traffic helped. She felt she was succeeding. Rick made no effort to lose her.

She followed his car into the parking lot of a huge apartment complex in the city of Warren. She parked as far away as possible while still keeping him in view.

He entered the building. She waited. He did not emerge.

Carefully—ready to turn and retreat if necessary—she entered the same lobby he had.

There were mail slots with name tags. She scanned them as quickly as possible. No box for him. But . . . "Niedermier L-103."

Metaphorical scales fell from her eyes. Things were so much more clear now.

"It's not fair. All you have to do is lie there!"

All sorts of retorts occurred to Lil Niedermier. One thing was certain: This was not a recommended way of healing a quarrel.

They had been at odds for only a couple of days. But it was a bitter separation. Perhaps it had not been an inspired decision to attempt lovemaking at their first opportunity.

She quickly resolved to be as conciliatory as possible. She would not respond to his rebuke. Both she and Rick knew well that she could participate in lovemaking as actively as he. It would help though if she were invited to play.

She didn't anticipate any long-term problem. She was far more concerned over the cause of his impotence.

He had seemed in such high spirits when they had talked on the phone this afternoon. He was clearly happy that she had taken the initiative in patching up their squabble. He wanted nothing more than reconciliation.

Between then and now something had happened. If she could learn what had upset the applecart, she might be able to help him. "Just because this has never happened to us before doesn't mean it's abnormal in any way. There's probably a reason."

He didn't respond.

"Everything was fine," she went on, seeming to ignore his silence, "when we talked this afternoon. The only thing you had scheduled was the Catechetical Committee meeting. And that was more or less a party. Was there anything else that happened that could have upset you . . . ?"

Still he didn't respond. She left the question dangling.

"The last thing I need," he said at last, "is to put my day under a microscope. I don't know what happened. I guess I'm distracted."

"You want to talk about it?"

"No! Definitely not."

"Okay. Let's talk about the Ursula get-together. What did you think of it?"

He couldn't bring himself to confess that, even though he had participated in the conversation, he couldn't remember much of what had gone on. "I think that might have been the last of those reunions." He was glad to change the subject.

"You think there won't be any more Ursula meetings? Why not? Not enough of the gang attending?"

"Yeah. That, plus the fact that the whole purpose is history. It was foresighted of Bob Koesler to start the thing. There were walking wounded shot up by Father Angelico. They needed strength to complete their assignments there and emerge in one piece. Even after they—we—moved on, the scars needed TLC. But that's all gone now. Angelico's gone. The school's gone. The parishioners are gone. Hell, the whole damn parish is gone!"

He sighed. "Even our memories of the place are softened by now. We don't talk about the Ursula experience anymore. It's just a debating society of—what else?—conservatives and liberals. Guys and gals who want to live either before or after Vatican Two."

"In one corner," she agreed, "there's Father Harry Morgan . . ."

"And in the other corner," he completed, "everybody else."

"As time goes on," she said thoughtfully, "there are fewer and fewer who can remember personally what the Church was about before the Council. That Church is becoming just part of Church history."

"Like everything else today. You, as a Catholic school principal, must bump into this all the time."

"Sure," she affirmed. "If it happened before today's kids and young adults, as far as they're concerned it didn't happen."

They laughed. It was their first light and bright moment of the evening. It felt good.

They were still chuckling when Lil touched Rick's cheek. He tipped his head to trap her hand. It was not a particularly erotic gesture on either part. Yet, suddenly, both were aroused. Slowly, lingeringly, tenderly, they made love.

Pleasantly relaxed, Rick lay on his back, cradling Lil's head in the crook of his shoulder. Whereas previously he had been angry and distant, now he was at peace with the world. At peace even with Dora.

"Honey . . ." His voice was low, husky, postcoital. ". . . school's over for you now, right?"

The question came out of nowhere. It took her a moment to return to the present. "Well, yeah . . . I guess so. Tomorrow the eighth-graders graduate and summer vacation begins. Yes, tomorrow is the last day of school. What brought that up?"

"I was just thinking: I've got a vacation coming. And you'll be starting yours. What do you say we go someplace?"

Lil sat up. "Do you think we could? I mean, is there somewhere we could go and not worry about being recognized? It sounds wonderful."

There she goes again: Worried out of her skull about being found out! He was certain they didn't need to be all that concerned. But . . . there was no sense spending what was supposed to be a relaxing vacation looking over one's shoulder for the Grand Inquisitor's secret police.

Wait a minute! Now he was climbing into a boat similar to Lil's. She was conscious of and nervous about everyone. And now he had become conscious of and nervous about Dora. Why else was he proposing this vacation? Why did it have to be now? Why couldn't it wait for even a week or so?

During a brief period of sexual delight he had forgotten all his troubles, even Dora. Now he was back in the land of reality. His going away might just give Dora an opportunity to put things in perspective. All she had to realize was that she'd had intercourse with a drunk. The sex had been fueled by the alcohol that had removed all sense of restraint, not to mention awareness.

He wanted this vacation as an escape. And, for the first time, he wanted anonymity as much as or more than Lil did. "Someplace we could go and not be recognized," he repeated. "How about Tom Becker's cottage? You know, the one on Old Mission Peninsula in Traverse City. It would be a miracle in reverse for anyone to recognize us there. The place is self-sufficient. All we'd have to go out for would be groceries. We don't have to do that together. What say a month—more if we need it?"

Her eyes were aglow. As if she were a child at Christmas.

Just as suddenly she grew serious. "I forgot about closing up—the school, I mean."

"Tomorrow is the last day! You already said that."

"I know. It's the last day and graduation. But there's paperwork to finish. It has to be done."

"But you don't have to be the one to do it. What about your assistant principal? You're always bragging about how efficient she is. Why not let her take this responsibility? It'll be good for her." Rick believed about three-quarters of what he was giving Lil as reassurance.

She twisted a lock of her hair. "I could do that." Pause. "But what about you? You can't just up and leave your parish."

"I've got that Basilian priest from Assumption University in Windsor. He lives in a houseful of priest-teachers. I can leave the parish in the capable hands of Father Chircop and never look back. Whattya say, kid? How about a little R and R? We've earned it."

"Oh yes, darling. When can we leave?"

"I'll just check with Tom and make sure the cottage is vacant. I'll call him now."

Rick got a reply on the third ring. Lil could tell by the growing smile on his face that the place was theirs.

She, of the two, always was the cautious one. It was a kick to be spontaneous for a change.

Things looked dark. But Dora was not about to give up.

She knew she would make Rick a good wife. And she'd be an excellent mother to his kids. *Their* kids.

Okay. So he had been under the weather the other night. Still, they had given themselves to each other with abandon. It would not be burdensome to engage in wild, steamy sex whenever they felt the urge. Why would he turn all that away? Why would he reject her? Her offer was on her part unconditional.

She thought she might have unearthed the core problem. It well could be Lillian Niedermier. If this were so, she, Dora, had been blind-sided.

Lillian! That sweet young thing! She too had served at St. Ursula's. But her life there had never touched that of Father Casserly. They were ships that never even passed in the night.

Was he actually shacking up with her? Dora didn't want to jump to conclusions. All she knew for certain was that after their tiff Rick left his rectory. He drove to a large apartment complex in Warren. He entered a building that did not list him as an occupant. But it did list an L. Niedermier. Coincidence?

It stretched credulity.

If Rick and Lil were living together without benefit of clergy, that would explain a lot.

Prescinding for the moment Rick's being a priest, he could qualify as one of the Detroit area's most eligible bachelors. All right, so he's sixty. He looks and acts anything from twenty to thirty years younger. He's a very successful priest. Whether it comes to raising money or giving spiritual direction, it would be nearly impossible to top him. Is he good-looking? Some people improve with age. Rick certainly started handsome and got better. He must have had a bevy of women throw themselves at him.

So why is he still a priest and still single?

Is it a triumph for celibacy? Is it an accident? Is God saving him for good old Dora?

Or—and this is the torturous—alternative, have Rick and Lil been playing house for God knows how many years?

Dora decided she would back off for a couple of days. Give the matter a little time for her to make plans and get on this case seriously in the coming week.

Dora got ready for bed, musing that the way this situation was playing out, there was good news and bad news. The bad news was that a woman, a younger woman, might have staked a claim on the man she herself loved. The good news was that Rick Casserly had had an ulterior reason in rejecting Dora's offer of herself. He hadn't turned her down because she was, somehow, repulsive.

No, Dora was confident of her beauty. If she could get rid of this female specter, she could land her man.

Eighteen

Dora had a fitful weekend. She vacillated between hope for a happy and assured solution and fear that the cause was already lost.

On this early June morning, at least the weather was promising. Not too hot, not too cool, and a high sky whose color would be described by Detroit Lions football fans as Honolulu blue.

She decided to try Rick first. She dialed the rectory number and was not at all surprised by the sound of the woman's voice at the answering service. Dora had been informed by countless clergy that in the good old days not having a priest available to answer a phone was a sin that cried to heaven for vengeance. Nowadays, it was as easy to get Donald Trump to answer his phone as it was to find a priest at the rectory. Without volunteering her name, Dora asked for Father Casserly.

"Father is not available. If this is an emergency, I can give you a number to call."

"This isn't an emergency, but I do have to talk to Father. Can you give me a number where I can reach him?"

"I'm sorry. I don't have that information. But if this is an emergency . . ."

"Can you tell me when he will be available?"

"I'm sorry. I don't have that information. But . . ."

"Can you tell me who is saying the Masses while Father Casserly is gone?"

"That would be one of the numbers you can call in an emergency."

"Would you?"

"Certainly. The priest is Father Chircop and the number is . . ." Dora quickly wrote down the number. *Thank you.*

The conversation had been calm and polite with no sarcastic overtones. All business. Dora's mother might have been dying and the service operator would have had the same rational, professional tone.

Dora dialed the Detroit number for Windsor's Assumption University.

"Assumption," the woman identified.

"May I speak to Father Chircop?"

"Father isn't here. He's helping out at Holy Redeemer parish today. Would you like that number?" There was the slightest French accent—not unexpected in this bilingual country. The secretary sounded chatty. An advantage for Dora.

"That won't be necessary. I'm sure you have the information I'm looking for. Is Father going to substitute for Father Casserly for weekend liturgies?"

"Let me look up his calendar appointments."

There was silence for about a minute. Then, "Yes."

"Does the appointment schedule say how long that will be?"

Another pause. "It says at least a month. Maybe more. Do you want to talk to Father Chircop? It's real easy to get him."

"No, that won't be necessary. Does it happen to say where Father Casserly will be?"

"No. Father Chircop doesn't know either. I remember him saying that before he left this morning."

So.

One down, one base to touch.

If Niedermier was at work, Dora would be willing to chalk all previous coincidences up to chance.

She dialed the number for St. Enda's school. Should Lil come on the line, Dora was prepared to hang up immediately.

It was Lil's secretary.

"No," the secretary answered Dora's question, "Ms. Niedermier is gone for the summer. You just missed her. If you want to get in touch with her, you might try about the middle of July. She may be back then."

Thank God for secretaries who talk too freely.

Coincidences!

It was now more than likely that they were together. And more than likely they had been together for a long time in the past.

Dora gave brief thought to tracking them down. She believed it would not be all that difficult. But what would she gain when she found them? Confrontation would be counterproductive at this point.

At this point, indeed, she had to step back and evaluate whether there was any hope at all.

Rick might have been right when he urged her to get a life.

She would have to give this serious thought. What she decided to do now, at this crucial time, surely would influence her entire future.

It had been a pleasant June if you liked warm, dry weather. Just a week ago, on the twenty-first, summer had officially arrived. Now municipalities and individuals were planning fireworks and patriotic displays honoring Independence Day.

The mother of all these area celebrations would be held a few days prematurely. It would be breathtaking. A barge would be anchored in the middle of the Detroit River. On the shores of Detroit and Windsor huge crowds would gather. Boat traffic on the river would be halted. And for about an hour, rockets, each more spectacular than the previous one, would light the sky and the booms would echo among the downtown skyscrapers.

Pat Lennon, editor-in-chief of *Oakland Monthly,* had invited Father Koesler to lunch. She had done that from time to time when she wrote for the dailies, sometimes to get reliable background on a "Catholic" story, sometimes just to renew their friendship.

They had first met over twenty years ago. The occasion was a series of murders of Detroit priests and nuns, a case that was popularly labeled the Rosary Murders. At that time, Pat had been premier reporter for the *Detroit Free Press,* while Koesler was editor of the weekly Catholic newspaper. Together, and with the work of others, they broke the case and solved the mystery of the killings.

From time to time they continued to be helpful in solving other crimes having to do with the Catholic Church—he as resource person, she as investigative reporter.

In between, they were just friends.

Today they were to meet at 11:30 A.M., "to beat the crowd," at the

Northern Lakes Seafood Company on North Woodward, in, appropriately, Oakland County.

As was his custom, Father Koesler had arrived ahead of time. Lennon spotted him immediately. He was wearing—what else?—black clericals and the roman collar. She smiled and wondered if he wore the uniform while bathing or taking a shower.

The few priests still in harness generally wore civvies when not involved in parochial duties. Some never wore clericals. A few, Koesler among them, dressed the way priests used to dress—because they were the priests who always used to dress that way.

When Lennon reached the table, Koesler was studying the menu. He made an awkward attempt to stand but it ended looking like an aborted curtsy.

"Chivalry is not dead; it's just a little ill," she said as she slid into the seat opposite him in the booth.

The two smiled. They were genuinely fond of each other.

The twosome did not draw any attention. It was a couple of generations since the days when priests were not to be seen alone with a woman. The days when, in case of an emergency requiring a priest and a woman to be alone in a car, one of them was to sit in the backseat.

Besides, if he were an Episcopalian priest, Pat could have been his wife.

After giving them time to consult the menu, the waitress came to take their order. Neither would have a drink. Both opted for a salad.

At the time of their last meeting, Lennon had not yet been hired at the magazine and Koesler had been contemplating retirement.

In response to his question, she was explaining life at a monthly magazine. "Actually," she said, "it suits an aging newshound. Things gradually slow down. No longer do I hit the ground running. Of course when you get down to deadline time, it gets frighteningly like a daily paper. But I'm fifty-five now and I can use the slower pace."

Koesler liked the unconcern with which Pat voiced her age. "I'm sure," he said, "that fifty-five sounds elderly to you, but just think of being a septuagenarian!"

She smiled. "You look as if you're holding on quite well."

"Thank God. And, please God, some more."

She told him about being practically shanghaied into taking over the then-failing magazine. "So, you see, I never really got to experience retirement. What's it like?"

"Retirement," he answered, "is pretty much what you make it." He told her of helping out at various parishes, and generally keeping busy accepting parochial invitations. "For me, the big thing was no more meetings or worries about the effect of rain on a patched roof."

Their salads were served. Lennon asked for decaf coffee. Koesler ordered iced tea. They ate for a while in silence, comfortable in not needing to talk.

Then, "There is something I wanted to talk to you about." It was said almost with a sense of embarrassment. Pat did not want to create the impression that this was turning into a business luncheon; that had not been her intent.

Koesler was unconcerned. "Ask away. If there's any way I can help, I'll be happy to. Part of the luxury of my retirement." He put down his fork and gave her his full attention.

"Okay." Her fork followed suit. "Remember the two people who hired in at the magazine—Dora Riccardo and Jerry Anderson? Each of them had a laundry list of references. Since she had been a nun and he had been a priest, I called you. I always do when I have a 'Catholic' situation."

"I remember, okay."

"And then you said you didn't know either one well enough to respond."

"Yeah. And I referred you to Father Casserly. I never heard from you again regarding the matter. I assumed Rick had answered your questions satisfactorily. I've seen their bylines and credits in the magazine. So you did hire them. Is something wrong?"

"Something troublesome, I think. Let me give you some background." She thought for a moment. "They came to the magazine at a perfect time. I was cleaning house and I wanted quality people around me. For the first time, the magazine could afford to pay a decent wage, so I wasn't ashamed to recruit good people."

"Has there been a problem with either Dora or Jerry?"

"No . . . not till recently."

"How long has the problem been going on?"

"About a month ago . . . maybe a little less."

"That would be approximately when we had the Ursula get-together."

"The what?"

As succinctly as possible, Koesler described the annual meeting of those who at one time or another had been stationed at St. Ursula's parish under Father Angelico.

"If you don't mind," she said, "that's weird?" She made it a question out of deference to Father Koesler. Lennon's immediate reaction to the Ursula routine was that it was weird, period. But just in case Koesler might have considered the whole procedure as normal, she left the door open with a question mark.

"And," she went on, "Anderson and Riccardo were in that category?"

"Both qualified."

"I guess that explains part of what's going on." Lennon resumed eating. So did Koesler. Then his brow knitted. "What do you mean, 'part'?"

"Dora came to the magazine just a tad before Anderson. In fact, she sort of steered him to us. In the beginning, everything worked out well. Both of them needed to learn a lot. But, as I correctly anticipated, they were good students and workers—"

"What made you think they'd work out?" Koesler interrupted.

"Partly their previous professions. I assumed they would be conscientious and have a good work ethic. Secondly, they were entering the marketplace considerably older than most beginners. They would know that they had to make up in a hurry for the deficit. They were starting on an uneven playing field. And they knew it."

"But they both did well."

"Un-huh. But as an aside, almost from day one, he was coming on to her like there was no tomorrow. Oh, no harassment or anything like that; he kept it subtle. And she seemed to handle it all right. Anyway, they kept their private lives pretty much out of the office.

"And," she added with an authoritative air, "I know what I'm talking about when it comes to office romances.

"Anyway," she continued, "something happened, as I say, about a month ago. She seemed to become somehow dependent on him. He covered for her. Oh, the work was getting done—which is all a manager should be responsible for—but I sensed this could blow up any day.

"So," she concluded, "I'm interested in what you have to say about that meeting."

He collected his thoughts before he began to speak. He told her, as best he could remember, about the argumentation and debate that had transpired. When he finished the narration he added, "I don't see how any of what went on during the meeting would have an effect on their work habits."

"If you'll pardon me," she said, "I'd like to go over this business of Anderson's leaving the priesthood."

"Sure."

"As one who keeps up with the news, and as a journalist, I know this quitting the priesthood is by no means rare. There was a time when they came pouring out. That's slowed now?"

"A trickle."

"So there's very little media coverage anymore? In effect, it's been done."

Koesler nodded.

"But Jerry's quitting got all that press solely as an aftermath of the wedding he performed?"

"That plus his work in the core city with his basketball program. Otherwise his departure would just have been noted in the *Detroit Catholic* as taking a leave of absence."

"Oh, yeah, I remember that box you used to put in. With the appointments, wasn't it? Father So-and-So is going to be pastor somewhere and Father So-and-So is taking a leave of absence. Page three, wasn't it?"

"What a memory! Yes, that's how it ran."

"I wasn't terribly interested in the thing. A leave of absence suggests that the person will return. Is that how it worked? And how come it didn't work that way for Jerry? He obviously didn't go back."

"Nor did practically anyone else who took a leave of absence from the active ministry. It was the extremely rare bird who returned. It's as some have charged: The Church has no words for saying 'Sorry, we were wrong.' So it seems to state in this case: 'Father So-and-So is leaving the active ministry.'"

"I'm still up in the air," Pat said. "Why should Jerry's relationship with Dora take a drastic turn now? What could it have to do with that Ursula thing a month ago?"

Koesler thought for several moments. "Maybe . . . yeah: It came out during the meeting that Jerry had been laicized years ago."

"Hold it. I'm familiar with the term. But not precisely. Fill me in on that, would you?"

"Sure. Laicization is a process by which a priest returns to the lay state—becomes a layman again. A priest may apply for such a release. The request may or may not be granted. If it is, then the man, while still remaining a priest forever, is forbidden—barred by the Church— from *acting* as a priest except in cases of serious emergency. But the priest, acting as a layman, *is* free to marry.

"By no means do all priests who leave go through the process. Some couldn't care less about the procedure. Others apply and are rejected out of hand—depending on the mood of the Vatican at that particular time.

"Now"—Koesler returned to the case at hand—"it was sort of obvious that Jerry Anderson did not go along to any great degree with Church law. You just have to look at that famous, or rather infamous, wedding he witnessed. You could presume he had done things like that in the past. Even without a history, there was so much canonically wrong with that wedding that it would be safe to conclude that Father Anderson did not much follow Church law."

Pat Lennon's brow unwrinkled. "I think I'm beginning to understand what's going on here: Jerry quits the priesthood. The people who know what's going on naturally assume that Jerry would not bother applying for laicization. He would not fool around begging the Church to free him.

"But it comes out at the Ursula thing that he has, indeed, applied for it."

"Not only applied for it," Koesler said, "but had gotten it."

"Then . . ."

"Then," Koesler interrupted, "it was at that party that everyone—including Dora Riccardo—would know for the first time what Jerry had done."

"Jerry," Lennon concluded, "is free to marry—and so is Dora. As a former priest and an ex-nun, they would have lots in common. Dora sets her sights on Jerry."

"Could be." Koesler finished the salad and sipped his tea. "It's entirely possible that Dora would not seriously consider marriage with Jerry because he was still bound to celibacy. Until it came out at the party that he was indeed eligible, Dora . . . none of us . . . had known that Jerry was already canonically "reduced to the lay state," as the Church terms it.

"Now, as a priest, Jerry and anyone he entered into marriage with would be excommunicated. However," he concluded, "for the past month Jerry and Dora have known they're free to court—and marry if they decide to."

"So—Lennon finished her salad, then motioned to the waitress for more coffee—"this could explain why Dora has let her work slip."

"I guess there could be lots of reasons. But the one we've just discussed is as good as anyone could devise."

That having been more or less settled, the two engaged in small talk as lunch wound down.

As they rose to leave, Pat extended her hand and said simply, "Thanks."

Koesler merely smiled and nodded.

As they parted, Koesler mused that their conversation had cleared things up for him as much as for Pat. If Dora and Jerry were an item, God bless them. They'd both paid their dues.

Nineteen

IT WAS NEARING the end of August.

Casserly and Niedermier had returned from their vacation a little more than three weeks ago.

It had been a glorious time for them. The only fly in their ointment was what Casserly termed Lil's paranoia about being found out. But he was willing to live with their situation. He smiled when he thought that years from now, when most likely there would be optional celibacy, she'd still be worried—just out of habit.

He'd had no further occurrence of impotence. It had happened just that once and never again. However, since he'd returned and assumed his parochial duties, he'd been walking on metaphorical pins and needles. *When would Dora drop the other shoe?*

Yet she was nowhere to be seen. He did not go out looking for her. However, as he celebrated the liturgy he would scan the congregation carefully. Day after day, weekend after weekend, there was no Dora. He felt particularly vulnerable in the confessional rooms. All she'd have to do was enter and he would be trapped.

He answered the phone tentatively. He opened the door to visitors warily. But—bottom line—no Dora.

After a couple of weeks, he phoned Father Koesler. Ostensibly, the call was just chitchat. How everyone was getting along. What had happened during Rick's vacation. And, oh, by the way, anything new with the Ursula group?

Nothing major, Koesler reported. There *was* a rumor that Jerry and Dora were dating. Nothing certain, just a rumor. "But keep that to yourself, won't you?" Koesler added.

Would he ever! His heart soared. Long life and abundant children to Mr. and Mrs. Jerry Anderson. After a couple of weeks of constant nervous exhaustion, he breathed freely once again.

Lil didn't know the cause for his great relief, but she was enjoying it.

Their dating was falling into a pattern. From two to four evenings a week they would meet at one of the suburban Detroit restaurants, of which there were very many. They would have a couple of drinks and order dinner. She stayed on veggies and fish. He was meat and potatoes.

The conversation was pleasant. Either they were dredging up stories about their years in the rectory or the convent, or they talked shop. The rectory/convent stories were fun and funny. Shop talk grew one-sided. Dora seemed to be losing interest in work. Up to these last couple of months, she had been completely taken up with the magazine. Now she gave every indication that her time there was coming to an end.

Jerry took that to mean that, just maybe, she was considering marriage. He would not mind at all supporting her and providing a good home for her and their family. But when it came to family, they should get serious soon about children. Dora was forty. The biological clock was running.

In the meantime there was fun to be had. Though it was limited to dinner and a show or movie and a good night kiss at her door.

Until this night.

Everything had progressed routinely until they reached her door. She invited him in. Eagerly he accepted. About all one could say about her apartment was that it provided shelter. It was neat but nondescript.

She brought out the fixings and asked him to brew some instant decaf. She disappeared into an adjacent room. It might have been the bedroom; Jerry couldn't tell, as she had closed the door behind her.

The water was boiling by the time Dora returned. She wore nothing beneath a diaphanous gown. The water in the kettle was ready, but so was Jerry. And his condition took precedence. He didn't want to misjudge this situation, making more of it than was offered. But she left little to no doubt that this was the supreme invitation.

She guided him backward to an upholstered chair into which he tumbled. Draping her legs over the chair's arm she settled in his lap.

She put her arms around his neck and began kissing him. He returned the kisses. Neither was an expert at this art, but both felt excited.

In no time he had her in his arms and carried her into the other room. It was, indeed, the bedroom. She moved from his arms and stood before him. She touched her negligee at the neck and it dropped to the floor. Jerry was dumbstruck. She stretched out on the bed. The light from the single lamp cast shadows that emphasized the deep curves of her body.

In no time Jerry was out of his clothes.

Somehow they were able to slow themselves down and make love lingeringly. They remained in each other's arms, both satisfied and relaxed.

After perhaps half an hour, Jerry was drifting toward sleep. Dora rose, slipped into a bathrobe, and said, "Jerry, you'd better leave now."

"What?"

"I said it would be a good idea for you to leave."

"What? After . . ."

"It's just that I have neighbors," she interrupted, "who are nosy busybodies. I wouldn't be surprised if some of them have spotted your car in the parking lot. They will make note of when you arrived and when you left. It's better this way, believe me." She smiled broadly.

Don't push her, he reminded himself. She had offered a lot—almost everything but permanent residence and marriage. He accepted everything she put forth. There'll be another day and another night.

Words were not appropriate now. He dressed, kissed her no longer as a mere friend, and left.

She finished making the coffee. She sat, and sipped, and thought.

Jerry was great. He could not have had a great deal of experience. His sensitivity made up for that. Lovemaking, she determined, could be all she dreamed of. Especially if it involved the one and only person with whom you wished to share your life, your all.

Unfortunately, Jerry was not that person.

213

Father Koesler was living in a private apartment in a priests' retirement compound on a Catholic college campus. In his opinion, the chief benefit of living here was the companionship of other Senior Priests.

He was pleasantly surprised when Father Rick Casserly phoned to arrange for a meeting. It was a bit of a drawback that there was not more contact from the world outside. While it could be fun swapping all the old stories with elderly priests, from time to time Koesler itched to hear the latest clerical gossip and, in general, to keep current.

So, at just a few minutes after two in the afternoon, Father Koesler welcomed the knock at his door. He greeted Father Casserly, who passed on anything to drink.

They sat opposite each other and Koesler prompted Casserly to reveal the latest scuttlebutt.

"Most of the talk," Casserly said, "is that we're going to get another auxiliary bishop."

"Another?" Koesler clearly was surprised. "Who's it going to be?"

"Disputed, as usual. It's been a long time since we've had an active Pole as auxiliary. The time gap is there, plus Detroit's still got a thriving and loyal Polish community."

"But another auxiliary!" Koesler couldn't get over it. "Pretty soon we'll have more bishops than priests. All chiefs and no Indians."

They chuckled.

"I hate to cut this visit short," Casserly said. "I really enjoy talking with you; you know that. But I've got something you could do for me. It'll take just a minute. And then I'll have to run."

"Well, sure. I'll be glad to help with anything I can. Watcha got?"

Casserly pulled out of his small, black valise a bound stack of looseleaf papers. Koesler looked at it speculatively. He had no idea what it was.

As if anticipating his question, Casserly said, "It's my Last Will and Testament."

"You've never had one?"

"Sure. I just wanted to update it. I did it myself," he added.

Koesler accepted the document. "Are you sure it would pass a judicial exam?"

"Yes, I'm positive. A lawyer gave me a model will. I just had to fill in the blanks and change what needed changing."

Koesler was unclear why Rick would not simply let an attorney handle this. Heck, next Casserly would be performing a self-appendectomy! Whatever. Koesler began to leaf through the document.

"Go ahead and read it, Bob. I'm going to ask you to witness it. And, more important, I'm naming you as executor."

"What! I've got a decade on you! What makes you think I'll be around when you reap your heavenly reward?"

"You're doing just fine. If you do leave before me, I'll try to get someone else. But . . . read it. Then I think you'll have a better idea why I'm asking you."

"All right." As Koesler scanned, he quickly skimmed to the salient parts.

"Clothing to the St. Vincent de Paul Society," Koesler said aloud. "Books to the seminary . . ." He looked across to Casserly. "Are you sure they'll want them?"

"I talked to the librarian. She said they'd be careful to absorb what they wanted and, more important, find a good home for the rest."

"Uh-huh." Koesler returned to the document. "Furnishings—again—to the S.V. de P. I don't think you could find a better organization." He was silent for many moments. He raised his head, a look of disbelief on his face.

"You're leaving everything else to Lillian Niedermier? Car? All financial assets? Are you serious?"

"Dead serious. Literally. Everything to Lil."

"Rick, I've been around a long time. Nothing much surprises me. But this surprises me."

Casserly replied with no sense of embarrassment. "Lil and I have been living 'the third way'—neither married nor celibate—for a long, long while."

"I never would have guessed. Does anyone else know?"

"Tom Becker. If you'll look at the last page you'll see that Tom is a witness. You're the other one. That's why I'm telling you our secret.

Tom's known about us almost since we began sharing our lives. So now, you're the only ones who know—at least as far as we're aware."

"Not even Peggy Becker?"

"Shows you how close-mouthed Tom can be. And so can you, I know. That's why I've told you. And that's why I'm asking you to witness. How about it, Bob?"

"Just give me a moment. At my age, I don't take shocks all that well. How have you pulled it off?"

"By being super-careful. Our success is almost entirely Lil's doing. She wanted to protect me as much as herself." Casserly glanced at his watch. "She is so much younger than I—she's got to outlive me by a bunch of years. I want to take care of her as best I can. Bob, I'm running a little late. How about it?"

Koesler flipped to the last page and affixed his signature.

They bade each other good-bye and Rick Casserly departed, leaving behind a somewhat bemused Father Koesler.

If any other clerical couples had managed to conceal their lifestyles as successfully as Rick and Lil, Koesler, of course, wouldn't have known about it. Just as he hadn't known about them. But he did not think many, if any, could equal their success.

Of course Koesler would keep their secret. In fact he felt honored that Rick shared it with him. It would happen, of that he was certain: There would be an optionally celibate Catholic clergy. He was also certain that that alone would not solve the priest shortage.

And as for Rick and Lil and their clandestine relationship without benefit of clergy, Koesler adhered to the biblical injunction, Judge not and you shall not be judged.

Indeed, this latest revelation seemed to put everything at rest. God's in His heaven, all's right with the world.

Tom and Peggy Becker are enjoying the benefits of a long, happy, and holy marriage, aided, perhaps, by Tom's ability to keep certain secrets. Rick and Lil are proving that love can protect its own. Jerry and Dora are entering a deeper and committed relationship. Father Zack Tully is fulfilled in his parochial setting and acts as a linchpin holding together himself, his brother, and his sister-in-law. Harry Morgan is sure he is right. And he himself, Father Koesler, is as happy a priest as Bing Crosby ever was.

All in all, a tightly held structure. Suddenly, a scene flashed before his imagination: cheerleaders piled together, forming a pyramid. If one of those cheerleaders were to falter, the whole bunch would come tumbling down.

Twenty

Enough time had passed that Rick Casserly did not panic when Dora Riccardo called. She needed to talk to him, she stated. Would it be all right for her to drop by late this afternoon?

He readily agreed and set four-thirty for the appointment.

Of course he speculated. His best guess was that she wanted to talk about Jerry Anderson, the new man in her life. After all, he knew Jerry quite well. If that was not it, perhaps she wanted to wind up their own relationship, if such it could be termed.

Either way it was fine with him. When he had heard that Dora and Jerry were linked, an intolerable weight had been lifted from him. So desperately did he wish to be free of Dora, he banked on rumor being fact. So, whatever Dora wanted, as long as it wasn't himself, he would help her in any way he could.

At precisely four-thirty, he happened to be passing the screen door as Dora was walking up the path to the rectory. He stopped to watch her.

She really was attractive. The soft breeze swirled the skirt of her light, summer frock against her legs. Whatever else, there was no doubt about it, she was a well-formed female. And, glory to God, she was not his.

She was about to ring the doorbell when she noticed he was standing just on the other side of the screen. His smile was genuine. She smiled back awkwardly. He opened the door and ushered her to his office. She looked around the businesslike room and said, "Do we have to be so formal?"

He hesitated only a moment. "Of course not." He led the way into the living room.

She sat on the couch and crossed her legs—demurely.

There was a period of silence that seemed longer than it was.

"We haven't seen each other for some time," he said, searching for a way of introducing the matter of closure.

She nodded. "For a while I thought we'd never see each other again."
Another drawn-out pause.

"I didn't sleep last night." Her voice was tight.

He began to grow uneasy.

"I spent all day yesterday and most of today trying to find a way of
telling you . . ." She paused an infinitesimal moment. "I guess there is
no way but bluntly: I'm pregnant."

Her last two words were a thunderclap. Limitless lines of faces passed
before his memory. All the people who had spoken the same two
words. They had come to him as their father confessor, their spiritual
guide, the hope in their desperate need. Pregnancy meant the end of
their world. The end to college dreams. The end of their hope for a new
house. A catastrophe as planned as a tornado.

Generally he had responded with sympathy rather than empathy. It
wasn't his problem. It never was his problem. It never would be his
problem. He could be objective and helpful.

Now, for the first time, the words "I'm pregnant" meant that he
would be a father in every sense of the word. His impulse was to question the condition before denying it. "Are you sure?"

"Of course. Do you think I would kid around about a thing like
that?"

"But it was only once—one time! And I was drunk!"

"Neither condition would prevent fertilization. For the past couple
of months I've put on a little weight. Most of all, I've missed two periods.
And this from a woman who could set her clock by the regularity of her
periods."

"That's all? That could be caused by any number of things."

"I've been to Dr. Green. He's been my ob/gyn for years. He'll be glad
to see you."

"You told him about me!"

"He's my doctor. I'm his patient. He isn't going to talk."

Briefly, Rick thought of the trouble he'd gone to with his Last Will
and Testament just to avoid another party to his secret bequest. Lawyers
and clients had protected relationships as well as doctors and patients.

If she'd gotten a diagnosis of pregnancy from a doctor, that pretty well nailed down the truth of her condition. Although, just to be sure, he would contact her Dr. Green.

However, there was another logical question: "Are you sure I'm the father?"

"Yes. I'm sure."

Wait, there was one other clutchable straw. "What about Jerry Anderson? I heard you were going with him."

She cleared her throat. This was embarrassing. All these demeaning questions. But, she told herself, she'd better get used to it. There were going to be a lot of demeaning, embarrassing questions.

"I dated Jerry," she admitted. "I tried Jerry. He's a lovely man, but he's not my man. And, so far as Jerry's being the father, my doctor says conception was about eight weeks ago. About the time of the Ursula meeting and our intercourse. A full month before I began dating Jerry. If there's any further doubt, we can get into DNA. If you want to know it, you're my man. You were from the beginning." She made an instant decision not to mention her visit to him when—bent on seduction— she'd worn a habit, a bathing suit, and nothing more. She had to focus on the here and now. "I dated Jerry. I didn't live with him!"

There was something about the way she stated the final sentence. Did she know about Lil? The question was irrelevant at the moment. There was a baby to deal with. The question was: What are we going to do about the baby? And the answer was: I don't know. All he knew was that he had never before felt so trapped.

"So," she said, "what are we going to do?"

He didn't know. Several options occurred. But none clearly. Actually he felt faint.

"You aren't thinking of abortion, are you?" she charged.

"No!" Although, honestly, the word had popped to mind. "What about adoption?" he offered.

She cocked her head to one side. "Would you really want to have a stranger raise your child? I would not."

He had used about all his options. There was only one more possibility before he had to face what he most feared. "What if," he said, "you have the child and I support the two of you?"

She hesitated. "I was about to say you couldn't do it. Not on your salary. But then I remembered, you have Tom Becker in your corner. So, okay, you probably could pull it off. But I would be joining the ranks of single mothers. Our baby would grow up without a father. Do you really want any of these things for your child?"

He hung his head. "All because I got drunk at a party! And you insisted on driving me home." He looked at her accusingly. "You orchestrated the whole thing."

"I've been waiting for you to dump it all on me. Tully was in his rectory when someone had to drive you home. Koesler might just as well been at home. He stayed there overnight. There was one driver. Me. Not only could I get you home, I was going in your direction anyway.

"I could have dumped you on this couch or on your bed. I thought you might be sick during the night. That's why I undressed you. Why did you undress me?"

The argument might have continued. But it was going nowhere. He faced the final option.

He gazed into her eyes. "This has been an unforeseen bombshell. I need a little time, Dora."

"How much time?"

"A little. Honest. A little."

"All right." She stood. He did not.

"I can let myself out," she said. And she did.

The early evening sun warmed the rectory. He sat back in the chair. He removed his clerical collar and twirled it on his finger.

Thirty-five years. A career. A long time to do exactly what he'd always wanted to do. Five years away from retirement if he were in the real world. Ten years to achieve the status of Senior Priest.

He thought of all the parishes he'd staffed. The marvelous people he'd met and served and guided.

Again he thought of all those frightened faces, the trembling lips that spoke of pregnancy. *"I'm pregnant."* He'd done for these people what he thought was his best. If he had to do it again, after what had happened today, how much more compassionately he would have reacted. How much more honest he would be in mouthing that cliché, "I feel your pain."

He remembered how fearfully he had gradually intensified his association with Lil. There had been so many opportunities to alter the course of their relationship.

From the first time they'd met, on one of his return visits to St. Ursula's, she had been in awe of him. No, not him so much as his role as a priest. Their relationship had deepened to progressively more friendly and intimate levels. He had been conscious of this deepening. At any level he could have called a halt. Perhaps it had been selfish of him not to keep their closeness merely platonic. He'd heard the phrase, "theologizing a swollen prick." Was that what he had done?

But there had been other things going on. There was the exhilaration of Vatican II. It encouraged questions rather than blind rote obedience.

Was celibacy that precious? That necessary? Was he denying himself the intimate company of a woman for no good reason? Had he been born too early in the ecclesial scheme of things?

How much had been selfishness? How much had been common sense?

Slowly he became aware of place and time. Early evening had given way to late evening. Shadows were lengthening. He smiled sardonically. It was over, finished, done.

When Dora announced her pregnancy, he knew. He knew his dream was finished. He had launched a series of defense mechanisms, fighting off the inevitable. Deny the pregnancy. Deny his role in it. Deny his responsibility for it.

Finally, with all denial spent, relax into reality. His time as a priest was ended. Of course he would do the "honorable thing." No matter that doing so would cause lots of unhappiness to lots of people. That frequently was the cost for accepting responsibility.

Again, he was being selfish. He was forgetting Lil. All their years together. Their marriage without paper. Her trust and faith in him and what he had told her as he had led her step by step into intimacies she had considered forbidden.

He would have to tell her. He would have to tell her before there was the slightest possibility she might hear it from someone else.

In all his life he had never dreaded anything as much as he shrank from this.

He let himself into their apartment. He could hear Lil humming a show tune. She had a sweet voice. Almost no vibrato—like a boy soprano. One of the many, many things he loved about her. One of the many, many things he would sorely miss.

"That you, honey?" she called from the kitchen area.

"Yeah."

"Did you eat yet? I've got some stir-fry going. Just take a few minutes."

He made no response. He was swallowing emotion that rose in his throat like bile.

"Did you hear me, dear? Are you hungry?"

"No. Don't bother yourself."

She caught the tone of his voice. Something was wrong. She stepped toward the door so she could see him. She was wearing shorts, a tank top, and an apron. She was carrying a hand towel. And she looked very concerned. "Honey?"

Instead of standing up straight as he usually did, he slumped. His shoulders drooped.

"What is it, Rick?" Whatever it was, clearly it was serious.

"Sit down, please," he said as he, in turn, sat down.

Neither said anything for several moments. The verbal ball was in Rick's court, but he couldn't return it.

"Sweetheart," he began. "Remember a couple of months ago, the Ursula meeting?"

"Of course." She thought all this had something to do with their quarrel earlier that day when she had demanded to be put ashore. But that was now long over. They had spent a trouble-free vacation together. Nothing but good had happened between them since then.

No, it couldn't be that quarrel. It had to be something else.

Maybe her worst fear had come true: They had been seen together in some compromising situation and reported!

Part of her wished he would just spit it out while the rest of her didn't want to hear it.

"Maybe," he said falteringly, "you noticed that I was putting away the booze pretty heavily."

"You were putting it away like you owned the distillery." She smiled, hoping the smile would somehow alleviate the doom she felt.

"You didn't see the worst of it. In the time it took you to get from the basement to your car, I downed almost as much as I had drunk previously that evening."

She gasped. "You could have killed yourself!"

"It might have been better." This was no exaggeration. He meant it.

"After you and the others left . . ." He stopped. But he had to go on. "There were four left. Me—in a near stupor, I guess—Koesler, Tully, and Dora. The question was who was going to take me home."

"Why didn't they put you in a guest room and let you sleep it off?"

"A good question. Neither Koesler nor Tully could know whether I had anything scheduled early the next day. They didn't know whether I had morning Mass. They thought it a good idea to get me home. Whatever. Anyway, Tully was home already and Koesler had a room there. That left . . ."

"Dora," Lil supplied. "Dora Riccardo."

He didn't have to go any further. Lil knew. Suddenly she realized that being found out was not the worst thing that could have happened.

Rick went on to explain what had happened that night once it was determined that Dora should chauffeur him home. What he knew— outside of a few moments in bed—was largely hearsay.

Lil did not interrupt again. Numbly she half heard his narration. Dora was pregnant, bottom line, exclamation point, the tragic, tragic end. One single act of intercourse and all the years of double and triple prophylactic protection were as nothing. The years she had devoted to Rick—wasted. Their relationship—over.

All this and more thundered against her consciousness.

He must be finished; he had stopped talking. After she realized that Dora was pregnant and Rick was the father, Lil didn't care about any of the details. She knew it must have all been an accident. She knew Rick did not love Dora. She knew that Rick loved her.

But that didn't matter—none of it mattered. Rick would marry the mother of his child, that Lil knew. She did not know the battle Rick had fought within himself to submit to that marriage.

All the while Rick had been explaining the situation, choosing his words as carefully as he could, she had been absently twisting the towel in her hands. In so doing, she had exerted such pressure and friction that the skin of her left palm had broken. There was blood on the towel.

Rick's mouth continued to move. But she was oblivious.

"Honey! Honey!" Rick was shouting. Lil looked directly at him. But she didn't seem to comprehend anything he was saying.

Rarely had Rick seen anyone in a catatonic state. This, he was convinced, was one of those times. He shook her, then abruptly stopped. She was hurt, injured somehow inside. Shaking her might further damage her.

He was out of his league. He dialed 9-1-1. An emergency crew was on the way.

He held her close. He spoke to her as quietly and reassuringly as possible. After all, his guts also were wrenched.

When the E.M.S. arrived, he stepped back to let the professionals take over.

A crew member took down essential information. Rick was not dressed as a priest, nor did he identify himself as one. Lil, now on a gurney, was being wheeled to the ambulance. She would be delivered to Warren Emergency Hospital. Rick would follow along in his car.

The place was terribly busy. But he was able to ascertain that Lil had arrived and was behind the curtain in one of the cubicles. He identified himself as a friend, a friend who had given her cataclysmic news that undoubtedly triggered her present condition.

An emergency room doctor informed him that the initial diagnosis was an acute reaction similar to schizophrenia with a catatonic state.

At this point, Rick was abandoning the situation. He gave them the address and phone number of one of Lil's aunts. The two women weren't close, but they were related. He did not get further involved because he was certain his news had caused her reaction. He was the last person in the world she needed right now.

This assessment tore him even further apart. It was a self-contradiction: She needed his shoulder to cry on—but it was he who had caused her tears.

In a daze, he drove back to the rectory. He did not care what happened to him. But he had already done grave harm to the woman he loved; he did not want to cause injury to any one else. That caution alone made him drive as carefully as possible under the circumstances.

After debating briefly within himself he phoned Koesler. Rick gave the older priest a bare bones summary of what had happened, starting with Dora's volunteering to act as chauffeur. With no detail, Rick admitted having sex with Dora. He told of her pregnancy, his decision to do "the right thing," his finally telling Lil, and the tragic result of that revelation.

"She's in Warren Emergency?"

"Yes. I left her there."

"You left her!"

"If she comes out of this, I'm the last person she'd want to see."

"I understand. You want me to look in on her?"

"No," Rick demanded. "Not look in on her. Be there for her. I gave them the name of one of her aunts. I did it in a moment of panic. They hardly know each other. She hasn't got any one else. Well . . ." He thought again. "Maybe her assistant principal, Jenny Roberts. But would you be there for me?"

"Of course. I"ll keep you posted." Koesler paused. "What are you going to do?"

"Me? I'm going to do what I should have done with Lil. Get married."

Twenty-one

THERE WAS NO REASON to delay the inevitable. Within days, the red tape having been tied in an orderly bow, Rick and Dora became Mr. and Mrs. Richard Casserly. The presiding minister was Judge Timothy Kenny, a nice guy. Rick decided that if they couldn't have a priest witness their marriage, they might as well go for a nice guy. Judge Kenny was a friend of Rick's. The judge understood the groom's desire for a quiet, simple ceremony. And so it was. A few of Dora's coworkers at *Oakland Monthly* were present in the judge's chambers. Two of them acted as official witnesses.

There was little chance of any hoopla discomposing the summary nature of this ceremony. Unlike Jerry Anderson's headline-grabbing wedding of dual celebrities, Rick married Dora—both commoners. And the time had long passed when priests getting married, was, in and of itself, considered newsworthy.

Among those present was *Oakland Monthly*'s editor, Pat Lennon. She was at a loss to know what to think of it all. Dora didn't blend with this guy, Casserly. She was intended for Jerry Anderson. Even Pat's old buddy Father Koesler had confirmed that connection.

Intraoffice small talk had it that somehow Dora had engineered this merger. If that were so, Lennon did not know what to make of it all. Without doubt Jerry Anderson had set his cap for Dora. Dora seemed to be reciprocating. The dip in her office efficiency was attributed to her flirtation with Jerry, who would, according to rumors, marry and make a housewife of his beloved.

Since Dora's announcement to the magazine's staff a few days ago, Jerry Anderson had been conspicuous by his absence. What to make of that?

Better that Lennon stay abreast of developments. If Dora's work continued to slide, for whatever reason, this could be time to warn Dora that she might have to find work elsewhere.

True to his pledge, Father Koesler kept Rick Casserly informed as to Lil's medical condition. Her doctor attributed her remarkable progress to a strong will, good overall health, and a determination to cooperate in her treatment. In a matter of a few days she was well enough to be discharged. However, she remained hospitalized an additional two days for observation.

She had made no attempt to contact Casserly.

Immediately after their wedding, utilizing their combined Christmas card lists, Rick and Dora sent out a simple notice of their marriage. No matter how they were informed—by word of mouth or by U.S. Postal Service—recipients had varying reactions to the news.

Lil, of course, was in a stupor. She knew nothing of Jerry Anderson's role in this affair.

Tom Becker was furious with Dora for having robbed Rick of his priesthood. Peggy did not know of Dora's pregnancy. To Mrs. Becker, Rick was just one more priest failure who had looked back after putting his hand to the plow.

Zachary, Zoo, and Anne Marie Tully knew of Dora's pregnancy. They sympathized with both Rick and Dora.

Jerry, of course, knew about himself and Dora, but had been unaware of Lil's feelings for Rick. Where once he had loved Dora, Jerry now hated her for having manipulated and discarded him.

Father Harry Morgan didn't have a clue.

Father Koesler knew everything.

The newly civilly married couple honeymooned for a couple of days at the St. Clair Inn. The setting was beautiful. The mood left something to be desired.

The sex was satisfactory—no more—and that only because Dora put so much into it. It was as if she were going to make this marriage work, no matter the odds.

Rick struggled to forget what had brought him to this point in his life. He walked the beach endlessly, wrestling with Dora's essential question, "Why did you undress me?" And his answer to it all, "I was drunk." Finally he settled on a simile that seemed to help.

What of the man, Rick reasoned, who got drunk, took a handgun, and killed someone? Was the man not guilty of murder because he was drunk? Or was he responsible for getting drunk and thus responsible for what he did while drunk?

Rick knew darn well what he was doing when, motivated by anger at Lil, he began drinking too much at the party. After he passed out he was still responsible for having drunk too much—to the point of intoxication. And responsible for anything he might do while in that state. He was responsible for then falling into a sexual frenzy. Granted, his mind had been muddled at that point. But he was responsible for his muddleheadedness.

This conclusion helped a bit. But he was coming at it from two angles: cognitive and emotional. His mind dictated the complete acceptance of responsibility. But he felt he had been ensnared in Dora's orchestration, and, thus blindsided and trapped as he was, had been robbed of all he wanted in life.

He tried to see things from Dora's perspective. This was no unadulterated picnic for her. She was pregnant. He figured that most women considered that condition as good and bad news. It must be thrilling to have new life developing inside oneself. On the other hand, the baby was not going to painlessly slide into the outside world.

On the second and last day of their honeymoon he called Tom Becker to see if permission were still granted to use the boat. He had to play all relationships rather tentatively due to his status change. People who respected him as "Father" might despise him as Rick.

But Tom proved true (which was more than Tom could guarantee from Peggy). The boat was Rick's for the afternoon.

Brightly he proposed to Dora a leisurely ride on the lake. He'd never seen anyone exhibit such fear, instantaneous panic. She was terrified of the water. One more nagging difference from Lil. Accept your responsibility! his mind commanded. But it hurts, his heart replied.

It was a surprise to no one that Rick was offered a job in management in Becker's company. He spent his first day at work much the way Mary Richards—of the *Mary Tyler Moore Show*—had: sharpening pencils. Gradually, but solidly, he got a handle on the job and was making creative suggestions and moves.

He had to get used to being one of the bunch. In his former life when he uttered an unpopular opinion, others might react, "You've gone too far, Father." Now when he said something questionable, he might be greeted with: "You're full of shit, Rick." Oddly, he was not perturbed; he thought he preferred the latter approach.

One day after work Rick stopped in to see Father Koesler.

"I've been expecting you," Koesler said as they both sat down in the living room.

Rick smiled slightly. "I kind of thought you would."

"For one thing," Koesler said, "I expect you'll be wanting to change your Last Will and Testament."

"Where I name Lil as the main heir?"

"Uh-huh."

"No, I want to leave the will just as it is."

"But you're married now. Don't you want to name Dora as beneficiary?"

"No."

Koesler shrugged. "It's up to you. But I doubt it'll be legal unless you specifically mention your wife and your child. You'd better talk to a lawyer."

"I owe Lil just about everything. I've already told you how long we were together—how much we depended on each other." Rick shook his head and blinked away a tear.

"Anyway," he said after a moment, "I wanted to ask if you would be a sounding board, a listening post, whatever . . .

"From time to time it may be important for me to know who might still be speaking to me and who isn't."

Koesler smiled reassuringly. "You're a friend and a colleague. You shouldn't be concerned that you all of a sudden will be shunned."

Casserly looked purposeful. "There's Harry Morgan, for instance."

"If I were you I wouldn't count out Harry. I think you'll find that by and large you'll be pretty much accepted across the board."

"Maybe. I guess you're right." Rick shifted forward in his chair. "Maybe I am a little paranoid. But I don't want to barge in where I'm not wanted. I may want or need to talk to one of the guys, but if he doesn't want my company, it'll be an embarrassing scene for him. And I don't want that if it can be helped."

"Okay, okay. I'll keep a weather eye out. Is there anything else I can do for you?"

"How are you at changing the past? No . . . no," he interrupted Koesler's attempt to respond. "Forget it." Rick started to rise, then sat back again. "There is one more thing."

Until now Rick had been testing the water . . . seeing how his friend would respond to him. Both he and Koesler knew this. Games people play. "I was wondering," Rick said, "how's Lil doing?"

"Remarkably well," Koesler replied. "She started her comeback early on and has made good progress. She comes to see me from time to time. Would you like me to give her your greetings?"

"No. I don't want to mess up her life again. Best I stay out of the picture—hard as that is to do."

"Whatever you say."

"Oh . . ." Casserly did his up and down, jack-in-the-box routine again. "By the way, does she ever mention me?"

"Every time I see her."

Casserly beamed. "You don't know how much that means to me. I guess, if you don't mind, you could say hello to her for me."

They shook hands and Casserly left.

Koesler stood watching from the screen door as his friend walked to his car. I wish, Koesler thought, that I could do something about the past.

When Rick Casserly reached the inevitable conclusion that he would marry Dora—which was shortly after he learned of her pregnancy—he began the process of cutting his ties with the active ministry. Without his involvement, the all-too-familiar notice of his "leave of absence" was published in the *Detroit Catholic*. And a temporary administrator was appointed to Rick's former parish.

Shortly thereafter, Dora appeared at the *Oakland Monthly*. She had been granted vacation time. Now she was expected to return. She knocked on the door of Pat Lennon's office and was welcomed in.

"Thanks for the vacation time," Dora opened.

"You earned it. You ready to come back?" Lennon was not at all sure Dora could carry the load as she had when she first came to the magazine.

"That's what I want to see you about . . ." Dora nervously tapped fingernails on her purse. "I think I'm going to have to leave."

"Oh?"

"I'm pregnant."

Being pregnant was one of the few things Lennon had never done. Dora's admission was the final nail in the coffin. No one in the office would have bet against her pregnancy. "How about a maternity leave?" Pat suggested.

"Thanks. That's more than I deserve after goofing off lately. But I don't think so. I've got to take it easy. I'm spotting a bit. And after the baby comes, Rick and I have decided that I should stay home with the baby."

"If that's the way you want it, fine. I'll try to get you some severance pay. It's not yours by rights 'cause you're leaving voluntarily. But you'll just be settling in and the money couldn't hurt."

"Thanks again. But Rick is doing well. We're sure we can make it."

There was no point in small talk. Lennon had lots to do. So they said their good-byes.

Then Dora paused to look for a final time around the large editorial office. It held many memories, mostly good. She looked specifically for, and found, Jerry Anderson. He seemed absorbed with the screen of his computer. His back was to her and there was an air about him that said he didn't want to be interrupted. Particularly by her.

So she left—feeling she would never see this place again.

Women commonly complain about being used and discarded by men. Now, Jerry Anderson could sympathize.

Ever since Dora's wedding Jerry had had mixed emotions. He oscillated between embarrassment and hatred. And much of the time the two emotions meshed. He knew he wouldn't get over these feelings soon—if ever.

A few days ago he had heard from Father Harry Morgan, of all people. Morgan informed Jerry of Lil's hospitalization. There were no details—only that Lil had been in the hospital for several days. With the way patients lately were whisked in and out of hospitals, the fact that Lil had been confined several days spoke to the seriousness of her problem, whatever it was. All Morgan knew was that Lil was now at home, presumably convalescing.

All members of the Ursula group had the others' addresses and phone numbers. The apparent purpose of Morgan's call was to suggest that Jerry contact Lil and offer services if needed.

Anderson wondered why Morgan had selected him to visit Lil. If Jerry had to guess, it would be because, of all the members of the club, he and Lil were the only single and eligible people left. And since Jerry had been duly returned to the lay state, he could, if it came to that, contract marriage in the Church.

Jerry debated briefly with himself before deciding to follow Morgan's lead. He'd been out of the helping business—which came as a second nature to priests—for a long while. But maybe he *could* help in some as yet undefined way. Besides, he could use a little companionship himself.

It had been several days since Morgan's call. But Lil's condition, whatever it was, probably hadn't changed much. When he got home from work he phoned her.

Lil answered guardedly. As if the wrong caller might have seriously hurt her. Her voice then took on a puzzled tone; seemingly the last person in the world she expected to hear from was Jerry Anderson. Taken by surprise, she assured Jerry she was all right and needed nothing.

Jerry told her to feel free to call anytime if she changed her mind.

For the next thirty minutes Lil weighed the consequences of getting even slightly involved with anyone. In the end, she dialed Jerry's number. "Can a girl change her mind?" she asked meekly.

He laughed and said he'd be right over.

She was wearing a robe over her nightgown when she opened the door for him. It was a small apartment. He reminded himself that few people get rich working for the Catholic Church.

She had taken over—and seemed to be living on—one end of the couch. She invited him to occupy the other end.

They found it awkward beginning a conversation. He led her into narrating the responsibilities of a parochial school principal. From there he prompted her to remember and relate some of the anecdotes that went with the job. They both began laughing. It was doing her good. Then he launched into life at a monthly magazine. He wanted to keep things light. She laughed at his tales of office shenanigans.

It became clear to Jerry that it had been a spell since she'd been able to lighten up. He kept at it until the night sky was ending the day.

Lil was tired with a happy exhaustion. This was a difficult time for her. Rick had come to her so often as day ended. Anytime his evenings were unscheduled, he would come "home" to her. Her bodily rhythms prepared her to welcome him. And when he couldn't be with her because he was scheduled, he would be with her as soon as he could.

She had not yet adjusted to the fact that he would not be coming home to her ever again. Because that accommodation remained unresolved, this time of day was especially hurtful.

Jerry had changed things—slightly—but changed them nevertheless. Instead of crying, she'd been laughing.

But Jerry would have to leave soon. If only because she was so fatigued.

He sensed her weariness and prepared to leave. She saw him to the door. Haltingly she asked if he would come again. He told her he didn't want to become a pest. She said that was the last thing he had to worry over. So it was set: tomorrow early evening, same place, same people.

As he was leaving, she stood on tiptoe and brushed his cheek with her lips. It was as chaste a kiss as one would give one's parents. Yet there was something erotic about it.

This night she slept peacefully with pleasant dreams. He spent most of the night sitting in a chair, fixated on nothing. Letting Dora's attractive features slip out of mind—to be replaced by Lil's sweetness and delicate beauty.

Though Jerry and Lil had taken different paths, each was now filled with the other.

Twenty-two

By the time lil and jerry anderson enjoyed a memorable evening together, she had progressed from catatonia to merely a major league depression. Now, almost two weeks later, she was almost completely adjusted. The lion's share of the cure was due to Anderson.

He had supplanted Rick in Lil's life. Now it was Jerry, not Rick, who arrived as the sun was setting. Jerry had few demands on his time once the clock indicated the workday was finished. He anticipated her every need.

Sometimes they sat and watched the sunset, or perhaps television. Sometimes they did nothing but sit and hold hands. But that was in the beginning of their special relationship.

Soon, both felt that they should go out. Lil was strong enough now.

She couldn't believe the difference. They could go anywhere they wanted—as a couple. And they went. To the symphony. To a movie. To the theater. Swimming. Horseback riding. The zoo. Dinner with some of Jerry's friends from the magazine. Dinner with her assistant principal and some of Lil's teachers.

They were an ordinary couple. She found it difficult to believe. Occasionally she would glance behind her to see if there was anyone they knew. And then she would laugh to herself.

And, although they were in love, they hadn't made love. Their scars were too deep. They were sharing everything except what had brought them together in the first place: the unfaithful betrayal of the two people they had each loved exclusively.

It is unlikely that time heals everything for everyone. But it often aids the healing process. So it proved for Jerry and Lil. Neither completely forgot what had happened. While Jerry Anderson condemned what Dora had done to him as reprehensible, she had done him one favor: She didn't marry him. Comparing the generosity of spirit of the two women in his life, there was no contest. Dora manipulated people; Lil helped them.

While Lil Niedermier realized that Rick Casserly was not fully responsible for what had happened, he was the ultimate cause of it all. Hardest of all to forgive and forget was Dora, who had written the script.

However, without their being conscious of what was happening, time was performing its invisible miracle. Jerry was absorbed in Lil's goodness. And Lil was lost in her love for him.

It was October, early fall. School had been under way for nearly a month.

Oakland Monthly featured an interview with the newest Detroit Lion. Would the team recapture the splendor of the boys of the fifties when Bobby Layne and Joe Schmidt carried the Lions to championships? Would Detroit fans again be roused to the heady hopes and excitement generated in 1999 by Bobby Ross's heroic band of walking wounded?

There were fall fashions, personality portraits, interviews with a local TV meteorologist, and the ever-popular dining-out guide.

St. Enda's school got under way in its usual faltering manner. Students reluctantly had to forgo the constant play of summer and get down to work.

As always, parents who valued private school over public paid the extra load to send their children to institutions like St. Enda's. If a student didn't live up to the academic expectations, he or she would be picked up by the public school system, leaving that student's parents most unhappy.

But now, in October, the wheels of education were turning and everybody was doing about what was expected.

To say Lil Niedermier was a happy principal would be to undershoot the target. She could think of Jerry as "my man." And, of course, she need no longer fear anyone discovering her significant other. She stopped abruptly in reading a teacher's report. *My man?* she thought.

How did he happen to be her man? Nothing corroborated this title but their love for one another.

What was missing? The intimacy of love that sealed their relationship. Plus what Rick used to refer to as the paper chase.

That situation would have to be rectified. Suddenly she knew this beyond a doubt. *Tonight.*

With the help of her assistant, Lil was able to get away earlier than usual. She made a large tossed salad and cut into it some grilled chicken breasts. This constituted a pleasant surprise for Jerry, who had expected to eat out.

He watched her as she cleared the table and filled the dishwasher. It was a view that Rick had admired and that Jerry delighted in even more.

She lowered herself onto the couch, almost on top of him. They sat very still, holding hands.

After a period of silent commingled thoughts, she raised her face to his. He kissed her lightly on the lips. She took his hand and placed it on her breast.

He was startled—but he did not pull away. Rather, he fondled her. Finally he whispered, "Are you sure?"

"I've never been more!"

Each of them had had only one previous partner. But this was better than anything they could have tasted or imagined.

Meanwhile, in their home on Detroit's east side, Rick and Dora Casserly had just finished dinner.

Rick had said little since returning from work. He had not even complimented Dora on the gourmet meal she had prepared. It was par for the course for Dora. Ordinarily, Rick would have commented. Tonight, no.

Like most gourmet cooks, Dora had used most of the pots, pans, and cookware in the cabinets. Cleaning up, then, was a chore.

Rick looked up from reading the paper. He studied Dora as she cleaned. Her back was to him. Again he found himself comparing her with Lil. Dora had her own attractive features. Even though the two were both relatively young, it was like comparing apples and oranges. One thing he had to say for Dora: She kept trying until, generally, she got what she wanted.

She started the dishwasher for what would be the first of three full cycles. It would take that many to wash all the utensils, dishes, and flatware.

She stepped into the dining ell and sat across from him. That was a sign she wanted to talk. He recognized it and put the newspaper down to give her his full attention.

"Rick," she began, "we haven't entertained very much."

"Give us time. We're just getting started. My contacts at work haven't reached the stage of socializing. It'll come. You have to be patient. And you seem to have pretty much moved away from your former colleagues at the magazine."

"That's a good place for us to begin." She folded the dish towel carefully and laid it on the table. "We have a tendency to dance around the most painful part of our past. Take the gang at the magazine, for instance. Lately they haven't taken my calls or returned them. They've frozen me out. And I resent it!"

He hesitated to respond. He was sure her former coworkers had learned how she had treated Jerry Anderson and they were put out because of it. But he knew from previous conversations that Dora refused to accept responsibility for dumping Jerry.

In an effort at conciliation, he said, "Maybe there's a simple explanation for that. You're used to working with these people Monday through Friday, week after week. I suppose most of your contact at the magazine was work-related. It was constant contact, but most of it had to do with work. They all had an after-hours life that you weren't a part of. I mean, they went home after work just like you did.

"What you're missing, Dora, is the life on the job that you're no longer sharing with them."

"No!" she said with bitterness. "It's Jerry's fault. He's bad-mouthing me. They've got to work with him and they're taking his side about what happened.

"It's not that he got nothing out of this whole thing," she continued. "He got Lil—for all the good that'll do him. Probably she could have gotten you if she hadn't been so hesitant about going after you. I knew you were the prize catch aeons ago. I went after you. That was the difference."

This, too, was water under the bridge. Dora couldn't or wouldn't admit that the only reason she and Rick were together was because she was pregnant. Without that condition, he and Lil would still be sharing life on his terms.

The fact that Lil didn't "get" Rick, in terms of a formal marriage, was his doing, not Lil's. She would have loved legitimacy. He wouldn't hear of it.

The reason Rick was no longer a functioning priest was because Dora had found the one chink that would force him to leave. Lil, on the other hand, had respected his wish to remain in the active ministry.

Rick and Dora had discussed this many, many times. She had blind spots that conveniently resisted remedy.

"Then," Dora went on, "there's Tom and Peggy Becker. They are—or were—maybe the best friends you ever had. Where are they now? Okay, so Tom got you your job. Is that the end of it? You got together with them regularly before this happened. So, what about Tom—and especially Peggy. Once again, she doesn't return my calls. We have so much in common, Peggy and I. Neither of us is in the workplace. We're homemakers, essentially. What could those two possibly have against me?"

She knows, Rick thought. He had never met anyone who denied reality more often or more tenaciously than Dora. Peggy came to her own negative opinion of their former friendship when Rick announced his intention of leaving the priesthood and marrying Dora. The man Peggy had grown to admire exposed his feet of clay. Later, when she discovered the real reason Rick had taken this drastic step, she was doubly furious with him. Not only now for leaving the ministry but also for getting a woman pregnant. On top of everything else, Peggy was disgusted with Dora for bringing all this about. Peggy was of the school that believes that not only does the woman always pay but that the woman *should* always pay.

Things had become dicey for Tom Becker too. While he was furious with Dora for—in his view—robbing Rick of what he most dearly loved, his friendship with Rick remained as strong as ever. However, he was on tenterhooks with his wife over the matter.

Until recently Tom had needed to keep his wife from knowing about Lil. Now, in addition, he needed to hide the fact that his rapport with Rick was as firm as ever.

"Anyway," Dora was steaming toward her conclusion, "I thought that we ought to try to get everybody together. A party. Just to see if getting all of us together in person couldn't make peace all around."

Bizarre! It was the only word to describe what Rick felt about Dora's solution. To postpone a response to her proposal until something adequate could be formulated, he asked what he thought was a logical question. "What about the priests who, to one degree or another, had a part in this? Koesler and Tully and Morgan?"

"They come later," she answered brightly. "First we patch everything up with the people most directly and personally involved. We don't have to worry about the priests; I know their friendship is steadfast."

Silence.

"So," she prompted, "what about it? What do you think?"

More silence.

Then, suddenly the figurative lightbulb lit. "You know, it might just work," he said.

Dora's countenance brightened. She'd expected a heavy measure of opposition. "Good!" she exclaimed. "We should do it soon—the sooner the better."

"Yes," he agreed. "And aboard Tom's boat!"

Her countenance fell immediately. "Boat! On the water? No, no, no! You know how I'm afraid of the water! No!"

"Yes, I know your fear . . ." His tone was supportive. "That's one of the main reasons we should have the reunion on the boat."

"No! I couldn't!"

"Yes you could. If you want this as much as you seem to."

"Why?" She asked in a near-whine. She did want this reconciliation badly, indeed. She was weakening perceptibly.

"Because everyone knows—or will know before we get on board—about your fear of the water. If you are willing to be fearless and come aboard, the others will have to be impressed with your sincerity. It will be a grand bargaining chip to convince them to take a step closer to reunite themselves. Don't you see . . . ?"

Again silence. "Well . . ." Her voice trailed off.

"That's not all," he enthused. "Once we get aboard, it's going to be very difficult to give up on our effort easily. I mean, they're scarcely going to jump overboard and swim to shore. We'll have them in the best possible position to work this all out."

More silence. Then, "But it's October . . ." Dora was now pleading. "Nobody takes a boat out in October." She sounded close to tears.

"You'd be surprised. There are lots of times in October when conditions are perfect for boating. And Tom Becker is famous for going into dry dock later than just about anybody."

Now his eyes were almost boring into hers. "If you really want this, Dora"—his voice was steely—"you'll do it my way."

Silence, this time for several moments. Rick's argument made sense. There was no rejoinder but her unreasoning fear. And she really did want this matter settled. There were ways of carrying such things off. She had never been on Tom's boat. But she'd seen pictures of the boat and Tom and Peggy and Rick on it. There was ample space below deck to stay and not get frightened or sick. "All right," she barely whispered. "I'll try it."

"You've got to be more positive than that."

"Okay. I'll do it. When do you think would be a good time?"

"Tomorrow."

She paled. "So soon?"

"Strike while the iron's hot. Tomorrow is Saturday. Everybody will be off work. Besides, we're getting some Indian summer. It should be ideal for the weekend. I'll get on the horn right now."

He got up and headed for the den to make the necessary calls. Dora

was left alone to fight off second guesses that were blooming everywhere. Actually, she was being quite successful.

Rick's first call was to the Beckers. Fortunately Tom answered; Rick
was certain that no way would Peggy be moved to take part in this.

Yes, the boat was in the marina. Yes, it was unscheduled both tomorrow and Sunday. As for Peggy, Tom hoped that time would change
things. Absolutely nothing else stood a chance of working. Peggy had
a lot of forgiving to do. That was a large order and her sensibilities, not
to mention her moral judgments, were delicate. But Tom would come
and together he and Rick would pilot the boat.

After hanging up, Tom checked maps and forecasts. Tomorrow's
weather would, as Rick had said, be just about perfect. If anything, too
perfect. It would be hot and humid. So hot and humid that there was a
chance of scattered squalls and thunderstorms. But only a chance—at
this point, a 40 percent chance. Not threatening enough to keep them
off the water.

So far, three would be going aboard; there were two more to contact.

Once again, Rick thought himself lucky: Jerry answered the phone.
Chances were better trying to convince Jerry than Lil.

Neither Jerry nor Lil considered themselves friends of Rick's. But
neither were they embattled enemies. The couple's animus was directed
toward Dora. Especially was this true of Lil.

Rick explained the enterprise to Jerry.

"Boy, I don't know," Jerry responded. "I don't much care either way.
About the only positive thing I can think of is it would be nice to be
out on the lake. Lil is going to be a different case altogether. This isn't
going to be easy. Tell you what, I'll talk it over with Lil and get back
to you."

"Tonight, okay? This is supposed to go off tomorrow. And if you two don't sign on, the ship isn't going to sail."

"Tonight," Jerry affirmed.

It was an hour and a half later when the phone rang. Rick took it in the den.

On the other end of the line was Lil. Rick's heart skipped a beat at the sound of her voice. The last time she had spoken to him was the evening he told her of Dora's pregnancy.

"We'll be there, to fill in the bottom line," she said, coming straight to the point. "It wasn't an easy decision. Our agreement to accept your invitation is a tribute to Jerry's power of persuasion. It was a particularly rough decision for me. I've had a hard time putting you two— especially you, Rick—out of my mind. But we've pretty well done it . . . I guess I should say we *almost* did it. This invitation to get back together again sort of took us by surprise and stirred up old memories. I don't hold too much hope that we can accomplish what you propose. But we'll give it a try. See you tomorrow."

It had been a running monologue. Rick had no chance to get a word in edgewise. He had achieved what he and Dora proposed, but with Lil's reluctant and negative attitude, it seemed a rather hollow victory.

It didn't make him feel at all good to hear Lil say that she had tried to and had almost succeeded in wiping him from her memory.

Twenty-three

It was a few minutes before noon on Saturday.

Tom Becker had been doing odd jobs around his boat. This probably would be the final outing of the season. For October, the skies scarcely could have been more promising. Yet there was an outside chance of inclement weather.

The water temperature was 74 degrees F. The temperature on land was between 90 and 100 in the sun. October readings were not normally this high. It just reinforced Michiganians' boast or complaint that if you don't care for the immediate weather, just wait a few minutes; it'll change. That's Michigan.

The Casserlys, picnic basket in hand, arrived exactly at noon. Rick had planned on arriving much earlier, but Dora took extra time what with makeup and indecision about her outfit. The effort proved worthwhile: She looked quite attractive in white short shorts and a Ralph Lauren halter. All the curves were in the right places; her pregnancy didn't show at all.

While nowhere close to being tipsy, she'd had a couple of drinks before leaving home. She knew she shouldn't be drinking, but she needed alcoholic courage to carry this through. Now she was somewhat further reassured by the condition of the Beckers' boat. It gleamed like a polished diamond. She knew it was in perfect running condition; Rick had assured her of that.

Tom and Rick hailed each other. Tom's greeting of Dora was considerably more reserved. That might be attributed to the fact that they were only casual acquaintances—but also Tom bore a grudge for what Dora had done to his friend.

Rick tried to assist Dora into the boat but she was aboard before he could take her arm. God bless a couple of drinks, he thought. He went to join Tom at the wheel.

"Well," Tom said, "what do you think?"

Rick looked about him. "It's a little chancy, huh?"

"A little. It could go either way. It stays like this and you couldn't find a better spot for a cooling cruise. Or, it could get a bit dicey. How bad do you want this get-together?"

Rick didn't have to reflect. "It's almost a miracle that I got you and Jerry and Lil to agree to come today. I think the element of surprise had a lot to do with it. If we call this off, I'm not sure we could do it again. But . . . on the other hand . . ." Rick left the thought unfinished.

The two men looked down the dock. Jerry and Lil had arrived. Lil was carrying a picnic basket—two. Both Lil and Dora had brought food. Rick hoped this wouldn't prove divisive. He was an expert on both women as cooks. And while Lil was more than adequate in the kitchen, she could not hold Dora's spatula.

The four greeted each other and Jerry and Lil went to join Dora in the aft stateroom. From what conversation Tom and Rick could overhear, everyone seemed to be behaving in a mannerly fashion.

Rick turned to Tom. "Well, what do you think?"

"This is your party and your call. I'll go along with whatever you say."

Rick clenched his jaw, then said, "Okay. We're never going to get a better chance to patch things up. Let's go."

"Right. But before we cast off, I'd like a little prayer."

Rick was surprised. Tom was the sort who made his entire life a prayer and didn't need anything for special occasions. But Rick offered a short prayer for a safe journey and added a request for peace among friends.

No one said much during the early stages of the cruise. Lake St. Clair was so calm it was like glass. Tom was at the wheel. The others sat in the aft cockpit and soaked up the sun.

From time to time one or another of the group would visit the refrigerator for a snack, a soft drink, or a brew. Dora was particularly pleased that she was keeping a lid on her pathological fear of the water. She kept sipping beer. It couldn't hurt.

The conversation was stilted and forced. Rick, more than the others, wanted to patch things up. Dora wanted the same, but on her terms. Rick knew if this effort were to be successful there would have to be a healthy amount of compromise.

One of the drawbacks to meaningful sharing of thought was that they were seated above decks outside. They had to almost yell to be heard above the engine thrust. Finally Rick invited them into the main salon where there was plenty of room and it was quiet enough that they could speak in normal tones and be heard.

"I suppose you're wondering why I called you together," Rick began. It was an ancient comic opener. But in this gathering it got at best some patronizing smiles. "Look," Rick continued, "once upon a time we were all friends—and not so long ago at that. We—Dora and I—thought that if we could all get together, maybe we could talk it out."

There was a measure of hostility in the silence that greeted Rick's invitation.

"I know I'm the Judas goat in this, and I resent it!" Dora said forcefully.

Jerry shrugged. "You're the one who got pregnant."

Dora glared at him. "You could have been the father, you know! Does Lillian know that?"

"Lillian knows that," Lil responded. "We've talked about that. We've been over that."

"Well, anyway," Dora returned, "I didn't get pregnant all by myself. Why do you hate me and not Rick?"

"We don't hate you, Dora," Jerry said. "We just don't like you very much. We could get along very nicely without you. The world could get along without you."

"Now, just a minute . . ." Rick said.

Tom was at the helm. He could hear snatches of the conversation going on below. When they spoke in anger he could hear the tone. But he couldn't quite make out what they were saying, only that they were angry.

He was seated in a shadowed area and the breeze should be cooling him. But he was perspiring freely. Something about the weather disturbed him. It was *too* calm. It was the atmosphere—something about the atmosphere. Left to his own better judgment he would have turned toward shore. But Rick wanted this meeting to succeed. From what Tom was hearing this group had a long way to go before it found the peace for which Rick had prayed.

While Tom sat and thought and was hypersensitive to the weather, the conversation below went on. Both the atmosphere and the group were unstable. Something was about to happen, Tom felt sure of that.

Rick was trying to defend his wife and simultaneously wishing she'd shut up. It became clear that she was demanding complete vindication while shouldering no responsibility. And Jerry and Lil were not about to concede anything resembling that.

It also became clear that Lil had lost everything she had once felt for Rick.

The way this was working out was that Jerry and Lil were in love. They needed no more affirmation than their own feelings. More and more Rick was beginning to feel "stuck" with Dora. And Dora searched in vain for validation.

"The bullet had your name on it" is a popular expression for destiny or fate. Later, a storm would be said to have had this group's name on it.

A gale from hell was coming together hidden in the upper altitudes. The history of the Great Lakes was cluttered with skippers who had ignored storm warnings. Sometimes they'd gotten away with it. But when they took the risk and lost—it was on their own heads. The fresh water of the Great Lakes flows over the wrecks of vessels whose captains chanced it and failed.

Tom knew that. This was the first time he did not follow his gut reaction to get out of the way of whatever was coming.

In the main salon the conversation-turned-argument continued.

"We're not getting anywhere," Rick pleaded. "We're not going in the right direction. It can't be that difficult to find common ground."

"Maybe," Jerry said, "we're beating a dead horse. It's just possible that what we once felt for each other can no longer be retrieved. Maybe we ought to agree that we should just go our separate ways. This is a nice boat ride, and that's that."

"If that's the way you want things," Dora said, "it's okay with me. This animosity hurts Rick more than it does me."

"It's not just me," Rick added. "I don't believe it is helping any of us. It seems to me, with our backgrounds in religion, we ought to be capable of salvaging something that was . . . well . . . beautiful."

At that point, Tom stuck his head in the cabin. "Rick," he said, "could you come up for a minute?"

"Sure." Rick took the stairs two at a time.

His abrupt departure startled the other three. They had been oblivious of any warnings. But Tom's voice throbbed with urgency.

Dora's eyes darted from one person to another. From one object to another. She fought against losing the defense mechanisms she had carefully constructed. She grabbed another beer and chugalugged it.

Jerry and Lil merely showed interest in what might come next. The many times Lil had been on this craft, the violent storms she and Rick had weathered, gave her confidence in the vessel.

On deck, Tom let his concern show. "Rick, I feel like there's something big coming. I can't raise anybody on the radio. Same with the phone. Too much interference. It could be Selfridge Air Force Base. It's right around the bend and they've got all that radar. Probably all of it's in operation now."

Rick frowned. "This boat can take a beating and hang in. I know it from experience."

"Nevertheless . . ." Tom left his doubt uncompleted.

After a moment, Rick said, "You're right, of course. Better safe than sorry." Looking around, he added, "We're out quite a ways. Let's head in. I'll get some precautionary procedures started."

Rick returned to the cabin. He looked at the other three occupants. It was a captive audience, eager to hear him out.

"Don't anyone get worried," Rick began. "We're heading in. There's a storm coming. It may very well miss us completely. But it's a good idea to be ready. So"—he reached into a cabinet—"we'll all put on life jackets." He passed them out. "Lil, you help Jerry with his. I'll help Dora."

Jerry welcomed the assistance. Dora balked at fastening the jacket.

She complained that it was uncomfortable. That drew a guffaw from Lil. Granted, Dora was busty. But Lil thought it silly, at a time like this, to call attention to her endowment.

Rick quickly decided not to insist. If leaving her jacket unfastened bolstered Dora's confidence, he would not press the issue. Time enough later if the storm did hit.

Through the radio's on-and-off broadcast an announcer's preternaturally calm voice said something about approaching clouds at fifty thousand feet. Tom was able to make that out. And one word came menacingly to mind: microburst. If this was what was coming, they might well not survive it. In any case, it was useless to speculate. These storms were so unstable that it was next to impossible to predict their path accurately.

There was little warning. The water's surface was the first to break the secret. Some called it the bathtub effect with the water sloshing around. Steering became impossible. The ship was at the mercy of the lake. And there was no mercy to be found.

The erratic tossing of the ship reached Dora first. She made a dash to the head, slamming the door behind her and locking it. There was little room—but it had a toilet bowl and that was what Dora needed most.

No one could spend time trying to comfort the sick woman. Each was trying to survive, while helping the others do the same.

The boat featured extra-large transom lockers. Tom opened two of them. He handed out pieces of three-quarter-inch rope to each of the others and set aside one for Dora. He didn't bother trying to yell; they couldn't have heard him. He pantomimed what he wanted them to do.

As he began his demonstration, ultracool air in microbursts of energy slammed over the craft and into the lake at a speed of seventy-five miles an hour, creating waves of four to six feet.

As the group tried to comply with Tom's instructions, they fought to remain standing. It was near miraculous they could do just that. Tom and the others each wrapped the rope around their waists and made a loop at the belt. Once that was accomplished, Tom fed a separate rope through each loop. They had become a human chain. All immediately saw the wisdom of the move. The boat could be demolished in minutes at most. Their only chance was to abandon ship before that happened; otherwise their craft would then become a weapon against them. It might do anything from knocking them senseless to burying them in the shallow waters. They must get on deck.

But first they had to get Dora out of the head. The door stayed locked. After pounding on the door fruitlessly, Jerry kicked it off its hinges.

She was an odorous mess, covered in vomit.

In unspoken agreement, they resolved to reach the deck, then tie Dora to the chain.

With great effort, they stumbled up the stairs. Waves periodically knocked them back down again. Only adrenaline kept them moving. Without it they would have given up, and surrendered to the lake's demand.

Dora's life jacket was hanging loose. It didn't matter, it was imperative to get her in the human chain. Her face was a mask of panic and stark terror. Tom got the rope around her waist and tied the loop.

None of them saw Jerry look up, nor did they hear his screamed warning. But everyone's eyes followed his finger as he pointed toward the sky, his shrieks sucked into silence by the howling wind. There, seemingly poised over them, was a wave almost twice the size of the boat. Dora reached out to Rick just as the wave smashed over them. The five were washed overboard, one of them torn loose from the rest.

In those waves their life jackets gave little help. The rope holding them together was of more benefit. It linked them in their battle with this suddenly monstrous lake. They could at least try to help each other. And if help reached them in time they would all be in the same areas.

All but Dora.

The other four thrashed about, calling her name, trying to locate her. A huge piece of white fiberglass almost took their heads off. It was the boat's foredeck, the largest intact piece of the now disintegrated vessel. It may have been a stroke of good luck that they had been thrown overboard. They might well have been killed by the force that had demolished the boat.

A stroke of good luck for everyone but Dora. She was the one who so desperately feared the water. She would know of no way to handle herself in the angry sea. Her life jacket had long since left her.

The four others were trying to breathe as the waves gave them opportunity. Out when submerged, in when their heads emerged.

The ultimate fear they shared was that no one might know they were out there. They could not know that as the thunderhead passed from shore to the lake, the marina manager had contacted the St. Clair Shores Police, who, in turn, had contacted the harbormaster and the aviation section of the Detroit Police. A helicopter and two rescue vessels were on their way to the scene.

The storm itself did not hold, but the roiling water continued to churn and affect anything or anybody in its unpredictable path.

Time, of course, was vital. The longer these people were in the water the more chance there was of their tiring and succumbing. The direction taken by the chopper pilot in locating the survivors was crucial.

Guessing that the craft had been trying to return to its dock, the pilot started there and thence flew in concentric circles. Within minutes the crew spotted the four victims. The chopper descended as far as was prudent to examine the scene.

Four in the water, linked by rope. Excellent. But the marina manager had said five. One was missing.

The chopper pilot directed the first of the two rescue boats to the swimmers. That done, he began the search for the fifth. Forty-five minutes later, Dora's cold body was pulled from the water. Both rescue vessels returned to the dock, where ambulances took the living to St. John's Hospital Emergency.

Dora was pronounced dead at the scene. Her body was taken to the morgue for autopsy.

Anne Marie Tully happened to be listening to the all-news WWJ radio station. A reporter was announcing the bare bones essence of this tragedy with a promise of greater details as they happened. Of importance to Anne Marie were the names—all people who had been at that meeting some months back.

She phoned her husband and asked him to get involved. It hadn't happened in his jurisdiction, but that didn't bother her.

Zoo promised to try. He called a Grosse Pointe detective he knew, told him that he was familiar with the rescuees, and asked if he could look in on the case. Zoo was heartily welcomed aboard—no pun intended.

On his way out of the city, Zoo called his brother and Father Koesler. Neither had known of the accident; both were deeply shocked. Zoo asked if they wanted to ride out with him. They did indeed. Picking them up lengthened the drive time, but with one dead and the others hospitalized none of the victims was going very far.

Zoo's badge gained him admittance to the emergency department. The collars did the trick for the two priests.

Zoo quickly located his Grosse Pointe colleague, who briefed the three Detroit visitors on what was known.

"What we got here," said the suburban cop, "is a party of five. Out for a cruise on the lake. The storm—at least the intensity—fooled just about everybody. Pretty well made matchsticks and slivers out of the boat.

"One dead"—he consulted his notes—"a Dora Casserly. Not a swimmer, refused to fasten her jacket. Got carried off before the others could tie her to the human chain. The four survivors got pretty well bounced around. Some contusions, lacerations. Possible closed head injury for a guy named Becker. He's gonna be admitted for observation.

"The others are pretty shaken up. But they can leave soon as they get patched up and put together. They were lucky about lots of things, but most of all for getting thrown out of the boat. If they'd been on board when the boat fragmented, they could've been run through like pincushions."

"Any sign of foul play?" Tully asked.

The Grosse Pointe officer shook his head. "Who could've known about the storm? Besides, they were all in this together. Nobody stayed on shore. I wondered about the dead woman . . . the only one not linked up. But I'm convinced they did what they could for her before she was swept away. Accidental death, I'd say.

"I guess that's why they call it an Act of God: nobody else to blame."

Tully remained with the detective. Zoo had more questions that needed answers. The two priests were eager to comfort the survivors. So they did not linger for the police discussion.

The victims lay on gurneys in adjacent cubicles. The partition curtains had now been drawn back.

The four, obviously exhausted, and to varying degrees perilously close to shock, were incoherent. Koesler listened attentively to their babble. He did not mind at all that he couldn't, in any case, have gotten a word in edgewise.

As he listened to what, more often than not, seemed more rambling than substance, Koesler's thoughts went back to Casserly's overindulgence at the recent Ursula bash. Guiltily, he reproached himself, remembering how he and Father Tully had excused themselves from driving Rick home. This, selfishly, so that neither he nor Zack would have to play chauffeur. So that they could retire for the night.

All of this had led to an unwanted—at least on Rick's part—pregnancy. Then, all hell had broken loose, culminating in Dora's death.

The more he chased these events through his mind, the more questions remained, multiplied and crescendoed.

As he listened to the four rehash, rework, restate, rework, rework, restate, elaborate, and repeat, new answers popped into Koesler's mind. Along with new questions.

At long last, he thought he saw light at the end of this maze.

The question that continued to nag at him was: What, if anything, was he going to do with this new insight?

Twenty-four

THIS WAS WHAT EARLY OCTOBER in Michigan should be. Brisk, with the smack of footballs in the air. The leaves had begun to turn. Soon they would fall.

Ideal weather for a funeral. The mourners would not be inconvenienced by rain or snow or any sort of punishing weather.

It was Thursday, five days after the storm. A drawn-out interval made advisable by Rick Casserly's recovery time. The other three survivors, in bandages and immobilized to whatever degree necessary, were in attendance.

The autopsy revealed that Dora had drowned. Her unborn infant was male.

None of the four survivors would talk about the accident. Immediately after their rescue they had given statements to the police. After which they had not been able to restrain themselves from running on to Fathers Koesler and Tully. After that, though, there was no expressed consensus, they refused to say more.

Pat Lennon had tried in vain to coax Jerry Anderson into doing a first-person piece for the magazine. Lil Niedermier said she needed virtually complete bed rest. Casserly and Becker refused to answer either bell, door, or phone.

The incident was a major news story for twenty-four hours. Then, as with almost all news, once the sun guns and mikes were turned off and the notepads tucked away, the affair suffered a lingering death.

The funeral site was chosen mostly by elimination. St. William's, Casserly's former parish, was rejected because it held too many conflicting memories for him. In the end, they settled on St. Joseph's downtown.

As pastor of the parish, Father Tully would be the principal celebrant of the Mass of Resurrection. Fathers Koesler and Morgan were invited to concelebrate. Koesler accepted readily. Morgan declined. Dora and Rick were "living in sin." So, in Father Morgan's version of Christianity, Dora did not deserve the rite of Christian burial.

A sizable crowd filled roughly three quarters of St. Joe's capacity.

Dora had lain in state since yesterday afternoon. Now, just at 10 A.M., the lid to her coffin was closed for the final time. The pallbearers accompanied the casket down the middle aisle while everyone was encouraged to sing the hymn "Grant Them Eternal Rest." The pall, a large, rectangular white cloth, was spread over the coffin and Mass began with the traditional Penitential Rite. Father Tully led the congregation, as all read from the missal: "I confess to Almighty God, and to you my brothers and sisters, that I have sinned through my own fault, in my thoughts and in my words, in what I have done, and in what I have failed to do; and I ask blessed Mary, ever virgin, all the angels and saints, and you, my brothers and sisters, to pray for me to the Lord our God."

A muffled sob came from Rick Casserly. The sound was particularly poignant; he had held up so strongly through this entire ordeal—to this point.

The Mass proceeded. To Catholics the familiar words were consoling.

Since Father Tully had barely known Dora, Father Koesler gave the eulogy. He spoke of the dedicated years she had given to teaching children, in a parochial setting, not only the three R's but of Jesus who was their Lord and brother. He spoke of the special sorrow in her death: She had been about to give birth to a child whose future opened wide before him—only to be crushed before it was begun. He ended by commending the souls of Dora and her son to the welcoming arms of their God.

The Mass proceeded in the familiar traditional universal form. At Communion time, the four principals, along with most of the congregation, presented themselves. All four happened to be in the line leading to Koesler, who gave a consecrated host to each. While some might have questioned his decision, he felt it was thoroughly justified. He would not and could not be each one's conscience.

Harry Morgan would not have been pleased.

At the conclusion of the service, the organist led the congregation in the hymn "On Eagle's Wings," and then the Latin *In Paradisum*: "May angels guide you and bring you to paradise; and may all the martyrs come forth to welcome you home; and may they lead you into the holy city, Jerusalem. May the angel chorus sing to welcome you, and, like Lazarus, forgotten and poor, you shall have everlasting rest."

And that was it.

It was a small procession to the cemetery and a lonely burial. Dora's parents, her only close relatives, were dead. Six young men who worked for Tom Becker and with Rick Casserly acted as pallbearers. The undertaker, his assistant, and the four survivors attended. Fathers Tully and Koesler presided. A few prayers, the sprinkling of holy water, and it was over. Without another word each went his or her separate way.

Father Koesler was one piece shy of completing this jigsaw puzzle of a mystery. He knew full well that whether or not he was able to put it together to his satisfaction, he might well carry the secret to his grave.

The next several months passed quickly. It was January. Those who favored winter sports were delighted. Snow continued to fall in abundance. Michigan's ski resorts did not even need to "make snow." Those interested in and/or captivated by football had their fill of the college bowl variety over the New Year's holiday. And there was still more to come from the postseason pro games.

Most of the rest of humanity was in the doldrums, waiting for Lent to pass, Easter to come, and spring to arrive.

One distinctly bright spot had been the marriage of Jerry Anderson and Lillian Niedermier. Father Robert Koesler had witnessed the ceremony, which took place in St. Joseph's—downtown—church just before Christmas.

Lil's maid of honor was her friend and assistant principal. Most of the school staff, as well as many of the students, attended. Nearly the entire editorial staff of *Oakland Monthly* was there, led by editor Pat Lennon.

Conspicuous by his absence was Rick Casserly, who had not been invited and would not have participated in any event. He had just barely gotten over the pain of thinking about Lil with another man; he did not need to be reminded so vividly by the reality of her marriage.

For Lil and Jerry, this Christmas was the happiest of their lives. They had each other. They loved each other. And neither would ever have to be lonely again.

Jerry's mother was a bit confused by this turn of events. One day, her little boy was a priest—the answer to a mother's prayers. Then suddenly, he was no longer a priest—even though he was "a priest forever." Then that was okay because the Pope let him be a layman again. Now he was married—even though he had a lifelong commitment to celibacy. But it must be all right since it had happened in a Catholic church with many of Jerry's priest friends and classmates in attendance.

Her head was reeling.

In an undemanding moment, she decided that God was good. She'd had the button-popping pride of having her son a priest. And now, one of these days, maybe she'd be a grandma. The best of all possible worlds.

Tom and Peggy Becker thanked God every day they were together.

Tom decided it was past time to retire. He put his business up for sale and was considering the offers. Already he had enough money for the rest of his life. And with proceeds from the sale his children would be set till the end of their days.

Tom and Peggy cherished life after he had come so close to losing his. The boat was a total loss, but it had been completely insured. He would not buy or build another. From now on he would drink water, not travel on it.

Rick Casserly returned to work a month after his wife's funeral. But his heart wasn't really in it. And he had lost his angel/protector, Tom Becker. Becker could not guarantee that his present employees would be retained. To try to find a buyer who would agree to that might take more years than Tom had.

Casserly, then, had to give some attention to his future. He spent the next few months debating within himself what he might do next. Clearly, he was at a crossroads. To stay with the present job with the strong possibility that new owners would clean house and bring in their own personnel. Or, to anticipate such a move and try another company. Or . . .

☙   ❧

Father Koesler would always remember that it was Palm Sunday when Rick Casserly called for an appointment. As luck would have it, Koesler happened to be helping during Holy Week at St. William's, Casserly's last parish. The chancery still had not found a permanent replacement for Rick.

They met that afternoon in St. William's rectory. Casserly was unwilling to suffer the memories evoked by this building so he repressed them.

They sat in the living room, each with a cup of coffee fortunately not made by Koesler. Though a mite stale, still it was infinitely more potable than anything the elder priest would have brewed.

"Bob," Casserly began, "I've been thinking a lot about my future. I could use a little help. I've got a good job with excellent pay now, but once Tom sells the business, the new owners may want their own team. And sixty, leaning on sixty-one, isn't the best time of life to start hunting for work."

"I see what you mean." Koesler nodded. "But if you wanted advice regarding the job market, you probably would have gone to some sort of employment agency. So, to make a long story short and to get down to what we might more realistically consider—you're thinking of returning to the active ministry. You didn't get laicized—and you figure that opens the door for you. Anything else you—or an agency—could have figured out. That about it?"

Casserly nodded and smiled. "In a nutshell, yes. Only thing is . . . I don't know how to go about it. First, I wanted to know what you thought of the idea. Then, maybe you know something about the procedure."

Koesler stood and began pacing the large living room. "If I can believe the *Detroit Catholic,* you are one of the many on 'leave of absence.' Few guys with that label ever return. Those who do generally are gone a short time, during which they do little or nothing to compromise the possibility of their returning. You weren't gone long—so far so good—but you did get married."

"But it was invalid and never convalidated."

"Right. But you'd have to prove that. And, of course, you know that and you also know how to get a declaration of nullity. My point is, even 'attempting a marriage' kind of compromises the possibility of returning."

For the first time, Casserly looked concerned. "I'm not sure I understand."

Koesler stood still, hands in pockets, looking down at Casserly. "It just so happens that I counseled one of the fellows who came back. So I have a pretty good idea of what to expect in this archdiocese. You know about Fred Doyle?"

"Only that he was activated after being gone a long time."

"Twenty years."

Casserly gave a low whistle. "That long!"

"Uh-huh. He tells his story to anybody who's interested. So I don't think he'd mind my telling you—so you know what's ahead."

Casserly sat back. "I'd appreciate knowing."

"It starts," Koesler began, "with Fred—or in this case, you—getting together with a chancery official. You formally state to him that you want to return to the active ministry—and that you want to be incardinated in the Detroit archdiocese. Then, after a couple of months you arrange for a conference with the chancery man and one of the auxiliary bishops."

"Two months!"

"They're in no hurry. If everything goes well up to that point, you take a semester to make sure your theology is kosher. If you're still on track, you spend three days being interviewed by a psychiatrist or psychologist. That goes to a psychological evaluation. And you take tests: Rorschach, MMPI. Then . . ."

"There's more?"

"Oh yes. The chancery people take all of this for their assessment."

"And if they're satisfied?"

"You make a thirty-day retreat at the retreat facility of your choice."

"Holy cow!" Casserly breathed.

"One more thing," Koesler pressed. "And this you've got to expect, I think: With Fred, somewhere during this procedure, they found out that he had gotten somewhat involved with the Episcopal Church."

"He got ordained?"

"Not nearly that involved. Just received into that Church and became a Eucharistic Minister. Nothing more than that and that only for a short time. But the chancery people came this close"—Koesler held up his thumb and forefinger barely an inch apart—"to washing him out."

"It sort of makes you wonder, doesn't it? If they get their noses out of shape because somebody is just distributing Communion for Episcopalians, what are they going to think about someone who 'attempts' marriage?"

They were silent for many long minutes. Koesler resumed his chair.

"I had no idea," Casserly murmured finally. "My wedding was as clearcut a case as you can think of for an invalid marriage. I had not been dispensed from the obligation of celibacy. I hadn't even requested a dispensation. Any marriage I attempted in that state was invalid on the face of it. All I would have to do was prove I was an undispensed priest and I'd get an annulment in record time."

"But it makes you wonder, doesn't it?" Koesler mused. "I mean, if you leave the active ministry and you are not laicized, theoretically you can return to the active ministry. Nowhere, however, does it say the Church has to take you back.

"But in the final analysis," Koesler concluded, "I don't know. I'm not sure anyone knows. Maybe there aren't any cast-iron categories. Maybe it's a fresh decision for each case. I just don't know." He looked at

Casserly with great seriousness. "If I were you, I don't think I would give up my day job."

Casserly looked somewhat numb. Clearly he hadn't expected any information resembling this.

They said their farewells. Koesler urged his visitor to "Keep in touch." And then watched as Casserly went weaving down the walk to his car.

Suddenly the final piece in Koesler's jigsaw puzzle fell into place. In fact, he might even have a couple of pieces in reserve.

Twenty-five

R_{ICK} CASSERLY not only thought mightily about his future and the Catholic Church; he prayed over it.

Something about Koesler's explanation of how reentry into the active ministry worked suggested that the procedure might not be identical in every diocese. At least that's the way it seemed to Casserly. Sometimes things happened so quickly or abruptly that it took Mother Church by surprise—before She could make up any governing rules and regulations. Wandering in and out of the ministry just might be one of those instances.

Just about every diocese was hurting for priests. But not to the same degree.

The longer he thought about these possible differences, the more convinced he was that he wanted to test his theory. And his theory definitely did not include the Detroit archdiocese. Not after hearing what Fred Doyle had gone through

Casserly considered that he himself might not live long enough to qualify for reentry. Not to mention the serious possibility that his own diocese might not welcome his return.

In the state of Michigan there were eight dioceses, Detroit being the chief or metropolitan diocese, and Flint the most recently created diocese. Casserly wanted to stay in the state if possible, though not in Detroit. The question was, Which of these sees was most desperate for priests? If the rules for reentry were uniform, it would make no great difference where one applied. But if his hypothesis was accurate, he should at least try to find the weak link.

After study, research, and prayer, he picked the runt of the litter—Flint. That diocese had been created, largely, by taking a small chunk of the Lansing diocese and a big bite of the Saginaw diocese. Priests in the affected areas were given a small window of opportunity to remain in their original, now shrunk, dioceses. Otherwise they would belong to Flint. Most chose to depart Flint and relocate in either a Lansing or a Saginaw parish. Thus leaving Flint with the majority of its clergy on the brink of retirement and not at all disposed to work twice as hard as they had hitherto.

Flint it would be.

The first bishop of the neonatal diocese of Flint was the Most Reverend Harold J. Waldo, former auxiliary bishop of Grand Rapids, home of Gerald R. Ford, once President of the United States. The bishop, in his forty-five years as a priest, had been stationed all over the large Grand Rapids diocese. It was the rare parish that hadn't been served by him. This peripatetic history, along with the popular book, prompted the sobriquet "Where's Waldo?" He had five years to retirement—and everyone, including the Pope, was counting. He made a nice interim Ordinary. Those who created bishops were sure they could find a decent replacement in five years. Just hang in there, Waldo, they prayed, until we cut you out to pasture.

Rick Casserly knew who the bishop was, but knew nothing about him. Detroiters, particularly Detroit priests, tended to know nothing about the rest of Michigan, including where anyone else was located.

Casserly made his appointment with Waldo for 1 P.M. Holy Thursday. Tradition had it that this was the day Jesus instituted the priesthood of the Apostles during the Last Supper. Appropriate, Rick thought.

The bishop himself opened the door and invited Casserly in. They settled in the kitchen over coffee and cake.

"Now," the bishop opened, "what was it again that you were interested in?" He was wearing black trousers, not well pressed, and an open-collared white shirt.

"I want to be a priest in your diocese."

As far as Bishop Waldo was concerned, this was a by-damn miracle. This man, to all appearances in full command of his faculties, wanted to be a priest. In this diocese. And on Holy Thursday. There must be some catch. The bishop was soon to discover there was.

Casserly held nothing back. He was loath to go over his time with Lil when they'd lived in fear that someone would discover their secret.

But—no more secrets. When he finished his autobiographical sketch the two men sat in mutual silence.

"As I understand it," Waldo said, after a thoughtful minute, "you left the priesthood to marry. That was about ten months ago. You didn't petition for laicization, nor were you granted it. A few months ago, your wife died in a tragic accident. So, now you want to return to the active ministry. But not in your home diocese, Detroit. How so?"

"Too many memories. Too many explanations." These reasons were valid even if they weren't the essential cause of his leave. Of course, if this request to belong to Flint required the time and effort of that Detroit rigmarole, it would be back to the secular workforce for Rick Casserly.

But Waldo simply nodded, indicating understanding. He rubbed his hands together as if completely satisfied. "Well, since your impediment is deceased and you haven't been laicized, I guess I'll just incardinate you into the Flint diocese."

Casserly was too stunned to utter a word.

"Wait a minute," the bishop wondered aloud. "Can I do that? Just accept you into the diocese?"

As rapidly as Casserly's heart had soared, that quickly did it plunge. Was this going to be another Detroit?

"Do you know anything about this, Richard?"

"Uh . . . no. I've never done this before."

"Neither have I," the bishop said. "It makes sense though, don't you think?" he asked brightly.

Casserly nodded happily.

"After all," Waldo continued, "you're a validly ordained priest. You just don't have any bishop's permission to function. If there are any rules and regulations about how this is to be done, I've never seen them. Still, it does make sense. Rome probably will be making up some folderol about it in time. Why don't we do this . . ." He rubbed his hands briskly again. "We'll make all that you told me earlier your confession. I'll give you absolution. And I'll take care of that little matter of excommunication you incurred when you attempted matrimony. I know a couple of lovely canons that will do the trick. Then, just after

Easter we'll talk, and figure out what assignment will be best for you. Now, kneel down."

Casserly did.

"God, the Father of mercies . . ." Waldo began the rite of absolution. After concluding, he held up a finger, indicating that Casserly should wait a minute or so. He then disappeared to another part of the rectory, shortly to reappear, bearing a sheet of paper that he handed to his still stunned guest. It was a document granting Rick power to again function as a priest. Once more Father Casserly was a priest in the active ministry.

Later, reflecting on what had transpired, Casserly thought it extremely odd that the bishop had referred to Dora as an "impediment." However, Rick was not about to argue the point. He had learned to accept what was offered and be grateful.

Twenty-six

LITURGICALLY IT WAS still the Easter season, though it was now the middle of May. Spring, thus far, was mild and dry and extremely welcome after a harsh winter.

Father Koesler was still parish-sitting St. William's. He had finished the weekday morning Mass and was sitting down to an oatmeal-and-banana breakfast when the phone rang. He almost jumped. This phone, unlike in former times, hardly ever rang.

"You told me to keep in touch." Rick Casserly's voice was oddly upbeat.

"Yes, indeed I did. The last time we talked was . . . what? . . . almost a month ago. Did you ever follow up on getting back into the active ministry?"

Rick, condensing as he went along, related what had happened in Flint with Bishop Waldo.

Koesler chuckled. "It reminds me of Pope John the Twenty-third. The Cardinals couldn't agree on anyone in that consistory who was acceptable to the majority. So they elected that old man, who overturned everything.

"I remember when they made Flint a diocese. Neither the Michigan bishops nor the Vatican could agree on anyone, so they appointed Waldo to do nothing for five years. And then, good-bye. From what you two worked out, I'd say he's going to make some pretty sizable changes in the time he has left until retirement." He chuckled again. "Well, congratulations, Rick. Welcome back."

"Thanks."

"I thought you'd dropped off the face of the earth."

"The bishop wanted to keep it quiet. There was a brief notice in the Flint paper. But if you weren't a Flint priest, it well could slip by." Casserly hesitated. When he spoke again, his voice seemed to have lost some of its buoyancy. "Say, Bob, I wonder if I could have some of your time? There's something else I'd like to talk over with you."

"Time is something I've got a lot of. You're calling from Flint?"

"Uh-huh."

"Suppose we make it late afternoon. Then maybe we can go out for dinner. You wouldn't like what I could fix for you."

"Sure. About four?"

"Fine."

As time passed that day, Koesler grew somewhat uneasy. He thought he knew what Casserly wanted to discuss, and it would not be small talk. Koesler wished he had suggested a much earlier meeting. He would have had less time to be preoccupied about it.

At several minutes before four, Casserly arrived. They arranged themselves again in the spacious living room. "We could talk about how things are in Flint," Koesler began. "But that's probably not why you wanted to see me. So let's start with that."

"Okay." Casserly's hands were busy, fingering various parts of his suit. Fiddling with the buttons on his sleeve, touching his pockets, running a finger between his neck and the white, starched clerical collar. "I haven't been feeling well, Bob." He held up a hand. "And before you mention doctors, I've been to a few."

Koesler didn't respond. He sank deeper in his chair. "What's the trouble?"

"It's sleep—or rather the lack of it. I went to my G.P. He sent me to a couple of specialists. Nothing. They didn't find anything."

"Tried a psychologist?"

"That's next on my list if you can't help."

"Why me?"

"The trouble seems tied up with the priesthood. I thought you'd be more informed about that phase."

"Okay. Let's try it. You say it's the lack of sleep and it's tied up somehow with the priesthood. Let's get specific."

Casserly cleared his throat, stood, removed his suit coat, draped it over the chair and sat down again, this time on the couch. "It started sometime—maybe a week—after that storm and the accident."

Koesler thought he knew where this was going and he feared the direction it would take.

"I started having these dreams—I guess you could call them nightmares. I never had problems with sleep before. But since the storm, I go to sleep, after a couple of hours I have the nightmare. Then I can't get back to sleep. I've tried a nightcap. I go to sleep then, but it isn't restful sleep. And after tossing and turning, I have the dream again. And I can't get back to sleep.

"It's driving me nutty, Bob. It's getting so I'm afraid to go to sleep."

"What's the dream about?"

"It's different every night. But basically it has the same theme. I'm supposed to do something—but I don't know what . . . I don't know how to do it. I wake up in a panic. I'm drenched."

"Give me a for-instance."

"Okay. I'm in the vestibule of a church. I'm familiar with the church. It's one I worked in. But it's a different church each night. I haven't even read the Scripture readings for the day. I'm supposed to give a sermon based on those readings. It's going to happen in a few minutes. But I can't do it. I'm not going to do it.

"Or take another dream. I'm in a stage play. I'm standing backstage in the wings. I'm supposed to go on any minute. I don't know what play it is. I don't know my role. I don't know any lines. The other actors are going to depend on me for cues. I can't give them any help. And in neither of these dreams, or any others that are like them, can I leave the scene. The dream always ends with my failure. That's when I wake up. It's driving me crazy!"

"I can well imagine."

"Have you ever had this happen to you? Dreams like these? I mean, you were in lots of plays in school. You've certainly been celebrant of a Mass when you weren't as prepared for the homily as you'd want to be. Have these sorts of things ever been the manifest content of a dream or nightmare?"

"Maybe. I can't think of one like you're describing. But certainly I've never had it as bad as you have." Koesler began to revise his thinking. Maybe Casserly had to go back through dangerous memories. Maybe his subconscious needed to face reality.

"Do you suppose," Koesler said, "these dreams have anything to do with that storm?"

"Are you kidding? That's the first thing I thought of. I went over it more than once, I can assure you. That's not it. It was an accident. The storm itself they call an 'Act of God.' And the police officially declared Dora's death an accident."

"Would you mind," Koesler said, "going over it one more time? With me leading the way?"

Casserly seemed a bit reluctant. But he was the one who'd asked for Koesler's aid. "Okay, if you think it'll help. I'll try anything at this stage. 'Once more unto the breach . . .'" He shook his head in irony. "Tonight I'll probably be standing in the wings knowing nothing about Shakespeare's *King Henry the Fifth*."

"The meeting we had at St. Joe's almost a year ago seems to be the starting point of everything. Is that party clear in your mind?"

"Crystal."

"You drank too much that night. Do you remember why? I mean, I've been with you many, many times, but you've never overindulged like that."

"I was sore about a tiff I'd had with Lil earlier in the day."

"Tully and I never should have sent you home in the care of Dora. Do you remember any of that episode?"

"Fuzzily. But clearly enough to know that I did what she accused me of."

"Okay. Fast forward to the day of the storm. Why did you want to get together with the Beckers and Jerry and Lil?"

"It wasn't my idea. Dora was upset that one-time friends were friends no more. This was supposed to be a healing experience." Casserly snorted, "Some healing!"

"Whose idea was it to have the get-together on the boat?"

"Mine, of course. Dora was scared stiff of the water. Everybody knew that."

"Did Dora agree readily?"

"She dragged everything she could. I wanted a setting where, if things got too argumentative, nobody could up and leave. The only two places I could think of were a plane or a boat. We didn't have a plane. Once I made her see that, Dora went along with it."

He was rattling off answers as if they'd been rehearsed. Koesler wondered how many times Rick had gone over this in his mind.

"There was a threatening weather watch on that day," Koesler continued. "Did you consider postponing the gathering?"

"Michigan's weather is notoriously fickle. There was a better chance that we would have ideal weather than that we'd run into a storm."

"Even though any kind of storm would terrify Dora?"

"I thought a postponement would develop into a cancellation."

"Just before the storm hit, you began taking precautions. The first thing you did was issue life jackets?"

"How did you know that?"

"Some of what we're discussing I knew about because I was present at the St. Ursula gathering. Some I learned from others telling me. Most of what we're talking about now—what went on in the boat—I learned in the emergency room when you all were babbling compulsively." Having explained that, Koesler returned to the question at hand. "So, how about the life jackets?"

"I handed them out. A little later, Tom got out the rope that would link us together."

"Lil helped Jerry with his jacket. And Dora?"

Casserly hesitated. "I was trying to help Dora with her jacket."

"And you did?"

A longer hesitation. "She refused to buckle it. Said it was uncomfortable."

"And with a storm like that coming on, you let her get away with that excuse? Knowing on top of it that she would be the most vulnerable of anyone on the boat?"

Casserly did not reply to either question. "What's going on here, Bob?" he said. "This is some kind of inquisition?"

"You said you would go with me on this."

Casserly hung his head. After a moment, he nodded. "I thought I . . . we . . . could get the jacket fastened when we went on deck. It would be easier than in the crowded conditions of the cabin. Debris was flying everywhere." He looked at Koesler as if begging him to understand.

"So," Koesler said, "this time it was Dora who had too much to drink. She went in the head to be sick. And, probably because she was embarrassed, she locked the door. You let her get away with that? The one most likely to react irrationally to the storm?"

"It . . . it seemed best at the time." Angrily, "We didn't have time to sit down and plan what was best to do. This is hindsight! This is Monday-morning quarterbacking!"

"Take it easy, Rick. You wanted my help. For good or ill, stay with me." He paused to give his friend time to pull himself together. At Rick's nod, Koesler proceeded. "Now, when it became imperative to go up, Dora was still in the head. Jerry kicked the door in and got her out. Not you, her husband?"

"Jerry was . . . was closer to the head."

"This is crucial, Rick. When you got up on deck, you all were linked together—all but Dora."

"We only had time to get the smaller length of rope around Dora. The giant wave hit us before we could link her to us."

"The giant wave . . . the giant wave. If memory serves me, it was Jerry who spotted the wave. He pointed at it and caught everybody's attention. How much time would you think passed between everyone's seeing the wave and the time it hit?"

Casserly considered briefly. "It hung there for a . . . a . . ." He squinted, as if trying to recall. "That type of wave . . . well, waves like that, when they're about to break, they sort of hover . . . I'd say for a second . . . maybe two."

"Rick, it always surprises me what people can do in a second—even a fraction of a second. Athletic events—football and basketball, for

272

instance, that depend on a period of time for the game—sometimes they use a clock or a stopwatch that records tenths, or even one hundredths of a second. Skiing, for instance: It's amazing what they can accomplish in less than a second. A basketball player can get the ball in play and another player can take a shot—all in a fraction of a second."

"Bob!" a shocked Casserly exclaimed. "What are you saying?"

"It put me in mind of an Agatha Christie mystery, *Murder on the Orient Express*. Each and every one of the suspects stabs the victim. No one can be the murderer because it's impossible to determine which of the stab wounds was the fatal blow."

"Bob!"

"This would be just the opposite," Koesler continued. "No one killed Dora. She died because no one helped her. During her funeral Mass, in the Penitential Rite, we recited these words: '. . . I have sinned through my own fault . . . in what I have done *and in what I have failed to do*.' After that I heard a sob. Was that your subconscious, Rick? In being particularly sorry about what you failed to do?"

Even in the fading light of early evening, Koesler could see that Casserly's countenance had become ashen.

"It hasn't taken you long," Casserly said, "to narrate what happened on that boat. It took even less for the actual event to happen. Do you mean to say that in that brief and pressure-packed time the four of us entered some sort of conspiracy to kill Dora? Did we have time to plot all this?"

"No, not plot. Time enough to create an atmosphere in which this could happen. Look at it this way, Rick: Before Dora took center stage in your lives, everything was sailing smoothly. Then she got pregnant and you lost your most precious possession—the priesthood. Lil lost you and you lost Lil. Tom Becker ached for you, his best friend. Jerry Anderson lost Dora. Dora managed to foul everyone's life. Dora was Public Enemy Number One. The atmosphere was created to take revenge on Dora.

"If you want another indication of how long-standing this atmosphere was, look at laicization. At the meeting at St. Joe's, Jerry told us how quickly he had been dispensed. You came out very forcefully in favor of playing by the rules. For someone at odds with the Church, it was strange to hear you argue for laicization as the honorable path. Yet in all the time between the wedding and her death, you never even began the process—although you knew this was an opportune and appropriate time to apply. Why not? Because if you were laicized, as was Jerry, you never would be readmitted into the active ministry?

"When Dora reached out to you to save her, in that split second, did all that atmosphere overwhelm you? You didn't need time to plot; your subconscious had done it for you over a long period of time. In a sense, you, as well as the other three, choreographed the whole scenario."

Rick recalled charging Dora with the same accusation: that she had choreographed the situation.

"Is it possible then," said a shaken Casserly, "that we are—all of us—guilty of murder? That I am most guilty of all? I was her husband. Yet I took every aid, every help, every support she needed away from her. In her last moment, she reached out to me—she literally reached her hands toward me. And I stood there and watched her be swept away."

Koesler thought he saw tears coursing down Casserly's cheeks. The shadows were growing long.

"Rick"—the priest's tone was compassionate—"whatever went on in that boat, it wasn't murder—not in the legal sense." Koesler paused to reflect. "Once I formed this theory," he said, thoughtfully, "I asked around—discreetly—and learned that there is no Michigan law that demands one citizen help another." He paused again. "Now, if any one of you had, say, pushed Dora overboard, it would have been murder, plain and simple. But with no law in Michigan regarding this matter, we're considering not legality, but morality. And that judgment is within the conscience of each one of you.

"That's why I was so reluctant to bring this up . . . to mention your possible involvement from a moral standpoint. But you are the one having nightmares. You wanted my help to get rid of them. You couldn't—because I think you've blocked it out—recognize what was going on beneath the manifest content.

"Remember just a few minutes ago telling me about your stage-acting dream? You spoke about the other actors needing you, depending on you for their cues. You couldn't give them any help.

"Remember when you were on that boat? And Dora needed, depended on you, to save her? You didn't—you couldn't, perhaps—help her. You didn't insist she fasten her jacket. You didn't force her to unlock the door to the head. You didn't get her out of the head—Jerry did. And, most definitively, you didn't try to save her when she was swept overboard."

Rick looked like a limp washcloth. It was obvious he was overcome with guilt—deep, encompassing, pervasive guilt.

"Now," Koesler, not unkindly, "it's time to hear from the defense. Rick, I don't think any of your actions were premeditated in any way. You had an excuse for everything you did. The boat was a means . . . it was supposed to prevent an angry exit. It would be easier to get Dora's jacket on after you left the cabin. And so on.

"Do I think you committed murder? Obviously, in the legal sense, absolutely not. There was no law for you to break. Morally? I don't think so. Just as your immune system fights off infection, so your psychic personality fought off the block to your priesthood. It went on fighting even after you lost that priesthood.

"It might not have been your finest hour. But you would never, under any circumstances, have deliberately killed that woman—or anyone else, for that matter." Koesler sat back, but looked at Rick intently. "One more thing: I don't think you'll ever have those nightmares again."

Silence. Not a sound in this old house but floors that squeaked in memory of priests who had served here through the years.

There is an expression: a shadow of one's former self. It applied to Rick Casserly now. He took out a handkerchief and dabbed at his eyes. He would do that many more times in days to come.

Father Koesler moved to the couch and sat down next to his friend. Koesler put his arm around Casserly's shoulder and held him. Nothing more. Just held him. Occasionally Rick would sob softly. But neither man said a word. Dinnertime came and went. Still they sat together.

It grew very late.

Casserly rose mutely, donned his suit coat, and stood motionless for a short time. He took Koesler's hand and held it tightly. And then he left. He was composed, but shaken to his core.

Koesler watched him leave. And then it was night.

Twenty-seven

"WELL," FATHER TULLY SAID DULLY, "here it is Wednesday. I'm well and I don't need a priest or a doctor."

"Too bad," Father Koesler replied, "you've got one right next to you."

"A doctor?"

"That'll be the day. Even *honoris causa*."

The two, in their clericals, were waiting for the start of a movie in a dingy theater on the outskirts of Detroit. The choice had been Tully's. He was a movie buff and this theater had a policy of showing film classics. Koesler came along to ride shotgun. This neighborhood was *not* Detroit's answer to New York's Fifth Avenue.

Koesler smiled at Tully's large tub of popcorn and giant soft drink. Zack indulged in this gastronomic madness only and always at the movies. "Do you remember," Koesler said, "what we were doing a year ago tonight?"

"How could I forget? We were hosting a reunion of St. Ursula survivors. Speaking of survivors, whatever happened to Rick Casserly? I haven't heard much about him after that storm and the boat incident."

"Oh, he's in Arizona, working things out." Koesler didn't add that Rick had joined a religious order called the Theresians—the male counterpart of Dora's order. When Rick explained what he'd learned about himself and Dora, Bishop Waldo gave him permission to join the strict group with the proviso that should he wish, Rick could return to Flint. Rick had only one reason for joining that order: atonement. He could not bring himself to believe he was innocent of Dora's death. He had to make amends; to God and to Dora. But his nightmares had not recurred.

"Strange, isn't it," Koesler asked rhetorically, "what the choices we make can do to our lives?"

"Uh-huh." Tully nodded, and filled his hand with popcorn.

"Take Dora Riccardo, for instance. If she had chosen practically any other religious order than the Theresians, this whole thing we've lived through this year probably wouldn't have happened. Any other order that had paid attention to Vatican Two would have utilized her talents to the maximum, instead of going nuts over rules and regulations.

"Whereas, getting pushed and abused by her religious colleagues, Dora set her cap for Rick. Rick had already chosen Lil and Lil had reciprocated. Jerry had chosen Dora. And Tom Becker chose to be Rick's best friend. A lot of choices going on. With lots of strange effects."

"Uh-hmm," Tully agreed through a mouthful of Coke.

"I mean," Koesler continued, "there's the maxim, Play the hand you're dealt. I think most people who cite that expression believe that God is the dealer in this game of life. If they suffer great evil, they may do the best they can and they figure they are shouldering their burden: They are playing the hand they've been dealt. But they blame God for dealing that hand.

"Actually I think most people never consider that in large part they themselves are the dealers. We have no choice about our parents; God may have dealt that. But shortly, the hands are dealt by us. And we have to take responsibility."

Koesler was aware that Tully was not paying much attention. It didn't matter. Koesler wanted to sound himself out on the matter of responsibility.

"Rick," Koesler continued, "dealt himself a relationship with Lil. It changed his life. For one, he proved a man could be a superior priest when married—for all intents and purposes—to a strong, beautiful woman. But he had a lot of cards to shuffle. Dora dealt herself a high card when she seduced a drunk.

"And on and on it goes, Zack. We've got to play the cards we're dealt. But we have to realize that most of the time *we* are the dealers and we have to take responsibility for the way we play the game as well as for who dealt them. *We* did!"

"Uh-huh."

It was one "Uh-huh" too many for Koesler. He nudged Tully. "How much time before this movie starts?"

Tully glanced at his watch. "Five minutes."

"What do you know about this flick—besides the fact that it's supposed to be a classic?"

"Harry Morgan tipped me off on this one. I was talking to him the other day and he recommended this movie highly."

"What's it about?"

"Sort of a sequel to *All the President's Men*. It's about Watergate and the downfall of Dick Nixon."

Koesler slumped in his seat. "I don't know, Zack. Haven't we seen enough of Nixon and his gang?"

"No. Morgan said this film centers on the guy who gave all those leads and tips to Woodward and Bernstein. The guy whose identity the reporters never revealed. Even in the movie with Redford and Hoffman, all we saw was a shadowy figure. All we could hear was his voice. This picture, according to Harry, is all about the guy who really brought the Nixon administration down."

"Hmm . . ." Koesler wondered. "What's the name of the movie?"

"*Deep Throat*. Remember? That was the alias they used to identify the guy."

"Hmm." Koesler thought again. *Deep Throat*. The name rang a bell.

The house lights went down and the movie began. Within two or three minutes it became all too obvious this had nothing to do with Washington or Watergate.

"Zack!" Koesler exclaimed. "I know what this is. It's a classic all right! It's one of the earliest—if not *the* earliest—hard-core pornographic films ever distributed in America! Zack, this is one of the dirtiest movies ever made! Now I know why everybody in the theater was looking at us in that peculiar way! Let's get out of here—fast."

"But my popcorn . . . !"

"Bring the damn tub with you!"

As they exited the theater, Tully wanted to get a refund. Koesler pulled him away. "All I've got to say is that Harry Morgan has a weird idea of revenge."